Private Johnnie Jackson has got himself classified as a nut case to avoid the front line. The time is the last days of the war and the first days of peace. But Johnnie and his mates don't care about the battlefront nor what the politicians are doing. Arch-scrounger, black marketeer, lady's man and general no-good, Private Jackson is sublimely indifferent to it all, so long as he doesn't have to fight, get shot or bombed, and so long as he can carry on his usual shady and lusty activities.

Also by Ray Rigby in Panther Books

Jackson's War

Ray Rigby

Jackson's Peace

Panther

Granada Publishing Limited
Published in 1976 by Panther Books Ltd
Frogmore, St Albans, Herts AL2 2NF

First published in Great Britain by
W. H. Allen & Co Ltd 1974
Copyright © Ray Rigby 1974
Made and printed in Great Britain by
Hazell Watson & Viney Ltd
Aylesbury, Bucks
Set in Linotype Times

Chapter 1

Colonel Franshaw smiled pleasantly and handed Jackson his AB64.

'Open it,' he said. Jackson, trying to look as casual as possible, opened his Army Identification Book, turned a few pages, then slowly exhaled his breath. His medical category had been altered from A1 to B2 – Base duty permanently. He stared for a long, long moment at the neat handwriting.

'Well?' inquired Colonel Franshaw.

Can't be, thought Jackson, then he swallowed hard as he stared at the Colonel.

'Base, sir, Base. That means . . .'

'Your activities from now will be confined to the Base.'

I've really got away with it, Jackson thought. I've beaten the trick cyclists at their own game. Bullshitted Major Buncroft, old Freud's disciple, right out of business, and now the Medical Board – including a full grand Colonel with a score of great hospitals, all the better for his devoted services; a real first-class specialist consultant in the events that happen in a poor fellow's head; an expert in the waves of grey matter that go soggy and refuse to function properly. I can almost see his smiling face peering into many a crazy-house ward. I've baffled him. Jackson's heart was swelling with pride. My truth, my truth baffled him. Well, now I've got it all written down in this horrible little book. But before I bid him farewell, I'm going to let him know I'm not one of the phonies, like those idiots waiting outside, all trying to work their ticket and hopefully – some hopes – sail away from Suez on a steamer heading for England. The poor, daft bastards, some hopes they've got. I didn't try and pull anything. I told the truth, didn't I? I answered all the puzzle games Major Buncroft set me, with total honesty.

'Sir,' Jackson said quietly and sincerely. 'It seems the war's over, sir.'

Colonel Franshaw smiled at his fellow officers seated at the table. All pleasant-looking blokes, and they responded with smiles.

'Jackson,' said the Colonel. 'The war's not over yet.'

'For me, sir, I mean.' Jackson couldn't help boasting.

'Ah, well . . . not really . . . in a sense perhaps. I do see what you mean.'

'Base, sir. The war shouldn't be noticed, at Base, I mean.'

'Quite.'

'I want you to know, sir . . .' This was very important to Jackson – a matter of honour, something he seldom thought about. Trying to live honourably – he had attempted to on a few rare occasions, and it had only increased his day-to-day problems past the limit of his endurance. 'I didn't try to work my ticket, sir.'

'Of course not.' Clearly the Colonel believed him.

How odd, thought Jackson. How bloody odd. Then how the hell did I baffle all of them? Truth. My burning honesty. Simple as that. Obviously this dear old Colonel wasn't used to meeting with total honesty every day. That must be the secret.

'As long as you understand, sir.'

'I do, I do indeed, Jackson.'

'Now what, sir?'

'Report back to your training camp. They'll know all about you. I'll see to that. By the way, if you meet with any problems, any problems, contact me at once. Understand?'

'And you will sort them out?' The Colonel nodded.

I don't believe it, Jackson thought. Is this the army I've been trying to dodge all along? I settled for NAAFI because I was sure it was a safe billet. How could I run into danger selling chocolates and cigarettes to the poor bloody soldiers? And what happened? They dumped me in some bloody queer places and I was bombed and stukered from arsehole to breakfast. Three years of it and I thought it was a safe billet. So this is the army? Base duties permanently. Can't believe it. They couldn't treat royalty better. He smiled at Colonel Franshaw.

'I don't expect to have too many problems now, sir.'

'That's the spirit. Keep your chin up and do your best.'

The old army clap-trap's even got through to him, Jackson thought. Then, picking his words carefully, 'Sir. Why did you medically downgrade me?'

The Colonel pondered for a moment. 'Does it really matter?'

'Yes, sir, I think it does.'

The pleasant smile again. 'Most of the chaps aren't too much bothered about the why or wherefores.'

'I'd like to know.'

Another pause. Then the Colonel shrugged. 'The technical word is psychotic.' Jackson stared blankly at him. 'Don't you understand what the word means?'

Jackson blurted out, 'Of course I know what it means. I'm crazy. I'm a head case. That's what you think, isn't it?'

'Jackson,' the Colonel spoke in a calm, assured voice. 'Can you give me one good reason why a medical board should grade you B2 if we considered you to be perfectly normal?'

'Then why aren't you sending me to the crazy house?'

'In civilian life you no doubt encounter problems and face up to some and wonder about others as . . . er . . . many people do. But your basic reactions to problems are no doubt accepted by most people as reasonably normal behaviour. But now there's a war on, Jackson. Do you think you function at your best when there's a war on?'

Jackson automatically dismissed the latter part of the Colonel's statement. He knew. Ever since the war had started he had functioned at dead stop. Not a bad guess, he thought. In civvy street I'm too bloody normal. So he thinks I'm crazy? Good. That can't hurt and I've got proof. I've got it in my little book. B2. Base permanent. What a gift, and what does it mean? It means I'm crazy. That can prove to be very useful. If I'm crazy – and everybody had better believe it – I should be able to get away with everything. Just short of murder.

Jackson was delighted and at the same time deeply offended. He had never seen himself as a sick mind. He was Jackson the wheeler-dealer. Charming Jackson, whom everyone just couldn't help liking. Irresistible Jackson, whom all the girls were absolutely mad about, and who couldn't wait to drop their panties for him. If I'm crazy, he reasoned, how come no one, except this idiot and his 'yes men' and possibly Major Buncroft, noticed it? These trick cyclists, head shrinks, they had to be crazy. Didn't they spend every working hour of their lives with nuts?

Jackson had worked in an asylum for six months as an orderly and it had almost sent him crazy. So he'd got out. He had seen them. God! Ugh! Holy Christ! The bearded nut who had walked about the ward wearing a blanket, bare-ass naked under it, convinced he was Jesus Christ. Lying on the floor, on his back, arms held out in the crucifixion while the grinning patients stood on his hands and Jesus Christ wriggled and panted and jerked his body up and down until he got his jollies. Ugh! The patients in the padded cells, withdrawn, standing still against a wall for hours and days on end; then a terrible burst of violence, then the strait-jacket. The silly ones who crapped in their beds. The persecuted ones. The lethargic ones. The megalomaniacs. The melancholics. Poor miserable bastards, and this smiling Colonel is convinced that I'm a head case. The idiot. Good. Let them all think that. I'll show them. I'll show everybody. Jackson switched on his most charming smile.

'Then you've done the right thing, sir. Be terrible if you sent me up to the front. I could disorganize the attack and turn it into a full-out retreat.'

The Colonel's smile was tolerant. He won't accept the truth, of course, he thought. Just as well. Years on the couch. He wouldn't stand for it anyway. As he is now, he's happy. Really enjoys living. That's the basic reason why he's such a coward. He loves life and in wartime chaps like him can be a major problem. The Colonel smiled pleasantly.

'We won't have to put it to the test.' Under his breath, Thank God. 'Now run along and don't forget, if you have any problems, come and see me.'

'Back to the training camp, sir. Don't think Captain Rainbow will be too pleased to see me.'

'Probably not, but as I said . . .'

'Any problems, come back and see you, sir. I won't forget.'

'I'm sure you will be posted out at the first opportunity. Good luck, Jackson.'

'Thank you, sir.' Jackson did a smart turn about and marched out.

The Colonel sat brooding after Jackson left, then jotted down some figures and stared at the sheet of paper thoughtfully. Then he addressed his fellow officers.

'It's only a rough guess, but close enough, I think. During the last fifty years, and up until now – and it's still patriotically going on – normal men have probably killed about seventy million of their fellow men. At this rate, we could, given more time, wipe out the entire human race. Jackson obviously hasn't killed anyone and clearly doesn't intend to, so we have to put a label on him. Psychotic.' His pleasant smile again. 'Worth thinking about, isn't it?'

The loonies outside the tin-topped hut were still going through their routines. The soldier who went down on all fours and barked like a dog. The soldier whose hands shook so much he couldn't hold a rifle. They looked at Jackson with inquiring eyes.

'I'm crazy,' said Jackson cheerfully. 'I'm a supreme head case.'

The soldier's hands stopped shaking. 'Got your ticket, mate?'

'Flying me home to Blighty in three days' time.'

'To the crazy house?'

'No. Buckingham Palace.'

'Buckingham bleeding Palace?'

'That's right. George Six wants me to teach his kids unarmed combat in case there's an invasion.'

The soldier who barked like a dog slowly nodded his head. 'This one's not kidding. He's a real head case.' Then he went down on all fours and started barking again.

Jackson watched him. 'You're trying hard enough but if you're a real head case you don't have to try.' Then he thought, my God. That's true and it isn't even funny, and immediately began to worry. He walked slowly across the desert, pondering about it. Then a smile began to spread over his face as he increased his pace. 'Bonkers!' he said, out loud, as he went into a run, his ammo boots sinking into the soft sand. He ran faster. 'Bonkers!' he shouted, and began laughing. He was laughing but a rage was building up inside him and it was directed at the pleasant, smiling Colonel.

Sergeant Major Hopper stared at Jackson with deep loathing. He was hoping that the worst possible fate had overtaken Jackson. The Medical Board must have realized that he was a dodgy boy, a lead-swinger, a con artist. All that's wrong with him, he reasoned, he's a dirty, bloody coward trying to work his ticket back to England and once there he would probably take up poncing for a living. Colonel Franshaw was a bit on the soft side. Too lenient, but he was no idiot. Hadn't he sent Franshaw a few smart alecs and hadn't they come back tail between their legs, eyes bubbling over with tears? Oh, yes, the soft bloody articles, and hadn't he gleefully marched them into Captain Rainbow and listened with unconcealed delight as Rainbow, in his clipped, over-posh, very minor public school accent, had told them their fortune, cut them down to size and then posted them to the Infantry or Tank Corps? Yes, yes. The only way to treat the horrible, scrounging bastards, and now it's Jackson's turn. Good, very good. Infantry. That's the mob for him. Into battle with the dirty bastard and no doubt he'll get a bullet up his arse – sure to be trying to go the wrong bloody way.

'Well, Jackson,' he said with a horrible smile. 'So you've seen the medics, eh? Seen the vets?'

'Yes, sir.' Jackson was standing stiffly at attention gazing at the endless shimmering sand. The glare hurt his eyes, and sweat trickled down from his armpits.

'And the verdict, eh?' Hopper gloated.

Jackson undid the breast pocket on his shirt and handed Hopper his AB64 and watched, poker-faced, as Hopper thumbed through the book until he found the magic page and he observed with interest Hopper's face crease up with pain and his sun tan change to a violent red as he gaped at Jackson's AB64. He stared for a long moment at Colonel Franshaw's neat handwriting. The words swam before his eyes, then he got them into focus again and the words slowly registered in his mind. He's done it, he thought. He's bleedin' well worked it. First he baffles Major Buncroft, the crazy trick cyclist. Now the Medical Board. Fooled the lot of them. The horrible little pisspot's got away with it. He glared at Jackson, who stared innocent-eyed past him at nothing. He wanted to smash his fist into the handsome face. The cocky, dirty little fart.

He began shouting, the words grating and bumping into each other, eyes glaring insanely.

'See about this . . . see . . . yes see, we will. We'll see about this. Yes we will. You won't get away with it. Oh, no . . . no . . .' He turned on his heels, kicked the door to Captain Rainbow's office open and confronted the startled Rainbow.

'He's bloody worked his ticket!' he bellowed.

Captain Rainbow jumped to his feet and stared at Hopper in amazement. 'Sergeant Major, what in God's name . . .'

'Jackson ! !' It was a scream straight from the guts.

'Calm down. Just calm down. And the next time you want to see me . . .'

Hopper threw Jackson's AB64 on to the desk. 'It's all there . . .' There was a red haze before his eyes.

Captain Rainbow was alarmed as he stared at Hopper's beef-red face and crazy eyes.

'I said, calm down! Calm down!' Then realized he was shouting. For God's sake, hadn't he got enough on his plate without Hopper ranting and screaming at him? 'Just calm down,' he repeated as he seated himself again. 'If you have any problems, I'll do my best to deal with them. But damn well control yourself. Now, what is it?'

Hopper pointed a thick finger at Jackson's AB64. The nail was bitten to the quick. Then he remembered to stand to attention. Get a hold of yourself, he thought. Calm it down and do some quick thinking.

Rainbow scanned the book, then glared up at Hopper. 'I see, so the Medical Board found him . . .'

'Wanting, sir. Wanting in the bloody head. A few screws loose. He's pulled the bloody wool over their eyes, sir. Now what do we do?'

'Post him out, of course.'

'Ah. That's it, sir.' A conspiratorial wink. 'Post him out.'

'Of course.'

'Infantry, eh, sir? Infantry!'

'What?' Rainbow was startled.

'Screw the verdict, eh, sir. The medics don't know what the hell they're talking about.' Hopper began ranting again. 'Put the bastard in the Infantry. I've trained him well, sir. The assault course, route marches. Rifle drill. He's busting fit, the bastard. Wasn't too hot on the rifle range. Couldn't hit a barn door at ten paces, the crafty article. Put him up front, sir. He'll learn. Oh, he'll learn fast when the Hun comes at him.'

Captain Rainbow thought, so it's true. Hopper is crazy. Absolutely out of his mind. He groaned inwardly. So I'm landed with a crazy Sergeant Major, as if I haven't got enough problems. If he doesn't stop smashing my ear-drums with his ranting I'll post *him* out. Back to the bloody Infantry. He stared cold-eyed at Hopper.

'The Medical Board have confirmed my secret opinion of Jackson. He's mentally unstable.'

'Not you, too, sir!' shouted Hopper. 'He's not fooled you, too?'

'Sergeant Major!'

'I was up there two years. Wounded, shot at. Wadi this, Wadi that. Fighting. Now it's his turn. It's that bastard's turn. He's fit. Fit as a bleedin' commando. Fit ...'

'Shut up!' Rainbow was losing his temper. 'Damn well shut up and listen!' This halted Hopper with his mouth open and Rainbow stared with disgust at his yellow teeth. 'I stand by the Board's verdict. Now, you march out, Sergeant Major, and tell Jackson I want to see him.' He paused and stared at Hopper. 'I pride myself on being a fair man.' He knew he was. No one could be fairer. 'I've no time for prejudice, understand? Now march out.' As Hopper tried to speak again, he raised his hand. 'I said, march out. That's an order.'

Jesus Christ. Hopper took a deep breath. Jesus holy Christ. What's the army bleedin' well coming to. He wheeled about, crunched his way to the open door and yelled, 'Get inside there you! Hef . . . hef . . . hef . . . move . . . move . . . move!'

Jackson entered the office like a tornado, a blissful smile on his face and the moment Captain Rainbow set eyes on him, all his good resolutions evaporated. I really do dislike him, he thought. If only I could find just one redeeming feature. That smug smile.

'Close the door,' he snapped.

Jackson smartly about turned, slammed the door shut, marched back to the desk and stood firmly at attention and waited.

Captain Rainbow stared at Jackson's AB64. It had been his intention to be . . . well, not exactly sympathetic – bit much to offer sympathy to a chap who has just been judged crazy by a Medical Board. Tolerant, that was the word, and send him on his way, wish him the best of luck. He's keeping his face straight now, but does he think I don't know he's laughing inside? Laughing at me.

'I see you got away with it, Jackson.'

Jackson's eyes went blank. 'I don't understand, sir.'

'No?'

'No, sir. I saw the Medical Board . . .'

'I know.' Rainbow handed Jackson his AB64. 'That's pretty obvious.'

'And that's their verdict, sir,' said Jackson as he pocketed the book. 'Their honest estimate of my state of mind.'

Rainbow was now convinced that there was absolutely nothing wrong with Jackson, and he felt a passing sympathy for Hopper. But how had this smug young bastard fooled the Medical Board? And, even, almost convinced himself? He stared at the young, untroubled face. Of course he was fit. Sun-tanned, clear-eyed, not an ounce of spare flesh on him. Hopper had most certainly got him into splendid shape. How the hell had he managed to get away with it?

'So you won't be going up to the front line after all, eh?'

'No, sir, seems I won't.'

Jackson's heart was singing. Maybe I'll get a posting to Cairo, he was thinking. Not a bad place to be when there's a war on. Can't see Rainbow going along with that idea, though.

'Where would you like to be posted?'

Jackson pretended to ponder the question, then said very seriously, 'Cairo, sir.'

'What?'

'Or Alex, or what about Cape Town?' Jackson was smiling.

'You insolent young prick,' snarled Rainbow, in a voice with the ring of bow bells backing it, as he pushed himself out of his chair and glared at Jackson. 'I'll post you to a company that still knows there's a war on. An RASC company that . . .'

'That transports ammo and bullets and petrol to the front line.' Jackson remembered Colonel Franshaw's parting words and felt at ease and very safe. He leaned his hands on the desk and stared directly into Rainbow's eyes. Then he lowered his voice. He didn't want to be overheard. No witnesses.

'When are you going up the front? How much longer are you going to skulk down here at Base? You want to send me somewhere you're shit scared to go yourself.'

For a moment, Rainbow did not believe that Jackson had really said . . . simply wouldn't have the nerve.

'Repeat that. I want you to repeat . . .'

'You just post me out and no sweat. But don't forget I'm Base duties. There's no front line for me.'

'You repeat . . .'

'You're the prick. I know who I am. I'm Jackson. I'm a coward and that makes me survival prone. Coward and head case. But who the hell are you, you poor bastard? You strut around the Base, playing at soldier. You send every poor bastard you can get your hands on up front . . .'

'Jackson. You be careful, very . . .'

'While you piss it up in the officers' mess at Base, and

good luck to you, but just don't kid yourself. You're a bloody coward, too.'

'You're on a charge!' Rainbow slammed his fist on the desk.

Jackson looked at him with contempt. 'I didn't forget to drop a hint to Colonel Franshaw that I might have trouble with you, so why don't you post me out, or I'll have to see Franshaw and believe me, I'll drop you deep in it.'

'Get out!' Rainbow was beside himself with rage. 'Get out before I . . .'

'Sir!' shouted Jackson as he threw up a derisive salute, turned and marched to the door. Jerked it open and marched out. As he passed Hopper he was delighted to see that he looked totally and completely shattered.

'Name and number,' shouted Sergeant Major Hall. 'And hands, lad, hands in line with the seams of your trousers.'

'441, Private Jackson, sir,' shouted Jackson as he stared at Major Stevens seated at his desk. Rainbow had posted Jackson to the transit camp ten minutes after the interview. And here I am, thought Jackson, going through the same old bullshit. He watched Stevens examining his army record, idly turning the pages. Then he glanced up at Jackson.

'You were in NAAFI, I see.'

'Yes, sir.'

'Why did they post you out?'

'It's a lie sir,' said Jackson, switching on a cunning look.

'What?' Major Stevens looked surprised.

'I'm as sane as you or any other man.'

'Did I say you weren't, Jackson?'

'Don't believe it, sir. That's all. Medical reports can lie.'

'Now, look here . . .'

'Not that I mean Colonel Franshaw deliberately lied, sir. I mean, he's a gentleman and he wouldn't deliberately, but he's overworked, you know, sir.'

'Another one, sir,' groaned Sergeant Major Hall, casting his eyes heavenwards. 'He's been in front of the Medical Board and the vet's found out he's barmy.'

Major Stevens had caught on. He nodded to Hall. 'Jackson, don't feel too badly about it.'

'If my family ever find out about this, sir, the disgrace . . .'

'They won't,' Stevens interrupted Jackson. 'Absolutely no reason why they should. It's strictly confidential.' He stared at Hall. 'No need for anyone to know outside ourselves.'

'I wanted the Infantry.' Jackson sounded bitter.

'Bad luck.' Stevens thought it best to humour him. 'I'll post you to a decent company. No doubt we'll find other chaps who are . . . er . . . in a similar mind to your own. Decent chaps, of course.'

'I promised my girl a VC,' said Jackson, his voice even more bitter. 'VC and Bar. Do it twice and nobody can doubt you, can they?'

'Yes,' said Stevens. 'Quite.'

'Those bloody Huns have got to be stopped.'

'Of course,' said Stevens, then with a forced laugh, 'Suppose someone else will have to stop them now, eh?' And before Jackson could reply, 'March out and good luck.'

Jackson saluted, turned smartly and marched out, thinking. For a trial run that didn't go down too badly. Puzzle them with sincere bullshit and baffle them. It's crazy – I have to join the army to find peace.

'501 RASC Company, eh, sir?' inquired Hall.

'Yes, think so,' agreed Major Stevens. 'How many like him have we sent to date?'

'Eight, sir. But I fancy there'll be a lot more.'

Major Stevens sighed. 'You know, the poor bloody OC of 501 Company must think by now somebody's got it in for him.'

Chapter II

501 RASC was a transport company and had never seen any action. They had left England in September 1940 and been transported to Syria and later to Palestine. They were now destined for Italy where they would again be a strictly base company. The reason why they had not seen any action was

quite simple. With very few exceptions, the personnel were either considered over age or were low medical grades.

Watson was one, and he was constantly amazed that no one had thought to post him out to a younger, better company. Not that he had any complaints. The last thing he wanted to see was action. He was speaking to Jackson, trying to weigh him up and filling him in on all the latest gen. For reasons he could not fathom, he was not particularly popular, so he was pleased to have an audience, and Jackson was patiently listening because he was eager to learn all he could about the company.

'The OC's a bastard,' said Watson in a reasonable tone of voice. 'But he's a fair bastard. Goes by the book but he could be a lot bleedin' worse. Captain Butcher's a fly bastard. I wouldn't trust him with my grandmother, but he's easy to get along with. Over there,' he added, nodding to a recumbent figure, dressed only in his underpants and lying on a dirty blanket, 'that's Dusty Miller. He's a looney boy.' He raised his voice. 'You're a looney boy, ain't you, Dusty?'

Dusty turned over and switched on a winsome smile. He had beautiful, dark blue, empty eyes. 'Yes.' He always agreed with everybody, no matter what they said, and this way he was never in trouble.

'He can't read or write,' said Watson, then raised his voice again. 'You can't read or write, can you, looney?'

Dusty had great difficulty even trying to decipher a kid's comic, and hated to be reminded. But, as usual, he switched on a simple smile. 'I can't read or write,' he agreed. 'But I can count up to fifty; what's wrong with that?'

'He's a wanker,' grinned Watson, thinking himself no end of a wit. 'He's got a terrible bloody problem, he's suffering from wanker's doom.' He shouted at Dusty, 'You're a terrible bloody wanker, ain't you, looney?'

'Yes,' agreed Dusty. 'I'm a champion wanker.'

'All night long he's wanking,' grinned Watson. 'How many times, Dusty?'

'All night long,' agreed Dusty.

'Why don't you fuck a bint?' shouted Watson. 'Tell me why.'

'They want paid,' said Dusty with a crafty smile. 'I do it myself and it's free.'

'That's Paddy over there,' said Watson, lowering his voice. 'Paddy Fitzroy. He's a new intake. I haven't worked him out yet.'

Paddy was stretched out at the far end of the tent. He yawned, slowly stood up and flexed his muscles. He was a handsome young man with a friendly, open face and black curly hair.

Jackson was staring at him with mixed emotions, something between horror and awe. He was thinking, he's tattooed from arsehole to breakfast. Just above the wrist on his left hand was printed in splendid Technicolor, BRIDGET MY BELOVED, and above that, MOTHER I LOVE YOU on a bleeding heart with an arrow through it. Above his wrist on his right hand was MARY MY BELOVED, and above that was MOTHER I LOVE YOU across a purple bleeding heart, and over it Jesus Christ on the cross. The rest of his body was something to marvel at. A fantastic hunting scene – a horse, rider, hounds and a fox with a long, splendid brush. The chase started on his left shoulder, carried down his left arm, up the under part of his arm, across his chest, around a large bleeding heart with MOTHER I LOVE YOU over it, down his right arm and up again under his arm. Then the chase circled madly over his trunk and disappeared into his underpants and Jackson was curious to know what happened under the pants. The chase continued up and down both legs and again disappeared into his underpants. Then all over his back and once more into his underpants.

Paddy was aware of Jackson's interest. He switched on a charming smile.

'Me name's Paddy Fitzroy and us bloody Fitzroys have got royal, bloody blood in us veins and so we have. It was King Charles who made us the gift and I hear he was a randy man who was too fond of his cock. Sure, it's a lie, he was led by his nose. He was led by his cock. Wasn't Nell Gwynne one of his and a hundred and more others and maybe Madam DuBarry? I'm a bit short on me history but every time Charlie jumped on a lady or old whore or whatever was moving, didn't he give her a title of Duchess and a pension for his bastards and so that's how it came to be. His royal cock cost a fortune and I'm descended from a long line of Dukes and some terrible bastards. Sure they had to be because I'm so bloody broke it's bloody ridiculous.' Changing the subject, he added, 'You're wondering where the bloody fox winds up. Is that so?'

'I am,' said Jackson.

Paddy dropped his underpants. The fox was chased around his buttocks, in and out of his pubic hairs. Then Paddy turned around. The huntsman and hounds were in a circle around Paddy's arsehole and the fox's brush was bravely sticking out. The fox had made base.

Jackson was deeply impressed.

The rumour was on the grapevine – Italy. The rumour was spreading fast. Italy. All those beautiful little dark eyes. Italy. All those delightful, warm, emotional, little, sweet, tempting pussies. Italy. The men were groaning in their sleep. This is it. This is where it's at. It's Italy. We're going to Italy, where the wine flows and the girls are heavy-breasted and slim-legged and begging for it and loving English Tommy because he's brave and kind and wonderful and will freely give away the bully beef and the cigarettes and chocolate and forget his wife and promise anything. Put them all up the spout, the little black-eyed darlings. Italy. Here we come.

They were in for a bitter disappointment. They were going to southern Italy. Where the girls, and their mothers, kneeled to kiss the priest's ring and curtsied to him in the street and had to be chaperoned all the time, and it didn't matter that they were coming in their panties at the fearful, delightful, crazy, joy thoughts of a man, British Tommy, or any man, pushing into them as they spread their legs wide open on the bed.

But they were chaperoned, by their mothers, or aunties, or brothers. They were part of a non-sexual society. It was the gold ring on the third finger, left hand, or nothing.

The soldiers in their groaning sleep were convinced that

Italy was Mecca. The world's love-nest, and they were going to Italy.

The flat-bottomed ship on the tideless Mediterranean Sea floundered, thumped, swayed, farted, rose and fell and looked like sinking every other second. 501 RASC Company were on their way to Italy. No one was seasick. They were all too frightened. The three-ton, five-ton and ten-ton trucks were heavily secured by screaming steel chains on the deck. The ship listed. Jackson, who lay in a hospital stretcher that fitted snugly into both sides of his truck, watched his legs rear up in front of him, then sink seemingly into the steel floor of the truck, then up again, feeling dizzy and convinced the next lurch would end in his watery grave. He closed his eyes and prayed once more, 'Oh God. Please God. Oh God please . . . I'm excused . . . excused . . . Please God let up . . . up we go again . . . please help, stop the ship, where now? Please . . . it's a hell of a long night. Please . . .' Then he was sick and felt pleased to have something else to worry about.

In the shimmering dawn Toranto was paradise. White with a golden glow. Holding his breath Jackson, unshaved, still feeling seasick, waited, longing to land. Longing to feel firm land under his ammo boots. He wanted to smell the pure air of Toranto. To sample the bars, to drink the wine. To gaze lovingly at the beautiful women. To sample the beautiful women. To live. It was four hours later that the ship docked.

As the trucks roared through Toranto, Jackson realized that it was nothing but a dirty black shit-house of a town. The golden dawn sunlight had deceived him. He watched Toranto retreating from him from the back of a truck with bitter hostility. Another disaster area, another dirty, wog-ridden town like Benghazi. Another terrible disappointment. But he was determined to return and check out the main streets and the back streets and the hovels, and most of all, the girls.

He lay in a hastily erected tent. A blanket beneath him, a

rock almost breaking his back and still he thought about Toranto and the women and the bars. He was trying to convince himself again that Toranto was paradise. Well, maybe a third-rate paradise, but it just had to be better than Benghazi. Around him the men muttered and groaned as they moved their aching backs trying to find a comfortable space on the iron-hard ground. Trying to sleep. It was too hot. There were too many buzzing, dive-bombing flies. The air was blue with language and violent rebellious farting.

Then the voice of Regimental Sergeant Major Tompkins was heard shouting orders. 'Up on yer feet. Let's have yer. Come on now, move!' The voice was a deep bass, frightening. The owner of the voice was one of the most nervous men in the company. He was an ex-bus driver and an ace bullshitter. Any orders thrown at him by his commanding officer, Major Holland, he picked up as quickly as a dog picks up a bone. Holland only had to yell 'Sergeant Major!' and a cloud of dust tore at hurricane speed in the direction of the voice. Tompkins probably was the worst RSM in the British Army. He fawned on the officers. He shouted and screamed at the men under his command, and under no circumstances would he stand by them or stand up for them. He was a creep.

The Sergeant Majors, Sergeants and Corporals now all started shouting orders. 'Out of your flea-pits. Let's have you on parade. Move.'

Groaning and swearing, the men tottered out of their tents, pulling their shirts over their heads, pulling up their stockings. Checking on their puttees, straightening their caps, sweating and hating the loud, abusive voices. The blazing sun overhead. The dry, dusty camp. The buzzing angry flies. Moving sullenly, wearily, heavy legged to the parade ground, wondering what this parade was for. Why couldn't they be left alone for once for Christ's sake? Stupid bastards. Always shouting orders.

'Parade attenshun! Stan' at ease. Let's have it again now. Parade attenshun! Better, that's better.'

RSM Tompkins turned like a guardsman, slammed to attention and saluted Major Holland, who stood with Captain Butcher and Lieutenant Randall in a small listless group. It was really too hot for all this nonsense, but Holland straightened up and smartly returned the salute. He was a handsome man, iron-grey hair, grey military moustache, slim, erect, fifty years old, a non-smoker and strictly tee-total and in splendid physical shape. He despised Tompkins, but found him useful. He did keep discipline, and would obey any order, short of murder, without question.

'Stand the men at ease, Sergeant Major.' God, it was damn hot.

'Parade . . . now, wait for it. Parade, stan' at ease!' bellowed Tompkins, who dearly loved the sound of his own voice. 'Now let's have that again and this time, move! Parade . . . shun! I saw you move, didn't I? Now this time I don't want to see you move, do I?'

Major Holland spoke quietly but his voice carried, as he interrupted the idiot Tompkins. 'It's rather too hot for all that, Sergeant Major. Just stand the men at ease.'

'Sir!' bellowed Tompkins. 'Stan' at ease!'

The men thankfully stood at ease.

Holland's careful, well-modulated voice carried clearly even to the men in the rear ranks. 'Men, I have just been instructed that you are all to undergo a short-arm inspection.' He paused and smiled as a titter of laughter rustled down the ranks of waiting soldiers. 'It seems you should have undergone this most important of all medical inspections in Suez before we embarked for Italy. Apparently, it was overlooked. However, it seems, it's never too late.'

A voice from the ranks called out. 'Too late for me, sir. Mine fell off on the bloody boat coming over.'

This remark was greeted with a great good-humoured gust of laughter.

Major Holland smiled even more broadly, but Tompkins wasn't going to allow any one to speak to the Major like that. His voice boomed over the laughter. 'The man who made that insulting remark, step out of the ranks.'

This halted the laughter, but Major Holland dismissed Tompkins with a wave of his cane as he stared towards the ranks of waiting men. 'Sorry to hear that, whoever you are. I call that jolly bad luck.' The men burst out laughing again and the officers joined in and Tompkins stood red-faced and thin-lipped. Holland addressed him. 'The medical officer should be here soon to inspect the men. Line them up over there.' He pointed his swagger cane in the general direction of a tarmac road that ran through the camp. 'That's all for now.' Holland threw up a casual salute and sauntered away, followed by Captain Butcher and Lieutenant Randall.

Once again Tompkins boomed orders and the men marched to the tarmac road and made a long single line, two paces from the next man, and waited in the hot afternoon sun. And waited, once more bored out of their minds.

When Tompkins heard the sound of a car engine in the distance, he gave the order. 'All right, men. Drop yer shorts and drop yer pants.'

The soldiers responded with laughter as they fumbled down their shorts and underpants and stood exposed in the hot sun. Some of them were embarrassed, standing like idiots on the side of the road with their limp cocks hanging down. They cast furtive glances at each other, made embarrassed jokes, lewd, obscene remarks, or stood shifty-eyed, staring ahead, trying to pretend it wasn't happening.

A battered old Italian truck was on them almost before they were aware of it. In the front of the truck were two weather-beaten, middle-aged Italians. As they drew level with the men at the beginning of the line they looked sideways at them. Then away. Then together, turned their heads and stared at the soldiers' baggy shorts hanging around their boots and private parts exposed. They stared incredulously. They simply could not believe it. The driver almost ran off the road and only straightened out in time. Then their arms began waving, and their faces creased into smiles as they stared at the long line of limp cocks.

In the back of the truck were six girls, buxom, heavy-breasted, dressed in oil-stained sweaters and skirts. They were employed by the British Army to load and unload oil drums on to trucks. They were powerfully built and worked harder and better than the Italian men.

As the soldiers became aware of them, at first, they could

only stare foolishly. The girls stared back, open-mouthed. Then the girls and the men, at almost the same instant, started to turn away. The soldiers reaching for their baggy shorts, the girls covering their faces with their hands. Then the laughter broke out simultaneously. The girls dropped their hands and shrieked with laughter and made rude gestures. The soldiers left their shorts and underpants where they were and laughed back and blew raspberries and returned the gestures and lifted their limp cocks in their hands and danced a little and threatened the girls with their secret weapons. And the girls were clinging on to each other and almost weeping with laughter. Tompkins, in a red-faced rage, was shouting orders to get dressed, which no one heard and there was now absolutely no embarrassment, because the girls were so earthy and real and obviously enjoying every moment – happily throwing obscene gestures and kisses at the soldiers and almost helpless with laughter because the scene was so absurd and the men could not feel sexy. They were simply happy and enjoying the humour of the situation and the girls' laughter.

The driver slowed down the truck and he and his companion saluted and waved to the soldiers and passed comments and, on occasion, compliments to the soldiers who, for reasons that they could not understand, were standing on the side of the tarmac road, exposing their cocks. They would tell the story when they got home to the older members of their families, and they would repeat the story many times in the bars to their friends, and their friends would laugh, and some, of course, would not believe the story. Oh, they knew the English were crazy, but even the English were not as crazy as that.

As the truck slowly cruised along the long line of men the laughter increased and the girls became more and more hysterical and found and even invented more gestures and blew more and more kisses to the long line of dangling cocks and their eyes and their gestures expressed equally compliments and insults. It was a day they would remember too. Tompkins was marching along the side of the truck, bellowing at the driver to 'Move, move, move bleedin' faster!' But the driver was almost helpless with laughter and was trying to ask Tompkins in his fractured English, to show his cock. But he was shaking with laughter and nothing he said was even remotely comprehensible.

Jackson was laughing so much that he began to pee, and soon most of the men lined along the tarmac were laughing helplessly and pissing on to the road. Some laughed so hard they fell down and finally the truck, still driving at a snail's pace, came to the end of the line and, with last hysterical waves from the girls, increased speed and disappeared into the distance. It took Tompkins a good ten minutes to restore some kind of order.

Major Holland had witnessed the scene, standing outside his tent, and had decided not to interfere. He was not particularly amused, being at heart a puritan. But he was determined to speak to Tompkins about the incident.

A motor-bike roared up the tarmac road, slowed down, then stopped. Seated on it was the medical officer. The men by this time were correctly dressed again. Tompkins marched to the medical officer and threw up a salute. The medical officer, who was drunk and impatient to get back to his friends before they finished the second bottle, instructed Tompkins to order the men to disrobe.

Three hundred pairs of shorts were dropped to the ground and three hundred soldiers stood exposed and grinning again. To Tompkin's amazement, the medical officer revved the engine, put it into gear and drove along the line of men, slowly at first, as he waved his cane and yelled, 'Passed passed, passed. My God, that one's healthy. Fit, fit, fit!' The soldiers did not comprehend what was happening at first. Then the laughter began to build up once more as they realized that the medical officer was either drunk or crazy. He was giving them a short-arm inspection from the seat of his motor-bike. Solemn face, not a trace of humour, he was passing everyone A1, fit and pox free. The laughter increased and so did the speed of the motor-bike. It reached the end of the line, turned, then roared back at full speed and was soon out of sight. The short-arm inspection was over.

Chapter III

The monsters stood in a long neat line. Five-ton Morris Cowley trucks that supported AA guns pointing to the sky. The orders were that A Company were to transport them over the mountains to an RA company somewhere near Naples.

Jackson, inspecting them with a jaundiced eye, realized that he would not be seeing Toranto after all. He felt regret at missing exploring that scruffy-looking town and acute alarm at the thought of driving one of the monsters over the dangerous-looking, towering mountains that reared up, a giant backcloth in the distance.

Jackson had been passed as a driver on a dusty, bumpy pavement in Ismailia alongside the sweet water canal. He had found driving a truck over the deserted desert track comparatively easy, and even a night drive in convoy through empty villages, no great strain. But his one encounter in daylight driving against fast-moving traffic in a town had proved to be too much. An approaching tank had finally done for him as, in a panic, he swung the driving wheel away from the tank, lurched on the pavement and hurtled down it with Arab women, old men and children screaming ahead of him, then he'd darted off the pavement just in time and almost been mangled under the tracks of the tank. He finally managed to slam on the anchor and come to a shuddering halt.

The Sergeant Driving Instructor had sat stock still for almost a minute, then had slowly and deliberately lit a cigarette. He turned his head and stared balefully at Jackson. Then his expression had changed to one of total disbelief. 'Jackson,' he picked his words carefully. 'You'll never be a driver as long as you've got a hole in your arse.'

It dawned on Jackson that his momentary panic had probably been incurred because the last thing he wanted to be was a driver. He just couldn't see any future in it. Jackson stared back at the Sergeant Instructor, glad that the idiot had thought that one out all by himself. Then he had stared in total disbelief as the Sergeant Instructor continued, a stream of smoke pouring out of his nostrils. 'Passed, Jackson, you're a bleedin' brilliant driver.'

Jackson thought he hadn't heard him right. 'But Sarge. I thought you said . . .'

'I know, son. But if I don't pass you, see, then I'll bleedin' have to keep instructing you, won't I, and you'll end up bleedin' killing me, won't you, son? Not out of spite, of course.' His voice rising and becoming almost incoherent with rage and fear. 'Not out of spite, no. But because you're bleedin' bonkers. A rare, screaming, bleedin' head case. A walking, fucking disaster. Move over, you horrible bastard. You're passed! Passed! You're me star pupil. I'm gonna sing your bleedin' praises and get rid of you.'

He had pushed Jackson out of the driving seat, reversed the truck and driven it back to base.

Staring at the monsters, Jackson thought, I'm stuck with it. I'm a driver, first class, and I've got to drive one of those bloody awful-looking trucks over those bloody awful mountains. Then a more cheerful thought. I'll have a co-driver. I'll let him drive it. I'll put him in the picture, scare the pants off him and he'll be only too keen to do all the driving. Wonder who my co-driver will be?

Dusty Miller with his simpering smile and wondrous, empty blue eyes stared fondly at Jackson. 'I'm your co-driver, Johnnie.'

Jackson stared at him aghast. 'No. Can't be.'

'Oh, yes,' said Dusty. 'It's you and me.'

'No. Not you.'

'Yes, me,' smiled Dusty.

'I'll speak to Tompkins. Don't worry, Dusty. I'll work it out.'

'He spoke to me,' said Dusty, with his beguiling smile. Empty as a vacuum. Vacant as a painted doll, sweetly, enchantingly, childishly innocent. 'It was his idea and I'm glad because I like you, Johnnie. You're nice. Not like some.'

That bastard Tompkins, thought Jackson. He's planning to get rid of us both at the same time.

'Listen,' Jackson put his hands on Dusty's shoulders and bestowed on him a warm, friendly smile. 'I'm a terrible bloody driver. I'm a nervous wreck behind the wheel. Don't you understand? I can't handle a bloody truck. It won't do what I tell it to do. I passed out as a driver on the bloody pavement by the sweet water canal. I nearly killed half the population.'

Dusty looked absolutely delighted. 'Not bad, Johnnie.' Then stuck out his chest and boasted, 'But I did better. I passed out as a driver *in* the sweet water canal.'

Jackson shut his eyes and shuddered. 'Who passed you?'

Dusty switched on his most innocent, so innocent it was almost heart-rending, smile. 'Sergeant Donleavy.'

'The bastard!' shouted Jackson. 'That crazy, cross-eyed bastard! He was the one who passed me!'

'See?' said Dusty. 'So it was meant to be.'

'No. There has to be a way out. No, Dusty. Not us two together. That's pushing our luck.'

'I'll drive, Johnnie. Not to worry. I'll drive.'

'No you bloody won't,' said Jackson, coming to a decision. 'I'll drive. You just sit next to me and keep your trap shut and look at the scenery, or wank off. But don't speak to me. I'll need all my concentration to get over those bloody mountains. Why I had to get you . . .' He stopped and stared into Dusty's eyes. No expression. But he sensed his hurt feelings. 'We'll make it, Dusty. Somehow we'll make it.'

Dusty's beautiful innocent smile returned. 'We'll beat them all,' he boasted. 'We'll show them we ain't head cases.'

Oh, God, Jackson inwardly groaned. This looney boy is putting me in his category now. Then remembering RSM Tompkins. He's not the only one, he thought. Christ, I'm burdened with the label 'head case'. It's supposed to be useful, but it could be the death of me.

*　　*　　*

The transport convoy left the camp one hour after dawn. They had been driving for six hours and Jackson was exhausted from concentrating on the dusty winding mountain tracks. The trucks behind were honking their enraged horns again. The gap between Jackson's truck and the one ahead was at least a mile. Once again, Jackson's careful driving had split the convoy in two, but he was not going to press on at speed to please the stupid bastards honking behind him. What's all the hurry, he reasoned. The object of this exercise is to get there all in one piece.

He glanced sideways and down at a beautiful valley and shuddered again. He had been shuddering for six hours and by now most of his muscles ached. On his left-hand side was a sheer drop of at least five hundred feet and no barricades to protect him. He could almost hear his nerves screaming. How much more can I take, he wondered. The mountain track was very narrow. One false move and he knew he and the truck and Dusty would plunge to their deaths. He was seized by another shuddering fit. He glanced at Dusty, who was blissfully sleeping, mouth open, breathing like an innocent babe. Jackson was almost overwhelmed with hatred. How could that looney sleep through such a hair-raising experience? His brain signalled him to watch the turn ahead. He approached it cautiously, swung the wheel hard, then just in time applied the brakes. The turn was so sharp and narrow his front wheels were on the edge of an abyss. Another few inches and they would have been over the top and plunging to their deaths.

He sat, frozen, holding on to the steering wheel, too afraid to move. Then, dimly at first, he heard the horns honking behind him and voices shouting insults. He ignored them. He stared at Dusty, who stirred in his sleep, then slowly opened his eyes and smiled. 'Are we there, Johnnie?'

'We,' said Jackson, speaking slowly, 'are sitting on the edge of a mountain track, overlooking a panoramic view that stupid fucking tourists have paid a fortune to visit and gasp and coo over!'

'Oh, good. Let's look.'

'Shut up!' screamed Jackson.

Dusty's sweet smile did not switch off, so obviously he wasn't offended. He glanced ahead at the front wheels, then down into the beautiful, fruitful, farm-filled valley. 'We have to back it up, don't we?'

'Yes! That's right! We have to back it up!' Jackson was still screaming and the trucks were still honking their horns, and the soldiers were still shouting withering insults, and Jackson was still ignoring them. Then he had an idea and he turned to Dusty again and got his voice back under control.

'The thing to do, Dusty, is to back it up.'

'I said that,' agreed Dusty, who felt a sudden glow of pride because, for once, he had thought of something first.

'Now the way to handle this little situation,' said Jackson as he slowly, carefully, climbed out of the driver's seat and thankfully felt firm ground beneath him, 'is for you to get into the driving seat. But carefully, don't rock the boat.'

'I was about to say that,' said the delighted Dusty, who all his life had longed to be called on in an emergency. 'I'll back her up and you steer me back.'

'Of course.' Jackson smiled fondly at him. 'Know which is reverse?'

'It's one of them.' Dusty revved the engine madly and the truck shuddered.

Jackson shouted over the roar of the engine, 'I know it's one of them, you daft bastard! The secret is to find the right one.'

'I'll find it,' Dusty shouted back. 'It's here somewhere, so I must find it.' He was slamming the gear handle around the box in the most reckless manner.

'You can't work on the law of averages,' shouted Jackson. 'That's a five-gear job so you're on a five-to-one shot and you'd better pick the winner.' He stepped away from the truck as far as possible and said a short simple prayer. 'God look after the poor daft bastard.'

'This is it!' shouted Dusty. 'I think.'

He grated the gears and the truck leapt back and made a small dent in the mountain. Then it sprung forward again and stopped on the lip of the abyss. Then it purred backwards and Dusty, with a blissful smile, purred it forward again and Jackson leapt aboard and the truck purred smoothly round the mountain track, followed by ironic cheers from the soldiers in the convoy behind.

Dusty, still wearing his blissful smile, glanced at Jackson. 'I'm a good driver when people don't make me nervous.'

'Drive on. Don't talk, Dusty.'

'I'm a smashing driver,' boasted Dusty, stepping on the gas and making a smooth turn. 'All I need's encouragement.'

'You're a smashing driver,' Jackson enthused and thought, I'll say anything to keep the idiot happy. 'You're doing great. Just great.'

'I'm better than Malcolm Campbell and Henry Seagrave,' shouted Dusty. 'I'll catch up with the convoy ahead.'

'Just take it easy.'

'I'll drive the rest of the way, Johnnie. You sleep and don't worry.'

Sleep, thought Jackson. Sleep. Some hopes. But he soon fell into an exhausted sleep.

When Jackson opened his eyes again he had no clear idea where he was. He stared about him. The dusty track that had been hewn out of the mountain twisted and turned. The mountain loomed above. Stunted trees jutted out of the side of the mountain and down below was the same beautiful valley, or perhaps another one. Farmland with a few grazing cattle, specks against the green and red earth. Another turn on the mountain track and ahead a small, dazzling white village.

But higher up the mountain, Jackson sat up straight and stared ahead. Dusty, by some miracle, had caught up with the convoy ahead. Jackson turned in his seat. The rest of the convoy, correctly spaced, was lined up behind him. No honking horns, no abusive screaming drivers. Jackson looked at Dusty, who beamed back. 'I've kept up with them all the way, Johnnie. Fact, I could beat the lot of them I could.'

'Just keep your eyes on the road, Dusty.'

'All the time, Johnnie. I watch it all the time.'

'Keep watching it, Dusty.' Then Jackson remembered to throw in a compliment. 'You're doing great.'

'I'm the best, Johnnie.' Dusty swung the driving wheel with one hand and the truck went into a waltz.

'Hold that bloody wheel with both hands and don't fart about!' Jackson was screaming again. 'Don't take any chances with my life, you stupid bastard!'

'You got the wind up, Johnnie?'

'Shut up! Concentrate on the road.'

'I'm feeling great, Johnnie.'

'Just drive it. Drive it carefully. Don't take any chances. Just drive it.'

'That's what I'm doing.'

'Do it then. Don't fool about.'

They were much closer to the village and it was no longer dazzling white. Jackson stared at it gloomily. Then had an idea. 'Dusty. When we get to the village, turn down the first street we come to.'

'Why, Johnnie?'

'Because I need a drink.'

'What if the convoy goes straight on?'

'The convoy will go straight on, but we're going to stop and have a little drink. Okay?'

'Could go for a beer,' Dusty agreed.

'Don't suppose there's any beer but I could sink a bottle of vino.'

'I could go a bottle of vino.'

'Okay, Dusty. The first turning.'

'The first turning, Johnnie.'

Dusty drove on in silence and soon the wheels were bumping over the cobbled main road in the village. Jackson indicated a turning and Dusty nodded and swung the truck down a narrow street. Behind them the horns started honking again, but Dusty ignored them. The street was so narrow there was only just room for the truck to pass.

They came to a plaza with a fountain in the centre and slowly circled. Dirty white houses, a few shops and a dilapidated-looking bar with iron tables and chairs on the pavement. Jackson pointed to it and Dusty pulled up outside. Jackson eased his cramped limbs out of the truck and slowly walked to the bar and sat down on one of the chairs and Dusty joined him.

They sat there for some moments before Jackson became aware of eyes watching them. He stared at the shuttered windows on the opposite side of the plaza. The shutters moved, just a little, and cautious faces peered out. He continued staring at the shutters and one by one they closed. Then he turned his head and saw an old woman who had left the bar and was standing at his elbow. She was a very ugly old woman, dressed in black. Jackson thought, she has to be eighty, but more probably, a hundred. Her wrinkled face was impassive, but her eyes were watchful and alive.

Jackson smiled at her. 'Vino, my old lovely,' he said, making the shape of a bottle with his hands and gesturing the bottle to his lips. 'One bottle vino, my old sweetheart. Pronto, compree? At the double, you dear old thing.' The old woman's expression did not change, so Jackson repeated the gestures. 'Vino, sweetheart. One bottle quickly-o. Vino, vino. Very importanto. Vino. Booze, darling.'

She turned slowly and walked back to the bar and in a few moments she returned with an opened bottle of red wine, two glasses and a saucer of olives. 'That's my girl,' enthused Jackson. 'The service is pretty good, eh, Dusty?'

'She looks like my old Gran,' beamed Dusty.

She would, thought Jackson, as he poured the wine and bit into an olive, spat out the pip and swallowed the warm red wine, felt it course down his parched throat, and waited for the first tender glow and began to feel good as he emptied his glass and refilled it. This poor old bag just has to look like one of Dusty's family. He clinked glasses. 'Cheers, old son.'

'Cheers.' Dusty bestowed a fond smile on the old woman, who was holding out her hand for payment, then turned to Jackson. 'Good idea stopping off.'

'I'm full of good ideas and lousy intentions.'

'Wouldn't old Tompkins be mad if he knew we'd stopped off?'

'Go out of his raving mind.'

'He's horrible. He's a nasty fella.'

'He's all shout. Pay the old girl, Dusty.'

Dusty smiled. 'Ain't got any money.'

That figures, thought Jackson, as he turned to the old woman. Dusty just has to be broke. 'How much?' he inquired as he pulled out his wallet. 'You want lire or cigarettes?'

A dim light awakened in the old woman's eyes. 'Cigarette.'

Jackson held up a packet of Players and a gnarled hand grabbed the packet and the wrinkles on her face moved. She may have been smiling. Then she slowly walked away again and shortly she returned with another opened bottle of red wine and again the wrinkles moved as she indicated the bottle before shuffling off again.

'That one must be on the house, Dusty. Not bad. Two bottles of wine for a packet of Players. Think I'm going to like Italy.'

He sat in the warm sun and refilled his glass and watched the small children whispering and nudging each other as they moved towards the truck, then cautiously on to the truck, glancing all the time at Jackson and Dusty, ready to run at the first sign of danger. When they saw that neither Jackson nor Dusty were over-interested in their activities, they swarmed all over the truck, pushing and shoving to take turns spinning the wheel that manoeuvred the gunbarrel. Their excited voices rose now as they swung the gun-barrel in all directions, honked the horn, sat behind the steering wheel and climbed all over the truck.

Dusty and Jackson, aglow with kindness as they poured vino down their throats, watched the children with tolerant smiles. Some of the shutters opened again and smiling faces peered down at the happy, excited children, who were playing their own war game, shooting down raiding planes from the clear blue sky.

A jeep roared into the plaza, circled it and came to a squealing halt beside the truck and RSM Tompkins was standing up in the jeep next to his driver and his voice boomed and smashed against the walls of the houses. 'Get out of it, you little wog bastards! Get out of it!' The children scattered in terror.

Dusty slowly stood up, his eyes growing larger and larger as the booming voice beat in his eardrums. He turned to Jackson for advice, help, support. But Jackson remained seated, his body glowing from the warm dry wine. He was half-happily drunk and full of vino courage. He stared at Tompkins and thought, might have expected that stupid prick to track us down. Oh, well. Let him shout. Who cares?

Tompkins walked slowly round the truck, glaring at the gun-barrel, which was pointing directly at the middle house on the opposite side of the plaza. Then he confronted Jackson and Dusty. 'You,' he pointed at Jackson. 'Up on your bloody feet.'

Jackson slowly stood and deliberately drained his glass before replacing it on the table. Then he refilled the glass. 'Like a drink, sir?'

'I'll give you a bloody drink. Put it down.' Jackson put the glass to his lips and drained it. 'I said put it bloody down!' shouted Tompkins.

'I did,' said Jackson with a cheerful, reckless grin. 'And it went down jolly well, too.'

'I'll have you grinning other side of your face. You left the convoy without permission.'

'Had to, sir.'

'Had to?'

'Wouldn't have got permission otherwise.'

'Comic lad, ain't you? A little comic lad, eh?'

'Yes, sir.'

'Bleedin' bonkers the pair of you. Am I right?'

'Bleedin' bonkers, sir,' agreed Jackson cheerfully.

'I know Miller is. How they ever let him out of kindergarten is a bleedin' mystery. Stand up straight, Miller, when I'm talking to you.' Dusty did his best to stand ramrod stiff but his knees were trembling. 'Know you're a looney, boy. Mystery of the age how they ever passed you for the army. Whose pissing idea was it, Miller, to stop off for a drink, eh?'

Dusty turned his beseeching eyes on Jackson, frantically

appealing for help, his adam's apple dancing like a yo-yo.

'My idea,' smiled Jackson. 'I had a sudden inspiration.'

'You did, eh? Oh, you did.'

'Over six hours' steady driving, sir. Thought it was time for a stop and a rest.'

'There was no bleedin' place to stop and rest on that bleedin' road. No place.'

'There was here,' smiled Jackson. 'And very nice it turned out to be.'

Tompkins stared at Jackson for a long moment. 'You two get back into that truck and catch up with that bleedin' convoy and when we get to our destination, you're both on a charge. Now move!'

Dusty ran to the truck and revved the engine like mad and Jackson just made it as the truck roared into life and circled the plaza and sped into the narrow street, on to the main pass through the mountains. Dusty was driving like the wind and Jackson, glowing with vino and in a happy state of mind, sat relaxed in his seat.

'Jankers for us,' muttered Dusty. 'Or the glass-house. What will they do to us, Johnnie?'

'Nothing.'

'Jankers or the glass-house.'

'Nothing, Dusty. Don't worry.'

'Jankers . . .'

'Shut up, Dusty. Stop sweating. Tompkins is all shout. Anyway, we're both looney boys. How can they expect us to behave in a rational manner?'

'What will you say to Major Holland?'

'I'll worry about that when the time comes.'

'What can I say, Johnnie?'

Jackson started laughing. 'Dusty, honestly, you don't have to say anything. All you have to do is look at him and he'll tell you not to be a naughty boy again and send you home to your mother.'

Dusty smiled his sweetest smile. 'Tell you the truth, Johnnie. I've always been a naughty boy. It's much more fun, ain't it?'

Jackson lit a cigarette, still laughing. 'Dusty, you're a hell of a lot brighter than most people give you credit for.'

Dusty was delighted. 'I'm not so daft as I'm green looking. Ain't I driving good, Johnnie?' The truck was eating up the miles, now the dusty track had turned into a good tarmac road, and the frightening bends were easy curves.

'You're a great driver, Dusty. Better than Malcolm Campbell. But don't go too mad with joy. Slow down on the curves.'

Chapter IV

501 Company reached their destination – a farmhouse, meadow lands, and several farm workers' cottages – at five in the afternoon. They hastily set up tents and before darkness descended, Sergeant Leadbetter had set up his field cookhouse in and outside one of the farm cottages and served the first hot meal of the day. Bully beef stew, hardtack biscuits, and piping-hot sweet tea. The men ate ravenously, then wearily turned in for the night. No one, apart from Major Holland, had any idea why they were setting up camp in the fields of a deserted farm and no one particularly cared. Most of the men were convinced that the camp had to be a temporary halting place. It didn't make much sense to the men, being dumped in the middle of nowhere. Living in tents. Sleeping on rock-hard ground. They had had a comfortable war and were a disgruntled company before they finally groaned and bitterly complained themselves to a restless sleep.

RSM Tompkins was reporting the inexcusable conduct of Jackson and Miller to Major Holland, who was listening with growing impatience. It had been a long day and he was tired. He finally interrupted Tompkins. 'Listen to me, Sergeant Major. It must be fairly obvious to you that Miller is mentally retarded and Jackson's got a bad mental history, too, and there are others. Fitzroy, for example, and Watson. We've had quite a few of them fostered on us and if I get any more, I'm sending them back. Damn it, it's hard enough trying to run a company with supposedly average, mentally normal chaps.'

'But, sir. Boozing outside a bar. Kids swarming all over the truck, fooling about with the AA gun . . .'

'Were they drunk and incapable?'

'Jackson, sir, I would say was drunk.'

Holland interrupted again. 'They got here all in one piece?'

'Well, sir, yes. But an example ought to be set.'

'Both of them are mental cases. I'm only surprised they didn't give the truck away, or, more probably, try to sell it. I'll have them on the mat, of course, and give them a good dressing down. Stop them seven days' pay. But no jankers. We need every man. Know why we're here?'

'No, sir.'

'This place is going to be one of the biggest petrol and oil dumps in Italy, and I've got to get all the labour I can from the village or wherever. I've rather a lot on my plate, Sergeant Major. Understand?'

Tompkins understood very quickly when the old man decided to be tough. 'Yes, sir. I understand.'

'Good. Now I'm going to turn in.'

Tompkins saluted and marched out, thinking. Those two loonies should be on a charge. Jankers or the glass-house. If the Major lets them get away with it, be no holding them.

Reveille next morning found the men still disgruntled and back-weary from sleeping on the hard ground. But breakfast – tinned bacon and beans, hardtack biscuits and the inevitable sweet tea – restored them a little, and the usual moans and complaints were mixed with jokes about the fate in store for them.

Drivers from 17 RA Company appeared on the scene and the trucks were handed over to them and forms were signed and a lot of saluting went on before the trucks were driven out of the meadows and the drivers of 501 Company were happy to see the last of them.

Major Holland had taken over the farmhouse. The living-room was now the Company office. The upstairs bedrooms were shared by himself, Captain Butcher and Lieutenant Randall.

Butcher had grown a large moustache. His habitual expression was one of cynical amusement. He was thirty-five years old and still could not understand why he enjoyed the good luck to be posted to a company that obviously would not be seeing any action. At least, so far, 501 Company hadn't, and he fervently hoped it never would.

Randall was twenty-three. An earnest young man with poor eyesight. He was secretly ashamed of the thick spectacles that were so necessary to him, and also ashamed that he had been posted to a company that had never seen any action and probably never would. Major Holland was briefing them.

'My orders are that we build and maintain an oil and petrol dump. A and B Companies will maintain it, C and D transport.'

'How long will we be here?' inquired Butcher.

'Don't know. It looks like the last place on God's earth to me, but don't let's start worrying about that now. Our first job is to get organized.'

'Will the men be sleeping under canvas until further orders, or is it only temporary, sir?' Randall peered at Holland through his thick spectacles.

'As I understand it, yes.'

'When winter comes, sir ...'

'And we'll worry about that when the time comes.'

'The men are already complaining about sleeping on rocks,' said Butcher.

'Then get them busy digging them out. They'll have to make themselves comfortable the best way they can. I need hardly add that the men in the front line experience even more discomfort. Now, we'll have to rig up a canteen as soon as possible.'

Randall eagerly interrupted. 'I'll get the canteen under way, sir. But the beer ration's only three bottles a man a fortnight.'

'Isn't that too bad. So they won't be drunk every night.

We must find other ways to entertain them. Any suggestions?'

'Might form a concert party, sir.'

Holland looked at Randall and thought, you really are rather a simple man. 'Any other bright ideas?'

'Er . . . what about forming a discussion group, sir?'

Can he be serious, wondered Holland. 'Butcher, there may be a film unit in Naples. Check it out and if there is, try and persuade them to visit us at least one a month.'

'Yes, sir,' agreed Butcher.

Randall had another brilliant idea. 'And talks, sir, we could organize . . .'

'Talks on what? The political situation? Art? The ballet? You'd better get to know the men. Pitch up a tent as a reading room.'

Randall was still eager beaver. 'And a library. Sir, with your permission I'll see if I can scrounge some decent books from the Red Cross or somewhere.'

'Cowboys and thrillers and all the copies you can lay your hands on of *Blighty* and *Lilliput*. Any mags with a pin-up on the front page.'

'Yes, sir. And some decent books.'

'I'll leave it to you.' Holland turned to Butcher. 'I'm putting two of the village cafés in bounds. One for NCOs. One for ORs. This is important. All houses barring the two cafés are out of bounds to all ranks.'

'Right ho,' smiled Butcher, and thought, I can't see that working. Poor old Holland ought to know better than try and pull that one.

'Food is very scarce,' continued Holland. 'Damn scarce, so no meals must be served to the men. Make that very clear. Drinks only.'

'I'll do what I can, sir,' nodded Butcher.

Holland stood up. 'There's sure to be a pretty brisk black market trade in the village, so any man caught bartering with the villagers is for the high jump. Understand?' Both Butcher and Randall nodded. 'The small hotel on the outskirts of the village is in bounds to officers only and the same rules will apply there. Drinks only will be served.' Corporal

Mills entered the office and waited. Holland turned to him. 'Yes, Corporal?'

'There's a priest waiting outside, sir. He wants to have a word with you.'

'Do you mean an Army Chaplain?'

'No, sir. Think he's the village priest.'

'Better show him in.'

Butcher, followed by Randall, moved towards the door. 'We'll get busy, sir.' They walked into the bright sunlight.

A tall, thin, haggard, grey-haired man slowly entered the room and stared intently at Holland. Then he smiled. 'I am Father Raffio.'

Holland shook his hand. 'How do you do. I'm Major Holland. What can I do for you?'

'Sir. I have come . . . It is for the people of the village. I have been to Napoli and I return and the English are here, making this camp.'

'Just the thing I want to speak to somebody about. I was going to see the mayor, but you'll do. We're building a petrol dump here and I need labour. All the men I can get my hands on.'

Father Raffio looked happy. 'This is excellent, all will be joyed.'

'The payments. Father . . .'

'Food is badly needed.'

'As soon as they start work. I can pay them daily if you wish.'

'You can give them food, Major?'

'Food? Sorry, no. But there's a fixed rate of pay. Now, how many men do you think . . .?'

Father Raffio interrupted Holland. 'But no food?'

'Well, I'm afraid not. You see . . .'

'The children of the village. You have seen them?'

'Only just got here, Father.'

Holland had seen a few of the children as he drove through the village. They had sat listlessly on the pavements staring large-eyed at the convoy as it drove in a cloud of white dust down the village main street. 'Yes, I saw some of the children.'

41

Father Raffio would not permit himself to show any emotion. 'All need food. All.'

'I'm only permitted to draw rations for my men. I'm sorry. But we are paying four hundred lira a day, you know.'

'Would not buy a loaf of bread.'

'Come, now.'

'I speak of the black market.' Holland stiffened. 'How else will the people buy food?'

A hard look crept into Holland's eyes. 'You sound as if you approve.'

'Approve!' Father Raffio became angry. 'The black market must stop.'

Holland nodded grimly. 'It will. I'll see to that. I promise you if I catch any of my men dealing with the people in the village . . .'

'If my people do not deal with the soldiers, many will starve. But, sir. If you give them food. Money is almost useless, but if you give them food then this way we can help to end the black market, yes?'

Holland adopted a stern attitude. 'I'm sorry, but rules and regulations make it quite clear how much I pay for labour, and I must stand by the rules.'

'Rules.' Father Raffio shook his head. 'This means nothing to my people. With cigarettes they can barter for food . . .'

Holland interrupted. 'Any man I find selling cigarettes to civilians will find himself facing a court martial.'

Father Raffio stared long and steadily at Holland. 'Then my people will starve.'

Holland spoke crisply. 'Sorry, but rules and regulations are made to be obeyed.'

Father Raffio looked at Holland more in sadness than in anger. 'Si. But your rules will not help to keep my people alive. Please think over all I have said. I will come back.' He slowly moved to the door. He looked a very tired old man.

The midday meal was over and the men in line were emptying their slops into a filthy dustbin. The usual moans and jokes were repeated. 'Bloody bully beef again . . . roll on demob . . . who called the cook a cook.' Some of the men flicked their cigarette butts into the dustbin before wandering away.

Four barefooted children watched the last man leave, then they swarmed around the dustbin. They carried tins with wire handles and struggled and pushed and shoved each other and dipped the tins into the dustbin and collected the soggy food. Watson, who was removing the remains of a dixy of tea and hardtack biscuits from a trestle table outside the cookhouse, pretended he had not seen them.

Sergeant Leadbetter left the cookhouse and shouted at the children. ' 'Op it. 'Op it, you lot.' The children, clutching their tins, ran away as fast as they could. Leadbetter now turned his attention on Watson. 'Ain't I told you to chase those kids?'

'I do, Sarge.'

'You'd better make a better job of it. Holland's orders, no kids allowed in the camp.'

'Poor little bastards.'

'Poor little bastards is right, but orders is orders.' He snapped to attention and saluted as Major Holland walked past, then stopped and inspected the dustbin. He sniffed. 'Don't smell too healthy, Sergeant.'

'No fatigue party yet, sir.'

'Speak to the Sergeant Major.'

'Yes, sir.'

'I saw children.'

'I chase them, sir. But I can't keep them all away.'

'Don't encourage them.'

'I don't give them nothing, sir. It's the swill they come after.'

Holland leaned forward and stared into the bin. A soggy mess of bully beef, vegetables, tea, hardtack biscuits, and cigarette butts.

Leadbetter was staring at him. 'The kids is near starving, sir.'

Holland spoke harshly. 'I've instructed the Regimental

Police to keep the children out of the camp.'

'Yes, sir.'

Holland walked away, then had a change of mind and returned and stared at the dustbin again. 'Get three new dustbins. New ones. Try the QM. If he hasn't any, find some.'

'Yes, sir.'

'Make sure they're thoroughly scoured. Put a notice on each of them. MEAT AND VEG. DESSERT. TEA. Understand?'

Sergeant Leadbetter smiled. 'Yes, sir.'

'And if you catch any of the men carelessly unloading all his leavings in one bin or dropping cigarette ends, send him to me.'

'I will, sir,' beamed Leadbetter. 'Will you be having a word with the Regimental Police, sir?'

'Yes,' snapped Holland as he marched away.

'What's all that about?' inquired Watson when Major Holland was out of earshot.

'Giving me a few tips about how to feed the five thousand.'

'He can be a hard bastard, Sarge.'

'Maybe. The other order still stands. Don't let me catch you slipping grub to them kids.'

It was the last thought in Watson's mind. Any food he gave away would not be for humanitarian reasons. He grinned. 'Now would I, Sarge?'

'Just don't let me catch you. If we feed them our own lads go short and I ain't having that.'

Watson laughed. 'Some wouldn't mind.'

'Great comic you are, but there's nothing to laugh about.'

'No offence, Sarge. But I ain't had a square meal since I joined the bloody army.'

'No? Tell that to them poor little bastards who were bloody near killing each other to get at the swill.' A burst of anger. 'I'm about sick of looking at them, I am.' He turned and walked back into the cookhouse.

It was early evening and Jackson, Fitzroy and Watson stared about them. A large stone cross stood in the centre of the village square and close to it an old stone bench, a few dusty, shrivelled flowers in a bed beneath the cross. All three sat on the bench and stared at the houses with very little interest. Paddy, staring about him as he lit a cigarette, said, 'It couldn't be more deserted now, could it?'

Jackson stared at the closed window shutters. 'It's not.'

Paddy pulled on his cigarette. 'We haven't run into nobody now, have we?'

'I can feel them, Paddy.'

Watson nodded. 'They're maybe waiting to see what we're up to.'

Paddy smiled. 'Sure we're not going to eat them.'

'They're a shower, anyway,' grunted Watson, who was bored almost out of his mind.

Paddy stood up to inspect the village more thoroughly. 'We didn't bash this place about at all. Sure, they must have had a cushy war.'

Watson nodded. 'One bomb and the lot would crumble.' Jackson was observing Watson. There was something about him he didn't like. 'Did you notice all the farms we passed?'

'What about them?' Watson moodily lit a cigarette.

'Dead. No animals. Nothing.'

'That's so,' agreed Paddy. 'And what about this dump?'

'Dead,' agreed Jackson.

Paddy, still searching about him for the one place that interested him most, said, 'Where's the pub old blow-hard Butcher was shouting about. Couldn't I use a drink now.'

'Jerry did it,' said Jackson.

'Now what did he do as if anyone bloody cares, Johnnie?'

'Cleaned them out. Livestock, grub, farm equipment, the lot. Left them with exactly bugger all.'

'Yeah,' agreed Watson. 'Old Jerry don't mess about. Got to give him that.'

God, thought Jackson. Nearly three years in the desert, Wadi this and Wadi that and Wadi nowhere. Sidi Barrani, nothing there but an old Italian fort and a couple of wog houses. Tobruk, a dustbowl. Derna, dead. Benghazi, what a dump, and to think we all started to cheer when we learned we were sailing for Italy. He was laughing and couldn't understand why. Maybe I really am crazy, he thought. Now I'm stuck in this dump, I'm laughing. One thing's sure, we'll all die of sheer bloody boredom here. Watson was looking at him with a sour expression.

'Watty, those mountains we came over from Toranto. Did you ever see anything like them?'

'Sod the mountains. Remember that village we came through? Remember the bint doing the washing in the square with the lovely round little bum, who turned and laughed. Then she waved to me.'

'Bints,' yawned Paddy. 'I don't fancy our chances. I've not met the good living Catholic girl yet who's prepared to open her little fat legs until after you've danced into the church with her. I'm telling you the good believing lot of them are all terrible con artists. Sure now we must be able to get a drink some place.'

'All houses are out of bounds except two bars. We'd better track them down,' said Jackson.

Watson nodded. 'Here, what's this?'

They all stared at a small skinny girl in a threadbare dress. Jackson guessed her age as thirteen, possibly fourteen, but she looked older.

Father Raffio passing her, stopped for a moment and patted her face then placed a hand on her head. She smiled then walked away. He watched her, then stopped smiling and crossed to a small church and entered it.

The girl glanced at the soldiers as she was passing and Paddy smiled at her.

'Hello, me little darlin'. Will you come here a minute now?' The girl paused and stared, big-eyed, at the soldiers. Paddy held up a bar of chocolate and the girl made a grab at it, but Paddy held it higher in the air the way one would hold up a bone for a dog. Still smiling he spoke very clearly. 'Me . . . looking . . . for . . . drink . . . understand? Drink . . . me . . . want . . . drink . . .' He allowed the girl to take the bar of chocolate. She clutched it in her hand and stared silently at Paddy.

'Let me try,' said Watson, as he handed her a cigarette. 'Here. Cigarette for Poppa.' Then aside to Jackson, 'If they're watching, and I bet they are, they'll catch on we're friendly.' 'What's your name, eh? Me . . . Walter . . . what's your name?' The girl made no reply. 'Name. Understand name, you sloppy little bitch.' An aside grin at Jackson, who was watching the pantomime with a bored expression. 'Wonder if she's got any big-titted sisters? What's your name, love?'

The girl stared blankly at Watson. She had made no attempt to unwrap the chocolate bar. Jackson watched her carefully place it in a little pocket in her dress, and she kept her hand over the pocket, guarding the chocolate bar. Jackson realized that it took a great effort of will on the child's part to simply leave the chocolate bar in her pocket. He didn't want to look at her another moment so glanced at Watson and observed that he was fast losing patience, but still trying to keep up a pretence of friendliness.

'All I want to know is your name, dopey. Is that much to ask?' The girl was smiling to herself now and staring at the chocolate bar in her pocket. Watson exploded. 'Aw. Go on, beat it. She's dumb or daft like everybody in every stinking country we've soldiered in. They stick out their hands. Gimme. Gimme.' The girl flinched, but stood her ground.

'No need to scare her,' said Jackson. 'She's only a kid.'

'Gimme, gimme. It's all they bloody know. That and British Tommy no good.'

Jackson watched a young Italian as he crossed the square and came up behind the girl. He walked slowly and was smiling. He touched the girl lightly on the shoulder. 'She's a little crazy.' He smiled down at the girl. 'My name is Tony. You like this village, yes?'

'He must be joking,' said Jackson.

Tony smiled. 'It's very good if you got chocolate, cigarettes. You soon find you like it then.' He was watching the soldiers for their reactions. 'You got bully beef maybe you've got a nice time.'

'The different-coloured bastard's a pimp,' said Paddy, as a delighted grin began to spread over his face. 'Tony, we've got all that, and more, so we have. Now what have you got to offer?'

Tony winked, then he sniggered. 'You like dance? You like sing? You like the music?' A broad smile. 'Tell me what you like?'

'I'd like to fuck your sister,' said Watson.

The smile froze on Tony's face as he stared at Watson. Then he decided to ignore the remark. 'You like beautiful girls? That's what you look for, yes?'

'Wow!' said Jackson, without even a trace of joy in his voice as he imitated Tony. 'We wanna dance, we wanna sing. Music, champagne, beautiful girls.' He moved close to Tony, a belligerent look in his eyes. 'You understand bully beef, buckshees, cigarettes, chocolate, gimme, gimme. You understand?'

'Sure I understand.'

'I bet you bloody do.'

'You like good time, dance, sing, drink, girls. I have it.'

'He's going to take us to the local Palais,' said Jackson. 'Now we're going to start living.'

'Will you all stop beefing now,' said Paddy. 'An' listen to the dirty-minded, different-coloured bastard.' He put a friendly arm about Tony. 'Look, I'm needing a drink. I've a terrible thirst on me. I'm not so crazy about the girls now. Having had thirteen packets from wog bints, but wid a good drink inside me, maybe I'll chance the black pox again. Now you show us the pub first an' we'll come up wid all the luxury goods, understand?'

'I understand.' Tony was smiling again, as he put a friendly arm around Paddy. 'I got all the good times laid on.'

'Where, you darlin' little charmer?' smiled Paddy.

'No far from here.'

'You've got it. You wouldn't be putting us on now?'

'I got everythin',' he winked. 'I got the drink. I got the nice ladies.'

'Wow!' Watson danced a few steps. 'Wow! Let's go.'

'Hold it a minute,' said Jackson. 'I've seen this scene too many times before. Up comes a spiv and soon you're diving down some bloody awful back alleys. If you're lucky you don't get kicked to death and if you're unlucky you end up in some hovel and get filled up with jungle juice. I saw two New Zealand soldiers in Benghazi as they staggered out of a bar, both blind and dying on their feet.'

Paddy's eyes were cold but his smile was strangely gentle.

'This fella will take the first drink and if it's rot gut, sure I'll kick him to death. Johnnie, I've been in the worst places in the world an' come out smiling an' smelling of roses.'

Tony protested. 'We go to grand casa. Big home. Colonel.'

'Who?'

'Colonel. Big officer. His family nice people.'

Watson laughed. 'Entering high society.'

'Si,' agreed Tony. 'One time plenty money. Tell you true. Good people. Povero now. This business for me.'

'You worry too much, Jackson,' sneered Watson. 'Let's get going.'

'Si, let's get going,' said Tony, as he walked away. 'Girls multa bella. Come on.'

The soldiers followed a few paces behind him.

Chapter V

Major Holland, Captain Butcher and Lieutenant Randall were relaxing in the bar of the Mirima Hotel. A gaudy but comfortable little room. Butcher and Randall were drinking wine, Holland coffee. Not very good coffee and he was vaguely troubled. It was a drink, of course, but surely, unlike the wine, it had to be rationed. Therefore, it could be black market coffee. Perhaps in future he had better not drink it. He noted that the barman, who, he had discovered, was also the owner of the pension, did not look as if he was starving to death. He made a mental note to check on him in the near future.

He wanted to relax, but it was not in his nature. 501 Company problems were always his first waking thoughts, and his last, before he fell asleep. He seldom thought about his wife. Their marriage had been a disaster. For once in his life he had allowed passion to rule him. She had been a pretty girl, but empty. A shallow, selfish, demanding child, and had never grown into a woman. Worst of all, she was common.

'I'm not too happy about the transport,' he said.

'The trucks have had some pretty hard wear, sir,' explained Randall. 'And the fitters tell me . . .'

'Don't let them tell you anything. You tell them . . .'

'Yes, sir,' Randall hastily agreed, then tried to change the subject. 'Not a bad little bar, sir.'

'I wouldn't know. I seldom use bars.'

Butcher grinned and thought, it wouldn't be a bad idea, old boy, if you just once got absolutely pissed out of your mind. 'Any further news about home leave?'

'You shouldn't listen to rumours, Butcher.'

'The men are getting thoroughly browned off.'

'Getting browned off won't do them a damn bit of good. But let them moan.'

'What good does moaning do, sir?'

'Helps let off steam. Nearly three-quarters of the men are married don't forget, Randall.'

'Were, you mean?'

'All right, Butcher. I've a full record of all the wives who've fallen by the wayside since we embarked.'

'Of course, sir.'

'Our chaps are a lot of whitewashed saints, so it's extra hard on them when they discover their wives can't be trusted.'

'Either,' smiled Butcher.

Holland stared a long moment at Butcher, then returned his smile. 'Think I'll make an early night of it.' He nodded briefly, then left.

Butcher waited, listened to Holland's car drive away, then beckoned to the barman.

'Do you think you could lay on a decent meal?'

The barman looked troubled. 'Sir, excuse. It is not possible.'

Butcher lounged over to the bar, seated himself and stared at his reflection in the mirror. 'Why?'

'The Major, sir. He gives the orders.'

'I know the rules, old boy. Cigarettes, chocolates, you name it. You've got a little room tucked away somewhere haven't you, where a chap can have a quiet little dinner?'

The barman still looked troubled. 'If the Major finds out, sir.'

'Why should he? He's an awfully decent chap. Doesn't drink. Doesn't smoke. In bed most evenings by nine. The festivities will commence after he's pissed off to his billet.'

The barman smiled. 'Si, sir. That is different.'

'And how about girls, eh? Rather lonely dining alone, you know.'

'I think, sir, that is also possible. But tonight I do not think . . .'

Butcher smiled. 'Not to worry, old boy. Now, what's on the menu?'

'We have something very good. You call it octopus, yes?'

Butcher shuddered. 'You can stuff that, old boy.'

'We have chicken, sir, and with this I will make a sauce . . .'

Butcher looked happy. 'Don't give me all the gory details. Just pull your finger out and get cracking.'

'Yes, sir. Take a little time.'

'I can wait.'

Randall joined Butcher at the bar. 'I couldn't help over-hearing . . .'

'It wasn't exactly top secret, old boy.'

'I think it's a bit much.'

'What?'

'I mean, after all the old man said about buying black market food.'

'Oh, that,' Butcher smiled. 'Not a bad wine this.'

'It's on Regimental orders. Anyone buying black market food . . .'

'For Christ's sake, old boy. I pinned it on the board.'

'You're setting a pretty poor example, if you don't mind my saying so.'

'Not in the least. Going to join me for dinner?'

'No, thanks. You know there are people in the village going damn hungry?'

'You mean the enemy, old boy?'

'Not our enemy now, as you jolly well know.'

'Sorry, but the change over from enemy to friend has been rather too sudden for me.'

'If you caught one of our men dealing on the black market . . .'

'I'd put him on a charge.'

'And you see nothing wrong in that?'

'Listen, old boy. In the army it's not do as I do, but do as I say.'

'I still think it's a damn poor example to set.'

'How long have you been overseas, Randall?'

'Four months. But look here, that's got nothing to do with it.'

Butcher smiled. 'You've got plenty of time to learn the ropes.'

'I'm damn sure I don't want to learn tricks like that.'

Butcher bestowed on him a cynical smile. 'You'll finish up like the rest of us. You know, this really isn't a bad wine.'

The soldiers sat on uncomfortable old-fashioned chairs in the main living-room of the Colonel's house. The furniture was ugly but there was a look of solid prosperity about it. Near the window stood a grand piano, on it a bowl of faded flowers and framed family portraits. On one of the walls was a large photograph of a handsome army officer.

Seated beneath the photograph was an old man. Jackson had been staring at the photograph, then at the old man, for some time. The resemblance, considering the passage of the years, was remarkable. The moustache was grey on the old man and the brown liquid eyes faded, but the firm chin, the way the old man held his head, was unmistakable. He was a very handsome old man and Jackson felt uncomfortable in his presence and an intruder in the house. The old man sat very still. It seemed that he was totally unaware of the soldiers, who sat in line on the uncomfortable chairs facing him. Only Paddy appeared to be relaxed and at ease. He crossed to the man with a pleasant smile and offered him a cigarette.

'Colonel, me old darling, have a cigarette now.'

The Colonel's eyes were frigid. 'Thank you, I do not smoke,' the voice cold, correct.

Paddy stared at him for a moment before he retreated back to his chair.

'Okay, Colonel. You speak good English, sir.'

'I speak very little English.' The words stiff, over formal, pronounced carefully. 'Not since many year.'

'In the First World War, eh?' coaxed Paddy, who was thinking, the old goat's going to be hard to get along with. He's putting a hell of a damper on the party.

'I have not the remembrance,' said the starchy old Colonel, and added, 'And not the interest,' as he picked up a book, opened it, and began to read.

'Enjoying the party, Watson?' inquired Jackson pleasantly. 'How do you like high society?'

Watson scowled, lowered his voice and said, 'How do we get out of here?'

'Stand up and walk,' said Jackson, but he had no intention of moving on yet. He was curious about the old man and his middle-aged daughter, who sat on another high-backed uncomfortable chair, seemingly at a loss to know what to do with the soldiers. Jackson knew she should really be plump. Instead, she looked like a woman who had taken a crash diet course and was suffering because of it.

'I don't think they've been in the entertainment business long,' smiled Jackson, as he watched Tony cross over to the vaguely smiling woman and speak urgently to her. She rose from her chair, nodding her head, and moved to the sideboard and began pouring wine into glasses, turning to smile at the soldiers.

'Vino, si.'

'That's it, Momma,' beamed Paddy. 'Pour out the vino, me old darlin'. Loosen our tongues for the love of God and have some yourself and pour some into the old man and put a bloom on him, the starchy old sod.' Taking a glass from the smiling lady and toasting her. 'Here's to me and myself and the top of the beautiful morning to you.' He drained it and took another glass from the tray. 'Let's make

it a party now, you dear woman. Here's to you, Colonel.'
The Colonel took his eyes from the book, stared through
Paddy for a long moment, then returned to the book. 'I'm
still wishing you luck anyway, Colonel,' chatted on Paddy,
who had lost his sense of ease and well-being since his encounter with the Colonel. 'Here's to everybody now.'

A smiling Tony sat down next to him holding a glass of
wine. He spoke softly.

'I tell you this nice people, yes?'

Paddy smiled and nodded. 'The best, so they are.'

'You say you have cigarettes. It is for the vino, understand?'

'No problem,' winked Paddy, throwing a package of cigarettes on the table. 'We came prepared, so we did.'

More packages of cigarettes were thrown on the table by
the soldiers and Momma looked embarrassed and happy at
the same time and kept repeating 'Gracia' and smiling. Then
she carefully locked the cigarettes away in a drawer and
served more wine and the soldiers warmed to her.

'Seems a nice old girl,' said Watson, as he helped himself
to another glass of wine from the tray.

'Sure, she's like me old mother,' said Paddy. 'Anxious to
please.' As he stood up, he took the bottle from Momma's
hand. 'Let me do this now and you yourself go and sit down
and take it easy and I'll do the pouring.'

Momma, who was clearly very anxious to please, spoke
her thanks in Italian and seated herself next to Watson and
sipped her glass of wine and smiled sweetly at the soldiers,
trying to make them understand how welcome they were.

Soon the soldiers responded to her and her kindness,
speaking in as clear English as they could muster, and not
forgetting to put an 'o' on the end of most of the words, believing this would help simplify communication. They relaxed a little on their hard chairs and made complimentary
remarks about her, smiling at her and nodding their heads
and Tony helped as best he could by translating some of the
things Momma said.

'Sure she's a good old soul. Likes a gas and a bit of a
laugh, you can see that.'

'Lady says always welcome you nice boys.'

'We're getting the old feet under the table, eh?'

'Have a drink, Colonel. Come on now.' A remark the Colonel preferred to ignore.

Proud old bastard, thought Jackson. He hates us being in his house. Who can blame him?

'Pour a drink for Tony, Paddy.'

'Sure I'll do that. It's a great harbour we've sailed into. They'll have me carried out, so they will.'

'What's she saying now?'

'She say thank you, you very kind and she is happy.'

'We'll have her reciting "Dangerous Dan" before she's much older. Better get some more booze, Paddy.'

Paddy, who had made himself barman, couldn't pour the wine fast enough. Momma had stacked the sideboard with bottles. She repeatedly asked Tony what the soldiers were saying and laughed and was obviously enjoying herself.

'They do not know how long they will be in the camp. They think a long time,' Tony translated in Italian to Momma, and she hoped these nice boys with their cigarettes, which she could barter for food, would stay a very long time.

'Sure what wouldn't I give for a good pint of stout.' Jackson inquired. 'Were you in the army, Tony?'

'Excuse?'

Jackson, glowing, laughing, beginning to feel good. 'Army. You fight? You kill English?'

Tony laughed. 'Si, me soldier. But not kill. Not like kill.'

'No soldier now?'

'I finish. I say hell with this, it's no good to fight. Better drink. Better be happy.'

Watson called out, 'More vino, Paddy.'

Paddy, who thought he was picking up the language, quickly poured wine into Watson's glass. 'Si, si, more vino.'

Jackson, glowing and cheerful, watched the scene with amusement. Not so very long ago the English and Italians were killing each other in the desert and now, here we are, drinking and laughing together. It just doesn't make sense. Then he corrected himself. It does make sense. This definitely makes sense, but not to the old hide-bound Colonel.

Of course not. He's on the losing end. A house like this. A lifetime of devoted service to the army, pensioned, retired, and now he has to sell vino to English soldiers to survive. I suppose that wouldn't make sense to me if I were in his boots, come to think about it.'

He thought about finishing his drink and leaving, because suddenly the Colonel and even happy smiling Momma depressed him. He knew, under normal circumstances this family would not even give him the time of day and he resented it. The only thing that kept him in his seat was his curiosity about the beautiful girls, and he was none too sure that they even existed.

As he was thinking this, two young women entered and stood shyly in the doorway looking at the soldiers. The Colonel lowered his book and shouted something in Italian, but Momma shushed him. The soldiers gaped at the girls, who were in their early twenties. Momma introduced them, Cristina and Maria. Paddy became bashful and tongue-tied. Watson held their hands too long, and Jackson stared boldly at Cristina and thought he had never seen any girl as beautiful and for once in his life he was lost for words. As they shook hands, he was aware of her staring into his eyes before demurely glancing away. Suddenly he felt exhilaration as he realized that she was interested in him.

The girls walked over to the Colonel and greeted him with playful kisses on his stern cheeks. In return the Colonel was clearly trying to lecture them, but they were laughing and so obviously charming him that, against his wishes, he began to relax and even smiled.

Tony said in Jackson's ear, 'The girls are bella but also innocent, understand?'

'Yes.' Jackson was still watching Cristina.

'I want you all understand that.'

Jackson glanced at Tony and realized that he was in love with Cristina and he thought, poor old Tony. He hasn't got a chance in hell. He smiled. 'Don't worry, Tony. The boys know how to behave.'

'They better,' said Tony.

'What's the entertainment?'

'Maria play the piano. Cristie, she sing.'

'What does she sing?'

Tony smiled broadly. 'She like sing opera. You like?' He walked away.

Watson joined Jackson. 'Did you get those two bints?'

'That's the snag. Nobody's going to get them.'

'Yeah? You watch my smoke.'

'I will,' said Jackson, then motioned Watson to be quiet. Maria was playing the piano and Cristina began singing in a small, sweet voice and Jackson knew she would never make an opera appearance. She moved and the last dying rays of the sun shone on her and Jackson saw her for the first time clearly and thought, Oh, my God. The poor, skinny bitch. The poor skinny bitch, with more love than he thought he could ever be capable of.

A week had passed since 501 Company had set up camp and still Major Holland had no labour from the village, and the men under his command were complaining bitterly. They toiled in the hot sun, humping and loading oil drums on to transport trucks. Stripped to the waist, their bodies covered in oil, foul tempered, and no matter how hard they worked, they were always behind schedule.

Holland was interviewing the Mayor of the village. A pot-bellied, sly-eyed, pompous man. Tony, aided by Jackson and Paddy, who had sung his linguistic prowess to Butcher, had been appointed official interpreter to the Company. Holland was listening impatiently to a flow of Italian that issued from the thick lips of the Mayor. Turning to Tony, he inquired, 'What is he saying now?'

'Sir, he say you not understand the people.'

'Tell him we must have labour.'

The Mayor interrupted, speaking in faltering English, 'Food. Un'erstan', food.'

Tony backed the Mayor. 'All anybody is interest in, sir, is food. Give them food and all work like crazy for you.'

'I've specially asked permission from the area command for extra rations. But my request has been refused.'

The Mayor interrupted again, this time speaking in

Italian and with a belligerent look in his eyes.

'What does he say now? Does he keep saying no?' Holland turned to Tony. 'I can give work to more than half the men in the village. I'll even go further. I'll employ every man in the village. Now, that may well cause me problems, but I'll chance it.' Tony interpreted.

The Mayor merely pulled a sour face and replied in Italian, 'Tell him the cost of one loaf of bread. Tell him how much we pay for meat, when we can get meat, or fish.'

'Sir,' said Tony. 'The Mayor say we have to buy food on black market.'

'Rubbish.' Holland stood up. 'I know damn well you are issued with ration cards. On short measures, sometimes, no doubt.'

Tony shrugged and switched on a plaintive smile, thinking, how can this Major be so stupid. 'Sir, shopkeepers say very little food this week, a little flour perhaps, spaghetti, maybe some bread, no butter, meat, fish, coffee, no milk for babies. But we give cigarettes. Ah!' His ever-moving hands and alive eyes were as expressive as his words.

'And what are your police doing about this?' snapped Holland.

Tony's smile was splendidly cynical. 'Police okay, sir. Shopkeepers looking after them.'

'The bastards,' said Holland bitterly.

'Food. Un'erstan', food,' interrupted the Mayor.

Holland began to lose his temper. 'I've no authority to give you food. No authority. Tony, tell him I will put the village out of bounds and close his café to my men unless I get labour.'

Tony interpreted and the Mayor flew into a rage and spoke in Italian, 'This is criminal. The filthy soldiers allow us to survive a little with their cigarettes.'

Holland smiled grimly. 'Tell the Mayor the filthy soldiers, as he calls them, will definitely not be allowed to patronize his café unless I get labour.'

Tony laughed. 'Sir, you understan' Italian, si?'

'A little, but not enough. Say I have reason to believe that he is behind most of the black market operations and the moment I get proof I'll put a stop to him.'

The Mayor's fat face was frozen in shock for a few moments, before he launched into reasonably good English. 'Sir. No black market. I am Mayor. Sir, I would not permit the black market if I could help it.'

'I rather thought you understood English,' snapped Holland. 'You'd better think over all I've said, that's all.'

'People hungry, sir. People will die. Give food.'

Holland roared back at the Mayor. 'Open your shops, damn you! Sell the food to the people and not on the black market. You're the Mayor. You've got a police force. Start looking after your people instead of crawling here begging.'

The Mayor's eyes were now tragic. 'My bambino sick. My son. I sell food on black market. I watch him die?' He slowly turned and walked out of the office. Holland watched him, then glanced at Tony and nodded to the door. 'That will be all.'

'Yes, sir.' Tony threw up a salute and left.

Holland picked up papers from his desk, scanned them, then in a rage threw them down. Then he saw Butcher watching him. 'Yes. What do you want?'

'Did you get anywhere with him, sir?'

'No.'

'Stubborn lot aren't they?'

'They won't work unless we feed them.'

'Couldn't we give them a midday meal?'

'On our rations? Feed at least another hundred men? Then what about the women and children? They won't benefit.'

'We're not exactly living off the fat of the land ourselves.' Butcher paused to light his pipe, staring over the bowl at Holland. 'Would you care to pass the can and let me see what I can do?'

'What have you in mind?'

'If we don't get labour, what happens?'

'There'll be hell to pay. You damn well know that. Now what's your idea?'

'I think I can straighten out this little problem. Will you leave it to me?'

'Not unless you tell me exactly what your plan is.'

'There's a new man recently joined the Company. Jackson.'

'I remember him and I wasn't particularly favourably impressed by him. The ex-NAAFI chap. Go on.'

'Exactly, sir,' smiled Butcher. 'The thought's crossed my mind. He must have friends in the NAAFI.'

'Come to the point.'

'With the help of his friends, he might be able to wangle something.'

Holland stared grimly at Butcher. 'Do I understand you correctly? Jackson may be able to wangle . . . wangle . . .?'

'He's the only man I know who may be able to get us out of this hole.'

'Don't let me hear you mention it again.'

Butcher sighed. 'Very well, sir. But we've been here a week now . . .'

'I'm very much aware of that.'

'The chaps are working damn hard, sir. But we're not moving even half the stuff we're supposed to.'

'And we won't without help and I'm very much aware of that.'

'You can't blame the chaps for moaning. I mean, sir . . .'

Holland was almost shaking with rage. 'They'll do any damn job I order them to do, and if you hear anybody moaning, send him to me.'

'Yes, sir.'

'That's all.'

Butcher saluted. 'Yes, sir.' He turned on his heels and marched out.

Holland sat down and stared furiously ahead of him. He felt spent and defeated.

Chapter VI

Butcher decided that it might not be a bad idea to speak to Jackson, anyway. He might prove to be an ace up his sleeve for the future. Butcher's concern was totally selfish. He knew perfectly well that if labour wasn't soon forthcoming, he would have more than enough trouble with his men. It was impossible for the men to keep up with the work load so questions would soon be asked and the area commander would, without doubt, one day descend on the camp and then heads might fall. They would probably transfer Holland, and in the general shake-up, horrible thought, he also might be transferred to a company much closer to the firing line.

Butcher was not in the least concerned about Holland. The man was an ass who lived by the book. An honourable idiot. Probably still thought he was in the Boy Scouts. The interview with Holland, although none too successful, had not defeated Butcher. He reasoned that if no other solution was found, Jackson might – might – come up with an answer.

He decided to go in search of him and finally found him in the wet canteen. A dreary tent. Jackson was with Paddy, both brooding over a luke-warm cup of tea. Butcher pleasantly requested Jackson's company outside. Jackson joined him and they went for a walk.

'How do you like the army, Jackson?'

What a stupid bloody question, thought Jackson. Why doesn't he ask me how I would like to be hung, drawn and quartered. 'Not bad, sir,' he replied with a total lack of enthusiasm.

'How does it compare with NAAFI?'

'Absolutely no comparison, sir,' said Jackson, with complete sincerity.

'You had a good run with NAAFI, eh?'

What's he working up to, wondered Jackson, not deliberately looking at Butcher, but slyly eyeing him. 'They landed me in some funny places. Benghazi, Tobruk. Three years in the desert. Bombed and stukered.'

'Rough luck,' chuckled Butcher. 'But how does it compare?'

'Some of the time I lived like a king.'

'And,' sighed Butcher, 'all the booze you could lay your hands on. All the luxury tinned goods. All the cigarettes.' A meaningful side glance. 'Not to mention a jolly good fiddle on the side.'

'I was always completely honest, sir,' smiled Jackson.

'Of course.' Butcher's shoulders shook with laughter. 'So would I have been.' Their glances met and Jackson joined in the laughter. 'By the way, have you kept contact with any of your old friends?'

My old friends, thought Jackson, are lying under boxwood crosses in that stinking desert. Stuttering Hawthorne, Terry Lynch, Jock Cameron. The best of them all, and he knew that by now a few more must have gone and he didn't want to know the bad news. 'No, I haven't.'

'Some of them must be in Italy.'

'Sure to be.' He wondered where Taylor was, and Paddy O'Neill, and – but they had been thrown out of the NAAFI. And old Dodds, the old bastard. Old Dodds, he couldn't help smiling. But there was Wentworth, not a bad lad, and the idiot Green, and simple-minded Geordie, and Weaver, and dozens more.

Butcher interrupted his thoughts. 'Ever thought about tracking any of them down?'

From the first he had realized how thin Cristina was. Since then he had handed his cigarette ration into Momma's ever open hands, and chocolates and anything he could scrounge. When he ached for a cigarette, he tracked down Dusty and helped to smoke his. Had he thought about it? He had dreamed about finding at least one old friend who would supply him with the necessities of life. 'I've thought about it,' agreed Jackson, stopping in his tracks and facing Butcher. 'But I'll need transport.'

Butcher nodded. 'That might be arranged.'

'And then what?'

'For the moment, nothing, Jackson. If possible, I want to do it legally.'

'Legally?' Jackson smiled broadly.

'With Major Holland's consent. Make it easier all round if I can get it.'

'And if you can't?'

Butcher smiled. 'Then we may take a drive in the general direction of the nearest NAAFI Bulk Issue Store and you might check it out and see if you have any accommodating friends there. What do you think?'

Jackson returned the smile. 'I think that's a pretty good suggestion.'

'Good.' Butcher nodded in agreement. 'Now don't let me keep you away from your bloody awful canteen tea. They say it's the cup that cheers.'

'I'd sooner drink maiden's piss,' said Jackson as Butcher walked away.

Early evening and Momma with her vague sweet smile played the piano. Jackson and Cristina danced together.

Watson, with a brooding look, sat on a high-backed chair, drinking and paying very little attention to Maria. He was more interested in drinking and his maudlin thoughts. Nine days now and every night in this bloody dump and no nearer to getting anything from her than he was the first night. She smiled, she danced, she laughed. She talked to him in her fractured English and for some reason he could not understand, he hadn't put the bite on her yet.

A few other soldiers had chanced facing Major Holland by being discovered out of bounds, but when they had weighed up the situation they had quit. The wine in the Mayor's bar was just as good and a lot cheaper, and one could let oneself go there. The Colonel's dump wasn't even good for laughs with the old man on guard duty every night. The general opinion in the Company was, scrub the Colonel's house, there was no chance of getting into the girls' knickers.

The Mayor's bar was a thriving business. The Colonel's house a near disaster.

Watson was very well aware of this and he was beginning to think it was high time for Maria to be aware of it, too. He was waiting for the right moment to speak to her. Let her know that if Paddy and Jackson and he did not pay their usual evening calls, things would be very tough for the family. Most of his cigarette and chocolate ration, plus tinned goods he stole from the cookhouse, was given to Momma. He was getting a bad deal. One more drink and he would put Maria straight and take that stuck-up look off her face. Who did she think she was, the bloody Virgin Mary? It was time she learned about the facts of life, stopped this virgin act and opened her legs. Then, if she played her cards right, then he would see that she and all her bloody family survived this war in style. He could be generous. If it came to it, he'd pinch half the bloody Company rations. He'd look after them somehow. But now it was about time she started looking after him. Already he had helped to put a bit more flesh on her and she looked a lot better for it. He finished his drink. One more, he thought, and I'll give it to her straight. He wasn't going to be taken for a mug one more day.

Tony was talking to Paddy, who was cheerfully helping himself to more wine. He was on a warm, alcoholic cloud, and happy. He had found to his surprise that wine agreed with him. It created a warm glow, a feeling of well-being, a happy-go-lucky attitude towards life. Whiskey or other hard spirits had the reverse effect. It touched off the violence that was inherent in his character.

Tony was surprised that Paddy never danced with the girls. He was very friendly towards them, made jokes, was polite, but never got close to them.

'Why you not ever dance with the girls, Paddy?'

Paddy smiled as he stared into his glass of wine. Why the hell should I waste my time, he thought. There's nothing doing with those sweet little darlings. His approach to women was open and basic. 'How much do you want, me old darlin'? ' and if the price was right, he would climb on her, and when it was over, pick up his glass again. Women came a very poor third in his life. Gambling took second place. He smiled at Tony.

'Sure now, wouldn't it interfere with me drinking?'

Tony stared at him incredulously. There were two beautiful girls in the room and all Paddy could think about was drinking. What breed of men could the Irish be if Paddy was typical? Lost for a reply he called out to Jackson.

'Okay, Johnnie. Everything okay.' He wanted to hate Jackson because of Cristina's interest in him. But somehow he couldn't.

'Fine, Tony.'

'That's good.' He forced a laugh. 'You happy, si,' and before Jackson replied, he called out to Watson, 'Walter, you okay, Walter?'

Watson turned a surly look on him. 'Sure, why not?'

'You dance very good, Walter.'

'He's a great fella for the girls,' smiled Paddy.

Jackson stopped dancing and stood near the window with Cristina. 'I've been overseas three years, understand? Three years.'

'No,' smiled Cristina. 'You speak too quick.'

'Quickly.'

'Quickly.'

'It doesn't matter if you understand me, Cristie.'

Cristina laughed. 'I not understand.'

'Does it matter?'

'No.' She laughed again. 'I understand a little and will learn speak more.'

'I'm happy, Cristie.'

'Si, I happy.'

'Isn't it wonderful?'

'Si, I think.'

Speaking slowly and carefully, Jackson said, 'Fancy me meeting a girl like you. You're all such nice people, and it's funny, I feel at home here.' He was thinking, I feel like a kid on his first date, I even remember feeling like this when I was a moonstruck kid. It's magic and I don't understand it. He smiled at her. 'Cristie, you're beautiful.'

She understood, but pretended not to. 'You speak too quick.'

'I said, you're beautiful and you understood. You just wanted me to repeat it. You're beautiful and I love you.'

'Speak, slow, please.' Cristina knew she was in love for the first time in her life and she was frightened. He was a soldier. He could leave any day. Many girls must love him. She was frightened and terribly happy and wanted him and knew it was impossible and daydreamed about sharing her life with him. Jackson's eyes were burning into her and she wanted to throw her arms about him and feel his body close to hers. Her voice barely audible she said. 'We will dance, yes.'

He took her in his arms. 'You'll understand one day.' They danced close together with the frowning Colonel watching them.

Watson finished his drink and placed it on a nearby table. 'What about us going for a walk, eh?'

Maria smiled vaguely. 'No understand.'

'Don't give me that. Promenade . . . you . . . me . . . promenade . . . come on, let's get out of this dump.'

She shook her head. 'Not possible.'

'All you bints ever say is no. Now you listen. It's a smashing night.'

'No.'

'Why?'

'Why?'

'Yeah. Why, why, why?'

She did not like Watson. She did not like his touching her, but Momma was insistent she be polite to him. She forced a smile. 'Girls in Italy, not.'

'That'll be the day,' sneered Watson. 'If they don't, where do all the bloody kids come from? Now, stop kidding. You like me, don't you?'

'Like? What's like?'

She can't be as dumb as she sounds, Watson thought. 'Aw, you're enough to get anybody down. So no walk, so what do we do?'

'Do . . . please?'

'Yeah. Do . . . do . . . you . . . me?'

'Dance, yes?'

'Dance, yeah. You'll cripple me you will, dragging me around that floor.' He leaned back and scowled.

'No dance?'

'No.'

'Talk, yes?'

'No, I'm gonna get drunk.'

He picked up his drink, then turned and watched Bill Stone enter. He grinned and thought, he's pissed, old Bill might liven things up a bit.

'Hello, Bill,' he waved his glass. Bill was Corporal in charge of the Company rations. A very useful man to know. Watson stood up and put a friendly arm about Bill's shoulders. 'So you decided to come along, eh?'

Bill stood with Watson's arm draped around his shoulders, surveying the room. He nodded to Paddy, watched Jackson dancing with Cristina. He couldn't stand Jackson. He was convinced he was queer. Then he stared at Tony and decided he couldn't stand wogs either.

'You like to sit down somewhere, Corporal?' inquired Tony with a pleasant smile.

Bill moved away from Watson. 'You bought this place?'

Tony, catching the hostility in Bill's eyes, stood uncertain, not knowing what to do.

Paddy, sitting smiling and relaxed, interrupted, 'Sit you down and enjoy a drink now.'

'Is he the King Spiv, Paddy?'

Tony tried to pacify him. 'This is not my house. You like a drink?'

Bill poured himself a glass of wine. 'It's a queer-looking dump.' He was watching Jackson dancing. 'Glamour boy's here, is he? Those the two bints you was shouting about, Walt?'

'Yeah, that's them.'

'Those the only two?'

'Yeah.'

'Not bad,' as Jackson danced past. 'How's Romeo this evening?' Jackson looked at him and danced on. Bill, still watching Jackson, spoke to Watson. 'There's a new place opened up the street. It's a kind of cellar.'

'You don't say. Any bints?'

'There's a couple there look like film stars.'

'Yeah?' Watson looked hopeful.

'Dracula's daughters.' As Jackson danced past again, Bill cut in. 'This is an excuse me, ain't it?'

Jackson moved away from Cristina. She was watching him with an anxious look. He smiled.

'This is Bill, he wants to dance with you.' He backed off and watched him. He sat down next to Paddy and offered him a cigarette.

Paddy nodded. 'Thanks. Why did you let him cut in on your girl, now?'

'He's looking for trouble and if he's going for serious, I could end up in hospital.'

'Is that so?'

'He's a tough handful, Paddy.'

'So a lot of the fellas have told me.'

Tony joined them and watched Bill and Cristina dancing. He looked worried. 'Is he your friend, Paddy?'

Paddy smiled. 'When he's had a few jars taken, he's nobody's friend.'

Tony looked even more worried. 'Please, no trouble here.'

Paddy picked up his glass. 'Relax, will you now. Momma plays a great piano, isn't that so?' There was an amused expression in his eyes but he was not smiling.

Jackson could not keep his eyes off Bill as he glided smoothly around the room. He stood about five feet eight inches. All brute strength. Heavy broad shoulders, bull neck and massive hairy arms, yet he moved gracefully when he danced. He stopped near the window, offered Cristina a cigarette, which she declined. Then he glanced at the old man and grinned.

'Grand Poppa like cigarette?'

The old man stared at Bill with deep hostility. 'I want not your cigarette.' He wished he were a young man again. He would throw these English soldiers out of his house. All of them. He felt helpless and a rage was building inside him.

Bill laughed and turned back to Cristina. 'He can go and get stuffed then, can't he? Come on, let's go some place.'

Cristina did not look at him. Her pleading eyes were on Jackson. 'Scuse?'

'Scuse, scuse,' Bill was grinning. 'Look, don't kid me you don't understand. I've got money, or what you want – bully beef? Chocolate?'

'I not understand.' Cristina moved to walk away, but Bill held her arm. She glanced at him, frightened. 'Please. I go . . .'

Bill said, still holding on to her arm, 'Come off it. You . . . me . . . sleep. You understand that. Sleep. Let's go.'

Cristina understood. She shouted at him as she pulled herself away from his grasp, 'You idiot! Idiot!' and ran to her mother's waiting arms.

The old man was on his feet holding a heavy walking stick and shouting in Italian.

This is it, thought Jackson. Holy Christ, I can't back out of this one. But he did not move. He watched the old man threatening Bill with his stick and Bill was laughing, then he became aware of Paddy staring at him. He was still not ready. Still uncertain of himself.

'He came here looking for trouble, Paddy.'

Paddy's eyes gleamed, his lips a thin line. 'Fella, I'm waiting to discover who you are now.'

The old man still shouting, getting red in the face. Maria trying to restrain him. Tony speaking rapidly to Cristina and Momma, all flashing eyes and anger and moving arms, but doing nothing. Watson with a drunken smile watching the scene, enjoying it. Bill laughing, taunting the old man. Maria shouting at him.

Jackson walked over to Bill. 'Get out!'

Bill stopped laughing and turned to Jackson. 'What's that, glamour boy?'

'Get out of here!' Jackson was shouting. He was afraid. 'You bloody bastard! Get out!' Feeling humiliated because of his cowardice, raging against the man's brute strength, knowing he had no chance, he threw a left-hand punch to Bill's mouth. Felt Bill's teeth cut into his knuckles and saw blood and lost all control and threw a right hand, then another left with all his strength, taking Bill completely by surprise. Another blow and he saw Bill stagger, then he was lifted off his feet and crashed into a chair and it broke beneath his weight and he thought, oh, Jesus. My ribs. My bloody back, then twisted away as a heavy ammo boot slammed down, just missing his face. Blood in his mouth, rolling frantically across the floor, getting to his feet, legs so weak and losing vision in one eye. Moving to keep away from Bill, brain dazed, trying to locate something heavy to smash over Bill's head. Legs too weak to dodge another blow that only half connected, but sent him reeling into a wall.

Then in front of him, Paddy's back, arms and shoulders moving, pumping blows into Bill's body, face. Crunching, terrible blows, Bill shaking his head, moving in on Paddy, throwing punches. Paddy dancing on his toes, moving so lightly, then both feet firm on the ground, throwing more hard crunching blows, then Bill giving ground and retreating towards the door.

Jackson could see Paddy now, his eyes demented as he smashed blows into Bill's face, and Tony getting behind and opening the door and as it was half way open Bill crashed into it and the door splintered. A wild cry as Bill fell down the stairs, Paddy following. Another cry and the sound of a body falling down the stairs.

Jackson slowly got to his feet, and now there was total silence in the room. Then Paddy returned. He was smiling and the crazy look had left his eyes. He looked at Jackson and winked. Jackson felt weak again and sat down. Then Cristina was dabbing at his face with a ridiculously small handkerchief and he tried to tell her that he didn't want to spoil her handkerchief, but his tongue was thick in his mouth and he wanted to spit out blood, but some idiotic reminder in his head told him it wouldn't be polite, so he took a handkerchief from his pocket and on the pretence of wiping his lips, he spat into it and there wasn't as much blood as he expected, and that made him feel a little better.

One blow, he thought, and the bastard nearly took my

head off. And Paddy took him. Who the hell is Paddy? He broke that animal like a toy.

He got Paddy into range with his one good eye. The other was now firmly closed. He managed a grin and the thumbs up sign. If Paddy hadn't been on the scene, hospital for me. He still could not quite believe that Paddy, a light-middle weight at the best, had almost wrecked Bill.

Watson protested to Paddy, 'What's the big idea? Bill's one of us, ain't he?'

Tony, all courage now, shouted, 'One like you, yes!'

Watson ignored him, still speaking to Paddy. 'Where did you leave him?'

'On the street.'

'You gonna leave him out there?'

'You're the one to take him back to camp.'

Watson, still protesting, 'Now, look, Paddy, he's one of our mates.'

Paddy, smiling, relaxed, but with a hard edge to his voice, 'You take him back, will you, for it's clear to me you don't know how to behave yourself, you dirty bloody animal.'

Watson moved away towards the door. 'I won't forget this.' A hurried exit. Then Momma trying to sooth the old man, who kept repeating in tones of near despair, 'Soldiers . . . soldiers.' Momma murmuring, 'Si, Poppa, si.' Jackson nodding to the door said, 'Let's get out of here, Paddy.' Then Cristina holding his hand. 'No, please, no.'

'Cristie, we've done enough damage.'

'You stay.' She turned to Paddy. 'Please stay.'

The old man sat down again, trembling, speaking with deep anger in Italian. Paddy pouring a drink, smiling, relaxed and seemingly happy, not even breathing hard.

Then Momma moved to the piano and began playing and Cristina sat next to Jackson and held his hand and Maria joined Paddy and was thanking him as best she could in English, and Paddy was enjoying his popularity, and peace was returning, when the old man stood up again and shouted in Italian. Tony shrugged and said to Jackson, 'He says soldiers only want to fight, destroy. He's old. What else are soldiers for?'

The piano playing, Cristina's hand in Jackson's. His head throbbing, his body hurting, but beginning to feel good again.

Chapter VII

Bill dipped his head again and again in the plaza fountain, still dazed. Oh Christ, how he hurt, legs so weak, submerging his head again. The cold water increased the pain. The pain. The God fucking pain. Then momentary relief, still not believing it had happened. That dirty Irish bastard. Drunk. I was drunk. Sober now. Feeling his legs now supporting the weight of his strong body. Feeling better. I'll go back, I'll destroy the dirty Irish bastard. Face in the fountain again. Water a light blood red. Mopping his face on a dirty handkerchief. Feeling the bruises and the pain behind the fabric. Be a lot of curious bastards watching me tomorrow. Be a lot of talk. I'll get that Irish bastard when I'm sober. No . . . He turned to Watson.

'I'm going back.'

Nothing would get Watson back tonight, not with the crazy Irish bastard. He had to be crazy. Never seen anything like him. He grinned at Bill.

'Forget it. Let's get to this other dump you were talking about.'

'If he thinks he can get away with that, the dirty bog Irish.'

'He did,' grinned Watson.

'I was pissed.'

'Yeah, you're right.'

'But I'll have him. I'll nail him.'

Watson jeered. 'You go back then. He's about half your weight.'

'There's two of them.'

'Jackson?' scoffed Watson. 'There's only Paddy.'

'Aw!' Bill ducked his head in the fountain. Cold, and it stung the cuts and bruises on his face, but he was beginning to feel better. He would get Paddy one dark night. He would beat his brains in. He would get him.

'Where's this dump you were shouting about?'

Bill straightened up. 'There's nothing there except some rotten wine and a dirty old hag.'

'It's our lucky night.' Watson turned. There was the small, thin girl again, in the threadbare dress. 'Hello.'

Bill looked at her. 'Who's that?'

'Some dopey kid who's on the scrounge.'

The girl came closer and smiled at Watson. He remembered he had a bar of chocolate in his pocket that he had forgotten to give to Momma. He took it out of his pocket. It was limp and sweaty. 'You like chocolate? He held out the bar and she took it and she smiled again and looked childlike and almost pretty. Watson pulled her to him and kissed her savagely full on the lips.

Bill stared at Watson. 'What's it with you?'

Watson released her and she stood frightened, not knowing what to do. He eyed the girl sullenly. 'I was only kidding.' He pushed the girl. 'Go on, you. Go home.' He pushed her again. 'Go on, go home to your mum.'

Bill, with a look of disgust, walked away, calling back over his shoulder. 'It's you wants to go home, you dirty bastard.'

'That's the problem in a nutshell,' said Major Holland, leaning back in his chair.

Jackson turned from Major Holland seated behind his desk to Captain Butcher standing by the wall. Both watching him. Waiting. 'Yes, it seems to be a problem, sir.'

Holland, irritated, 'I've just said that.' The closed and discoloured eye across the desk was somehow confirming his natural distrust of Jackson.

'If I could make a suggestion, sir?'

'Why do you think I've sent for you?'

'Second thought, why don't you just leave it to me. I think I can feed any amount of labour you care to take on.'

'You do? Any amount. Interesting.'

'I mean, sir, enough for your requirements.'

'How? I have to feed at least a hundred men. Supply them

with at least a midday meal, and I'm prepared to listen to any reasonable, repeat, reasonable suggestions.'

'Will you give me authority to draw the company's rations?'

'What are your plans?'

'One of the NAAFI men in the Bulk Issue Store, sir, is an old friend of mine.'

'When did you see him?' Holland glanced at Butcher, who stroked his moustache.

'The Canteen Corporal saw him, sir, and mentioned my name, and they had a talk and . . .' He paused, eyeing Holland, waiting.

'Go on.'

'Well, sir, I'm sure he would let me have some extra beer. Shouldn't be too much bother.'

'And then?'

'Most of the chaps aren't too crazy about wine, sir. Personally I rather like it. You know, sir, they'd give practically anything for a few bottles of beer.' Jackson knew he was talking too much. Something about Holland made him feel nervous.

'Come to the point.'

'Well, sir, as soon as I've got the beer I drive to the rations dump.'

'And then?'

Jackson thought, you can't be as thick as you appear to be. You must know I'm talking about a bloody fiddle and you're supposed to close your eyes to it and leave it to me.

He switched on a charming smile. 'Well, we'll get all the extra rations we need, sir. Tons of it. Meat, bread, tea, sugar, bacon, tinned foods. Some of the chaps there would open up the gates for a crate of beer.'

Holland leaned forward. 'Do you realize what you are saying?'

Jackson stiffened his back and managed to look suitably blank. 'I'm only making a few suggestions, sir.'

'I hope you realize that the officer in charge on the ration dump is also responsible for the stock.'

'Well, sir. That's fairly obvious.'

'All he needs, Jackson, is about half a dozen gangsters like you and he won't have any stock. If you can just breeze in and get anything you want, dam'it, the chaps who come after you to draw rations for their companies are going to be rather out of luck, aren't they?'

Jackson, with a cagey look in his eye, did his best to explain. 'That sounds perfectly logical, sir, but it doesn't seem to work out quite like that.'

'You've just told me that crooks like you can get anything they want. Now explain to me how you confound the stock-takers. How is it that they do not know that the stock does not tally?'

'The stock never tallies, sir,' said Jackson evenly. 'So nobody really gets into a sweat over it.'

Holland slowly stood to his full height. 'Do you know why I sent for you, Jackson?'

'I thought you were interested in feeding the village, sir.'

'I am. But I'm also interested to know just what kind of a brazen-faced crook you are, and now I know, don't I?'

Jackson straightened his shoulders. 'May I repeat, sir. I'm only making a few suggestions.'

'Now I'll make a few. Forget about your old NAAFI pal. Forget about making any trips to the NAAFI Bulk Issue Store. Do you think that's good advice?'

'If that's the way you want it, sir.'

'The way I want it, Jackson? You are at liberty to ignore my advice if you wish.' He leaned across the desk. 'I won't mind very much if you do. Go right ahead and I shall take the utmost delight in putting you exactly where you belong. In the glass-house.' Holland's eyes glaring. 'I've met all kinds of rogues in my time, but you . . . get out. Go on. Get out!'

'Yes, sir.' Jackson threw up a smart salute. 'Thank you, sir.' He about turned and marched out.

Holland glared at Butcher. 'You knew what he had in mind?'

Butcher nervously stroking his moustache, said, 'I didn't go into all the gory details, sir. He said he thought he could get extra rations.'

'You didn't give a damn how he got them?'

'As I said, sir, I didn't go too deeply into the matter.'

'Do you think he's in league with the Mayor?'

'I'm sure up to now he's clean, sir.'

'Stood where you stand now, whining about his son. Told me his boy was dying of starvation. The liar. He hasn't even got a son.'

'Hasn't he, sir?'

'Jackson and the Mayor, between them, could feed the village I bet.'

'I'm not interested in the Mayor, but if Jackson can help us . . .'

'If all the villages could afford black market prices . . .'

'But we would get all the labour we need . . .'

'I will get all the labour I need. I will not . . . repeat . . . will not . . .'

Butcher interrupted. 'At least half the village will be getting one square meal a day. Father Raffio was telling me . . .'

'Father Raffio . . .' Holland looked tired.

'Six villagers have died in the last month.'

Holland blazed at Butcher. 'And what will you have me do, appoint a crook like Jackson . . .'

Butcher spoke evenly. 'All I know is every time I step out of this camp I'm confronted with hungry faces. Jackson's a crook, but at least he could feed them.'

'Some of the men. What about the women and kids?'

'I don't know, sir. Maybe we could do something about that as well. I don't know.'

'I'll stop Jackson if it's the last thing I do. If he trades one bottle of beer, one cigarette, and I hear about it, I'll put him where he belongs. Do you understand?'

'Yes, sir.'

'If he applies for a pass to Naples and tries to bypass me, you'll refuse it.'

'Very good, sir.'

'And I want another dozen men appointed to the Regimental Police.'

'I'll see to it, sir.'

'And if that doesn't work, I'll put the village out of bounds. That's all.'

'Sir.' Butcher threw up a salute and marched out, fuming. Jackson was waiting for him. 'We blew that one.'

'He's a stupid bastard,' snarled Butcher, walking even faster.

Jackson marched with him. 'A complete prick. Now what?'

'Better forget all about it.'

'Why?'

'Because I don't want to be bloody well court martialled, you bloody idiot.'

'Plan A didn't work and I didn't expect it to. So what about Plan B?'

'Jackson, I'm not sticking my chin out.'

'You don't have to, sir.'

'If I'm involved . . .'

'You won't be.'

'What's Plan B?'

'When the Canteen Corporal goes to the NAAFI Bulk Issue, I go along with him.'

'And then you swap the beer at the ration dump. We've been into all that.'

'Then I dump the food on Father Raffio.'

'Not the Mayor?'

'I've changed my mind. The Mayor's a bastard.'

'And Father Raffio sells the food?'

'Gives it away.'

Butcher stopped in his tracks. 'And who the hell's paying for it?'

'Okay. Sod the Mayor, but we'll have to use him. I flog some of the stuff. Not too much. Soap. Razor blades. Toothpaste. To the Mayor. That pays for the grub for the village.'

'Nothing left over?'

'Cigarettes and booze for the Sergeants' mess.'

'Free?'

'Of course.'

'And the Officers' mess?'

'Holland would rumble it.'

'Do I get my private stock?'

'Of course.'

'And what about you, Jackson?'

'I've got a girl, and she's got a family. I'll be looking after them.'

Butcher raised one eyebrow and smiled. 'Jackson, now, come on. No little fiddle in it for you?'

'What fiddle?'

'You aren't stupid. You could bloody well make a fortune.'

'And what do I do with it? Paper a bloody room with lira notes? Have you been to Naples? Tried to buy anything? Tried the once-upon-a-time jewellers' shops? All you can buy is a few lousy tin watches. I know I could make a bloody fortune, but Jerry has taken everything worth having. There's damn all worth having in the country.'

Butcher nodded. 'It seems we're in the wrong place at the wrong time. But your plan is remarkable in its simplicity. You'll finish up a reluctant philanthropist.'

'I'm counting on them building a statue to me after the war,' said Jackson with a cynical smile.

Butcher grinned. 'People have bad memories. I've got a girl you'll drop some stuff off for as well, and don't forget.'

'Then it's a deal?'

'I can't give you permission of course. Not even a pass.'

'I'll wangle it somehow.'

'Just a minute. Saint Jackson feeds the village. Splendid. But we still haven't got any labour.'

'Father Raffio only issues food to families where at least one of the men works in the camp.'

'But we don't feed them in the camp.'

'Of course not.'

'And if Major Holland finds out?'

'Who's going to tell him, the villagers?'

'Jackson, you're on your own. Good luck.'

Jackson, watching Butcher walk away, smiled to himself. Of course he was on his own. Hadn't he always been?

Major Holland looked up. There was Father Raffio standing

in the doorway. Holland was irritated. Thinks he can walk in here any time he likes. 'Father, I'm very busy at the moment, so I hope you will excuse me if I . . .'

'I have spoken with my people; they will work for you.'

Holland did not even attempt to hide his relief. 'I see. Please sit down.'

'One man from each family will work. Where there are no men, a boy.'

'That's very good. I promise you every one of them will be employed.'

'Major, I beg one more time. Can you not give them a little food?'

'If it were possible . . .'

'A little something to take home to the children?'

'Father, do you think I enjoy seeing children go hungry?'

'You know, sir. The Germans took everything. You know, of course.'

'Yes.'

'When the English came we were full of hope, you understand? We knew the Germans, we believed the English were not like the Germans.'

Holland tightened his lips. 'What exactly are you trying to say?'

'The Germans take everything. The English give nothing.'

'We've damn little to give. How many more times must I tell you.'

'If you spoke with your soldiers, asked them to give a little . . . just a little . . .'

'They probably would, but it's my job to keep them fit – not half starve them. When will the villagers start work?'

'Tomorrow.'

'Thank you.'

Father Raffio moved to the door. 'I believe you are an honourable man, Major, but also a very foolish one.' He left with a faint smile.

Late one night, after the Regimental Police had checked, as best they could, that all the soldiers had left the village, they returned to camp.

Then the church bell rang and doors opened and the people left their houses, carrying their bibles. They also carried sacks and they entered the church and silently lined up and waited patiently to draw their week's rations. Flour, sugar, tea, hardtack biscuits, tins of bully beef, tins of stew. On rare occasions, they would get fresh meat. There was always powdered milk for the babies.

The people knew how Father Raffio obtained the food, but the people were careful not to be over friendly to Jackson. They were afraid the Regimental Police might become suspicious. So, apart from the odd smile, or greeting, they ignored Jackson.

Every day men and boys from the village reported for work at the camp and they worked hard.

Major Holland would pause on his inspection rounds and observe the villagers slaving under the hot sun. They were respectful and politely answered questions through Tony, the camp's official interpreter. But Holland was aware of a certain hostility beneath the polite smiles. Holland was fully prepared for this and could even understand it, but he could not quite understand their willingness and cheerfulness when he was not present. He would stand at his office window watching them, listening to their voices and their laughter. Then one of the men would start singing and the rest would join in. They were looking more healthy, too. At times he would feel uneasy and could not understand why everything was going as well, even better than he had hoped. He should count his blessings, he told himself.

Jackson imagined that his major problem would be to absent himself for long enough from the camp to drive to the NAAFI Bulk Issue Store, purchase whatever he could, then drive to the Army Ration Dump and, in exchange for cigarettes, beer and spirits, load up with food, drive and meet Father Raffio and numerous women helpers at a deserted farmhouse, dump the food and drive away to the camp. He realized that this would have been almost impossible, but he found an unexpected ally in RSM Tompkins, who had been briefed by Captain Butcher.

Some of the soldiers had to be looked after. Some out of

friendship, like Paddy, others because they could either be useful or not trusted. Bill, the Rations Corporal, was one. He had to pick up Jackson at the NAAFI Bulk Issue Store and transport him to the Ration Dump and help load the truck and unload it at the deserted farmhouse. As he repeatedly and sourly informed Jackson, he was taking a hell of a chance. Another man Jackson took care of was Watson. He knew if he didn't, Watson might decide to turn informer. A dangerous game to play, but Watson was totally unpredictable.

Jackson nodded to a stone against the cookhouse wall and Watson grinned and moved to the stone and slipped two cartons of cigarettes under his white cook's coat.

Sergeant Leadbetter left the cookhouse and watched Watson sauntering towards him, then he glared at Jackson. 'What are you two up to?'

'Nothing, Sarge.'

'Come here, Watson.'

'What's up, Sarge?'

'Give them to me.'

'Give what?'

Leadbetter made a grab at Watson's coat and the cigarettes fell to the ground. 'Right, I'm dropping you both in it.'

Jackson smiled. 'Take it easy.'

'You're both on a charge.' Holding up the cigarettes. 'And here's the evidence.'

Jackson spoke quietly. 'I'd have a word with the RSM first.'

Leadbetter stared at Jackson. 'What's that?'

'You like a drink, don't you?'

'Bribery, eh? It won't wash.'

Jackson's smile was confident. 'The Sergeants' mess hasn't been doing too badly. Extra scotch, gin, beer . . .'

'Ration increase, so don't you try any games with me.'

Still smiling, 'By courtesy of Private Jackson. They weren't your bloody rations. Monty's a bloody teetotaller, he wants you all drinking tea, you know that. I fiddled it for the RSM and you and all the others.'

'Why you . . .' Leadbetter grabbed Jackson by his shirt.

'So let's forget about it. Live and let live. All good pals and jolly good company.'

'You little shit, so if I put you on a charge, you'll drop the RSM in it and the whole bloody lot of us, that's what you're saying.'

'No, I'm saying live and let live.'

Leadbetter released Jackson. 'One day you'll slip up and it can't be too bloody soon.'

Watson, wearing an ugly grin of sheer relief, interrupted, 'Sarge, can I have 'em back?'

'Have 'em back? You can watch me bleedin' burn them if you like.'

'Blimey, of all the daft . . .'

Leadbetter was raging. 'You shower. You dirty arseholes. Women and kids all round you half starved and what do you do? You rob 'em. You starve women and kids.'

Watson groaned. 'Sarge. Blimey, Sarge you're burning them.'

'You horrible bastards!' Leadbetter was still shouting as Jackson walked away. 'I'll get you one of these days. I'll get the pair of you . . .'

Jackson smiled to himself. He knew Leadbetter. He knew a dozen like him, the moral bastard. But it won't stop him getting pissed out of his mind in the Sergeants' mess tonight.

He wouldn't do anything. Couldn't do anything, only shout. If Leadbetter or any of the idiots put him on a charge, all he had to do was mention names.

A month passed. The hot sun seemed to hang in the sky longer each day. The villagers sweated as they loaded the waiting trucks with oil drums and petrol cans. There was more swearing than smiles. The work slowed down and Major Holland's anxiety increased daily.

A Colonel made a visit of inspection, blasted Holland and his officers and kept repeating, 'You have all the labour you need. More than enough. I don't want excuses. I want results.'

Holland sent for Father Raffio. The same futile arguments

and disagreements were expounded, but Father Raffio promised to do his best.

That night he rang the church bell and informed the villagers that there would be no more free rations unless they worked harder than they had ever worked in their lives. The villagers left the church grumbling.

Jackson met Father Raffio in the plaza. He was ashamed because his flock were not keeping their end of the bargain. Jackson remembered Butcher's cynical observation – 'People have bad memories.'

Next day the villagers worked with a will. No one sung. No one laughed. They worked with savage fury, swearing, spitting, taking out their rage on the oil drums as they strained and heaved them into the waiting trucks. Backbreaking work, soul-destroying work,. but it was the only guarantee they had for staying alive. Many would never forget the days they spent under the hot sun. Some would never forget or forgive the English for using them as they used their donkeys.

The old man worked in the hot sun, but because of his age and the rank he once held, Major Holland made him one of the checkers. He would count the barrels of oil as they were loaded on the trucks, but at the end of the day, he was as exhausted as any of the younger men from the village. The hot sun took its toll on everyone. Major Holland would make a point of stopping to speak to him. The old man would stiffen his shoulders, answer Holland graciously, then excuse himself and return to his labours.

In the Sergeants' mess, there were very few bottles of spirits on display, but no shortage of wine bottles. The drinking would, on many occasions, continue until well past midnight. RSM Tompkins had lectured the NCOs about drinking quietly and no singing. There was no real problem. Major Holland normally retired to his bed by nine o'clock each night, and by the time the drinking really got under way, he was usually fast asleep. The NCOs began to be bored with the gentlemanly drinking. Christ, they were well covered. All those bloody rotten bottles of wine behind the bar covered them, didn't they? The drinking became heavier. The nights longer and in the morning when some of the more bleary-eyed NCOs reported to Major Holland, his nostrils would twitch. Not being a drinking man himself, he could smell sour whiskey breath a mile away. Once a week, perhaps, they could stink of whiskey, but the rationing did not permit it every day. He pondered over it. He pondered over the savage but willing workers from the village. He pondered over his bleary-eyed NCOs and the villagers looking fitter and stronger as the days passed. How could this be on their insufficient diet? The work should be killing them. The women and children in the village were also looking more healthy. He did not want to delve too deeply into it. Everything seemed to be working smoothly, but somehow it didn't make sense and everything had to make sense for Major Holland. It was Captain Butcher who opened the door for him to broach the subject. He reported that two Sergeant Majors and three Sergeants were on sick report.

'Why?'

'Dysentery, sir.'

'Or the whiskey shits?'

A long pause as Butcher wondered how much Holland knew. Would he go as far as to inspect the Sergeants' mess? Wouldn't get much joy out of that, the stuff was well hidden. Why the hell did I get myself into this? Face him out. Smiling, Butcher replied, 'Not much chance, sir, unless they booze their ration in one horrible go.'

'NCOs report to me daily stinking of whiskey and gin.'

'Can't say I've noticed it, sir.'

'Perhaps because you don't damn well want to. Just what's going on?'

'As far as I know, nothing.'

'Butcher, if you're covering . . .'

'Sir, that's the last thing I would do.'

'Have you been in the Sergeants' mess?'

'Haven't been invited, sir.'

'Jackson.'

'I don't understand.'

'He's carrying out his damn plans. I want to see him.'

An uneasy smile from Butcher. 'I'll track him down.'

'I hope Jackson's on his own. I sincerely hope no one is in cahoots with him.'

'So do I, sir.'

'Get him here.'

A worried Captain Butcher found Jackson as he was leaving the latrines. Oh, God, thought Butcher as he faced him. Another one of the bleary-eyed brigade. (Jackson had given a vodka party the night before for some of his friends and was now wishing he hadn't.)

'The Major wants to see you, Jackson.'

Jackson turned his throbbing head. 'Trouble?'

'He doesn't know anything, but to say the least, he's highly suspicious.'

'Of me?'

'Who else? What do you plan to do?'

'Can't plan,' mumbled Jackson. 'Rusty wheels in my head sending me crazy. I'd better have a fix before I see him, don't you think?'

'Go in and see him stinking of whiskey. That's all I need, Jackson. Half the bloody NCOs are staggering in to see the old man still half-pissed out of their minds. The rest have got the whiskey shits.'

'That's the trouble with people, they aren't too bright. I tried to switch them on to vodka. It doesn't stink on the breath. But they were too bloody traditional. Whiskey or gin or nothing.'

'The old man doesn't know anything. Remember that.'

'He won't get a damn thing out of me.' Jackson unwrapped a package of chewing gum and popped it in his mouth.

'He'll try to work you over. You give one name, just one, and everybody's in it.'

'No problem,' said Jackson. 'I've got a terrible memory.'

'Come on then . . .'

Major Holland stared into Jackson's bloodshot eyes. It was obvious he had the mother and father of all hangovers. Butcher stood near his desk nervously stroking his moustache. Holland glanced at him and Butcher automatically straightened up. Then Holland stared hard at Jackson.

'Have you been on sick report, Jackson?'

A surprised look. 'No, sir. Why should I report sick?'

'Because you look as if you're on your last legs and there's been a sudden outbreak of dysentery in the camp.'

'I'm fine, sir. I mean, apart from a slight hangover.'

'So are the NCOs on sick report.'

'The wine's pretty heavy, sir.'

'And the whiskey, and the gin.'

'That's true, sir. Not much to choose between one poison or another, if you overdo it.'

'I have proof you've been supplying the Sergeants' mess with spirits.'

Jackson looked blank. 'You have, sir?'

'So you may as well confess . . .'

Jackson managed a stricken smile. 'If I could get my hands on the stuff, sir, I wouldn't pass it on to the Sergeants' mess.'

'What would you do with it?'

'Drink it, sir.' Jackson willed himself to sound cheerful. 'I've a drinking problem. I can't get enough of it.'

'Now let's stop playing games.' He stood up. 'Breathe.'

Jackson looked surprised. 'I am, sir.' Then a pained expression. 'At least, I think I am.'

'I want to smell your breath.'

Jackson leaned slightly forward and exhaled a deep breath into Major Holland's face. 'Spearmint-flavoured vino, sir.'

'You think of everything, don't you, Jackson?'

'Not at the moment, sir. I'm really in pretty bad shape.'

'Who is feeding the villagers?'

'How would I know, sir?'

'You damn well know.'

'It's on orders, sir. We are not allowed to fraternize with the villagers.'

'You outlined a plan to me . . .'

Jackson interrupted him. 'I told you how we could feed them, sir, and you invited me to try it and my own common sense told me it wouldn't be such a bright idea.'

'Someone is damn well feeding them.'
'I hope so, sir.'
'You are.'
'No, sir.'
'Don't lie to me.'
'If you have any proof, sir?'
'Don't be bloody impertinent.'
'I'm simply trying to answer your questions, sir.'

Holland sat down again. 'If you make a full confession, I'll be as lenient as possible with you. I give you my word.'

'There's nothing to confess.'

'I see.' Holland looked thoughtful. 'So you aren't feeding the villagers?'

'That's correct, sir.'

'And you don't mix with any of the people in the village?'

'No, sir.'

'Then some of the men in the Company must be feeding them.'

'Not to my knowledge, sir.'

Holland glanced at Butcher. 'Only one thing to do. Put the village out of bounds.'

Butcher protested. 'You can't do that. We've no evidence that any of the men are dealing on the black market.'

Holland shouted, 'The NCOs are boozing it up every night. The villagers are obviously being fed and I know and you know who's behind it. Jackson!' He pointed a finger. 'You, Jackson! Now, I'll give you one last chance, and as I said, I will deal leniently with you.'

'So you're convinced I'm feeding the villagers.'

'Of course you are.'

'And if I were, would it be a crime?'

'Dealing on the black market, yes.'

Jackson knew he should guard his tongue, but suddenly he didn't care any more. 'King's Rules and Regulations. That's all we're talking about. The bloody KRRs. People can starve but we must live by the bloody book.'

'Watch your tongue.'

'You've got your values fucked up.' He knew his hangover was making him stupidly reckless.

'Another word out of you and you're on a charge.'

'But you can say anything you like to me. An officer can say and do any damn thing he likes, backed by the KRRs. But if a soldier answers back, he's on a charge. None of it makes sense to me. They throw a uniform at us, bawl, do any bloody thing they like . . .'

'Jackson, I'm warning you . . .'

'I'm a bloody head case, for Christ's sake. Put me on a charge.' Jackson was shouting. 'Do what you bloody well like with me, but you won't stop me saying what I think is the truth. The army's a joke. A big, stupid, dirty joke!'

'You've gone too far.'

'You wanted to charge me with dealing on the black market. No proof. So you incite me to violence. One way or the other you're going to have me. All right, put me on a charge.' Jackson glimpsed Butcher's stricken face. 'But I'll claim a court martial, and I'll bloody well fight.'

'Get out!'

'Sir!' Jackson slammed to attention.

'I'll consider your case before I make a decision.'

'Sir!' Jackson threw up a salute.

'Wait outside.'

'Outside, sir!' Jackson slammed his ammo boots on the tiled floor, about turned, and marched out.

There was a long silence as Holland sifted through some papers on his desk, then turned to Butcher. 'I'm still convinced . . .' He watched Butcher fumbling with his pipe. 'Damn well smoke if you want to.' Butcher gratefully lit up. 'He's a crook.'

'Sir. He's a neurotic mess and not completely accountable for his actions.'

'If I get proof that he's implicated, he won't be alone, will he?'

'If you get all the proof you need to convict Jackson . . .' Butcher chose his words carefully. 'Others might be involved.'

'So you know?'

'I don't know anything.'

'In short, you aren't backing me.'

'If, as you say . . .' Butcher's pipe had gone out and he relit it. 'Or, rather, as you suspect, the Sergeants' mess is being supplied with booze illegally, then you've got quite a case on your hands, all the NCOs who drink in the Sergeants' mess are equally guilty. I wouldn't want to be involved in that.'

'So you're worried as well?'

'Sir, there's a war on. Thousands of people are being killed daily, and you're worried about a few bottles of booze.'

'I don't want a lecture.'

'What's your problem, sir?'

'You're suggesting I cover everything up.'

'I'm not suggesting anything.'

'What's the alternative?'

'I don't know.'

'I think I do. I post Jackson out to another company.' He leaned back in his chair and smiled. 'Then if the NCOs still report to me stinking of gin and whiskey, then we'll know Jackson's innocent, won't we?'

'Maybe that's the best thing to do.' Butcher felt relieved. He would miss Jackson's services and he wouldn't be alone, but things were getting too hot. Much too damn hot, and he wasn't any too sure of Jackson if there was a showdown. He really was a head case.

'And the village will be placed out of bounds.'

The old idiot, Butcher thought. No Jackson and the village out of bounds. That meant no more labour. Back to square one.

'Yes, sir,' he said with a bleak smile. 'Village out of bounds.'

Chapter VIII

'You don't know what it is, then?'

'No, sir,' said Jackson as he stared at the monster truck.

'You're a driver and you don't know what an articulator truck is?'

'I've never handled one.'

'You telling me you've never seen one?'

'I've seen them, but kept out of their way.'

'This one's yours.'

'Mine?' Jackson switched on a delighted smile. 'You mean it's mine?'

'I'm making you a present of it.'

'That's big-hearted of you, sir.'

'Now, get in the cab.'

Jackson slowly climbed into the cab, then looked down at Sergeant Major Withers. 'It's high up, sir.'

'It is,' Withers agreed.

'Does a parachute go with it?'

'Another bright little music hall comic, eh? Let's see you back it up.'

'Back it up.' Jackson switched on the engine and it roared into life. The cabin shook and so did Jackson. He grated the gears and Withers' face screwed up in pain. Jackson slammed the gears around and hoped he was in reverse; if not, the low wall just ahead of him was in trouble.

To Sergeant Major Withers' astonishment, he closed his eyes and let it go. The truck roared away in reverse. 'Stop it!!' screamed Withers. 'Put the bloody anchors on!'

Jackson slammed on the brakes and stared out of the cabin window and looked at a truck almost level but at a slant a few feet away. Where did that one come from? he wondered. He looked out of the other window at Withers' stricken face. 'That was a near miss.'

'That's your own bleedin' truck, you dope!' shouted Withers.

'Oh, is it?' Jackson realized that Withers was right and felt greatly relieved. 'Want me to try again?'

'Get out.'

Jackson climbed down from the cab and faced Withers. 'Not easy to handle, are they?'

'I'm beginning to catch on why 501 Company posted you out. That the best you can do?'

'Yes.'

'Honest?'

'I couldn't handle one of those if my life depended on it.'

'I'm convinced.' Withers climbed into the cab, smoothly straightened up the truck and parked it, then joined Jackson. 'The old man had better have a word with you.'

'But, Jackson, you're a driver. It says so in your AB64,' protested Major Patterson.

'Yes, sir. But I'm a lousy driver.'

'Better make you a dispatch rider. You can handle a motorbike?'

Jackson looked terrified. 'No, sir.'

'You've got to be able to drive something. This isn't making sense to me, you know.' He stared thoughtfully at Jackson. 'You look intelligent.' He thumbed through Jackson's AB64. 'Oh.' He stared past Jackson at Sergeant Major Withers, who responded by tapping a finger on his forehead. Major Patterson gave Jackson a sympathetic smile. 'You're a nervous chap, eh?'

'Yes, sir.'

'Hmmm. What can we do with him, Sergeant Major?'

Withers wanted to reply, 'Drown him.' Instead he switched on a thoughtful expression and appeared to be mentally debating Jackson's future. He wasn't going to be responsible for Jackson. He had enough problems.

'Maybe an office job, sir.'

'Ah. Can you type, Jackson?'

'No, sir.'

'Well, suppose you could learn.'

'Machinery, sir.'

'What?'

'Anything mechanical, sir, doesn't seem to work out for me.'

'Any chap who puts his mind to it can learn to type.'

'My spelling, sir.'

'You can't spell?'

'No, sir.'

Patterson looked at Withers, hoping he would come up with some kind of solution. 'What do you think, Sergeant Major?'

Withers found the answer, aided a little by some animosity. 'Latrines, sir.'

'Nothing mechanical about the latrines, sir.'

'Think you've got the answer,' smiled Patterson. 'I'm putting you in charge of the latrines, Jackson.'

'Doesn't a responsible position like that carry rank, sir?' inquired Jackson as he stared earnestly at Major Patterson.

Quite insane, thought Patterson. Seems such a willing, pleasant chap, too. 'Could make him up to Lance-Corporal, couldn't we, Sergeant Major?'

'Yes, sir,' agreed Withers.

'Unpaid, of course.'

'Yes, sir. Unpaid, of course.'

'That suit you, Jackson?'

'May I think it over, sir?'

'What's to think over?'

'It's a big step to take, sir.' Jackson spoke in a confidential tone of voice. 'The Board, sir. You know, the Medical Board warned me about taking on responsibilities I mayn't be able to handle.'

'Look here, Jackson. Being in charge of a shithouse isn't all that much of a responsibility.'

'If you're not a responsible kind of chap, perhaps not, sir. But I am. Any job I tackle, any job I can tackle, I mean, I take very seriously, sir. And if I'm going to be in charge of a shithouse, I've got to be sure I can make a success of it. I've got to be convinced, sir, that I can make it the best shithouse in Italy, sir.'

The poor, daft idiot is absolutely sincere, Major Patterson inwardly marvelled. God, he's absolutely eager beaver about his glowing future prospects. Humour him. 'Jackson, I'm convinced you're the man for the job.'

Jackson was clearly overwhelmed with gratitude. 'If you've got faith in me, sir.'

'I have,' Patterson heartily agreed. 'Go to the QM and get your stripes. That should give you confidence, eh?'

'Sir,' said Jackson, using his burning sincerity voice. 'You'll have a shithouse in this camp you can really be proud of, sir.'

'Splendid!' bellowed Major Patterson, knowing he couldn't take any more. 'Action stations, eh? Get on with it.'

'Sir!' yelled Jackson, as he threw up a splendid salute, stamped his ammo boots, made a dazzling about turn and marched out.

'Whew!' breathed Major Patterson. 'Why did we get him, I wonder?'

Got to keep my mind busy, thought Jackson. Got to get posted back to 501 Company somehow. Got to get back. The village out of bounds. That bloody, cunty Holland, the good, believing, dead square, honest, noble KRRs prick. He's sincere, deadly sincere. Believes he has a cause. Believes he's right and everybody else is a horrible, thieving villain. I should have kicked him in the balls. Thrown me in the glasshouse then, wouldn't they, and never get out. Oh, what a prize prick Holland is. The village out of bounds. The poor bastards will starve. Oh, Cristie, the grub I left you will see you over for a while, but how long? Holland, you bloody arsehole, don't you know what you're doing? I had it organized. No problems. Villagers fed and working their guts out. Now you've got it ballsed up again, Holland. How to get posted back, but how? Send this mob mad. That's how. Baffle them with bullshit. I'll get back. I've got to. Oh, Cristie, how are you managing? I've got to get back.

Jackson stitched on his Lance-Corporal stripes, then marched towards the company latrines, accompanied by his two assistants, Ginger, a work-shy Scot, who seldom spoke a word, and Alfie, a gnome whose feet smelt like bad cheese. Jackson kept to the windward side of Alfie.

Jackson's job was to keep the Sergeants' and the other ranks' latrines operational. There was nothing to choose between them. A six-foot-high screen hid them from public eye. Inside, built over a long, deep trench was a long wooden box with twelve cut-out toilet seats. The other ranks' latrine was a favourite hide-away for soldiers to sit and smoke a cigarette, tell dirty stories or moan about any subject that caught their fancy. Flies had taken a liking to it as well.

There was always a cloud of them hovering overhead or dive bombing the seated, sweating soldiers.

Jackson marched in, accompanied by his assistants, and announced to the half-dozen soldiers on their thrones, 'There's going to be some changes made here. Unbelievable changes.'

'Who's this nutter?' inquired a soldier with a screwed-up face, who was having trouble evacuating his bowels.

'I'm the new OC Shithouse,' explained Jackson. 'You can sit at ease.'

A chorus of 'fuck-off' greeted this remark.

'Alfie,' said Jackson. 'What kind of bum paper is that?'

'Anything we can find. *Blighty, Lilliput*, any old mags.'

Jackson picked up some sheets of paper. 'Pin-ups. Are you trying to send them mad? Aren't their minds warped enough? And you encourage them to wipe their bums on all these bloody gorgeous-looking film stars. The first thing we do is indent for some real army issue crap paper.'

A stream of protest came from the seated soldiers.

'It's like bleedin' sand paper.'

'Mind yer own business.'

'Fuck off out of here.'

'We need a path leading to it,' said Jackson, 'and it's got to be whitewashed. All right men, carry on shitting.'

'He's a looney!' shouted the soldier with the screwed-up face. Then his agonized expression was changed to a smile of relief.

'Scrounged buckets of paint from the paintshop. Other ranks' latrine – one screen painted with the Union Jack, the other with stars and stripes,' said Sergeant Major Withers.

'Go on,' said Major Patterson, with a puzzled expression. 'Haven't noticed it.'

'Inside, sir. The Jack and the bloody stars and stripes.'

'Sounds rather odd.'

'The Sergeants' latrine, sir. Red, with bloody hammers and sickles.'

'What?'

'And little garden paths and little bleedin' gardens. Got the two loonies with him watering the gardens all hours and we're short of water.'

'I'll see him,' said Major Patterson, looking grim. 'Maybe I'd better have a word with him alone.'

'If he goes mad, I'll be outside.' Withers opened the door and shouted, 'You! Inside. Double!'

Jackson doubled in and faced Major Patterson pounding his boots on the floor.

'At ease, Jackson.'

'Sir.'

'Hear you've been doing a painting job.'

'Do you like it, sir?'

'Haven't seen it, but from what I hear, no.'

'Too much loose talk in the Company, sir.'

'Is there?'

'The men, sir. Unpatriotic talk.'

'Is that your problem?'

'I'm doing my best to straighten them out. Whenever they sit, sir. It's there to remind them. The Union Jack and the stars and stripes.'

'And the Red flag?'

'A compliment to our glorious allies, sir.'

'Jackson, sit down.'

'Sir.'

'Cigarette?'

'Thank you, sir.'

'What's the game?'

'I'm doing a good job, sir. I'm running an efficient, patriotic shithouse.'

'I'm pretty easy going, Jackson, but I'm not a bloody fool. The Medical Board regraded you, but they didn't give you your ticket home. Is that your problem?'

'Of course not, sir. I'm a bit on the nervous side, but I function, okay. The Colonel told me so himself.'

'Do you think I'm going to recommend you be discharged from the services?'

Jackson pulled on his cigarette and relaxed as he smiled at the Major. 'Everyone says you're a bloody decent chap and I'm beginning to think they're right. The game is, sir, I want out. Posted back to 501 Company.'

'Why?'

'There's a girl I'm crazy about.'

'Italian?'

'Yes.'

'You know it's forbidden to associate with Italians.'

Jackson smiled. 'Do the bloody generals think they can get away with that, short of cutting our cocks off?'

'You serious about her?'

'Yes, sir. I want to marry her.'

'Oh, Christ, Jackson. You know you can't.'

'I'm telling you the truth, that's all. It's no crime wanting to get married.'

'Except there's a war on and you aren't free to do as you wish. My advice to you is forget the girl. She spells trouble.'

'No chance of that.'

'If I send you back to your old company, I'll only be encouraging you and that's not on.'

'I've been honest with you. What I do once I'm posted out is my problem.'

'Sorry, I can't help you. Now, no more bloody nonsense. No more pretending you're soft in the head. You're going to soldier on.'

'It's a pity you aren't a bastard, sir. I could handle you better.'

Major Patterson smiled. 'You could be surprised. If I'm pushed hard enough, I can be a horrible bastard. Now I want your word. No more fun and games. No more tricks.'

'No point,' agreed Jackson. 'I wouldn't get away with it now.'

'I'm taking you off the latrines. After you've restored them to their former drabness.'

'Got a new job lined up for me, sir?'

'You were in NAAFI. You can help in the men's canteen.'

'Oh?' Jackson showed interest.

'What are you "oh-ing" about?'

'I might be rather useful to you.'

'I bloody well hope so.'

'I might be able to fiddle extra rations.'

'Good. The men can use extra beer and cigarettes.'
'And the Sergeants' and Officers' messes, sir?'
'Splendid.'
'I'll organize it if you'll post me back in, say, a month.'
Major Patterson thought for a moment. 'Three months.'
'Three, sir. That's a hell of a long time.'
'We've all had a very dry spell. I'll post you back to 501 if you organize things, but I'm holding you for three months. By then you might have second thoughts about the girl.'
Three, thought Jackson. It's a hell of a long time, but it's not for ever. 'I'm on, sir.'
'Good. Buzz off now. I don't think we'll have any more trouble, do you?'
Jackson smiled. 'I don't think so.'

The days and weeks dragged. Jackson kept himself busy by supplying the company with extra rations.

His new company was stationed in a small village some twenty miles outside Toranto. Two cafés were in bounds but were not doing much business, since Jackson was keeping the beer flowing in the men's canteen. Jackson made a few bored trips to the village. The people seemed to be better off than the people in Cristie's village. He noted livestock, and men worked in the fields. He could not work up too much interest in the villagers. He found them surly. Most of his waking hours he was obsessed by thoughts of Cristie. He wrote to Paddy Fitzroy several times for news but never received a reply. He supposed that Paddy either could not get a letter past the company censor or preferred not to chance it. In desperation he wrote to Dusty Miller and received a blue-pencilled letter, but it was almost incomprehensible. He couldn't make head or tail of it. For hours he puzzled over the blue-pencilled lines and finally decided that the censor must have been as bewildered as he was, and had simply blue-pencilled at random. Dusty had begun his letter, 'Dear Sweetheart', which finally Jackson deciphered as 'Dear Sweetheart'. Was Dusty queer? The rest was gibberish and must have given the officer who censored the letter a nightmare hour or two.

At last his posting came through and he gleefully and

anxiously packed and was driven out of the camp and back to 501 Company, his kitbag filled with cigarettes, chocolates and tinned goods. His new-found family must have had a thin time of it. Those days were over. Soon he would be back to take care of them again.

Jackson found Paddy in the wet canteen, brooding over a mug of tea. His face lit up. 'Jackson. It's old dodgy Jackson.'

Sitting facing him. 'You didn't answer my letters, Paddy.'

'Everything's censored heavy, and no way to smuggle them out. You're back soon.'

'Three bloody months.'

'Well, it's good to see you.'

'And you, Paddy. How's everything?'

'You might well ask that. Sure it's been a bloody disaster. You'll be seeing some new faces.'

'What happened?'

'Didn't all the wogs in the village go on strike. Didn't the top brass turn up and give us all hell. Holland's posted out.'

'Thank Christ for that. Where?'

'How the hell would I know? And Butcher and some of the NCOs.'

'What about the RSM?'

'Tompkins climbed right up the new Major's arse, disappeared for several hours and came out smelling of roses.'

'He would.'

'And that bastard Watson's inside waiting a court martial.'

'What did they get him for?'

'Rape.'

'He always was bad news. How's Cristie?'

'Oh.' Paddy picked up his mug and drank noisily. 'Sure, she's fine. Why wouldn't she be?'

'When did you last see her?'

'It was some time ago.'

'You said you'd keep an eye on her.'

'I did so, but with the village out of bounds, it got too hot.'

'How's the camp Police Patrol?'

'Bloody heavy.'

'But you can get out?'

'Some of the fellas do. Those that think it's worth it.'

'I'll get out.'

'You'll be welcome.'

'Of course I will.' Jackson stared at Paddy. 'What do you mean?'

'It's not worth the risk.'

'I've got to see Cristie.'

'The new Major's a bastard. He's on to anybody who's found in the village. If they pick you up, Johnnie, your feet won't touch the bloody ground.'

'What's got into you, Paddy? What are you windy about?'

'I'm warning you, that's all. I'd give the village a miss.'

'You must be crazy.' Jackson walked out of the canteen.

The room was half-filled with soldiers and thick with tobacco smoke. Squatting in a corner, three soldiers gambled. The curtains were drawn, the room strangely hushed. The piano lid closed. No sign of Momma, Cristie, Maria, or the old man seated under the large photograph of his once-remembered self.

It came as no great shock when a soldier Jackson only vaguely remembered said with an indifferent grin, 'The old man? He's dead.' Maybe it will register later, Jackson thought, as, puzzled, he stared around him. Most of the faces he recognized. He nodded greetings and some of the soldiers responded with sly grins and glances. Then he noticed Tony. He moved over to him. 'Hello.'

Tony stared at him for a long moment, as though he did not recognize him. 'Hello.' Then he half-turned away.

'Business seems to be picking up.'

'Always busy now, always.'

'Where's Cristie?'

'Cristie?' Tony watched Jackson's expression as he glanced about him. A bedroom door opened. A soldier stepped out and grinned and nudged one of his pals. Then Jackson saw Cristie standing in the doorway, a dressing gown tied carelessly about her waist. Their eyes met. Cristie's lips opened as she stared with a stricken expression at Jackson. The room suddenly felt intensely hot. He had to get out into the cool of the evening. He turned and walked to the door that led to the stairs and down the stairs to the main hall. The walk seemed endless. As he reached the door it violently opened and Momma stood there. Jackson saw at once that she was drunk. She was startled. 'Johnnie . . .'

'I . . .' He tried to push past her.

'Wait.' Her speech was faintly blurred. 'You have seen Cristie?'

'I just want to get out of here.' He pushed past her.

She followed him. 'You are sorry.' A stream of confused Italian, then struggling with her English, 'For who is you sorry? For you or for my Cristie?' Tears splashing on her cheeks. She was gripping his arm.

Drunken bitch, he thought, as he pushed her away. 'Let me go.'

'You are not man, but we have everything now. Everything!' She was screaming.

As Jackson stumbled down the stairs, he heard Momma say in a more controlled voice, 'What's this? Why you not happy, soldiers? Why you not enjoy?'

He sat on the bench in the plaza, staring down at his ammo boots. Then he became aware that Cristie was standing close to him. He looked up. She made a helpless gesture.

'I could kill you,' his words savage. 'I could bloody kill you.' Remembering holding her tenderly to him as they danced. Her youth. Her innocence.

She dropped on her knees in front of him and bowed her head. All his plans shattered. Marriage. A mirthless, shuddering sound in his throat.

'All right. Tell me you were starving. There was no other way out. There was another way out and you bloody well know it and so did the old man. I suppose you all waited for him to die. Look at me.' She looked at him. Her eyes were dry. 'Am I supposed to understand? You've suffered, haven't you, you poor bitch.' He was crying as he pulled her to her feet and pushed her roughly away. 'Go back, go on. Go back to your fucking soldiers.' The pain in her eyes was too much, he had to escape. Her hands fluttered, her lips moved soundlessly. He pushed her again. She stumbled and almost fell. 'Go on.' Her mouth working out of control. 'Get out of my life!' She turned and slowly walked away. He watched her, longed to call her back, instead he began walking briskly in the opposite direction, then had to stop.

Father Raffio was barring his way. 'Excuse, but I overheard.'

'She's a whore.'

'You must never forget. She loves you.'

A cry of despair. 'Love me! Laying on her back for anybody.'

'You would prefer her dead? You must know people cling to life. Cling to hope.'

'I'm supposed to understand?'

'That these people are defeated . . . yes. Have been degraded and are not to blame, yes.'

'But, Cristie. God. Cristie.'

'She is only one. There are many others. This is what you have made of their lives. But shall we blame anyone when we are all guilty? This is war and in war there are no victors, only the defeated. You and your army. My people . . . all, all defeated.'

'And I'm supposed to understand. The one girl I've ever loved.'

'You are romantic. That is not loving. That is self-love. Until you can truly love someone and can be charitable, no matter what. That is loving. It is not easy.'

'It's bloody easy to talk, Father.'

'If you walk away now, if you cannot even try to understand, you will be just like all the rest – defeated.'

'Watch my smoke.' Jackson began laughing and the tears still fell.

'She's a whore. They're all bloody whores. I thought I'd found someone different. But they're all the same, all bloody whores.' He pushed past Father Raffio and walked away.

Chapter IX

The largest petrol and oil dump in Italy had proved to be a total failure. After Holland, Butcher and others had been posted to other companies, a new commanding officer, Major Cobbey, had taken over. Even though the war was more than half-way spent, a regular soldier in his middle forties, he had only recently been promoted to the rank of Major. The reason why he had been passed over may have been because he suffered from an appalling inferiority complex, which he did his best to hide under a cloud of bombast. The men soon caught on that Cobbey and RSM Tompkins were two of a kind.

Another new face had the grapevine buzzing with excitement and amusement. Tony Dare. He had been posted to 501 Company under somewhat unusual circumstances. He had boarded a troop ship at Greenock, Scotland, a full Colonel and appointed Officer Commanding Troops. After a few drinks in his cabin he became bored with the company of his fellow officers and decided to go ashore alone for a farewell round of the pubs. At roll call, prior to sailing, all officers, NCOs and men were present except Colonel Dare. A shore patrol finally found him blind drunk in one of the pubs. He was carried aboard ship and, in due course, court martialled and reduced to the rank of Lieutenant, and, to add insult to injury, posted from the Infantry to the RASC. He had served throughout the First World War with distinction; among the ribbons on his chest were the DSO and MC. He had enjoyed every moment of World War I, as his uncompleted memoirs clearly showed. Jackson at a later date read them with increasing astonishment. The ex-Colonel had to be insane, Jackson finally decided. Dare's history of World War I made it appear to be nothing more than a joyous prank. He had waded through death and destruction with a total disregard for his own life and with an eye on the coveted VC, which by his own account, he richly deserved on more than one occasion. Now, at the age of fifty-two, he had finally been disgraced and demoted. He was, however, perfectly philosophical about it. He described himself as a country gentleman and owned a small estate in Suffolk. He was also a dedicated alcoholic.

501 RASC Company were posted to a small village on the sea coast, fourteen miles from Naples. A and B Company were billeted in stables attached to an old palace, closed for the duration of the war. The palace had seen better days. Lord and Lady Hamilton had resided there and so, of course, had Nelson. C and D Company were billeted in a school.

Jackson on his return had been posted to D Company, with no specified job, until one day Lieutenant Dare sent for him. Jackson entered Dare's office, a room he used for one purpose only. Each morning at 9 a.m. he would enter it and cheerfully sign any papers his Sergeant Major placed in front of him.

Dare eyed Jackson thoughtfully as he stood ramrod stiff in front of him. He came straight to the point.

'I'm appointing you my batman.'

'Sir.' A cagey look in Jackson's eyes. 'I can refuse, can't I?'

'Of course.'

'Then if you don't mind . . .'

'It won't pay.'

'How do you mean, sir?'

'Do you want to have a cushy war?'

Truth prevailed. 'Of course, sir.'

'Then be my batman.'

Be brutally frank, thought Jackson. 'How will that benefit me, sir?'

'Good,' smiled Dare. 'You don't beat about the bush, I see.' Laughter wrinkles about his eyes. 'You call me at seven every morning with a cup of tea.' Still smiling, he stared at Jackson.

Jackson waited, but seemingly Dare had lost track of what he was saying. 'And then, sir?'

'That's it.' More than puzzled, Jackson gazed at Dare's open, smiling face. He repeated, 'That's it.'

'You mean all I have to do is serve you a cup of tea?'

'Yes.'

'Sorry, I don't understand. I thought a batman had to look after your kit and . . .'

'No one touches my kit.'

'What do I do the rest of the day, sir?'

'Any damn thing you like.'

'What's the catch, sir?'

'Oh, a couple of times a week we drive to the nearest NAAFI Bulk Issue Store and you wangle a case of whiskey for me.' How did he know about that, Jackson wondered. Dare answered him.

'I had a word with that arse-crawler Tompkins, who seemed anxious to keep in my good books.'

'How about the new Major, sir?'

'An awful fart. Shouldn't even be in charge of the Boy Scouts. He won't give us any problems.'

'When do I start, sir?'

'Tomorrow morning, and no sugar in my tea.'

'No sugar, sir.'

'Do you play chess?'

'No, sir.'

'Pity. Second thoughts, why don't you start now.' He glanced at his watch. 'We could make the Bulk Issue Store in an hour.'

'Why not?' smiled Jackson.

'Better wangle some stuff for the Officers' mess as well.'

'And the Sergeants' mess.'

'Of course. And don't forget the men. You'd better get some cash from the Canteen Corporal. Stock the place with beer.'

'Not a bad thought,' agreed Jackson.

Jackson reported at seven a.m. to the Officers' billet the next morning – a charming villa overlooking the sea, with a good view of Capri.

Bristow, the Officers' cook, poured a cup of tea.

'No sugar,' warned Jackson.
'For Dare?'
'Yes.'
'He's crazy.'
Jackson probed. 'Why do you say that?'
'He doesn't make any sense.'
'How come?'
'Doesn't do anything.'
'What's so crazy about that?'
'Major Cobbey's keeping an eye on him.'
'Could be. Tea'll get cold.'

Jackson took the cup of tea to Dare's room, knocked on the door, got no reply so he entered. The room was in semi-darkness. Jackson located the bedside table, placed the cup on it, then moved cautiously to the window and drew the curtains. The early morning sun found Dare, hair dishevelled, fast asleep. Jackson shook him awake. 'Your tea, sir.'

Dare opened his eyes. 'Put it on the bedside table.'

'Good.' More awake now. 'There's a toothbrush glass by the sink. Rinse it out, will you.' Jackson rinsed the glass. 'There's a bottle of Scotch in the wardrobe.'

'There's a case.'

'Was. Two missing. Open another one and I'll say when.'

Jackson held up the half-pint glass and carefully poured, eyeing Dare as he did so. When the glass was almost filled, Dare said, 'Careful. Mustn't overdo it.'

Jackson walked the whiskey to Dare's bed, being careful not to spill it. Dare was half sitting up in bed. A hand reached out for the glass. The hand shook a little. The glass was held in front of Dare's bloodshot eyes. He smiled fondly at the whiskey and took a long swig, then removed the glass from his lips and sighed. 'Hair of the dog. What's the time?'

'Seven. Your tea, sir.'

Dare glanced at the cup on the bedside table. 'Probably cold by now.' Another swig of whiskey and a loud belch. 'Better. Ah, forgot something. You have to pick me up at nine.'

'Why, sir?'

'Because you've got my car, haven't you? And unless you

want to walk back to your billet.'

'Nine o'clock, sir. Shall I take the tea back?'

'No. Pour it down the sink. Musn't offend the cook.'

'He dropped a hint.'

'What about?'

'He said Major Cobbey was keeping an eye on you.'

Dare chuckled and took another drink.

'Cobbey's absolutely shit scared of me. I know too much for him; any problems and I'll pull rank on him. Y'know the bloody idiot doesn't even know how to hold a knife and fork. Bloody embarrassing having to sit at the same table.' He belched again and took a more cautious drink. 'The Scots knew something. This stuff starts the blood running again. Marvellous for everything except the liver, kidneys and heart.' Another belch. 'Pardon, but better a bad lodger than an empty house. Cobbey's already started sounding me out. He's a mine of absolutely useless information. If I cared to prick the bubble, it would burst. Have you read Shakespeare?'

'No, sir.'

'Tony when we're on our own. What's your name?'

'Johnnie.'

'But don't be too bloody familiar when people are around. All the stuff Cobbey doesn't know about how to run a company I've practically forgotten. I'm much too useful. Promise you we'll have no problems. Have you been to Pompeii? Like to?'

'Wouldn't mind.'

'Wouldn't mind, by God!' exploded Dare. 'It's a bloody marvel. I'll have to try and educate you, I can see. After I've signed the bumph, we'll take a trip. You'll find it interesting, unless you've got other plans.'

'No plans.'

'There's a lot of interesting places to see. Been to the opera?'

'No.'

'Not too mad about it myself. Caruso bellowed. Pretty building, though. We'll try the ruins first and see what you think about them.'

'Can you really get away with it?'

'I told you not to worry, I can handle Cobbey. They fucked me up, y'know, when they court martialled me. My fault entirely, of course, but posting me to the RASC. Really, nothing a chap does quite deserves that. Are you married?'

'No.'

'Keep it that way. I've been on the treadmill three times. It simply doesn't work out. We must get some girls.' Jackson didn't reply. 'What's the matter?'

'I'm not all that interested.'

'I say. Hope you haven't got a problem?'

'I'm just off them at the moment.'

'The wrong position. Let me suggest you regain interest and see if you can rustle up a couple.'

Batman, pimp, thought Jackson, as he stared into Dare's bloodshot eyes. But he seems a decent old bastard. What a bloody odd Colonel he must have been.

Every day the same routine. Tea at seven, which was always poured down the sink. A glass of whiskey as an eye opener. The return trip to collect Dare and take him to his office. Dare always drove the car. 'Never seen such a bloody awful driver as you, Jackson.' His somewhat erratic conversation amused Jackson. He had played county cricket. Gentleman player, of course, but never made the England team to his lasting regret. Driven racing cars – Brookland and the European circuits. Travelled widely. Could quote Shakespeare by the hour. An avid reader and a warm, kindly, rather crazy man.

He had made it clear from the outset that Sergeant Major Stoddard was running D Company, and this suited Stoddard, who had thought that an ex-Colonel would be one hell of a problem and hard to handle.

'I'm waiting for my bowler hat,' Dare had informed him at their first meeting. 'And I don't intend to do another fucking thing towards the war effort. I'll sign the bumph and you'd better make damn sure all the bumph is in good order. I can smell a bad egg a mile away, so don't try and slip anything past me.'

Dare and Jackson explored the ruins, Dare acting as guide. They basked on the black, volcanic sand beaches. Went sightseeing. Dined out at the few expensive restaurants which were still operating for the rich Italians. The days passed and Jackson was seldom bored in Dare's company. He realized how lucky he was. Life was a prolonged holiday. The only things unobtainable were the girls. The Catholic curse of virginity at all cost worked against him. He made contact with a family in the village. Momma, Poppa, three brothers and seven daughters. Four of them young and beautiful. All the daughters were chaperoned by Momma, Poppa, and several aunts. They were delightful girls but totally unobtainable. Even whores were in short supply, and the few he found were not to Dare's taste, and he was not interested. He was still brooding and grieving over Cristina. Many times he thought about driving over and visiting her, but he knew he could never face her again.

Summer turned to autumn. He constantly reminded himself how lucky he was, but he was often depressed. A new and unwelcome experience for him. He swore savagely when she invaded his mind, cursed her memory and joined Dare on his drinking bouts, which seemed to be his full-time occupation. Dare drank steadily and happily. If he was ever depressed or hung-over, it never showed. Jackson drank recklessly. He drank to blot Cristina from his mind, and each new day started with a new hangover.

Paddy was with A Company, billeted in the stables. He shared his den with Dusty Miller. They slept on hospital stretchers supported on boxwood cases. Orange boxes served as bedside tables. Two old beaten-up chairs helped furnish the room. In Jackson's absence, Dusty had adopted Paddy, and Paddy good-naturedly did not protest too often or too loud.

It was Sunday and a free afternoon and evening stretched ahead. Paddy decided to go in search of Jackson. He found him in the school billet, lying on his bed. An army blanket beneath him on the tiled floor and his pack for a headrest, reading a thriller and bored out of his mind. He quickly accepted Paddy's offer to make a trip to Naples.

'But first,' said Paddy, 'how about a little jar now to help us on our way.'

Jackson took a bottle of Scotch from his kit-bag and slipped it inside his battle-dress blouse and they left the school and walked back to the stables. A cloudless blue sky, bright sunshine and a nip in the air that was a foretaste of approaching winter. They locked the stable door and poured the whiskey into enamel cups, and Paddy was soon feeling more cheerful. Jackson was still hungover from the excesses of the previous day. Dusty quickly got tipsy and made even less sense that usual, but was delighted to be sharing Jackson's company once more. His dog-like devotion amused and irritated Jackson. As the bottle slowly emptied, Jackson's spirits rose, and finally, when the bottle was empty, he was convinced that he was ready for anything, but it was clear that Dusty wasn't. His eyes were bemused, his speech thick and halting and he staggered. Paddy gazed at him with pity.

'Sure the poor daft bastard's got no head for drink at all. We'll have to dump him.' Dusty bitterly protested but to no avail. Jackson repeated several times, 'We wouldn't get anywhere with you, Dusty. The Red Caps would pinch us. You're as drunk as a fiddler's bitch.' Dusty, tearful now, snot hanging from his nose, still begging to go along with them, as Jackson and Paddy left the stable. Dusty followed, still crying like an idiot child, but a sergeant who was passing at that moment bellowed at him, 'You there, Miller, you daft article, what's the matter with you? You're pissed out of your bloody mind.' Dusty staggered back to his stable and slammed the door shut.

In the plaza they had a drink on the pavement outside a bar, then hailed a passing taxi and were on their way.

First call in Naples was an old palace, converted into a NAAFI canteen for Other Ranks. A beautiful old building that they hardly noticed. They filled up with egg and chips, a mug of tea and almost indigestible sausage rolls, then moved from bar to bar exploring some of the back streets. Then made their way back to the main thoroughfare, both becoming more and more elated. Then they found themselves in the dock area. Another bar and Paddy was trying out his Italian. His attempts were greeted with good-natured smiles and laughter and he would turn to Jackson and say, 'I'm getting through to the different-coloured bastards and that's a fact, now.'

Then the change. At first Jackson wasn't aware of it. A subtle difference in Paddy's tone of voice. A look in his eyes as he spoke to the barman. Aggression building, and the Italians were quick to pick it up. The smiles and laughter were less frequent. Some of them pretended not to hear what Paddy was saying, others moved away, and Jackson felt increasingly uneasy. Paddy was smiling and staring insolently at the people in the bar. Smiling and staring at them coldly. A vein throbbed in his forehead. His smiling lips would suddenly take a downward curve. His voice louder as he ordered drinks. Then his expression would darken and his eyes turn bleak.

'Let's go,' suggested Jackson.

'And where to?'

'Some other place.'

'I like it well enough here.'

'I want to try something else.'

Paddy, with a brooding look, was staring about him. 'These dirty bastards are Nazis.'

Jackson spoke firmly. 'We'll drink up and leave.' He lifted his glass.

'And why the hell should we go?'

'I don't want any trouble.'

'Trouble?' Paddy stared at Jackson, then an ugly smile as he turned and gazed at the men in the bar. 'Who the hell's here who could give me trouble now?'

Jackson followed Paddy's gaze. The men were dressed in their Sunday suits. Lean, weather-beaten faces. Strongly built. Most of them probably worked on the docks, loading and unloading the ships.

'Nobody here who could give us trouble, Paddy? Are you joking?'

'The proof of the pudding,' said Paddy. 'is in the bashing. I'm in the mood, so I am, to take the whole fucking lot on.'

'I'm in the mood to leave you to it.'

A hard stare from Paddy. 'Is that so?' Then his expression turned sour. 'And what's scaring you now, me little man?'

'You,' said Jackson pointedly.

'Me?' Paddy switched on a look of mock horror. 'Now how could I scare you?'

'By going out of your stupid mind.'

'And what makes you think I'd do that?'

'I hope you won't. Come on, let's get out of here.'

'How about you answering my question?'

'You're looking for a fight.'

'Not at all. But if any of these wogs wants one . . .'

'They don't. They don't want to fight and they don't want to be bothered.'

'Sure. Haven't they proved it in the war?'

'And haven't we?'

'Careful.'

'For Christ's sake.' Jackson was losing his temper. 'Can't you have a drink and enjoy yourself? Do you have to get into a punch-up? Nobody here's bothering us. It's their country. They're enjoying themselves so bloody well leave them alone.'

A silence in the bar. Hostile stares. Jackson aware of the mounting tension. He threw a sidelong glance at the dockers seated at a table, steadily staring at Paddy. He offered them a friendly smile. Not returned.

'Who the hell are you grinning at, Jackson?'

'Them.' Jackson was still smiling. 'I'm trying to send them friendly signals. Trying to get on their wavelength.'

'You poor bastard.' Paddy spat on the floor.

Jackson observed that that did not go down too well. 'I'm leaving.'

'Leaving me?'

'No. Leaving with you.'

'I'm not leaving.'

'Okay, then, I'm leaving you.'

Jackson smiled at the frozen faces of the men in the bar

one more time and then he left. He walked at a steady pace, his ears listening for sounds of violence coming from the bar. A clatter of ammo boots behind him and then Paddy was walking abreast of him, smiling secretly. They walked on in silence, then Paddy, without turning his head, said, 'You're a terrible bloody coward.'

Jackson smiled pleasantly. 'I know.'

'And you own to it?'

'I'm the world's champ.'

'You've no balls.'

'That's right.'

'You should have been a fucking woman.'

'A fucking woman,' Jackson smiled.

Then unexpectedly, Paddy began laughing, and put his arm about Jackson's shoulders as he walked on, shaking his laughing head but clearly bewildered. 'We could have had some fucking fun there, so we fucking could.'

'Great fucking fun,' smiled Jackson. 'And later we'd have been fished out of the docks.'

'I could take them all,' said Paddy with total conviction.

They walked on and Jackson felt Paddy slowly relaxing. Then Paddy shook his head again. 'You're a queer fella. A a queer fella, so you are.'

'Queen of the fairies, dear,' minced Jackson, sticking out his underlip.

Paddy laughing. 'So you are at it?'

I've calmed him down, Jackson thought. 'What about getting back? I've seen enough of this place.'

'It's a dirty hole.' Paddy stared about him. 'A bloody terrible shithouse.' The late afternoon sun was sinking. The streets looked drab. 'Sure, we'll go back. What's here for anybody?'

With great relief, Jackson said, 'We'll find a taxi.'

They walked on, not sure of their directions and not caring much. Paddy was chatting away. His old, good-natured self. Then they heard singing and from a turning trooped a group of Italian sailors singing loud and clear and singing in tune. They were young and their arms were linked and they swaggered as they marched towards Jackson and Paddy and the line stretched almost all the way across the road.

Jackson made a quick count, twelve, more, fifteen. There was room on the pavement to pass. Jackson instinctively began drifting towards the safety of the pavement, but a hand with fingers that had the texture of steel bit into his arm. He yelled as he was jerked back close up to Paddy, then an arm was linked through his and he was pulled back to the centre of the road. Paddy was smiling his strange hard smile again. 'We walk through them.'

The sailors were still singing, but they had become aware of the two soldiers walking towards them.

'You stupid bastard,' said Jackson.

'Through them,' Paddy repeated.

'You have to be out of your mind.'

The sailors, still singing, now glancing at each other, and watching the two soldiers steadily moving towards them. Jackson's arm trapped, struggling to escape.

'They'll give way,' smiled Paddy.

'You stupid, stupid prick.'

'Or I'll beat the holy Jesus out of them.'

The singing muted. Prickles of fear moving over Jackson's body. Fifteen. There's fifteen of them. The singing ceased. Thirty yards, or ten, separated them. It felt to Jackson like walking slow time, almost drifting, then he collided with an Italian uniform and was bounced back. He found himself staring into angry brown eyes. The sailor was about Jackson's age, but bigger and heavier. Then his body was jerked forward and Paddy pushed and shoved his way through the line, dragging Jackson with him and the crazy smile was in his eyes again.

Then quickly a circle of sailors was all around them and Paddy, still arm-linked with Jackson, stood in the centre, still wearing his crazy grin, then slowly turned, still linked to the reluctant Jackson, who was staring at the unfriendly faces. Paddy suddenly released Jackson's arm. Silence, as the sailors watched Paddy slowly turning, the crazy grin slipping downwards, spittle about his lips, his fists bunched, head lowered into his neck. Jackson turning fearfully. The circle of sailors slowly crowding in, angry-eyed. Jesus Christ, thought Jackson. They even carry daggers. Fifteen of them. This is it. I know it. Unless a miracle happens, this is really goodbye. Angry voices. Hands gesturing. The circle closing in. Jackson felt claustrophobic. Try to keep calm. Calm? I'm panicking. Try the friendly approach, a pleasant smile, an 'I won't hurt you if you don't hurt me' kind of connection. Wiggle your fucking ears. Make them laugh. Do something. Nothing is going to make these bastards laugh. They've been insulted. They want blood.

A possible answer to the problem came as a shock, and for a moment he was almost overwhelmed with fear, so he forced himself to act. He turned to Paddy, whose smile was now completely savage, then bunched his fist and struck out with all the power he could muster. His fist struck Paddy's chin, a searing pain ran up his arm. Paddy blinked and his smile disappeared. He stared with a bewildered expression at Jackson, then lifted his arms, his hands open, in protest. Jackson struck again. This time he connected on Paddy's nose, a softer area but clearly it did no harm. Paddy simply shook his head, still bewildered. Another blow. Paddy wasn't even trying to defend himself. Jackson heard himself screaming, 'You bastard! I'll kill you! Kill you!' He rained blows into Paddy's unprotected face and still Paddy did not defend himself. Then the laughter began, and the jeers. The sailors were enjoying themselves, roaring with laughter, encouraging Jackson, who was hurting his hands more than he was hurting Paddy. Then Paddy's arms reached out and encircled Jackson's arms and body and he was staring into Jackson's eyes and shouting, 'You're a fucking head case that's for sure! It's them we're supposed to be fighting, you daft bastard!'

Jackson was struggling to get free and still screaming, 'It's you! You! And all the crazy bastards like you!' Struggling harder. 'I'll kill you! Let me go and I'll kill you!' Demented with fear and rage. Wanting to kill for the first time in his life. Wanting to kill his friend for leading him into danger. His friend trying to get him killed. What kind of a friend? Struggling, spitting out the words, 'I'll kill you! Kill you!' Tears of anger pouring from his eyes and now Paddy was trying to calm him. 'Okay, fella. Take it easy now. Okay. If I let you go, will you give over now and stop trying to give me a hard time? Will you give over now?' Jackson still struggling violently, helplessly, Paddy's arms about him like iron bands. Helpless as a child. 'Will you give over now, Johnnie? Will you for Christ's sake give over?'

Now the sailors, they were moving and bustling around them. What were they saying? Could it be true? They were still laughing but they were trying to break up the fight. They were being friendly. Jackson began to calm down. 'Let me go. Take your bloody arms away.' Paddy's face a sorrow. No anger now. 'Sure I will, but behave now.' The iron bands turned into brotherly arms. 'You're the queer fella, that's for sure.' Hands patting him on the back. One of the sailors handed him his cap which had fallen off during the fight. He automatically dusted it before replacing it on his head. Then he walked through the circle of sailors, friendly smiling faces, but he didn't want to know any of them.

He walked on, Paddy at his side again, looking sideways, anxious. He walked faster, turned a corner, and as he did so, glanced back. The sailors stood in a group, smoking and laughing and seemingly happy. He still walked fast, Paddy keeping step with him. Then he stopped.

'I'm going on alone.'

'C'mon now, Johnnie.'

'The last thing I want is your lousy company.'

'Johnnie, will you calm it, now that's a good fella.'

'Will you piss off.'

'What did I do?'

'You're so thick you wouldn't know.' A strangled shout. 'You scared the shit out of me!'

'Will you forget it. Sure, I got a bit excited.'

Calmer now, Jackson stared at Paddy. He spoke quietly. 'I want to be on my own. That's all. See you back at the billet tomorrow.' He walked away, increased his pace, and turned another corner. His last glimpse was of Paddy, standing where he had left him. He looked forlorn.

All the kids on the street seemed to be begging, shining shoes, or selling their sisters. Jackson threw coins on the street, but that was no way to get rid of them. More and more gathered about him, shouting, pulling at him, begging, beseeching, cigarettes, chocolate, money. He threw cigarettes to his left and right. They fought over them. He increased his pace and the small army of begging children still pursued him. 'Gimme, gimme – you like fuck my sister, George? Very nice. Very clean. Only fourteen. Gimme, gimme.' A nightmare of beseeching, innocent and evil, little faces. Practically running now, still throwing cigarettes. 'How much boots, George? How much pantaloon?' A slight, sly-eyed boy with a fist full of notes. Christ, they'd strip him naked if he didn't get away. He took refuge in a bar and the kids followed him, still shouting, beseeching. The barman finally threw them out.

He sat brooding as he automatically lifted his glass. The kids hung around outside the bar, then one by one or in small groups, they left. Jackson ordered a taxi. The barman shook his head. 'No phone.' All Jackson wanted to do was get out of Naples and back to the comparative sanity and the security of his billet. He ordered another drink, and another. He hadn't the energy or inclination to move. Somehow he would get back. Sitting brooding, a bad taste happening in his mouth. I'll know about it tomorrow. Old man hangover, going to give it to me tomorrow. Better move. Soon. Another drink. 'Where's the nearest taxi rank?' The barman finally understood and glanced at his cheap watch, then shook his head. 'Too late.'

'What time is it?'

The barman showed Jackson his watch. Ten o'clock. How the time had flown. Sitting brooding in this bar. That's how the time had flown. That bloody Paddy. Steer clear of him in the future. Mad. Stark, raving mad when he drank too much. Keep out of his way in future. The barman wanted to close. Now where to go? Get a taxi somewhere or you've a fourteen-mile hike ahead of you. Never make it.

Jackson left the bar and walked and kept walking. Kids sleeping in doorways. No taxis and not many people on the streets. A cold wind. Jackson drunk, not knowing where he was going and not caring and worried about how he was going to get home. Then he saw an American soldier leaning against a staff car. A surge of relief. That's how he would get home. In style. He stopped and offered the soldier a cigarette. Then noticed he was a Sergeant.

'Cigarette, Sarge?'

The Sergeant indifferently shook his head, then beat his arms across his body. It was turning very cold.

'Could you give me a lift, Sarge?'

'Are you crazy?' The Sergeant looked angry. 'I'm waiting for the fucking General, man.'

'It's only fourteen miles.'

'For Christ's sake. On your way, soldier.'

'I promise you . . .'

'Beat it.'

'A bottle of Scotch.' Jackson still held out the cigarette packet. The Sergeant took a cigarette and lit it. 'A bottle of Scotch,' Jackson repeated.

'You're kidding.'

'You give me a lift and you'll get the bottle of Scotch.'

The Sergeant glanced up at a large block of apartments.

'I'd better pray the old bastard's having his goodies. Get in.' He snapped open the back door and Jackson climbed in. As the car purred away, he remembered some American soldiers who were billeted in the next village. They had entertained him one evening and he had promised them a bottle of Scotch. The Yanks aren't too bad, Jackson thought.

Chapter X

Jackson was bored. More and more often he politely refused Dare's offer to go on sight-seeing runs. He had seen all the ancient monuments and churches he could stomach, and Dare's driving was daily becoming more hazardous. If a truck or car was in his way and wouldn't pull over instantly, he would run on to the pavement, where pedestrians would either freeze in horror against the nearest wall or scatter screaming while Dare leaned out of his car window shouting insults at the driver. The cases of whiskey he was tippling, and at an alarming rate, were at last taking their toll on the happy-go-lucky ex-Colonel. The early morning glass was no longer sufficient. It was two for eye-openers to help stop the shakes and more generous glasses during the day and into the night to help keep him in his normal cheerful frame of mind. And he was repeating his stories of his past exciting life and becoming something of a bore. Jackson was beginning to feel sorry for Dare and he knew that that wasn't the way things should be. Dare was cracking up. The men in the company were beginning to treat him as a joke, and he didn't appear to be aware of it. Or, if he was, he didn't care. Each morning the forms were signed carelessly. He didn't even pretend to show the slightest interest. Then he would be off on one of his jaunts with two bottles of whiskey in the back of his car. Jackson came to realize how lost and lonely the man was. His demotion, because of his drinking problem, had soured and finally embittered him. His one interest was to get his bowler hat and return to his estate in Suffolk, where most probably he would drink himself to death whilst he brooded about the ignominy that had finally caught up with him. Jackson liked him but he was becoming a bore. Even his movements, once brisk and alert, now had a zombi quality about them.

Sergeant Winters, billeted at the stables, finally helped to relieve Jackson of his second most pressing problem – boredom. Cristie's memory still haunted him. She was his major problem of course.

One evening Winters said, 'Let's go for a drink.'

'Sergeants aren't supposed to drink with privates,' grinned Jackson, who wasn't sure that he liked Winters.

'Shit. This is business and I know a little bar where we won't be disturbed.'

Seated at a table in the corner of the bar they were served wine by the owner, a man approaching ninety years, still active and alert and a perfect advertisement for the wine he sold. His complexion was a deep blue; even his eyelids were blue. Jackson idly wondered how many thousands of gallons of wine had contributed to the masterpiece. Winters bluntly came to the point.

'I want to go into business with you.'

'No point in it,' said Jackson. 'We can make a fortune, I know, but what do we do with the money?'

'I'll be getting home leave in a few months. There must be ways of exchanging lire in England.'

'I won't,' Jackson replied. 'And by the time I get leave the money will probably be useless.'

'I could take your share as well and bank it for you.'

That's why I don't like you, Jackson thought. You really are a bloody awful crook. I wouldn't trust you with sixpence. He almost laughed out loud. 'I'll think about it.'

'There must be something to buy in this country.'

Jackson nodded his head. 'Booze and whores.'

'A house, a farm, something.'

'It wouldn't be legal and the Ities know it. They'd have us over the barrel.'

'Something in Naples.'

'I've tried that. You can buy cheap watches that cost a small fortune. Jerry sacked the town.'

'I still want to go into business with you. Any stuff you get from NAAFI I can sell and you know the prices are high.'

'And the money practically worthless.'

'Must be gold watches, jewellery, something.'

'Think I haven't looked, checked, tried to find it.'

'Even the rich Italians are on strict rations, Jackson.'

'They get over that easily enough. They buy cigarettes and barter them. Don't you know yet it's only the poor who have a hard time?'

'If we keep trying we may come up with something.'

Why not, thought Jackson. Be something to do. Might get some fun out of it.

'We look after Tompkins and the Sergeants' mess, right?'

Jackson nodded. 'I always look after Tompkins.'

'So that gives us all the freedom we need. All you have to do is get the stuff. I'll be waiting and I'll take the truck and sell at the right prices.'

They shook hands, neither trusting the other an inch.

Everything worked smoothly. Jackson invested his capital in the business. Winters raised enough money at a heavy rate of interest from anyone who was interested in the prospective gold rush. It was almost too simple. Jackson, with a driver, Dick Bell, a cheerful smiling quick-witted Londoner, hand-picked by Winters, drove twice a week to the NAAFI Bulk Issue Store. The runs were made in the evening so that they would return by nightfall. First stop the car park, where they deposited two cases of whiskey into Dare's car. Then on to the Officers' mess, where the Sergeant in charge of the billet helped unload cases of whiskey, gin, and a few luxury food items. Then to the stables where beer was unloaded for the men's mess, then to the Sergeants' mess. RSM Tompkins would usually be waiting and his normal greeting was 'Well, here's our little old fiddler and dead on time.' Jackson would smile and reply, 'And there's more where that came from.'

'Sir!'

'I mean, sir, sir.'

'Just because you're the most popular lad in town, Jackson, don't mean you can be bloody impertinent.'

'No offence intended, sir.'

'Good lad. Piss off now.'

By the time Jackson returned to the truck, Winters would be seated in the driving cab. Jackson would hand him the NAAFI receipts, Winters would nod, give the thumbs up sign and the truck would drive away to a destination that Winters kept secret, reasoning that if Jackson knew where he sold the goods, he would no longer have any use for his services. Each trip Jackson purchased more goods. It was so simple it was almost farcical.

Returning from a trip, he had a sudden thought. Why not take a consignment of cigarettes, chocolate and food to Cristie? He felt generous-hearted and all-forgiving when the idea occurred to him. He could imagine her expression as he carried case after case into her house. He had no idea how the family was faring or if other troops were billeted in or near the village. He had deliberately stayed away. What would her reaction be? Surely overjoyed. Jackson the saviour once more to the rescue and no strings attached. How noble can one be.

One evening in the canteen, swilling beer, Paddy joined him at his table. They had not spoken to each other since that day on the town in Naples. Paddy smiled.

'So you're working with Winters then.'

'That's right.'

'Johnnie, you might have pulled me in on the fiddle. I could be useful as you well know.'

Lifting his glass of beer, Jackson grinned. 'Too damn useful.'

'You're still thinking about our little trip to Naples.'

'I don't think I'm ever going to forget it.'

'I'd had a skinful now. But if it was business, I wouldn't go about it pissed out of my mind.'

The beguiling smile. The easy manner. Jackson was finding it hard to hold a grudge against Paddy. A thought came to him. 'Have you been back to the village?'

'What village?'

'Cristie's?'

'Sure I have not.'

'Know anyone who has?'

'Who would want to go back there? Wasn't it a terrible place now.'

'I've thought about it.'

'You're still stuck on your little whore.' Jackson's eyes narrowed and Paddy smiled. 'Isn't that your name for her, now?'

'I'm wondering how she's getting on.'

'She was a nice girl, you know, Johnnie.'

'I was thinking about taking her a gift.'

'Why?'

Surprised, Jackson looked at Paddy. 'That's a stupid question.'

'Not so stupid. If the whorehouse is doing good business, she won't be needing your help, now will she? There'll be a few dozen more taking care of her in more ways than one.'

'Make her think, wouldn't it.' Jackson's smile was not pleasant.

'Punish her with kindness, do you mean?'

The truth, thought Jackson. Punish her with kindness, the bitch. That should make her feel very bad. He smiled again.

'Yes. Something like that.'

'Maybe I'll go wid you.'

'Tomorrow evening?'

'What else would I be doing?'

'Winters will lay on a waggon. Only one thing.'

'What's that?'

'No boozing until the job's over.'

Paddy chuckled. 'And one other little thing now. What's in it for me?'

Jackson carelessly pulled from out of his battle-dress pocket a bundle of notes and, not even bothering to count them, threw half on to the table.

Paddy whistled under his breath, then hastily stuffed the money into a pocket. 'Sure, you're a bad bastard where women are concerned, but you're generous enough to your friends.'

Jackson made out his shopping list before he retired to bed for an early evening. He lay on the hard floor, covered by a blanket, staring at the ceiling. He was alone apart from Corporal Simpson, who was seated with his back against the wall, writing a letter to his wife.

Twice a day, without fail, he wrote to her. He smoked heavily but did not drink. He would like to drink and promised himself he would again when he was home once more and the war was over. He was afraid that if he drank he might get involved with whores or another woman. He was saving himself for his wife. Daily he had to prove his love for her. Jackson watched him as his pen slowly moved over the page as he concentrated on his letter. The letters were all much of a sameness, but no less sincere for all that. He told her about his daily routine, trying hard to make his letters as amusing as possible. Assured her he was not in any danger, and always ended with his declaration of love in much the same stilted words, thinking as he wrote, she must understand how much he loved her, needed her. That under no circumstances would he ever be unfaithful to her.

He had met her when he was seventeen and married her on his twenty-first birthday. There had never been another woman in his life and he was convinced that there never would be. Her photograph stood on a boxwood case next to his bedspace. He glanced at it from time to time as though searching for inspiration. She was a pretty girl, like many others one would see working in shops or offices, but to Simpson she was unique, perfect and the mother of his two children, a boy aged six and a girl aged four. He kept their photographs in his wallet. They never received the same attention that he bestowed on his wife. But he was to the best of his ability a good father and he loved them only second to his wife. Carol Ann was only one year old when he had last seen her and Jimmy three. His common sense told him that they would not know him when next he saw them again, but he would not and could not accept it.

He paused and stared once again at his wife's photograph, then became aware that Jackson was watching him. He smiled a self-conscious smile. He was a big powerful man with an exceedingly gentle and quiet manner. Everyone in the company knew how devoted he was to his wife and many of the men joked about the old faithful. But he was liked and respected.

'Don't mind me,' said Jackson. 'And don't forget to tell her you had it off twice last night.'

Simpson chuckled. 'She's a good girl, Johnnie. I know how lucky I am.' A smile, then the pen once again moved slowly across the page.

Jackson thought, one of the few. A lot of the men in the wet canteen drinking all the beer they could lay their hands on and telling dirty jokes and getting drunk and pretending all was well with them had received 'Dear John' letters. It seemed almost normal. He turned his thoughts inward. What happened to you, Cristie? You were a good girl. The best. What ever happened to you, Cristie? He wanted to sleep, to dismiss her from his mind. He knew it would be a long night. He was desperately excited about meeting Cristie again, and afraid. Would he have the nerve to see her? What would he say? He could never forgive her, or could he? No. His love had turned sour. No love now. Hurt pride, yet a deep longing for her. If only he could be revenged, then perhaps he could be finished with her for all time.

'Drop me off here,' said Jackson.
'What?' Paddy looked surprised as he slowed down the waggon and stopped in the plaza near the café.
'I'm not going to see her.'
'Are you crazy?'
'Give her the stuff and come back and pick me up.'
'You can't face her, do you mean?'
'Don't be long.'
'You've got a bad case of it, that's for sure.'
Jackson climbed out of the station waggon and slammed the door. 'Don't be all night.'
A wave from Paddy and the waggon drove away.
A full moon and the plaza in deep shadows. Nine months since he had first driven into the village, totally unaware of Cristie's existence. So long ago.
He walked to the café and pushed open the door. A few soldiers loitered against the bar, others were seated at tables. A new waiter whom Jackson did not recognize. Incurious glances directed at him as he made his way to the bar and ordered a glass of wine. Now he wished he had gone with Paddy. Cristie's house was only a short distance away. He could easily walk there. He felt doubt and uncertainty and a longing to see her – take her in his arms – tell her he loved her – forget all that had happened . . . If only he could forget. But she had rejected him. No, he had rejected her. But first she . . . she's just another bloody whore, for Christ's sake. He tipped his glass and swallowed hard, then ordered another drink and brooded about what he should do.
He glanced at his watch. Ten minutes. Paddy won't be back yet. He now realized why he had chosen Paddy to come on the trip with him. Surprisingly, he could trust him to treat Cristie well. He had always liked her, behaved like an older brother towards her and he would report honestly all that

happened when he saw her. Suddenly cynical. Report to me exactly what is happening in the whorehouse, punch by punch and round by round. All the bloody details. A wave of jealousy as he stared at the soldiers sitting over their drinks as he wondered how many of them had slept with Cristie. Deep hatred directed at the soldiers smoking and drinking, laughing and snickering. He shook his head. Don't be a damn fool. She's for hire, isn't she? How many cigarettes to lay and pound away and sweat all over her body. Cigarettes! Christ, if it wasn't so sickly sad it would be laughable, so why blame them? They look such gormless idiots. How can you imagine any one of them in her bed. I'll be sick in a minute. Hold on. Have another drink.

The hands on the clock above the bar moved slowly. Go to her . . . don't . . . stay here . . . Paddy will be back soon. He'll give me all the gen, then maybe . . . I don't know . . . Maybe . . . Almost an hour. What the hell is keeping him? No. Paddy wouldn't do that . . . you fool, what makes you think you can trust him? You bloody fool, what difference would it make. She's a whore. That's her trade. Another drink. He'll be here soon. I know he's crazy when he's drunk but you'd have to go a long way to find someone better than Paddy when he's sober. He'll be back soon . . .

The door burst open and Paddy entered the bar in a hurry.

'Mission accomplished. Now what about a jar?'

'Didn't you have one in the house?' Jackson ordered two drinks.

'I did not.'

'How did you manage to resist?'

'Had I started, as you well know, I wouldn't be back now.'

They made their way to a nearby table and sat down. Jackson sipped his drink and waited for Paddy to speak.

'Well?' Jackson's anxiety was showing.

'I saw she got the stuff.'

'What did she say?'

'She howled a few Hail Marys and went on her knees and blessed your darling memory.' Paddy swallowed his drink.

'What did she say? Don't fool about.'

'She cried.'

'Is that all?'
'Did you want her to jump out the window?'
'I didn't mean that.'
'She didn't want to take it.'
'But she did.'
'Sure, wasn't Momma there and in a bloody terrible state, crying like crazy and drunk out of her mind and calling on all the saints to do you a favour and where's me darling Johnnie. The best boy in all the world and so he is and Cristie pleading with her to shut her gab.'
'She doesn't want to see me.'
'She finally thanked you for the gifts.'
'But she doesn't want to see me.'
'She knew you wouldn't call.'
'But did she want to see me?'
'I don't know. Maybe. But then maybe she doesn't.'
'That's what I thought.'
'That Momma's in a terrible bad way, getting fat and boozed out of her mind.'
'Suffering, the poor bitch, for the crimes against her daughters.'
'And what about yourself?'
'Shut up!'
'The answer I expected. If the old one's suffering, maybe she's still a good woman.'
'She's a dirty old bitch.'
'You see it your way.'
'Turned her daughters into whores.'
'Instead of into the graveyard.'
Jackson waved his arm in dismissal. 'Who else was there?'
'Tony himself.'
'What was he doing?'
'Pouring the bloody drinks and trying to keep Cristie calm.'
'He's still in love with her, the poor bastard.'
'It seems he is.'
'Anybody else there?'
Paddy drained his glass and called for two more drinks.

'A few of the boys and don't be stupid and ask me what they were doing.'

That sick feeling again. 'Business as usual, eh?'

'That's so, business as usual.'

Jackson started laughing.

'What's the big joke, now?'

'I don't know.' Still laughing. 'It doesn't make sense. They're still at it. Still whoring, and I'm playing Santa Claus. Still supporting them. I must like punishment. I must like pain. I am a bloody head case. Drink up, Paddy, and let's get the hell out of here.'

'You're a head case right enough. Always dashing out of bars.'

Half an hour later Jackson, who had been bleakly staring ahead through the windscreen, said curtly, 'Let's go back.'

'What's that?' Paddy took his eyes off the road for a moment. 'Go back where?'

'To Cristie.'

Paddy started laughing. 'I'm sober don't forget, and when I'm sober I'm a decent-living fella and duck out of trouble like being booked in after hours and chancing jankers and all that.'

'No problems.'

A pause as Paddy smiled to himself. 'I forgot you've everyone fixed.'

'That's right.'

'Okay. Back we go.' Paddy slowed down when he saw ahead a side turning, drove into it, reversed and headed back towards the village. 'And what's your plans?'

'Don't know.'

They drove on in silence for a while, then Paddy said, 'Have to be careful where we park.'

'You're a real Doctor Jekyll and Mr Hyde.'

'That's so and it's always been the mystery of the age to me.'

'Big hero when pissed out of your mind.'

Paddy laughed. 'Say anything you want now, but be careful, I might remember it next time I'm on a crazy run.'

'Then I'll shut up, Paddy.'

They both laughed.

They parked the waggon outside the village. It appeared to be deserted. Then they walked through the darkened main street until they reached Cristie's house. Jackson discreetly knocked on the front door and waited. No response. The house was in darkness. He knocked louder and called out, 'Open up. Military Police.' Soon a light in the living-room was switched on and a window opened and Jackson saw Momma leaning out of it. She called down, 'What do you want?'

'It's me, Momma. Johnnie!'

'Johnnie!' Momma sounded genuinely glad to hear his voice. Then softly, 'You wait. I'll be down.' The window closed and in a few moments, the front door opened and she enveloped Jackson in her arms. Her wine-perfumed lips found his in the semi-darkness and his first impulse was to roughly push her away. Instead he planted a Judas kiss on her cheek.

'How are you, Momma?'

'Happy for to see you.' She pulled him into the hallway, then she saw Paddy.

'So you bring him back. That's good.' She closed the door and they walked up the stairs and entered the living-room.

'I send everybody home. I hope you come.' The heavy velvet curtains were drawn. She switched on a table light.

'You like drink?'

She's soon picked up some English, thought Jackson. She was smiling fondly at him and wore the kind of welcoming smile usually reserved for the prodigal son who has returned home unexpectedly. She was wearing make up, clumsily applied and Jackson decided that she had very easily adopted the role of Madame. He was secretly amazed. How could she so quickly change character? Her drunken smile bothered him, but her delight at seeing him took him off guard. He found himself returning her smile the way he had smiled at her in the old days.

'How's Cristie?'

'She sleep, but I wake her.' The bemused smile again as she moved to the sideboard and poured three drinks and placed them on a wooden tray. A remembrance of her hostess days, Jackson thought, but her over-made-up face belied it. Again he wondered why he wasn't hating her. Paddy had a firm hand around his glass and an arm about Momma's waist and he was beaming down at her and she was smiling up at him, a drunken, motherly smile. Perhaps all the boys nowadays were her prodigal sons, in or out of bed. Jackson grinned at the thought. Funny, though, that he wasn't hating her.

'I'll go in and see Cristie,' he said.

'You have much to speak.' Her eyes smiled again and Jackson looked away. 'Be nice.'

'Why shouldn't I be? We're old friends.'

'Just be nice.' Her eyes implored him now. The drunken smile disappearing and replaced with sorrow. 'Be nice.'

Jackson gulped down his drink and moved to Cristie's bedroom. He opened the door quietly. The light from the living-room shone on a bed. He switched on the bedside lamp. A heavy pink shade allowed only a discreet light, but he could see Cristie's dark hair and her white face on the pillow. He closed the door and switched on the ceiling light. In the harsh glare he could see her clearly now as she jerked upright in the bed. He noticed the dark hollows about her eyes.

'I am sleep. Who are you?' Then she recognized him. He switched off the harsh light and waited.

'Johnnie!'

'Thought I would look in and say hello.'

Her hands were moving, touching her hair, arranging her nightdress. She was deeply embarrassed and lost for words.

'I know it's late.'

'What is you want?' Her voice hardly a whisper.

'I wanted to see you.'

'Why?'

'I thought you were my girl.'

She was trying to do something with her hair, then she gave up and looked sideways at him. 'Now you see me.'

'Yes.'

'You like?' He did not answer. 'Why you stand there?' He did not move. 'My English still is not good.'

'Not bad, but you could have picked up a better accent.'

'What is it you want?'

'Do you practice? English?'

'A little.'

'During the day?' She bit her underlip. 'Or mostly at night?'

She bunched the pillows behind her, then leaned back and reached for a packet of cigarettes and lit one. 'You remember before I not smoke?'

'Before there were a lot of things you didn't do.'

Suddenly she smiled and leaned back and made herself more comfortable. 'Before? When was that?'

'Before you were a whore.'

She pulled hard on her cigarette. 'I forget before.'

'When we were making plans for after the war.'

'We were children.' Smoke trickled from her nostrils. She beckoned. 'Why stay at the door, soldier? You shy, soldier? You look nice. Why you angry? You don't have to be shy, soldier.' Jackson bunched his fists and a white stain appeared around his mouth. 'So many English soldiers get angry. Why is that, soldier? They come here wanting make love, then get angry. Why is that? Is why you are here, to make love with me?'

Jackson slipped out of his battle-dress blouse and threw it over a chair. 'How much?'

Her smile mocked him. 'You special soldier. You pay too much already. Do you not forget how much you pay?'

'Too damn much,' Jackson agreed, smiling in smouldering fury. 'Do I get a long or short time?'

'As long as you like it, soldier. Come any time. You very special.' Her eyes a blank stare. The dark hollows had aged her.

'With the light on or with it out?'

'As you like.'

'Any position I want?'

'But not swing from chandelier, that is favourite English

joke, yes? I dive bomb you from chandelier, sweetie. Another one is, I come run up the stairs and don't take my pack off. The English have funny human sense.'

'Sense of humour,' Jackson automatically corrected her.

'Human sense. Is that not better? If they was human, that is.'

'You mean they aren't human. Dear, dear.'

'They have sense of humour. That is only little piece of human.'

'Move over.' Jackson climbed into the bed.

'You keep pants on, soldier. You still shy?'

'Take them off.'

'Si, I do most things.' She reached under the bedclothes and pulled down his underpants. 'You not happy yet? You not excite.'

'Give me time.'

'You young. Why you need time? Most soldiers not need time. Puff, puff, fini.'

'The poor bastards. You should give them lessons.'

'Some I do.'

'God, you're big-hearted, Cristie. Take your damn night-dress off.'

'I have no name, soldier. You take nightdress off.'

Jackson ripped her nightdress down to her waist and stared at her breasts, then threw back the bedclothes and ripped the nightdress, totally exposing her, then looked down at his own body. 'I seem to be ready now.'

'Then why you wait.'

Jackson jerked her legs open and plunged down on her, then forced himself into her. And she cried, her whole body shaking.

'Oh, Cristie, Cristie, Cristie,' he was moaning as her arms embraced him. 'Cristie, Cristie.' She was crying bitter tears as she found his rhythm and held him as if she would never let him go. 'Cristie, Cristie.' Holding her arms, bruising them, her nails ripping into his flesh. Then she stopped crying and found his mouth with her lips. Her mouth was soft and slack like a wound.

'I love this. More, more, more. I love this. This I love.

More, soldier, more, soldier.' His body stiffened and her legs curled about his waist.

'More, soldier. Give more.' He stared down into her eyes. They're open, he thought, blank. She's not seeing me. I'm just another soldier. She's not seeing me. She's not feeling me inside her. Not me. Me. I'm just another soldier.

'Who am I, Cristie?'

'Move, move, move. Why you not move?'

'Who am . . .'

'Don't talk.'

'Who?'

'Fuck. Don't talk.'

He plunged down on her again, madly, insanely, bruising her. Lifting up, rearing up, his mouth sucking her breasts as she moaned, 'Fuck, don't talk, fuck.' A spasm that thrilled into another and another, then a moaning scream as his whole body shook violently into a climax. He lay panting and sweating. He moved. His flesh was stuck to hers. He moved again, then rolled off her and lay staring at the ceiling. Then his thoughts returned, dully at first. Marvellous. She's good, good, marvellous. But I'm just another bloody soldier. He tasted the bitterness of that thought. The hurt that he forced to cynicism. She's marvellous but I've had it good before. What about Madge? Haven't thought about Madge for a long time. She was the best. No one like Madge. Must write to her again. Wonder how she is? Soldier, soldier. Don't talk, fuck. What's marvellous about that? He wanted to laugh. End of romance. End of that comic word, love. She couldn't remember my name. The bubble's burst. He laughed silently. So that was my great love. He climbed out of bed and dressed.

She turned over as he walked to the door and opened it and silently left. She stared at the closed door, then her face creased up in pain as she buried her face into the pillow and cried, 'Johnnie, oh Johnnie!'

In the waggon Jackson sat silent. Paddy had started swearing and shouting when Jackson had walked out of Cristie's bedroom, curtly nodded to him and said, 'Let's go.' Momma, showing distress but not bewilderment, had fled to Cristie's room, Paddy following him down the stairs still shouting.

'We had it made, you daft bastard, wasn't I going to give Momma a good old seeing to.' At this, Jackson had stopped on the stairs and started laughing. It hadn't dawned on him that anybody could fancy Momma. Paddy had to be a head case. What was wrong with Maria? Still laughing, he had walked down the village street with the complaining Paddy trailing behind him, in half a mind to punch his head in. Who the hell did Jackson think he was?

As the miles ticked by, Jackson was surprised to discover that he did not feel deeply unhappy. First reaction, he remembered to warn himself, but it doesn't feel too bad, hope it lasts. More than anything he was feeling a sense of relief. For months he had convinced himself that for the first time in his life he was deeply in love. But it had only been moon and June time, he now thought, cynically. Kids' stuff.

Like when he had been sixteen and put all his dreams on a little Jewish girl, what was her name? Renee. Of course, Renee. And a phony name at that. Her real name was . . . he couldn't remember, not that it was important. Provocative Renee. He would wait outside the station every evening for her arrival, but was too shy to speak to her. Then one day he just didn't turn up. And years later when he had met her by accident, he just couldn't believe it. She had married a Jewish boy, of course. A barber, but he had a good business and was making a few quid.

Now he had built a dream around Cristie and – cynical again – she had found her true vocation. No one in their right mind could seriously complain about her. She didn't put her heart into it but she put everything else into it. She was born to be a whore, and the best of Italian luck to her. The only real woman he had ever known was Madge. This thought came as a great surprise to him. Wonder how she is and what she is doing now?

Paddy interrupted his thoughts by spitting out of the window and growling, 'What the hell are you grinning and snickering about?'

'I was thinking what a great lover I am, then I remembered something.'

'Sure, you're dying to tell me.'

'I remembered something I read. The common fruit fly . . .'

'The bloody what?'

'Some scientists put a fruit fly under a microscope and he jumped on a lady fruit fly and went at it non-stop for three hours and eighteen minutes.'

Paddy spluttered with unbelieving laughter. 'Then what did the little fella do, handstands?'

'He fell off.'

'I can well imagine. And then what?'

'He lay doggo for half an hour, then went back to the job again.'

Paddy looked amazed. 'You have to be joking.'

'I'm telling you what I read in a scientific magazine.'

'Jesus, the little bastard deserves the VC. How long did he keep it up this time?

'It didn't say if he beat the fruit fly Olympic world record again, but he kept it up for a week, with rests between rounds, and then he dropped dead.'

'I don't believe a word, but it's a great yarn. You don't show up so good. You weren't in the bedroom half an hour.'

'I had a better track record with Madge.'

'You finally make it with Cristie, then all you can gab about is fruit flies and who's Madge?'

Her memory was suddenly very clear to Jackson. Almost as though their first meeting had been yesterday. Nostalgia is just another phony escape, he warned himself, but she had been good for his ego – anyway for a time.

'Want to hear about it?'

Paddy yawned. 'Sure, if it helps keep me awake, but none of your crazy lies now.'

'I met her soon after I got out of France. May, nineteen-forty.'

'The great victory trip, via Dunkirk.'

'No, Boulogne.'

'I forgot. You was in NAAFI. Jesus, you've had a great war, Johnnie.'

'I was posted to the West Country. A little village. Well, not so little. It had three hotels. Officers only, of course. And four good pubs.'

'Other Ranks. Sure, I know.'

'Think we were better off for a change. They were decent pubs. I was sitting in the Rose and Crown with three rather snooty public school type RA's. All of them gabbing about when they were going to go after a commission. Madge walked in with an old bag, who I somehow knew wasn't her mother, and we all sat up and took notice. Madge had a figure that would stop the traffic anywhere.'

'Better than Cristie's?' Paddy shot him a sly grin.

'Yes. It wasn't Cristie's figure that attracted me. Her eyes, and that beautiful face, like a . . .' He almost said, Madonna; instead he smiled cynically again. Some bloody Madonna. Thinking about her again. Don't.

'You were telling me about Madge.'

Was she really the way he was imagining her now? Highly doubtful. And wasn't she a little on the stupid side? Very trusting, that's for sure.

'Madge beamed out sex. The three public school blokes started mentally wanking off the second they set eyes on her.'

'And so was yourself, I bet.'

'If I'd stood up my gong would have knocked the pints off the table. The boys started a debate about who was going to make the first move and how they were going to get rid of the old bag and they seemed to be under the impression that I wasn't even in the running, and while they were doing all the talking, I was doing my best to send her signals and I got the idea that she had picked up a message.'

'See you outside the cowshed when the moon's full.'

'They were still trying to make up their uninteresting minds when Madge and the old bag finished their drinks and left.'

'So?'

'I'd noticed that they both carried small brown paper parcels, and it dawned on me that there was a dance in the village hall that evening and I decided that they were proably going to the dance.'

'How so?'

'The brown paper parcels would be their dance shoes.'

'Sherlock Holmes.'

'The RA's got moody and stuck into their beers again, so I gave it about five minutes, then put a fiver on the table, and bet them I would be back with the sexpot in five minutes. They couldn't cover the money fast enough. They were gurgling and gloating and convinced I was pissed, so we set our watches and then I ran like hell out of the pub, with my last half crown clutched in my sticky hand. Dived into the dance hall, paid. Madge had just sat down, and the band at the same moment struck up. I said, "Thanks", pulled her to her feet, danced a few steps, then said, "Let's go".'

'Jesus, you're good at saying that.'

'I pulled her to the exit, nearly knocked the old bag over, who could only stand open-mouthed, and we were away heading for the pub with Madge protesting, "What is this? What's going on?" But not too loudly. We were back in the pub in just under four minutes and I only stayed long enough to collect the bet.'

'You're a miracle worker, that's for sure, Johnnie. Then did you give her the fruit fly treatment?'

Jackson was thinking, maybe I'd have made a good general. Shock tactics. Isn't that what it's all about? Then he remembered he didn't like bombs, or even small arms fire. Funny how that thought came to him.

Paddy interrupted his thoughts, 'So what happened?'

'We had dinner in the next pub, and I could see she still didn't know how I had got her out of that dance hall and I wasn't going to enlighten her, and then over dinner I did finally confess that I had just returned from France.'

'One of the NAAFI heroes?'

'I forgot to mention that,' grinned Jackson.

'Dunkirk, of course.'

'Of course. I could see she badly needed a hero, and I had exactly what she needed . . .'

'Sure you did now, but you don't get VCs with that, you're more likely to get the black pox.'

'In the breast pocket of my battle blouse.'

'Jesus, you're a miracle man, so you are. So it's detachable, is it?'

'The Croix de Guerre.'

'And where the hell did you get that?'

'I bought it from an old Frenchman in a bar in Boulogne, for a few francs and a hell of a lot of booze. She kept pressing me to tell her about my adventures in France, and after another pint or two and a couple of whiskies, I sort of felt inspired.'

'I get that way meself.'

'I decided that I'd been playing the modest hero long enough. She didn't want that. She wanted a man of action. A man with guts.'

Paddy snorted with laughter and Jackson grinned.

'I said we were retreating and Jerry was advancing . . .'

'She could read that in the papers, so she could.'

'Panza Divs breaking through. Tanks, the lot. The roads were filled with refugees. God, I was terribly sorry for them, of course. Old men, women, kids. And all the way we were dive-bombed and stukered. And then I lost my company . . .'

'Sure, what else would anybody with any sense do . . .'

'I didn't know what to do. It was black night and I took to the fields and in the morning I ran into Pierre . . .'

'Seeing you was in France, that shouldn't be too difficult. I take it he was a Frenchman?'

'A Captain in one of the crack regiments.'

'You should have taken off at once. Sure, a fella like that could get you into trouble.'

'I had to get into bloody trouble if I was going to be a bloody hero, didn't I?'

'That's a fact. Go on.'

'Pierre had lost his company, too.'

'The dirty, cowardly bastard.'

'In action.'

'The lone survivor?'

'What else?'

'It's pushing your luck, but it could go down well with a simple country girl.'

'So we joined forces. It was pretty tough going, then we ran into a German patrol in an apple orchard . . .'

'So you threw apples at the dirty bastards and drove them off.'

'Shut up,' laughed Jackson. 'I didn't mind confessing, after knocking off a few Huns, that we both ran like hell and made our get-away. Then we found an abandoned truck and drove it until we ran out of petrol, so we had to foot slog it again. I built up a few more near misses, like when we were spotted by a German tank. I forget how we got out of that. Anyway, after three days and nights Pierre and I had become pretty good chums.'

'So you would now, built on mutual respect.'

'Paddy. How did you know? I told Pierre the best thing we could do was head for the beaches and maybe he could get back to England with me. So we got our bearings and Pierre scrounged food from various farm houses and we ran into another advance German patrol and did our rear guard action thing and got away again. I confessed there were times when I was sweating but Pierre was fantastic. Absolutely fearless. Then we were crossing a field, Pierre in the lead, when there was one hell of an explosion. I threw myself down and when I looked up I saw Pierre. He was bleeding badly. We had walked into a mine field. Without thinking, I ran to him. He was really in a bad way. I knelt down beside him and do you know, he even managed to smile. He was sort of shaking his head. Then he said, "Johnnie, I'm fini, fini. You go on. You can make it." I put my arms about him. "No," I said. "I'm not leaving you." Then I noticed his legs. They were blown to hell. Then Pierre pulled the Croix de Guerre from his tunic and pressed it into my hand, then he smiled again, and he died. Then, Paddy, I took the medal from my pocket and pinned it on to Madge's dress and I said, "Darling, I think Pierre would like you to have this..."'

'Wow!' hooted Paddy. 'Wow! That's beautiful.'

'Her eyes filled with tears and I knew I was home.'

Paddy was still laughing. 'You bastard. How did it end?'

'Well, it finally blew up in my face, because she believed me and she bragged about her hero to the old bag she went to the dance with, and the old bag was having it off with an old Regular Sergeant Major and when I turned up at the pub the next evening, there she was with the old bag and the old fart of a Sergeant Major, and I joined them, after making a journey to the bar, of course. And the old SM said, "I say, lad. I understand you 'ad some terrible hair-raising experiences in France?"

'I eyed him cannily and said modestly, "Not much to speak of, sir".

'"Lass," he said to Madge. "Give it to me." And she proudly handed him the fucking medal and he examined it, and grinned and said, "Tell me more about this 'ere Pierre, now." And I thought, Christ, I hadn't bargained for this old bastard, so I went into my song and dance but he was sort of ahead of me and said, "Yes, lad I got all the rear guard action and daring do bits from Madge and poor Pierre blows himself up on a landmine and with his last dying breath Pierre decorates you on the field of battle." Then, examining the medal again, "It's a funny thing, lad. But this bleedin' medal was won by a bloke named Charles DuPont."'

Paddy started pissing himself laughing. 'You daft bastard. Now I know something else about you. You're like Dusty. You can't even read.'

'She could, though, Paddy. When we left the pub, she read me out.'

'She stayed with you after that?'

'I told you she was a good girl.' And so were you, he thought bitterly. So were you, Cristie...

Chapter XII

It was approaching Christmas and Sergeant Leadbetter had been preparing for it. He was going to give a kids' Christmas party in the men's canteen.

For months he had been saving his chocolate and sweet rations and so had some of his cronies, and he was now making a huge cake. He had plenty of soft drinks stored away and had bought Christmas crackers from NAAFI. Hopefully they would contain paper hats, whistles and other toys. He was missing his family. His wife and five children. He was one of the men who had not received a 'Dear John' letter. Possibly because an overweight careworn woman with five kids and a voice like a factory whistle was not considered the greatest attraction by the Yanks, Free French, Poles or Negro troops who were still left in England six months after the D-Day Landing in Normandy.

When news of the party came to Jackson's ears, he thought it only right that he should offer his services. He wandered into the cookhouse and watched Leadbetter icing the cake. Leadbetter without even taking his eyes off the cake said, 'I didn't give you permission to come into the cookhouse, Jackson.'

'That's a nice-looking cake, Sergeant.'

'Not interested in your bleedin' compliments.'

'Understand you're giving a party for some of the kids.'

'Did you now.'

'Can I do anything to help?'

'You?' The scorn in Leadbetter's eyes almost made Jackson flinch. 'How do you think you could help anybody?'

'Well, some people seem to . . .'

'Just 'op it.'

'Kids like tinned pineapple, pears, biscuits, chocs, jam, don't they?'

'I said, 'op it.'

'I can get you practically anything you want, Sarge.'

Leadbetter exploded in rage. 'I know you can, Jackson. You can get any bleedin' thing, you smart little bastard.'

'Charming. Do you want me to give you a hand?'

'I told you what to do.'

'No charge for kids, Sarge.'

'And maybe you'd like to dress up as Father Christmas too, eh?'

'Never wanted to be an actor,' grinned Jackson. 'You can do that. It's your party.'

'Right. It's my party.'

'But I'd like to help.'

'You'd like to help,' roared Leadbetter. 'Come on now, piss off out of here.'

Jackson was amazed. 'Sarge, it's no sweat for me to . . .'

'Rob your comrades,' shouted Leadbetter. 'You get extra rations and your comrades go short.'

'What bloody comrades?'

'The fighting men in the front line, for starters. The boys who are stopping the Germans sticking a bayonet up your arse, you dodgy bastard.'

'Sarge, I've been through all this before with Holland. It doesn't work out like that. NAAFI's one big fiddle. The stuff starts getting pinched from the moment they start loading it on the docks in England, Australia, Canada, or wherever, and when it's unloaded again, the dock-workers pinch it and the Red Caps who are supposed to be guarding it, pinch it.'

'And you, you bastard! So soon, there's sod all for anybody.'

'That's the mystery of the age, Sarge. Some of the stuff gets through. Now all you have to do is give me a list and I'll . . .'

'I'll give you a bleedin' thick ear if you don't 'op it.'

'So you don't mind if the kids go short.'

'The kids won't go short. I've seen to that.'

'You're using your comrades' rations to bake that cake, Sarge.'

Leadbetter felt guilty about the cake. He had used the

men's rations to bake it, but had reasoned it out that you could hardly give a kids' party without a cake.

'Get out!' he shouted. 'Before I give you a bunch of fives in your easy-talking, bleedin' mouth.'

'Okay. Good luck with the party, anyway.'

Leadbetter picked up a rolling-pin and Jackson hurriedly left.

The kids' party on Christmas Eve was a huge success. Brown-eyed little boys and girls, wearing their best clothes, drank soft drinks, ate the cake and other goodies Leadbetter had made, and there were tins of pineapple, pears, peaches and even tinned cream. Leadbetter, with a satisfied smile, knew that he and he alone had master-planned the party and was content. Some of the children were sick on such rich food and their parents, with many gestures and expressions of heartfelt thanks, took them home.

Jackson had been barred from the party on strict orders from Sergeant Leadbetter, but he watched them leave and listened to their chattering voices as they clutched their gifts of sweets and cheap toys and he couldn't help thinking, Leadbetter's a bastard, but he's a decent, kind-hearted old bastard.

At two minutes past midnight, Lieutenant Dare decided to turn out the guard. As he was Duty Officer, it was his right to do this. But the men did not appreciate it, as grumbling and swearing they climbed out of their blankets, checked their equipment and rifles and stumbled out of the guard-house into the cold night. The light from the guardroom illuminated them as Dare made his inspection. The only duty that Dare took any interest in was the guard-mounting. He was fiercely critical of the men's turnout and demanded one hundred per cent efficiency.

His inspections were thorough. Nothing escaped his gimlet, if somewhat bloodshot, eyes. The men quickly realized that Dare was very drunk – an unusual occurrence for him when he was Duty Officer. The men reasoned, well, it's Christmas, but the silly old bastard doesn't have to get pissed and put us through our paces in the middle of the night.

Dare addressed them in a whiskey-sodden voice.

'Men, your turnout leaves something to be desired . . .' A belch. 'However, Christmas Day . . . overlook . . . Jackson . . .'

A figure emerged from the darkness. 'Sir.'

'Give 'em their rations.'

An opened bottle of whiskey was handed to the Corporal of the guard. Much to his surprise.

'On the order, drink!' thundered Dare.

With a bemused expression the Corporal happily put the bottle to his lips and took a short choking drink, coughed and spluttered and drank again. The whiskey slowly poured down his throat and began warming his belly.

Then Jackson handed a bottle of whiskey to each member of the guard.

'Highly irregular conduct,' thundered Dare. 'Serving drinks to the guard. Good for a court martial. Had one of those, didn't care for it, so if any of you chaps let the cat out of the bag I'll have your guts for garters.'

Muttered promises of loyalty from the guard.

'One other thing. If any man is pissed when I dismount the guard, he's on a charge. Dismiss, and Happy Christmas.'

The guard, much cheered, still clutching their bottles of whiskey, managed a clumsy dismiss and walked back to the guardroom. All with kindly thoughts, for a change, directed towards Lieutenant Dare.

Christmas dinner was the same old routine. The officers waited on the men. Before this chore the officers had had a good session in the mess and the men had sunk a lot of beer so it was an alcoholic, relaxed kind of dinner. Fresh pork, apple sauce, baked potatoes and tinned peas followed by Christmas pudding. A feast fit for a king, the men thought. Bottles of beer lined the tables and a slightly alcoholic Major Cobbey made his speech.

'Men, another year has passed. One more year nearer to peace and a reunion with your loved ones.' This was received in cold silence and Cobbey was suddenly aware of it. 'Anyway, nearer home leave for all of you.'

Paddy, who had had a skinful, called out, 'Being meself from the land of saints and scholars, sir, if I go home, after fighting England's war for them, the bloody IRA will shoot me now, won't they?'

This was greeted with a gust of good-humoured laughter which Cobbey joined in.

'From all I've heard about you, Fitzroy, so they should.'

Another roar of laughter and Cobbey was delighted that he had got a laugh. He was not completely unaware that he was not popular. He continued, 'Don't want to take up your time with a lot of nonsense. Must say, though, that you've all done a fine job. Carry on, chaps, and do as well next year.'

The officers started hand-clapping and the men joined in. As the applause died down, Dare, who was busy opening bottles of beer on the tables, called out, 'Three rousing cheers for Major Cobbey. Hip, hip . . .' Jackson, watching him, grinned and thought, as the cheers echoed through the room, old Dare must be joking.

After dinner, Major Cobbey, who until now had appeared to be oblivious of Jackson's existence, took him on one side.

'Appreciate the good work you've done.'

'Thank you, sir.'

'Helped to make it a decent Christmas.'

'I did my best, sir.'

'NAAFI do rather a good line in watches, don't they?'

'Well . . .'

'Swiss.'

'Yes, sir, but . . .'

'Get me six.'

'Sir. It's not easy.'

'See you have one. Does it keep good time?'

'Yes, sir, it does. But you see . . .'

'Get me six.'

'They're in very short supply, sir.'

'That's an order and orders are meant to be obeyed.'

'If I possibly can, sir, I will of course, but . . .'

'No buts. Get them.' He turned his back on Jackson in dismissal and smiled at RSM Tompkins. 'A good spread. I'd better have a word with the cook.'

A worried Jackson made his way back to his table, thinking, the first time the prick even bothers to speak to me he has to ask for the impossible.

The cold winter nights ended and it was spring. The twice a week runs to the NAAFI Bulk Issue Store had passed without incident, then late one evening Jackson returned to the stables with another load of goods. Whistling to himself, he manhandled a case of whiskey from the back of the truck. As he approached the Sergeants' mess, he saw Winters standing near the main gate. He looked agitated. Jackson nodded to him as he kicked the door open to the Sergeants' mess and was confronted by an enraged RSM Tompkins, who hissed, 'You. Get out of here.'

Jackson halted in his tracks, still clutching the case of whiskey.

'But, sir . . .'

'Get out and take that with you.'

Bewildered, Jackson turned and stumbled out and back towards the truck, not quite knowing what to do with the case. Winters, looking all about him, walked over to Jackson. He was distinctly nervous.

'Get that stuff out of here.'

'What is this?'

'The bloody place is jumping with Red Caps and the SIB.'

'What!' Jackson almost dropped the case of whiskey.

'They're turning the bloody place over. Beat it.'

'But how?'

'They pinched my contact and they're giving him the treatment now.'

The driver had climbed out of the cab and was listening.

'Get back in,' said Jackson. 'And let's go.'

He threw the case into the truck, then turned. The driver was running as fast as his legs would carry him through the open gate of the stables. Jackson was about to yell after him, then changed his mind. It might bring the Red Caps swarming around him. He watched Winters' retreating back and thought bitterly, I'm on my own. That's all I need. He moved to the driving cabin but someone had beaten him to it. It was Paddy, wearing a large grin.

'Let's go. It's my turn to say it.' Jackson hardly had time to jump into the cab as the truck began moving towards the open gate. It turned left and headed towards the plaza.

'Where to, Johnnie?'

'Keep driving.'

'Sure, but where?'

'Where is bloody right. First we get out of the village.'

'I'm wid you there, then what do we do?'

'Keep driving. I've got to think.'

'Sure you have now.' Paddy flicked his fingers. 'Cigarette.' Jackson lit two and stuck one in Paddy's mouth. 'How come you were waiting?'

'When I saw the SIB and bloody Red Caps I guessed you might need some help. I knew your foxy bloody driver would take off if there was trouble.'

'The bastard. Where are we going to dump this stuff?'

'Dump?' Paddy looked shocked. 'I hope you're meaning to flog it.'

It dawned on Jackson that he had no one set up to sell the stuff to. Paddy interrupted his thoughts.

'There must be a hell of a lot of Ities who'd go mad for the stuff.'

'And where are we going to find them?'

'What about the old fella who runs the bar and has a face as beautiful as a bare-arsed baboon?'

The old man in his fractured English had dropped a hint or two that he would like to make a deal. But half a truck-load . . .

'The old man. How the hell could he afford to buy the stuff we got, Paddy?'

'He's not short of a penny or two. Half the village is his family. Didn't you know that? Dozens of sons and daughters and all the rest. I'm surprised he ever found the time to get that beautiful complexion. He's a rare old fella.'

'I'm worried about the parking. It's a narrow street.'

'I can get the truck through it.'

'What have we got to lose?'

Paddy drove around the plaza, then turned back towards the stables and took a left turn and slowly drove up a narrow street. He stopped by a passageway and nodded his head towards it.

'Make it fast.'

Jackson nodded and jumped out of the truck and walked up the passage and into the bar.

Giant wine barrels lined one wall. A few wine-stained tables and chairs were the only furnishings. The old wine-blue-faced man stood in his usual place behind the bar. About a dozen Italian men, the oldest about fifty-five, the youngest in his early twenties, were seated at tables. No English soldiers.

Jackson glanced at his watch. Six-thirty. Too early. Better get it over with before any of them arrive. If a deal was going to be made. He was doubtful on that score. He was suddenly aware that all the men were watching him. The old man's blue lips twisted. He could have been smiling as he poured a glass of wine and with a hand that was amazingly steady, considering his age, placed it on the bar. Jackson drank it in one gulp. He must be feeling nervous. The stuff in the truck must be worth three or four thousand pounds, in Italian lire. They wouldn't pay much for the whiskey, gin and beer, but the cigarettes, chocolates, razor blades, soap, tinned foods, all fetched good prices. Razor blades were a good line to carry. Compact, easy to hide, easy to get rid of. The men still carefully watching him. Wonder who bought the razor blades? Not this mob, surely. They contented themselves with a Sunday shave. He glanced at the old man again. He was smiling.

'Senor Jackson?'

'Hello, Poppa.' So my fame is spreading.

'You problems?'

Of course, Jackson thought. Everybody in the village knows. They aren't bloody stupid. He felt the tension in the bar and glanced about him again and spoke slowly and carefully.

'I've got a lot of stuff on a truck outside.'

The youngest man came to the bar. 'What you have?'

Jackson handed him the NAAFI bill of sale and the young man's eyebrows went up in surprise. He turned to the oldest man in the group and let loose a flow of excited Italian. Everyone stood up now, talking and gesturing. The young man with an eager smile said, 'You sell, Jackson?'

'The lot.'

'Bring it.' He held out his hand and Jackson shook it and ran out of the bar, down the short passageway and called out to Paddy, who was leaning against the truck, 'Unload.'

Paddy grinned and dropped the back of the truck. Piled three cases of whiskey on top of each other and trotted down the passageway with them. Jackson grabbed a case, then noticed an RAF Sergeant watching him.

'Hello,' Jackson automatically grinned.

'What are you doing?' inquired the RAF Sergeant.

'Minding my own business,' said Jackson as he almost bumped into Paddy running out of the passage.

'You're flogging the stuff.'

Jackson was looking down the passageway. The Italians were busy tearing open the cases and filling sacks. They don't waste much time, he thought. It almost looks as though they were expecting me. Wonder who's the mind-reader among them?

'I want your names and numbers,' said the RAF Sergeant. 'I'm arresting the pair of you.'

Jackson brushed past him and hurried up the passageway, dumped the case and trotted back.

Paddy was speaking to the RAF Sergeant. 'I said fuck off, didn't I?'

'You're both on a charge.'

Paddy left-hooked him on the chin and the RAF Sergeant hit the wall behind him, and crumpled unconscious to the ground.

Jackson climbed into the truck and lifted, pushed, and shoved cases out of the back of the truck. Half a dozen of the Italian men appeared and speedily and efficiently the cases were unloaded and carried into the passageway. None of them spared even a glance for the unconscious RAF Sergeant. From the back of the truck Jackson observed some of the Italians running up the street with sacks over their backs and disappearing down another passageway, dim figures in the gloom. If the whole operation had been planned to the last detail, he thought, it couldn't have worked smoother. All except the RAF Sergeant, that is. Wonder what we do with him? He pushed the last wooden case into waiting arms, jumped down, lifted the tail of the truck and was about to bolt it when Paddy pushed him on one side and dropped the tail of the truck again.

'What are we going to do with him, Paddy?'

'Sure we're not leaving him on the pavement now.' He easily picked up the RAF Sergeant and tossed him into the truck.

'We'll take him for a ride. Dump him some place out of town.'

Jackson glanced down the passageway again. No sign of any of the Italians now. Even the boxwood cases and shavings had been carted away. No tell-tale evidence left behind. Highly efficient men, thought Jackson. They got into the truck and Paddy reversed it down the narrow street, then straightened out and drove away.

'The best place to dump the fella,' smiled Paddy, 'will be on the main strada a hell of a way out of town. Somebody will pick him up.'

A thought occurred to Jackson. 'Paddy. They've got the goods. We can hardly scream blue murder if they don't pay us.'

'That's a fact,' agreed Paddy. 'They've got us by the short and curlies.' Then he bunched his fist on the steering wheel and grinned. 'But if they don't, I'll take payment out of some of their heads.'

They had travelled roughly fifteen miles when Paddy pulled on to the side of the road and hauled the still dazed and groggy RAF Sergeant out of the truck. As Paddy patted him on the shoulder and said, 'No hard feelings now,' he flinched away. 'Hard feelings!' The RAF Sergeant's voice was thick and muffled. He held his jaw. 'Hard feelings, you bastard!'

'If you come back looking for trouble, I'll break you in two.'

'Where am I?'

'On the road to Mandalay.'

'How do I get back?'

'Back where?'

'Naples.'

Paddy pointed back the way they had travelled. 'It's about thirty miles that way.'

'How do I make it? I'm not feeling up to it.'

'Jesus, you're a stupid bastard. You walk or thumb a ride. Now you heed me, don't come looking for trouble again.'

'If I see you again, you Irish mick . . .'

'Don't push your luck,' rasped Paddy. 'I'm in a highly excited state, so I am and might do you a rare injury.'

The Sergeant took the hint and walked away on wobbly legs. They watched him cross the road, his body erect, his legs fumbling. He stopped and looked back and called out, 'If I ever meet up with you two bastards again . . .'

Paddy made a move to go after him. Jackson put a restraining hand on his arm. 'Let him go.'

'Sure he's not worth wasting time on.' He mimicked the Sergeant's voice as he climbed into the cab of the truck. 'Give me your names and numbers, I'm putting you under arrest. Him and a bloody squadron more.' He made a U-turn on to the grass on the other side of the road, then straightened out on to the road again. As they passed the RAF Sergeant, Jackson waved and the Sergeant shook his fist.

A few soldiers were in the bar, beginning to get bleary-eyed drunk. The old man smiled at Jackson and put two glasses on the bar counter, filled them with wine and then nodded to the young man, who rose from a table in the corner of the room and joined them, placing his glass on the bar counter.

'You come with me as soon as ready.'

Paddy lifted his glass and gulped down the wine. 'Let's go.'

'Christ,' said Jackson. 'Now you're running out of bars.'

Paddy rubbed a thumb and two fingers on his left hand together and grinned at Jackson as he headed for the door.

There was hardly room to move in the living-room for furniture. Two sideboards, a large mahogany table, three antique wardrobes, a heavy old-fashioned bed, and chairs around the table and in any available space. Jackson pulled in his stomach and squeezed into a chair at the table and joined the man who was seated with an opened bottle of whiskey. The man filled four glasses and courteously handed a glass to Jackson, then Paddy, then to the young man, then waited, holding a crystal decanter, filled with water. Jackson nodded and as the man poured, after a brief moment he said, 'Thanks.' Paddy and the young man declined the water.

'Good,' the man smiled. 'Me Luigi, my son, Alberto.'

'Paddy and Johnnie.'

Luigi studied the NAAFI bill that was on the table in front of him, then spoke rapidly to Alberto, who listened with a serious expression, then lifted his glass and smiled at Jackson.

'Ciao. Poppa not speak good English. He say those not the prices for him.'

'Hardly,' smiled Jackson. 'You know the prices.'

'Si, I know when I buy on the street. I know those prices, now I know your prices.'

Jackson saw Paddy's lips turn down as he picked up his glass and eyed Alberto. Jackson smiled at him and winked, thinking, if Paddy gets on the juice any bloody thing can happen. He turned to Alberto, 'You knew we were in trouble when we came to you, right?'

'Si, everybody know.'

'Pity I didn't.'

'We try tell you. When you drive in, we try to wave you down.'

Jackson remembered quite a few people on the street waving and shouting at him and had wondered what all the noise was about.

'Okay. Alberto, I've got problems and we all know it. So . . .' He picked up the bill from the table and studied it. The NAAFI prices were bloody ridiculous of course. Cigarettes were eight pence for twenty and they sold on the street for ten shillings. What a hell of a profit and that applied to practically everything on the list.

'I'll give you the booze for exactly the prices on the list.'

Alberto's eyes widened and he quickly translated to Luigi, who nodded his head several times, then turned and smiled at Jackson and recharged his drink, then Paddy's. Then lifted his glass.

'Ciao.'

'Ciao.'

'You've a crazy way of doing business,' said Paddy.

'They wouldn't pay much for the booze, Paddy. That's the last thing on their list and where are we going to take it?'

Paddy nodded. 'Ciao,' and took a long drink. 'You're the boss.'

Jackson stared at Alberto's face for a long moment, then said in a casual voice, 'The rest of the stuff is just half the normal price. Just half. That gives you a bigger profit than me. Now you work it out and I'll check it, or the other way round, if you like.'

He glanced in turn from Alberto to Luigi as Alberto translated, trying not to appear to be too eager, but knowing it was bargain week. Luigi nodded his head several times, then slowly recharged all the glasses as he listened intently. Then he clinked Jackson's glass – 'Ciao' – and took a long drink, then carefully replaced his glass on the table, and a thick, hairy arm was placed around Jackson's shoulder and a gold-toothed smile switched on and the arm hugged Jackson until it hurt, then a stream of Italian and Jackson thought, 'I think I've made him so happy he's going to cripple me.'

'Poppa say forty per cent, not fifty.'

Jackson was amazed for a moment, then remembered that the Neapolitans had to haggle over prices like the Arabs. The bloody old crook, he thought, as he shook his head and watched the scowl spreading across Paddy's face.

'It's bargain week, that's why you're getting it for fifty per cent.'

Alberto was speaking in urgent tones to Luigi, clearly

begging him to settle the deal. Luigi listened, frowning, then suddenly the brilliant smile was switched on.

'Ciao.' Luigi's glass almost smashed Jackson's as he clinked it with enthusiasm.

'And what do I get out of this?' inquired Paddy.

'We share.'

Paddy's face brightened. 'Jesus, that's good.' Then his smile slipped. 'But why the hell are you giving it away so cheap?'

'It was you who said they had us by the short and curlies. So I'm making the best of it.'

Luigi was speaking rapidly to his son again, and Alberto nodded and translated.

'When we get the next stuff?'

When the swallows return, Jackson thought. Do they think I'm sticking my chin out again with the Red Caps and SIB looking for me? He shivered. In the excitement he had forgotten about them. God. If they pick up Winters he'll be the first to scream and turn King's evidence, if they give him the opportunity, or that foxy driver. Why hadn't he trusted his first impression of Winters? The shifty, yet bleak eyes. Give him the chance and he'll drop me and everyone in it, from Major Cobbey down, to save his own skin. I'll be lucky if I'm not thrown in the glass-house and this time I won't have to worry about the war. It will be over long before I come out again. Then a ray of hope. The evidence? Where's the evidence? I've never met his contacts, thank God, so they can't put the finger on me. Winters' word against mine. Let him scream. They'll have to have evidence before they can pinch me . . . three bottles of whiskey in my kit-bag, but that's at the school.

'Paddy, are the SIB turning over the school?'

'As far as I know, only the stables. Why should they turn over the school now?'

No reason why they should, Jackson thought. All the action's happened at the stables. Better get rid of the whiskey though. I'll dump it on Dare. They won't search the Officers' quarters. Dare will look after it. Then a slow grin. Down his neck he'll look after it. Well, let him have it. He'll be going dry for a long time, the poor old bastard, and he won't like my taking away his little bottle from him. He turned to Alberto, who was impatiently waiting.

'The next load,' he smiled. 'I think we had better let things cool down for a while, don't you? Two or three weeks and let's see how things are.' He picked up the bill and as Alberto translated to Luigi, he began jotting down figures on a piece of paper.

Paddy stood up and leaned over his shoulder. 'How much now is coming my way?'

'About a thousand quid.'

Paddy whistled. 'That's not bad. Not bad at all for a night's work.'

Jackson handed the paper to Luigi, who studied it, then passed it to Alberto, who finally nodded in agreement, and Luigi left the table, pulling his great gut in, and opened the nearest sideboard and took out a large steel box, and unlocked it, opened it, placed it on the table, smiled, and began counting the money.

Lieutenant Dare opened his eyes and thought, the drinking really started when I found out that it was damn hard work getting it up. The urge is still there, dammit. Still interested in the little darlings, but the flesh is not so willing, as Kate so often told me, the bitch. Drinking too much. Always on about my drinking. Glad when I sent her packing, and rather more glad when Chamberlain finally showed some balls that rather splendid Sunday and I could hang up my bowler hat again for a while. Otherwise, might have taken Kate back. Feeling rather lonely now I think about it. Glad to get out of mufti and back into business. Pity the flesh is not so damn willing. Still get the urge sometimes during the night, when I'm alone, dammit. By the morning though doesn't seem all that important. He put his hand on it. Wouldn't win a prize at the moment. Fifty-two and out of business. Damn bad luck. Cheers a chap up when he can jump on a gal and give her a jolly good seeing to. Maybe it's only temporary? Hope so. Who was the doc who once told me that chaps also go through the change? Always forgetting names nowadays.

Doesn't really make much sense, but still. A forced smile. Where there's life, there's hope. He waggled it. You're about as lively as a corpse, old boy. Then the thought – but the boozing, over all the years, well, it must catch up in time, mustn't it. He snorted a laugh. Stick at the thing you do best. Carry on drinking. Which reminds me, as if I have to be reminded . . .

The door opened and distracted his thoughts, and a dim figure entered the room. The clatter of a cup and saucer on the bedside table. The curtains drawn and there was Jackson, dead on time as always. Moving to the wardrobe. Ah, ah, pouring a good one. What a pleasant chap.

Jackson noticed that Dare was wide awake and watching him; the held-out hand was visibly shaking and some of the whiskey spilled as Dare placed the glass to his lips and took a long drink.

'Thoughtful of you to replenish my stock.'

'I had to dump it somewhere,' smiled Jackson.

'Can't think of a better place, but you've gone down in my estimation, y'know. Didn't realize you were running a black market racket. Why, for God's sake?'

'I just got bloody bored.'

Ah, it's touching the spot, Dare thought. 'Don't make sense, Johnnie. Cobbey's hopping mad.'

'I was afraid of that.'

'Sending out search parties for you last night. Better have a good excuse. Where were you?'

'Naples.'

'Of course. At the opera?' Another laugh snort.

'I don't know what's on.'

'Just tell him you were bar-crawling and send him mad.'

'Don't think I want to do that. He can make it rough for me, I suppose?'

'You should be worried.'

'I am.'

'My guess,' Dare took another drink. 'There's absolutely damn all he can do to you, because he knows you could pull down the house if you wanted to. But you've blotted your copy book, and he's not going to forgive or forget. I'd walk very carefully from here on if I were you.'

Jackson nodded. 'The party's over.'

Dare grimaced. His hand was still shaking, then he managed a wink. 'No reason to cut off my supply, is there?'

Jackson gave it a few moments' thought as he stared at the very shaky Dare and realized that he was not asking but pleading. Christ, the shock might kill him, he thought. He winked back.

'I'd better bloody well take care of that, hadn't I?'

'Good man. Knew you wouldn't let me down. Better cut along and see Cobbey.'

Jackson picked up the cup of tea and emptied it down the sink.

Dare was watching him. 'One thing I absolutely dread. The day I'm doomed to drink that ghastly stuff.'

Jackson knocked on Major Cobbey's door and was not surprised to discover that his knees were knocking. A pause, then a voice called out, 'Yes? Come in.' Jackson took a deep breath. Go on your usual run, he reasoned. Just try and bullshit your way out. He opened the door. Cobbey was sitting up in bed holding a cup and saucer. As he glared at Jackson, the cup rattled in the saucer. Jackson began to sweat and stood ramrod still.

'You wanted to see me, sir?'

'Where were you last evening?'

'Naples, sir.'

'Who gave you a pass?'

'Lieutenant Dare, sir.'

'He damn well would.' Cobbey placed the cup and saucer on the bedside table. 'I'm seeing you here, but don't think it's informal.'

'No, sir.'

Cobbey said bitterly, 'Damn you. I suppose you're aware that you're responsible for one hell of a bloody awful mess.'

'I didn't think that it would . . .'

'Of course you didn't think. You're a crook and it's well known crooks don't think or give a damn about anybody else.'

'I didn't think there was much to worry about.'

'What!' Cobbey went red in the face. 'I'm responsible for this company and everything that goes on, I'm supposed to be aware of it and take action. The SIB Major made that very clear to me. Have you got that through your thick skull?'

'Yes, sir.'

'If this blows up, it blows up in my face and if that happens, God help you.'

'It won't, sir. They've no evidence.'

'How do you know?'

'The men's canteen was almost out of beer and cigarettes and ...'

'So you've been supplying the men's canteen.'

'I thought you knew, sir.'

'And the Sergeants' mess?'

'Yes, sir.'

'The SIB checked the canteen and the Sergeants' mess. Lucky for you there was nothing there.'

'As I said, sir, there's no evidence.'

'Damn you. Because there's no evidence, do you think the SIB are simply going to scrub round the matter?'

'Without evidence there's nothing they can do.'

'Isn't there? Well, there's going to be an identification parade at ten hundred hours. The police have in custody two of the bloody Italians you were working with and I promise you they're shit scared and when they pick you out on parade ...'

Jackson interrupted him. 'I've never met them, sir.'

'Don't damn well lie.'

'I promise you I didn't sell them anything.'

'Then who the hell did?'

Jackson's mind was racing. If I tell him about Winters, he's in the shit, too. But if I don't and he's picked out from the parade, then everybody's deep in it, including you, bloody Major Cobbey, because Winters will scream his head off, the bloody fool. He won't take the rap alone.

'I'm speaking to you.' Cobbey was trying to remain calm. 'Who sold ...'

'Sergeant Winters.'

'Who else?'

'He was the only one who had any contact with the Italians.'

'You're sure?'

'Yes, sir.'

'Winters, eh? I won't forget him. Did you have a driver with you?'

'Bell, sir.'

'And I won't forget him. Now, listen to me carefully. Round up Winters and Bell and all three of you get lost. Do you understand? Dare will give you a three-day pass. You will stay away until this blows over. Do you understand?'

What a hell of a funny way to get a leave pass, thought Jackson.

'Better make it a six-day pass and have it back-dated three days.'

Oh, you crafty old bastard, thought Jackson, with a certain amount of respect. That looks after everything. 'Yes, sir. I'll see to it.'

'Make one more false move and I'll be on to you like a ton of coals.'

'Yes, sir, I understand.'

'You'd better. Now, get out.'

'Sir.' Jackson moved towards the door thinking, three days with Winters and Bell. Ugh. Well, I can always dump them. As he was closing the door, Cobbey yelled, 'Jackson!'

Jackson opened the door again. 'Sir?'

'Luck is on your side. In a few days we'll be sailing to . . . er . . . destination unknown.'

France, thought Jackson. Wouldn't mind seeing it again. No action there.

'That is lucky, sir.' He closed the door quietly behind him.

Chapter XIII

Another lurching, flat-bottomed, sea-sick boat, then Marseilles, and the convoy disembarked and they roared through the town to another transit camp; then across France, staying overnight in transit camps until finally they reached Menin Gate and the famous town which old soldiers – now nostalgic – fondly referred to as 'wipers'.

It's in a lot better shape this war, was Jackson's first thought. They parked in the streets and slept in the back of their trucks, but not the officers. They moved into a hotel.

The first parade at eight hundred hours the next morning was witnessed by none too interested Belgians from windows or vantage points on the pavements, and Major Cobbey made a speech.

'Men, we will be here, I really don't know how long. I'm awaiting orders, but don't count this as a rest period. The NCOs will allot you any duties I see fit. You will keep busy. This is as good an opportunity as any to overhaul your trucks. Dismiss.'

The men shuffled away, throwing sidelong or open glances at the girls and were waiting for the officers to piss off so that they could whistle them up and in their minds it was – what I couldn't do with you, darling. Gawd. Look at those tits on her. Look at the bum and wouldn't I like to get into her and, well, you know, and thinking about gleaming white, biting teeth and savage grinning soft mouths and smouldering eyes, and I've got to have it so shut up, and bouncing tits and . . . eh, steady darling, don't rock the boat you'll knock yourself off . . . and after . . . half a mo' darling, be back in a tick, and off to the pub, and whack hos, and the wink, and she expects me back. Mine's a pint, Charlie.

RSM Tompkins beckoned to Jackson, who stomped to attention facing his horrible smile.

'Got a job for you at last, Jackson. Something to keep you

busy, keep you out of bleedin' trouble, let's hope. You will sweep the pavements alongside the company lines and you will keep them spotless. Understand?'

'Yes, sir. But Lieutenant Dare?'

'Forget it. Now, get busy. Get a broom from somewhere.'

Jackson got a broom from the stores waggon. It wasn't too much of a problem, he only had to sign three forms, then he listlessly went to work. Dare, passing, paused for a moment, then smiled wanly and said quietly, 'Rather looks as though they've decided that your days of usefulness are over, Johnnie.'

'Who's your batman now?'

Dare grimaced. 'That poor idiot, Miller. He almost burst into tears when I wouldn't let him drive. I think Cobbey's trying to tell me something.' A smile and a nod, then he walked on.

By midday Jackson had swept the pavements on both sides of the road his company was parked in, and then it dawned on him that if he put his back into it he could be finished work by 10 a.m. and then what? Here was a town and there were bars and there were girls. That's what. He went in search of Paddy and found him overhauling his truck, grease stains on his face, arms and hands.

'When will you be finished?'

'We'll be at it 'til five, Johnnie. Now there's a bar with a big-titted girl.' He nodded. 'Over there.' The girl was standing on the pavement watching the men work and smiling to herself. 'That's to be the first port of call at the work day end, all the fellas are saying, and there's three of them.'

'We'll be killed in the rush.'

'I'll see you there anyways. Five it is.'

'Five,' nodded Jackson and walked away. Twelve now, he thought. That gives me five hours to explore the town and see how the action is. He returned to his truck and threw the broom into the back, then casually walked down the company lines, reached a corner, lit a cigarette, glancing about him to see that he wasn't observed, then nipped around the corner and hastened away.

He walked about half a mile before he decided that it was

safe to stop for a drink. The first bar was comfortably furnished and the shelves were lined with all kinds of drinks and his first thought was, with an inward smile, old Dare won't go thirsty in this town. Then he thought, maybe Belgium didn't have it so bad this war. Everyone looked remarkably healthy, including the dyed red-headed, buxom, middle-aged woman behind the bar. She greeted him with an automatic, totally phony smile.

'Hello, soldat.'

'Hello, dear.'

'What you like?'

'How's the beer?'

'It's good. You stay here long?'

'No idea.'

'Where you from?'

'London.'

'No, where you from?'

'Oh. Italy.'

'You like it?'

'No.'

'They say it's beautiful.'

'It's in bad shape now.'

A young man about Jackson's age, leaning against the bar, laughed. Jackson looked at him. 'You here 1940, soldier?'

'No. France. Didn't get to Belgium.'

The young man was still grinning. 'You know when British Tommy was here, 1940, he had it.'

'Had what?'

'The money for the drinks, for good nights out in the bars. For the girls.' An even wider grin. 'Now we have it.'

No politics, Jackson warned himself. Stay away from that old rubbish. He smiled pleasantly.

'Wonder how?'

'We've got it,' boasted the young man. 'And prices have gone up.'

He's had a nibble at the black market, thought Jackson. Ought to get to know him. He moved along the bar. 'What's your name?'

'Peter.'

'I'm Johnnie. Have a drink.'

Peter laughed. 'You buy me drink?' He turned to the red-head. 'Give him another beer.'

Jackson lowered his voice. 'What's the market price for Italian lire?'

Peter shrugged. 'Not good.'

'How much?'

'Not interested.'

'Look, the war will be over soon and the Yanks will have to throw money into Italy . . .'

Peter bellowed with laughter. 'And into fucking Germany, eh?'

'Fucking Germany,' the redhead automatically repeated.

Christ, thought Jackson. Will they do that? Then he grinned. 'I suppose they will. Then all the banks will be in business.'

Peter pondered for a moment. 'It's taking a risk.'

The con man in Jackson was getting to work. Here was a good town at last and all he needed was Belgian francs. 'It's not a serious risk, we both know that. You may have to sit on it a little while, that's all. Then you can make a killing.'

Peter pulled out a pen from his breast-pocket and a note-book from his jacket pocket, concentrated, then quickly scribbled some figures, then threw the paper on the bar.

Jackson picked it up and began working out the rate of exchange, then looked disgusted. Peter was offering him one-tenth of the current lire rate.

'You're right. You don't take risks.'

'Take it or leave it.'

Jackson calculated again. He had on him the equivalent of five hundred pounds, sterling, in lire. In his kit-bag about four or five thousand pounds more. Break that down and it could be five hundred pounds in Belgian francs. Safe money, but still a bad deal. 'Double it and I'm interested.'

Peter shook his head. 'I said take it or leave it.'

The redhead had been listening.

'How much you got?'

Peter was indignant. 'You keep out of this.' He turned

back to Jackson. 'Okay. How much you got?'

Jackson pulled a wallet from his pocket. It was stuffed with notes. The redhead moved to the door and locked it. Peter checked the money and the exchange was made. In business again, thought Jackson wryly, but on the wrong end of the deal. Why hadn't I thought of this before? But how was I to know I'd wind up in dear old Belgium where the morals seem to be about as good as mine? I could have brought a bank-load of lire with me, instead I handed it out like a millionaire with six hands.

He called for drinks and the redhead unlocked the door. Well, at least I've got moving money. About a hundred quid and a lot more where that came from hidden in my truck. The redhead's smile was more natural now and more friendly and Peter would meet him the next day and do another transaction, and he was much more friendly and called for more drinks. At three o'clock Jackson left them. He didn't mind doing business with Peter but he didn't want his company.

He found her in the third bar he visited. She had dark hair, green eyes, a flawless complexion and her lips were red and sensual. She had a beautiful body and she spoke almost perfect English. There was no one else in the bar. He ordered a drink and asked her her name. Her name was Marie.

He sat on a bar stool and remembered another Marie. He had met her in Boulogne in 1940. It began with visits to the cinemas, drinks in bars, then bed and they stopped visiting the cinemas but still used the bars. He had been running an officers' shop in the Hotel Imperial on the sea front and when it was bombed the first time, he had been inside the hotel and was lucky, but there were many who were not. The second time, the next night, he had made a point of being absent, despite being told by his officer, 'You don't leave; you guard the shop. Look here, Jackson, a bomb never drops in the same place twice.' Jackson smiled to himself at the memory, but he hadn't smiled then.

The day after the second bombing raid, GHQ, who had been bombed out of Arras in a similar fashion, wisely packed and got out. The day after that, the same officer, 'A bomb never drops in the same place twice,' scuttled into the shop (now somewhat cleaned up but still showing war scars) and yelled, 'Pack and get out. There's a boat at the dock. Board it!', and he ran like hell out again. A few minutes later, Jackson was running down the street, running with his big pack bumping on his arse like a parachute and carrying his kit-bag loaded with booze and cigarettes. He was going to give one hell of a party if he ever got back to England, and there she was, waiting. Marie, large-eyed, sorrowful.

'Where are you going, Johnnie?'

'What a bloody question. England.'

'And what about me?'

Did she expect him to stuff her in his kit-bag, or something, and smuggle her on board? He was in a terrible hurry and she was holding him back. He wanted to say something to comfort her. Take her in his arms. Instead he just stood there looking at her, increasingly aware that time was passing and maybe the boat wouldn't wait for him. Then the tears began to course down her cheeks. She was making gasping, hurt animal noises and then he realized for the first time something he had always suspected. That something they had never discussed. She was Jewish. He stared at her in horror and pity as though he were staring at a corpse. He moved to kiss her and couldn't. He knew, that she knew, how frightened he was, how anxious he was to run and get aboard the boat and back to England and safety.

'Sorry,' he said. 'Sorry, darling,' and he walked on. Now he couldn't run, much as he longed to. He walked on, thinking, you bloody coward.

Jackson lit another cigarette as he stared at the other Marie, who had seen the war through, been under German occupation, and survived. One thing was clear. This Marie wasn't Jewish. He didn't want to think about what had happened to the other Marie.

He ordered another drink and stared at her slim back as she stood slightly on tip-toes and reached for a bottle of cognac – Jackson was a careless drinker and sometimes switched his drinks, and he suspected it was a damn foolish thing to do. She had long, slim legs and a beautifully curved

– not football rounded, he noticed, but curved, arse. Backside, he mentally corrected himself, then with a schoolboy grin, bum. No words were adequate. He wondered why he thought of tits before breasts. A mother's breast. It just wasn't sexy was it? The naughty, dirty words always came to mind first with a guilty, gloating feeling. Why hadn't someone come up with more romantic names for those beautifully curved parts of a woman's body, he wondered.

She placed his drink on the bar counter and he sipped it, still smiling at her. He savoured it. Such a pleasant taste. Such a pleasant sensation. He felt greedy but nursed the drink, enjoying the taste. Enjoying the sensation. He was all mouth and stomach at that moment. Greedy mouth, the taste lingering on his tongue. All mouth and tongue and a warming sensation in his belly. All animal.

She was watching him with a half smile. Derisive? He couldn't be sure. Did she look at all the customers that way? With a vaguely distant, mocking half smile? How many open mouths had she stared into? Tongues flicking out savouring wine on lips, hands wiping away beer froth?

He discovered that he was lost for words. Strange, he seldom was, especially after a few drinks. That usually loosened the tongue, and brought a ready, easy smile to his eyes. He had been away from civilization too long, which to him meant away from the society of women. Southern Italy he could not count as civilized. The chattering girls in the casa, all virgins and acting foolishly, no doubt resenting their parents' and relations' strict control over them. Smiling and chattering and sometimes squirming. He knew they wanted it. Probably thought of little else. In a highly romantic way, or pure animal? He had never been sure.

The oppressive house with pictures of the Madonna and crucifixes everywhere. Rather gory pictures with bleeding hearts. There had been no freedom in his association with the girls. Old women sitting around knitting, watching. After a time he had almost felt like one of the family, like a brother, and then, of course, he had lost interest. No excitement. No secretive moments. No charged excitement. No touching of hands, lips. But here was an exciting girl and this was different and he was alone with her and he was searching his mind for something to say to hold her attention. He could hardly believe it. Then the words gushed out.

'You are beautiful.'

She looked bored. 'So I hear.' Her face turned away from him as she looked at the bar wall.

'Sorry.' A faint stammer. 'I . . . I'm out of practice,' he added lamely.

'You wish to practice?' she turned her head and looked at him. 'Don't practice on me.'

Was she laughing at him? 'You misunderstand.'

'Then explain.'

She knew she was in control and he felt awkward. 'Words can confuse. I mean, I haven't been near a beautiful girl in a long time.' Suddenly angry and making a bloody fool of himself. Confidence zero.

Her eyes were mocking him. 'Why not be you? Be yourself?'

'That's the problem. I am. I'm saying what I think is the truth.'

'Think?'

'Know is the truth.'

'Or what you think I would like to hear?'

It dawned on Jackson that this was an unusual conversation. Not the normal, customer–barmaid, first meeting routine, anyway. No forced laughter, no did you hear the one about the Catholic and the Rabbi, love? No searching for something funny to say. He was thinking, hoping, she was treating him as a special person. There seemed to be a hidden seriousness in their conversation, and there was something electric between them. He hoped she was feeling it. He began to brighten up a little.

'My name's Johnnie Jackson.' She had told him her name. Funny he hadn't introduced himself then.

She merely nodded her head.

'And I like you very much.'

'You like.' That smile again.

'Yes.'

'Isn't it too soon?'

'It's my first impression.'

'I think you lie. I think you know that girls like you.' An open smile backed with good humour. She was thinking, he looks like a little boy. A lost little boy, an inward giggle, probably a dirty little boy and he knows it and uses it. The way he smiles, playing shy. I would have to watch him.

'Perhaps if I get to know you, I will like you.'

I'm making headway, thought Jackson, with great good humour. I thought I hadn't just imagined that electric feeling between us.

'Are you sure you won't have a drink?'

'I have changed my mind.' She pointed to a bottle on the shelf. 'I usually drink the green one. It is sweet and I do not like it but I get commission.'

Jackson remembered Cairo, and the cabaret girls screaming for drinks, and thumping on the tables with the flat palms of their hands, and laughing uproariously, pretending to be drunk. The drinks were non-alcoholic, of course, like that green bottle on the shelf, and they got commission on all the drinks they ordered. He felt instant disappointment as he stared at her.

'With you I will have a cognac.' She knew exactly what he was thinking as he stared about him at the room.

'In the evening girls come here and drink with the men. With the soldiers.'

Jackson grinned. 'With the happily married men.'

Her amused smile. 'With the happily married soldiers.'

Together they said, 'I'm not married,' and they laughed.

'I'm not, honestly.'

A shrug. 'Does it matter?'

'And you drink with anybody?'

'Of course.'

'And go to bed with anybody?' A bitter taste in his mouth, bile rising. She certainly had a good routine. Really made you feel special, but a few drinks, money, of course, and anybody could have her. What a damn fool he was. But it wasn't the scene he had expected, somehow. He repeated with an edge to his voice, 'You sleep with anybody?'

Her eyes now angry. 'Yes, I can love, but I love not very often.'

What the hell business was it of his? He was behaving stupidly. Blame it on the drinks.

Her smile mocking again. 'When I say love, I mean make love.'

'You mean fuck.' You idiot, he thought. Why don't you shut up?

Her lips prim. 'I do not like the word, but that is what I mean.'

'Are you saying you've never been in love?'

'I am saying I will not fall in love again.'

'What's your problem?'

'They are always moving on some place, the men I have liked, and maybe could have fallen in love with. They never stay here very long.'

'What about the locals?'

'Who?'

'The men who live here.'

She laughed. 'Those. They only marry good girls.'

'What about the Germans?'

'There was one I liked.' A shrug. 'But that would be dangerous to be serious.'

'Why?'

'Because I knew he would go back to Germany and he would not take me with him.'

'I thought you meant dangerous to associate with him.'

'Oh, that. We did not think ahead. How could we believe at one time that they would lose the war?'

'But when they did?'

'Some of the good girls had a bad time.' A full clear laugh. 'Those who were supposed to be good girls. But for the girls in the bars, the prostitutes, our men knew who we were and knew we had to make a living.'

'Very rational. How was the occupation?'

A shrug. 'For me and girls like me not very bad. Mostly the Germans treated us well.' A thin smile. 'We were necessary. Some men were pigs. Some were not too bad. Some got drunk and sentimental and showed photographs of their wives and children. That kind could cry in their drinks. A few were kind. I think the occupation for girls like me was much the same as the occupation is now.'

Jackson found himself smiling. 'I thought that we were freeing you.'

'So many of the Germans said.'

'They never had much of a sense of humour. Anyway, you're very practical.' He took hold of her hand and his fingers tingled and the wonderful sensation made his arm shake and then his legs began shaking and there was a warmth about his crotch and when he spoke his voice sounded off key. 'Come round here.'

She gently released his hand, moved from behind the bar and sat on a stool next to him. Her knee touched his and he got an immediate erection and he felt the heat of it. He held her hand harder and now his body was shaking and the palms of his hands were moist. Filled with desire, he could only look at her with beseeching eyes. Like a sick dog, he thought unhappily. I didn't know I needed it so badly.

Clearly all his thoughts and emotions were picked up by her. There was an understanding look in her eyes.

'I will lock the door.'

Reluctantly he let go of her hand and watched her slim body move to the door. She bolted it, checked it, turned and smiled at him, then crossed the room and took his hand. He stumbled off the bar stool and dumbly followed her to a door and up a flight of stairs and they were in a bedroom. He only noticed the large bed. She pulled lightweight curtains over the window. She turned down the bedclothes and he feverishly undressed and got into bed and lay there shivering. Sound of water running from the bathroom and then she was beside him. His arms went out to her blindly, he found her lips with his and then he was on top of her and her legs opened and his erection touched hair and a softness and heat and dampness, then with closed eyes he was shuddering violently and then with open eyes he was staring down at her and filled with shame. It was all over. He lay on her a moment or two longer, then rolled off and closed his eyes again, too ashamed to look at her.

After what seemed a long time, he felt her move away. Still he did not open his eyes. Then the sound of running water again. She was washing him off her body. What a bloody disaster. He had always been proud of his control, felt masterful as he moved into a woman, and looked down at her, with love, or with amusement. He had really blown it this time. He had to escape.

When she returned he was dressed. She looked surprised. He could only mumble, 'I have to meet some friends.' A long puzzled look from her, but no comment. He thought, I should go and wash, but he had to get away from her and his sense of shame. He placed some money on the bedside table and almost blurted out, 'I'm sorry.' Instead, he said, 'I can see myself out.'

The sun was still shining as he closed the bar door behind him. Automatically he glanced at his watch. Five o'clock. He would go and see Paddy. But he wouldn't have anything to tell him.

The bar was crowded and four girls were serving beers and the soldiers were shoving each other at the bar and yelling to be served and making passes at the girls, who were giggling and seemed to be enjoying themselves. He found Paddy in a corner, propping up the bar, and Dusty was with him. Paddy greeted him with a sly grin and 'You're late. I suppose you found a piece for yourself.'

Jackson winked and wished he hadn't said that. When he had left Marie, he had wandered into another bar and sat brooding about his failure. It was like the end of the bloody world. Coming, and he wasn't even in her. Even on his first experience he had done a hell of a lot better than that. No one could have done worse. Puff, puff, finish. He was getting the horrors.

He finished his drink and wandered into another bar, still brooding over his failure. Great lover Jackson, you've beaten the world record. The woman behind the bar, obviously the owner, had broadly hinted about the good time he could have when the girls came on duty. The last thing Jackson wanted at that moment was to chance another good time, and to her surprise he told her so. She had arched an eyebrow and looked at the barman, who winked and grinned at her and then made a femme gesture. For a moment Jackson was darkly angry, then he had to grin sourly to himself as he thought, now I'm being taken for a bloody queer. This just isn't my day. He had moved on to another bar and again had been offered a good time and then he had decided to go in search of Paddy and they would try one of the good-time bars. He knew he had to prove himself but the thought of Marie still rankled. How could he ever face her again? Yet he was in two minds, to go back to her and be honest and explain that he really was out of practice – it had just poured out of him – and she probably would understand. But his pride would not allow him. It had turned out to be a farce, with the laugh on him. He hadn't even got into her. It shouldn't happen to a dog.

Paddy was nudging him. 'I'm thinking these girls fuck.'

Jackson stared at the four busy barmaids. The one facing him pouring a beer was heavy-breasted and didn't appeal to him. Bet she's got fat legs. He looked over the bar. She had. Dusty was tugging at his arm and he turned and stared into his empty eyes.

'Can you get me one, Johnnie?'

Paddy and Jackson both laughed, but Dusty persisted. 'I want it,' he said with his simple smile. 'And if there's any, you'll know where it is, Johnnie.'

'Okay. I'll see what I can do.'

'Knew you would.' Dusty happily guzzled at his beer.

'Jesus, the champion wanker's going in for the real thing,' grinned Paddy. 'We ought to be there to watch it.'

'Can if you like,' smiled Dusty. 'You're my friends.' He emptied his glass of beer.

'Money's the problem.' Paddy eyed Jackson.

'I can get your lire changed. But the rate's lousy. Only twenty per cent.'

'Better than nothing.'

As they left the bar, the girls were still serving beers and the soldiers were still shouting lewd remarks at them.

In the dim-lit bar, three girls sat round the table with Jackson, Paddy and Dusty, who by this time were all drunk. The girls had been steadily drinking non-alcoholic drinks for two hours, talking and laughing and putting on a great show as though enjoying themselves. Dusty had a fixed smile on his face and the girls were still teasing him, as they had been almost from the moment they had joined them at the table. Jackson, smiling drunkenly, thought, they treat him like a toy doll. I wouldn't be surprised if they started to dress him and undress him and put ribbons in his hair and old Dusty wouldn't mind. He was loving the attention they were giving him. If he weren't simple, if the light hadn't gone out of his eyes, he would be beautiful. The girls did seem to be happy and they were reasonably attractive, if not over-intelligent. Paddy was happily drunk, too, thank God, and not interested in going to bed with any of the girls, which was just as well, because Jackson was quite sure none of the girls had any intention of going to bed with any of them. He supposed they made a reasonable commission on the drinks, but it irritated him. Not that he wanted to sleep with any of them, just the idea of being taken. Good job Paddy was happy drunk or he might wreck the place. One of the girls in the other bar had taken his fancy. Jackson finally placed her. She wasn't the big-breasted one with the fat legs, but a skinny little girl with mournful eyes.

'She's the one for me,' Paddy kept repeating. 'She wouldn't be the forces' favourite, that one now, and that's why I fancy her and I'll have the drawers off her before long. You mark me word.'

Jackson nodded and grinned every time Paddy said this. He was trying to get one of the girls to take Dusty upstairs and the girls shrieked with laughter every time Jackson mentioned it. 'We do not sleep.' Laughing and shaking their heads and laughing again every time they looked at Dusty, who smiled drunkenly at them and ordered them more drinks, which Jackson knew he would have to pay for. But Jackson was determined that Dusty wasn't going to leave the bar a virgin, even though he knew the chances were he would. So drunkenly he repeated time after time, 'Take him upstairs. He's good at it, you'll be surprised.' And Dusty would wink and say, 'I'm not so green as I'm cabbage look-ing' and this made the girls more hysterical. They all seemed to be very fond of Dusty. Finally Jackson got angry. 'You look after Dusty or we're leaving.'

The girls went into a huddle, still giggling, then one moved very close to Dusty and whispered in his ear and Dusty turned his blue empty eyes on her and switched on his be-guiling smile and eagerly nodded. Then after a time, his eyes went really dead and his mouth opened and his head began nodding, then Paddy and Jackson caught on and it was Paddy who said it, 'Jesus, she's wanking him off,' and started laughing and Jackson laughed and croaked, 'He's doomed. Poor old Dusty's doomed to be a wanker all his life.' Then a great yell of joy came out of Dusty as he lurched to his feet, almost knocking the table over.

Late afternoon on the fourth day Jackson entered the bar and there was Marie. Again no customers in the bar. She looked steadily at him.

'Where have you been?'

'I'm a bloody fool, aren't I?' He knew at once that she understood.

'Have you been practising?' Her smile warm and open.

'No.'

She was questioning him with her eyes.

'Honestly.'

She moved from behind the bar and locked the door. He followed her upstairs and he took his time undressing, then climbed into bed and lit a cigarette and they talked, then his arms went about her and they made love and this time it was good. Then she went downstairs to the bar and returned with drinks and they laughed about the first time and then they made love again then bathed together and dressed and she opened the bar and they agreed that he would come back that night and stay with her. He walked down the street and felt good because they had really made it so well together and because there had been no mention of money. As far as he was concerned she wasn't a whore.

He was walking back to what was now generally recognized as the company pub, but there was something wrong. The streets seemed strangely deserted. No soldiers. He hurried his pace and finally reached the street where his company was parked. No trucks. His heart pounded and he began to sweat. He pushed open the door of the company pub. Apart from the skinny girl behind the bar, who was crying, it was deserted too. She stared hopefully and near-sightedly through her tears at Jackson, then registered bitter disappointment.

'Where's everybody?' he yelled.

'Paddy gone.' Her shoulders shaking. 'Paddy gone.'

'Where's everybody?'

'Paddy . . .'

'To hell with Paddy. Where are they?'

The door opened and Brewer, the thin, sly driver to Major Cobbey, entered. He looked surprised when he saw Jackson.

'Brewer, what's going on? What's happened to everybody?'

A nasty grin, then a titter. 'Looks like they've pissed off, don't it?'

'Where?'

'Don't shout. Give us a beer, dear.'

'Paddy gone,' said the woeful, skinny girl as she poured a beer.

'Make it two,' said Jackson.

She pushed a glass across the bar to Brewer, wet-cheeked and snivelling.

'Paddy promised to marry me. You his friend.' She pushed a beer towards Jackson.

He wanted to laugh. 'That's right. He told me he wanted to marry you. Don't worry, he'll be back. Did he say where he was going?'

She brightened up a little. 'He say he didn't know, but he be back.'

'See,' said Jackson. 'Didn't I tell you?' He turned to Brewer. 'Give it to me. Where the hell are they?'

'Don't know,' smirked Brewer. 'It's all news to me.'

'Then what are you doing here?'

Again the smirk. Jackson wanted to kick his teeth in. 'I

took the old man to the big city last evening.'

'What was he doing there?'

'What do you think? Boozing it up and having a bit of the other.'

So he's human, thought Jackson. I don't believe it.

'Where is he now?'

'He'll be along and won't you get it.'

'Does he know where the company is?'

'How could he?' sniggered Brewer. 'When I drove him back to his hotel with this old bag he'd picked up, he was pissed out of his mind.'

The door opened and Major Cobbey entered. He stared when he saw Jackson.

'Ah.' He moved to the bar and ordered a drink. 'So you're here I see.'

'Yes, sir.'

'Where's everybody, Jackson?'

Marvellous, thought Jackson. He really is as lost as I am. Couldn't be better, so we're both AWOL. Great, there's nothing he can do to me. Would you believe it. Old Cobbey getting pissed out of his mind and picking up an old bag. Bless him, there's hope for everybody. He relaxed and smiled.

'I'm as surprised as you are, sir. When I left they were all here.'

'Yes. Damn funny.' Cobbey was actually smiling and seemed not the slightest bit perturbed. 'No problem. We'll track them down.'

He must have had a hell of a time.

'I'm sure it won't be difficult, sir.'

'Where have you been?'

'Er, thought I'd chance a steak dinner, sir. The food in the company lines ...'

'Are you complaining?'

You ought to try eating it, thought Jackson as he smiled.

'No, sir. But when you get a chance to eat in a restaurant ...'

'Of course, and a good bottle of wine, eh?'

Oh you jolly old bastard, thought Jackson gleefully. And a good bottle of wine, eh? Dare had told him if you served him octopus ink he wouldn't know.

'Makes all the difference, sir. How was the big city?'

'Not bad.' He sipped his drink and smiled reflectively. 'I suppose you had permission to be absent from the company lines?'

A quiet voice nudged Jackson. Tell him you did. Then he thought, as he afterwards realized, very recklessly, are you joking, Cobbey? You're bloody well AWOL the same as me so there's damn all you can do. Oh, Christ, I won't be seeing Marie again.

Cobbey interrupted his thoughts. 'Did you have permission or not?'

'Well, I went looking for the RSM, sir, but I couldn't find him, so . . .' Jackson smiled pleasantly.

That grin, thought Major Cobbey. That cocky, insolent grin. All he had to say was yes, didn't he? Just say yes and I wouldn't have pursued it. But he has to be insolent. He has to provoke me. Very well. He can bloody well pay for it.

'So you didn't have permission?'

'Well, not exactly.'

The young bastard. The insufferable . . . I'm trying to be fair, trying to be reasonable, but it takes two, doesn't it? Well, if he thinks he can provoke me he's damn well right. Must be something wrong with his head. He's deliberately provoking me to punish me. A thin smile as he stared at Jackson.

'Get in the car. Consider yourself on a charge.'

'What?' Jackson stared back into Cobbey's cold, expressionless eyes. 'Are you telling me I'm on a . . .'

'Don't argue. Get in the car.'

You stupid bastard, thought Jackson as he walked to the door. All the hostility he felt towards Cobbey seething and boiling inside him. We'll see if you can get away with this or not. You're as deep in it as I am. You'd better watch your step. As he got in the car next to Brewer, he suddenly felt better. He wasn't going to crawl to the two-faced bastard. If he wanted a show-down, fine. He felt really good. Marie had been good for his ego. What a girl. What a pity he wouldn't see her again. And what a golden opportunity, he gloated, to take Cobbey to the cleaners. I really do hate the sight of him. A moment's panic, as he thought, I hope it's not the drink affecting my judgement. Then he dismissed the thought. No, I'm in the right. That's why I can afford to take chances and he's in the wrong so he really had better watch his step.

All night long they drove from check point to check point, with Cobbey inquiring after his missing company, until finally a Military Police Sergeant had the answer. Their destination was Holland.

Chapter XIV

Another village. Another school. A triangle of working-class houses – neat, red brick. The village green, badly churned up with tank tracks and hardened into a cement-like texture under the heat of the sun, and the red brick school squaring it off.

Jackson, standing outside Major Cobbey's office, looking out of the corridor window, watched the busy housewives cleaning the windows, scrubbing steps, sweeping the pavements. He had heard that the Dutch were very house proud and they looked it. There didn't seem to be too much gossiping going on. Busy, busy, heavy-bodied, square, bovine women. Some of the young girls didn't look too bad, and the kids were playing war games on the village green. Hadn't they had enough? Well, no damage at all to this village. The war had passed it by. Lucky sods.

His thoughts were interrupted by a voice next to his left ear.

'Take a good look, you won't be seeing that for a long time.' He jumped and almost bumped his head into RSM Tompkins' horrible grin. He automatically straightened up and thought, I suppose I'll be doing this in bloody civvy street any time anyone speaks to me!

'That's better,' scowled Tompkins. 'Hands in line with the seams of yer trousers, you NAAFI chocolate soldier.'

Tompkins smiled at his own wit. 'Head up, up. Shoulders back.'

That sinking feeling in the pit of his stomach. Trust Tompkins to spoil his day for him. He wasn't too sure now that he, David, could take on Goliath, Cobbey, because Cobbey wouldn't come into the arena alone and take his chance. He would have the whole bloody army backing him. All the generals, not to mention the King's Rules and Regulations, and that book of justice was unbalanced in favour of the officers. He couldn't help a shiver of apprehension, but he had decided on his tactics and hoped they would work.

Tompkins was inspecting him from head to foot, pulling at his blancoed webbing. He had sat up half the night scrubbing away and polishing the brass work. He wasn't going to be faulted on that, and his boots were beautifully polished. Dusty's contribution and Dusty was renowned as the best shoe-shine in the company and proud of it. Any spare time he had he would find a corner and sit himself down and bone and shine his boots, wearing his vacant smile. God knows what his thoughts were.

Jackson could see that Tompkins could not fault him by the disappointed look in his eyes. Then the bastard's eyes turned bleak.

'We'll see what the Major has to say to you.' Then in a lowered voice, 'You stupid young bastard.' The eyes gloating now. 'Walked right into it, didn't yer?'

A quick about turn, boots slamming on the tiled floor. A crashing thump on the office door, then the door bursting open and again the slamming boots.

'Prisoner all ready and correct, sir.'

Cobbey's voice. 'Double him in, Sergeant Major.'

The boots slamming again. Tompkins was trying to shame the guards at their own game.

'Prisoner, double!'

As Jackson doubled into the office, Tompkins yelled again, 'Hat off!' and before Jackson could reach for it Tompkins knocked it off his head. 'Keep them legs up! Up! Up! Double time! Up! Up! Up! Halt!'

Wow. Jackson was facing Cobbey, who was seated behind his desk thumbing his dossier.

Tompkins bawling, only half listening, it was too noisy. Jackson, J. 441. Absent from company lines. Shout, shout, bawl, growl.

You too, Cobbey, Jackson was thinking bitterly, you were AWOL. Finally Tompkins shut up and added, 'Sir!'

Cobbey still thumbing through Jackson's army record in the dossier and speaking in a level voice: 'Absent without leave from the company lines. I could take a serious view of that.' Thumb, thumb through the dossier, pausing to read, 'Not a record to be proud of, is it. Even NAAFI.' He poured all the scorn he could muster into the word NAAFI. 'Couldn't even stomach you and forty-two days' field detention and punishment. Absent again I see, that was Cairo.'

'Yes, sir.'

'Impersonating an officer as well and you were only awarded forty-two days.'

'Not proven, sir.'

'Wonder how you wriggled out of that?' He hadn't looked at Jackson once.

'British justice, sir.' An edge to his voice he tried to disguise. 'Didn't find me guilty, so they had to find me innocent.'

'Couldn't find you guilty.' Cobbey glanced up at Jackson and thought, that helps to explain his cocky grin, his insolence. He's been getting away with everything short of murder and that's why I'm going to punish him. For his own good. See if I can smarten him up a bit. Teach him.

'You have the right to demand a court martial, Jackson, or accept my punishment.' Cobbey waited.

'Accept your punishment, sir!' Jackson discovered that he was shouting. The anger inside him boiling over because his master plan had been to really fuck Cobbey up by demanding a court martial and letting him sweat it out and worry about what Jackson had to say about him being AWOL. Now he was quitting and he felt bad.

'What do you plead?'

'Guilty, sir.' The words almost choked him.

'Why did you absent yourself?'

'I wanted a steak dinner, sir.'

'What?'

'Some good grub, sir.'

'Is that the only explanation you have for your conduct?'

'Yes, sir.'

'It's no good.' Cobbey thought, I'm trying to be fair, but . . . 'What the hell kind of an excuse is that?'

'I'm not making any excuses. I'm guilty. Accept your punishment.'

'You impertinent young . . .' Cobbey's voice was going out of control. 'You just stand there. Stand there, with that damn smug grin.' He stopped speaking and took a deep breath.

Smug grin, thought Jackson. He's crazy. What have I got to grin about?

Cobbey started again. 'And tell me. Tell me . . .' Turning to Tompkins. 'Is this man in his right mind?'

Before Tompkins could reply Jackson shouted, 'Of course I'm not, sir. You've got my records. I'm a head case!' He knew he wasn't handling this very well, but he was getting into a fury with the shifty-eyed idiot behind the desk.

Now Cobbey was shouting. All the pent-up anger he felt towards Jackson. His black market activities in Italy. The SIB investigation. My God, he could have ruined my career.

'You won't get away with it. You damn well will not. I repeat, will not damn well get away with it. You've pretended, fooled some people, you're mentally unstable, but you don't fool me. So I'll punish you. Punish you as you deserve. Twenty-eight days' field punishment and detention. It's not in my power to give you more, otherwise I would.'

Jackson snarled, 'Accept your punishment, sir. You're right to punish me, I'm a very naughty boy.' I'll irritate the fuck out of him, he thought. I'll send him up the wall, the hypocritical old sod. I'll dig it right home to him. He switched on a phony pious expression and dropped his voice. 'I didn't tell the complete truth. I didn't go for a steak dinner only. I went round the bars boozing it up. Then I found an old bag and she wasn't bad at it. When a man goes AWOL, sir, and there's a war on, sir, that man, sir, isn't doing his bit for his King and country, sir. A man who gets up to the tricks I got up to, sir, when good men are dying up the front, deserves everything that's coming to him. Such disgraceful conduct deserves punishment.'

Cobbey listening, his mouth opening and going slack. The colour draining from his face, then up on his feet in a fury.

'You damned impertinent young bastard!' Raging. 'I'll punish you. It's the Field Detention Prison and they'll smarten you up. I'm awarding you fourteen days' punishment and . . .' His mouth dropped open again and he stopped shouting.

He got carried away and forgot. Jackson was gloating. 'Fourteen days' field punishment, sir. Thank you, sir.'

'Double him out!' shouted Cobbey.

Jackson doubled out of the office with a grin on his face. Fourteen days, the stupid bastard. That's not too bad. That will soon pass.

The truck pulled up outside the Field Punishment and Detention Centre. An old grey-walled prison and Jackson and his escort Corporal Simpson and two soldiers jumped out of the back of the truck and lined up between the two soldiers facing Corporal Simpson, who half whispered, 'If you've got any cigarettes, Jackson, now's the last chance to get rid of them.'

Jackson grinned. 'I've got five hundred fags and three bottles of Scotch. When I get inside there, I'm going to give a party.'

'Jackson!' Simpson looked shocked.

'Only joking.'

'Don't make jokes inside there.'

RSM Tompkins climbed out of the truck brandishing Jackson's crime sheet in a buff envelope with OHMS printed on it.

'No talking there,' he barked. Then he quickly inspected Jackson, grinned, nodded to the prison. 'They call it home, sweet home.'

A door in the main gate opened and a Staff Sergeant came out. The brim of his cap pulled down over his eyes, only half his nose and a thin trap of a mouth and rugged chin could be seen. Tompkins handed him the envelope and said, 'This one thinks he's a holy terror, Staff. Hope you can convince him he ain't.'

'A lot of them seem to think that, Sarn Major. Come in thinking they're bleedin' lions, go out like lambs. We treat them all the same.' He lifted his head to read Jackson's crime sheet, then handed the envelope back to Tompkins, then a voice pitched between a scream and a roar almost burst Jackson's ear drums.

'Fourteen days! Sarn Major, there's no room in the inn for minor offenders!'

'What?' Tompkins shouted back.

'No room. He'll have to do his punishment in the company lines.'

The door in the gate slammed shut.

Jackson's face muscles relaxed and he grinned. Thank God for the dodgy boys. Thank God for the real villains. No room in the inn, that's rich.

Tompkins was facing him. 'I'll wipe that grin off yer face. Think you've got away with it, do yer. We'll see.'

In a truck outside the school on the edge of the village green, Corporal Simpson handed Jackson a sheet of carefully typed paper.

'Read it.'

Jackson studied it carefully.

Parade with guard, 0600 hours.
PT 0630 hours, 0700 hours.
Clean equipment 0700 hours, 0800 hours.
Breakfast 0800 hours, 0830 hours.
Clean out cell 0830 hours, 0900 hours.

Jackson glanced at the truck. Some cell.

Drill 0900 hours, 1200 hours

Christ!

Lunch 1200 hours, 1300 hours.
Clean equipment 1300 hours, 1400
 hours.

 Restbreak, eh?

Full pack punishment drill 1400
 hours, 1600 hours.

 Wait a minute. That's abolished. I'm damn sure full pack
punishment drill's abolished. Don't argue. Only two weeks,
get it over with. Don't argue.

Tea 1600 hours, 1630 hours.
1630 hours, 1800 hours, dig holes.

 And plant me in one of them. Wow!

1800 hours, parade with guard.
1830 hours to 2200 hours, cookhouse
 fatigues.
2200 hours, 2400 hours, clean kit.

 'Wow!'
 'Satisfied?' inquired Corporal Simpson.
 'Crippled.'
 'No answering back.'
 'Fucked!'
 'I said no answering back.'
 'Ballocked.'
 'Watch out, Jackson.'
 'You aren't a bad bloke, Simpson. I'm not blaming you.'
 'And don't give me any bloody nonsense.'
 'I know your wife loves you.'
 'Jackson, I'm warning you.'
I'm going crazy, thought Jackson. Knowing what's in
store for me is sending me crazy. I had better watch it. Only
fourteen days. It will pass. Only fourteen days.

Simpson glanced at his watch.

'Fourteen hundred hours. Full pack marching order punishment drill. Get into your pack.'

Jackson looked at the badly churned-up village green. That's going to be heavy going. Then he noticed a small cluster of people outside one of the houses. They were taking an interest. More were leaving their houses. Looks like I'm going to be on exhibition, Jackson thought. Going to have an audience. Don't think I'm going to like that. Not going to like it at all. Three young girls gathered together and he decided that he didn't fancy any of them, but they were young and whispering and glancing furtively at him. I know I'm not going to like it. They can smell it. They know something funny's going on.

'Get into your pack, Jackson.'

Jackson bent down and picked up his big pack and was about to shrug into it.

'Not that one, this one.' Simpson picked up another pack and Jackson could see by the way he lifted it that it weighed heavy. 'Not my idea, Jackson. The RSM's.'

Jackson shrugged into it. It did weigh heavy.

'Rifle.'

'Rifle? Now look here.' Full pack marching order punishment drill. With bloody sand in the pack.

'Dirt.' Simpson lowered his voice. 'Three quarters dirt, the rest paper.'

'It still weighs heavy,' grunted Jackson. The straps already were beginning to bite into his shoulders.

'Don't give me a hard time.' Was Simpson pleading?

'Don't give you a hard time.'

'Don't come the old soldier.' Simpson stepped back. 'Shoulder arms, double!'

Jackson jogged away. The big pack bounced on his back muscles and spine. Don't like it, thought Jackson. Two hours. It's going to give my back hell. Shit! Tompkins is right. This is going to be worse than the glass-house. It's not going to do my back any good.

'Eyes up and keep that rifle up.'

Jackson was looking at the ground, stumbling and trying

to bypass the deeper ruts. Ruts! Christ, some of them could almost be trenches. Easy to break a leg if he didn't watch out.

'Eyes up.'

Jackson looked at Simpson. 'I've got to watch the ground or I'll break my fucking neck.'

'Eyes up. No talking.' Then in a lowered voice, 'Don't give me any trouble.'

He can't make up his mind if he's a sadist or man's best friend, Jackson thought, as he lifted his head, stumbled, almost fell, then dropped his eyes to the ground again.

'Eyes up.'

Jackson lifted his eyes again and saw the cluster of people had swollen. Their faces expressed sympathy. He glanced down again as he stumbled and almost fell.

'Head up. Up.'

They must think the Gestapo's back in town again, Jackson thought. Bounce, bounce went the pack. It didn't help his breathing. Try and time it. Stumble. Can't. Throws me off balance, straps beginning to burn. How long? Two hours. Joking. They must be joking. I won't last. Two hours. Joe Louis wouldn't last two hours.

'RSM's watching. Head up.'

'Fuck the RSM.'

'Don't give me a hard time.'

Give you a punch in the hooter, thought Jackson with a snarl.

Half an hour later, drenched in sweat. Sweat dripping from his eyebrows into his eyes, half blinding him. The pack loosened and punching into his back, beating the breath out of him in rasping gasps. Tight pains across his chest. His shoulders on fire with the rubbing of the straps. Stumbling, tripping, just managing to save himself. Rifle arm numb, no feeling but the weight of the rifle. The impossible weight of the rifle. The battle blouse rubbing his sweat-soaked neck. His body, underclothes, shirt, soaked with sweat. Sweat running down his body, running down his limbs. Lurching, stumbling, heart pounding, legs like lead weights. Then, weightless, stumbling over a field of cotton wool, then like lead weights again. Rifle slipping. Sweating palm of his hand somehow managing to save it falling.

'Keep it up, up. Keep the rifle up.'

Simpson, the friendly sadist. He'll kill me rather than get into trouble himself. Always been a pleasant bastard up till now. Writing letters to his fucking wife. Everybody likes old Simpson. Do anybody a favour. What's happened to him? Wait a minute. His name's on the home leave list. He's due for home leave. Home to his ever-loving after four years away from her. Of course the bastard will kill me if he has to. He's not going to miss seeing her for anything. Two letters a day for over four years. No boozing in case he's unfaithful to his ever-loving. Jackson spoke in gasps.

'You . . . didn't want . . . to . . . get . . . landed for . . . this . . .'

'Jackson.' Simpson was pleading. 'You know the RSM. You know he's a bastard. Jackson, he hinted if I don't make a good job of this . . .'

'I . . .' gasp '. . . know.'

'Bottom of the list, Jackson. Bottom of the list.'

'You . . . poor . . . bastard.'

'Bottom, Jackson, or even taken off it. Lost. Four years, Jackson.'

Gasping, Jackson said, 'Rest me.' Am I feeling sorry for him? Why the hell should I feel sorry for him?

'Only another twenty minutes, Jackson.'

No, thought Jackson. Twenty minutes, no.

'Then ten minutes' rest, Johnnie. Ten minutes.'

No, never make it. Know I won't make it. No. Can't do it. Twenty minutes. Blind, the sweat in my eyes. A gasping croak.

'Fuck your wife.'

'Don't say that, Johnnie.'

'Fuck her.'

'Nobody says that. I'm doing my best.' Simpson was thinking, I like him. He's a bit crazy, but I've always liked him. He got himself into this. The stupid bastard's always in trouble and the trouble is I like him and he's sticking it out pretty good. He's got guts, but if he says that about my wife again I'll kill him. Nobody says that about my wife. Three months and I'll be home. Fuck him. She's my wife. I need her and she needs me.

'Stick it out, Johnnie. Only seventeen minutes.'

'She's killing me. Your wife!'

'Stick it out.'

Seventeen. Can't make it. He knew he couldn't make it. The red haze. My chest. The pain. The pack. Wow. And then another hour. No.

'Here comes the RSM, Johnnie.' Voice loud giving the drill orders. 'Lef, right. Lef, right. Lef, lef, lef. Eyes up. Head up.'

'Everything under control, Corporal Simpson?'

'Yes, sir. Everything under control.'

Oh, the mealy-mouthed bastard.

'Doing a good job, Corporal.'

'Thank you, sir.'

Oh, you miserable bastard!

'Get that rifle up,' roared Tompkins. 'What you think it is, an umbrella?'

Jackson somehow pushed the rifle high up on his shoulder. A red haze, blurred faces. The houses tipping, blurring, fading.

'Up! The rifle up, up!'

The butt of the rifle hit Jackson on the chin. A glimpse of Tompkins' face behind the horny hand that thumped the rifle butt. He crashed to the ground. The sky was coming down on him.

'Up!' From a long way away Tompkins' voice. 'Get on yer feet. Up. Let's have yer on yer feet.'

The red haze and in the middle of it Tompkins' yellow teeth. Then a memory. Hawthorne. Poor old stuttering Hawthorne. Benghazi. The same thing had happened to him and what did he do? He got up and threw his rifle away, that's what he did. He threw his fucking rifle away, that's what he did. He quit and that's what I'm going to do.

'Get up. Up on your feet. Up!'

Jackson tried to stand, stumbled and fell back again.

Simpson's voice. 'Sir, I think he's had about enough.

Can't I rest him, sir? A short rest?'

'Up on yer feet!' roared Tompkins. 'Up! Up! Let's have yer.'

Red haze receding. Sky back where it belonged. Blue sky, floating white clouds. Clear and close, Tompkins' face bending down towards him. I'll punch it, thought Jackson. No. Couldn't hurt a fly, and that would be it. Assaulting an RSM. Then they'd really have me and they aren't going to have me. Put battle plan into action.

'Up on yer feet. Move!'

I'll make it in a minute, Jackson thought. I'll be up. But they aren't going to have me. He tried again and this time he made it. He stood on trembling legs.

Simpson picked up his cap and placed it on his head. Like mother used to do, thought Jackson, when I was a little kid.

'Now,' grinned Tompkins. 'Pick up yer rifle.'

Hawthorne, thought Jackson. Don't forget how Hawthorne handled it. Breathing becoming easier. 'You pick it up.'

'What!'

'And stick it up your arse.' He tried to slip out of his pack. A searing pain. Wow. But he just couldn't do it. Oh, well. Later. I'll get out of it later.

'What did you say?'

'I'm through.'

'Are you now?'

Jackson managed a lop-sided grin. 'You know I am. I'm stark, raving bonkers.'

'Pick up your rifle.'

'You pick it up.'

'I'm giving you an order.'

'And you can stick your orders up your arse.'

Tompkins started raving and Jackson thought, who's the crazy one?

'When I give an order. When I tell you . . . when I give orders, people jump. Now, you pick up that rifle.'

'I'm going home to my Mum,' said Jackson and turned and started limping away.

'What?' Tompkins was keeping pace with him. 'Simpson,

pick up that rifle. What? You're going home, you say. What?'

'She's a friend of Winnie's.'

'What you talking about?'

'How would I know?'

'Corporal,' yelled Tompkins. 'We'll give him a rest. Bring the rifle.'

'Yes, sir.'

'Well give you a rest, Jackson. Corporal, we'll give him a rest, then do it all over again. It's the first day. Maybe it's a bit hard on him the first day.'

Simpson walked on the other side of Jackson, carrying the rifle. 'Yes, sir. Must be hard going the first day.'

Tompkins was deliberately not speaking to Jackson. 'Yes, but in a couple of days, say three, he'll be dancing it. He'll be so fit he'll be dancing it.'

'Yes, sir. He'll be fit as hell and dancing it.'

'With Ginger Rogers,' said Jackson.

'If he sticks it out, sir.'

'If? Did you say if?'

'He'll stick it out, sir. I know him.'

'I've just remembered,' said Jackson.

'What?' inquired Simpson.

'My Mum!'

'What's he talking about, Corporal?'

'Don't know, sir.'

'She does Winnie's washing.'

'What's he talking about, Corporal?'

Simpson tapped his head. 'Don't know, sir.'

They reached the truck and Jackson slipped out of his pack. Christ! The pain was almost unbearable. Two hours, eh? Two hours every day. With the straps rubbing his shoulders raw and the weight of the pack and the bumping. If Tompkins had any bloody sense he should know that Jackson couldn't take it on that village green, which was more like a churned-up battlefield.

'Give him ten minutes' rest, Corporal, then take him out again.'

'Yes, sir.'

'And champagne,' said Jackson.

'Eh?'

'A bottle of bubbly to help me over the trenches; if I'm going into action, I want to be pissed.'

Jackson refused to smile, but now he had made up his mind he was beginning to enjoy himself. He was finished. He'd had it. He didn't know what they would, or could, do with him, but one thing he knew from experience, the Detention and Punishment Camp wouldn't be half as bad as the punishment Tompkins had planned for him. No room in the inn. Well, they'd bloody better find room.

Tompkins took his cap off and wiped his bald dome with a none too clean handkerchief.

'I'll give you bleedin' bubbly. Ten minutes, Corporal.' He turned to walk away.

'Haven't you got the message? I've quit.'

Tompkins jerked his head round and glared at Jackson and now it registered. The bugger meant it. The bastard was giving him problems; as if he hadn't got enough on his plate. He would have to report it to the Major and the Major wouldn't like it. Be some trouble when he told the Major. He had a horrible temper. Then a sudden thought, and he smiled. 'Corporal, rest him. I'll be back in a minute and I think he'll change his mind.' He hurried away.

'Have a smoke,' said Simpson, offering a cigarette.

'Prisoners aren't supposed to smoke,' grinned Jackson as he took a cigarette.'

'Shut up.' He struck a match.

Jackson inhaled. 'Thanks.'

'Look, Johnnie. We can take it in easy stages, see.'

'There's no easy stages out there,' said Jackson, nodding to the churned-up field.

'And I'll shift more of the dirt out of the pack.'

'I'm not wearing it.'

'You'll get yourself in dead trouble. And me,' added Simpson.

'Listen, you've done your job. I'm disobeying Tompkins, not you, so don't sweat.'

Simpson thought about it for a moment. 'He can't do anything to me, can he? I mean, you're telling him to stuff it.'

Jackson thought, how would I feel if my whole life revolved around a woman? To the point where anybody could make me do anything. Christ, he'd work in a concentration camp if that was the only way to get back to his wife. The poor bastard, what a state to be in. Hope she's worth it. No. Nobody's worth that. Simpson was anxiously waiting.

'Don't sweat. You're in the clear.'

Simpson was still anxious. 'I've got to get home.'

'You will.'

Jackson leaned against the truck enjoying his cigarette.

'Cigarette out.'

'Why?'

'The RSM's coming.'

Jackson dogged out his cigarette.

Tompkins carried a sheet of paper. He stopped and faced Jackson and switched on an unpleasant grin.

'See this?' He held it up.

It was the home leave list.

'Yes, sir.'

'And your name's on it, Jackson. Let's see. In about three months you're due for home leave. Funny. About the same time as Corporal Simpson.' Jackson nodded. 'Well then. I think you'd better do anything and everything you're told.' The unpleasant grin again. 'If not . . .'

'What?'

'Well your name will go right to the end of the list and maybe right off the list.'

Jackson said very clearly, 'I don't care if I get home leave or not.'

Tompkins stepped back a pace. 'What did you say?'

'Blackmail,' said Jackson with deep contempt. 'If the only way I can get home leave is to go out there and do a song and dance act for you, you can forget it.'

'I can stop your leave.'

'Stuff my leave. I'm not doing punishment drill.'

He's bluffing, Tompkins thought. Over four years overseas, and he's trying to kid me he don't care if he goes home or not. Then a thought. 'You got a family?'

'Yes.'

'Don't you want to see them?'

'I've managed four years without them.'

'You got a girl back home?'

'Had a string of them. Some may still be around.'

'Well then,' grinned Tompkins. 'You'll want to see them.'

'There's girls here.'

Tompkins stopped grinning. He couldn't figure Jackson out. Nobody in the army would turn down home leave except this stupid bastard.

He's backing down, Jackson thought. Think I've got him on the run.

Another idea came to Tompkins. The last thing he wanted to do was face the Major. How could he tell him that Jackson was refusing his punishment? What kind of a bloody fool would the Major think he was. He glanced at his watch. He won't be around just yet if I know him, the drunken old fool, but I'll have a word in his earhole. He's about the only one Jackson will listen to.

'Corporal, keep him busy cleaning his kit.'

'Yes, sir.'

'I'll be back.' Tompkins marched away.

RSM Tompkins came back another couple of times and each time Jackson noted that he was in a state of indecision. The booming voice sounded confident, but the eyes couldn't focus on anything for long. He was in the middle somewhere and he knew it.

'Just drill him,' he said the first time. 'Drill him for an hour.' Then a pause. 'No pack, no rifle,' and he marched away again.

So Jackson drilled, if that was what it could laughingly be called. He walked up and down on the tank-track-rutted village green. He didn't mind it. It didn't hurt. But he wasn't going to do full pack punishment drill, not even for Jesus Christ.

Tompkins returned again, still acting authoritative and shouting a bit. 'We'll see about you, Jackson. We'll see!' But his voice somehow wasn't convincing and his eyes were even more shifty.

Should have called his bluff a long time ago, Jackson thought. But then I didn't have much to call his bluff on. He was feeling pleased with himself and at the same time nervous about the outcome of it all. They probably would foul up his home leave and this thought got him feeling mad and vicious, but cancelled home leave or not – no field punishment drill. No bastard was going to put him through that again.

After the walking about drill it was 'Get him to clean his kit.' Tompkins must be running out of ideas. Then, 'Parade with the guard,' and after, 'Cookhouse fatigues.'

At Simpson's earnest request, Jackson opened his tin of blanco and placed his brushes near at hand in case the RSM returned, and Simpson kept a lookout while Jackson relaxed and smoked cigarettes and Simpson talked about his wife. Again Jackson found it strange that this basically decent man would do just about anything to any human being, if it would in any way interfere with his ten-days' leave of which Simpson obviously intended spending as much time as possible in bed with her. He had always been reticent about his wife. Now he opened up to Jackson and even used the word fuck twice. Jackson had never heard him swear before. Simpson had been quite prepared to half cripple him on orders, and now here he was treating him like a brother and to Jackson's amazement, he found he still couldn't help liking him. There was something bloody queer about their relationship that he didn't like and didn't understand.

He expected Sergeant Leadbetter to sadistically enjoy his present predicament. Instead old Leadbetter gave him a quiet talking to.

'You've got fourteen days to weather, lad. They won't be easy but just do what I tell you and do it best you can. No shirking and try and put a cheerful face on it.' Jackson started scouring out some pots and pans while Leadbetter was talking to him.

'I won't be hard on you. You're a bloody young fool, of course, and probably always will be, but they ain't giving you a square deal and I bloody know it, and if they think

I'm staying here to bloody midnight keeping you busy, they'd better think again. And that bleedin' full pack punishment drill, that ain't right and in front of women and kids. No call for that.' He was gruff and fatherly, much to Jackson's surprise. Not that he was too well up on the father scene. His father, the poor old sod, had never found the time to be fatherly. He was too scared of Mum for one thing.

Around nine o'clock, when Jackson was finishing scrubbing the mess tables, supervised by Leadbetter – 'when you've finished that you can 'op it' – Lieutenant Dare entered, reasonably sober. He politely and correctly asked permission to speak to the prisoner alone, and Leadbetter threw up a salute and left them.

They sat down at a table and Dare gave him a cigarette, then looked thoughtful.

'My experience has been you can't beat the army, Johnnie.'

'Full pack punishment drill.'

Dare nodded. 'You're on a good wicket there. It's abolished.'

Jackson was glad about that and showed it with a quick smile. 'And Cobbey was AWOL.'

'He really is a damn fool.' Dare was frowning. 'It's a bloody disgraceful state of affairs. If he had any brains he would have scrubbed round the whole stupid, bloody business. What are you going to do?'

'Tompkins threatened to cancel my home leave if I didn't obey orders.'

'Blackmail. God, they really are a bright pair.' A flicker of a smile. 'They deserve each other. Want my advice, for what it's worth? Soldier on. Obey orders, then complain after.'

'What good would that do?'

'You could request to see the Area Commander.'

'And what would happen?'

'What should happen is that the Area Commander investigates the whole stupid business and, at the very least, Cobbey would get one hell of a rocket up his arse.'

'And if I can't get to him, or if I do and he does nothing?'

'That, I suppose, depends on the Area Commander.'

Jackson thought for a moment, then said, 'There's one real problem. The punishment drill. I did forty minutes and I know I can't take it.' Was Dare looking somewhat disappointed in him, Jackson wondered. 'I mean it, Tony. On that churned-up ground there's no way to keep balance, to pace your steps, and with full pack I can't physically do it. Forty minutes and I was knackered and I mean knackered.' Was Dare still looking doubtful? 'I did a spell of detention in the Suez Area. Three hours' drill every day, bar Sunday, and humping rocks in the afternoon or digging bloody great holes and filling them in again. A hundred and ten, twenty in the shade if you could find it and I came out fit, no complaints. But that track out there. I can't do it. Simple as that.' Jackson wanted to convince Dare that he wasn't a quitter, and he knew that he was feeling sorry for himself, then that passed to anger. Why the hell couldn't Dare understand a simple thing like that? 'I know my capabilities. I've tested them. I can't bloody do it and I'm not going to let those bastards cripple me.'

Dare looked convinced. 'I'll tell Tompkins the good news. He'll have to haul you up in front of the old man.'

Jackson grinned. 'I'm sweating to know what his reaction will be.'

Major Cobbey stared at Jackson.

'When I give orders I expect them to be obeyed. You deserve the punishment and you will carry it out to the letter.'

He's not saying anything, Jackson thought. Just reeling off all the old army bullshit.

'Request a court martial, sir.'

'Request?' Cobbey's eyes turned stormy. 'Did I hear you right? You accepted my punishment and now you request . . .'

'Yes, sir.'

'Are you really a damn fool? I gave you a light sentence. Only fourteen days. If you take a court martial, know what will happen? They will have to give you a sentence to fit the crime. You accepted my punishment. Now you will carry it out. That's all.'

RSM Tompkins bellowed, 'About turn, double!'

'Full pack punishment drill is abolished. Your punishment is out of date. I think the court martial will take that into account.'

Tompkins roaring, 'I said double!'

Cobbey waved him to silence. 'One last thing I have to say to you, Jackson. Apart from the charge AWOL, others will have to be added. Disobeying orders, for one. That's very serious. In the army you obey orders and complain afterwards and if I think you have a serious complaint then naturally I will pass it on to the Area Commander. I know him well. He's a very fair man. Do you understand me?'

'No, sir.'

'I think I speak the King's English.'

'I accepted your punishment, but I'm not doing full pack drill. It's abolished. You know it, I know it. The other punishments I accept.'

'You accept!' Cobbey was shouting.

'I'll do it, but not full pack. I'll chance a court martial instead.'

Cobbey had risen from his chair. Now he slowly sat down again. His face flushed.

'Jackson, I think I've had about enough of you. You will do your punishment, then I'm posting you out to another company. Sergeant Major.'

'Sir.'

'Jackson will do his punishment, but not the full pack drill.'

'Not the pack drill, sir. Understand, sir.'

'You should have known it was abolished. I take a poor view of that. Double him out.'

The Sergeant watched Jackson pile his kit outside the front door of a large, rather grim-looking house. He had hardly spoken to Jackson all the way on the drive from the OC's office. Private billets, thought Jackson. Sleep in a bed and sheets for a change. Can't be bad.

'What's Eindhoven like, Sarge?'

'All right, but we won't be here long.'

'Oh?'

Clearly the Sergeant wasn't going to enlarge on his statement.

'I'm a driver but I can't drive.' He scowled. 'You went off to a flying start. That didn't go down with the old man.'

'I always believe in telling the truth,' smiled Jackson. 'Better than wrecking a truck and explaining why afterwards.' He looked up at the large grim house.

'That's a good billet.' The Sergeant was grinning. 'You'll feel at home there.' He got back into the truck and drove away.

Jackson pressed his finger on a bell and then waited. Presently the door opened and Jackson automatically smiled. She was small and dainty and wore a scarf on her head and a pinafore down to just above her knees and she held a broom. She returned the smile.

'Come in, love.'

A husky voice. Hardly any make-up. A little dark shadow on her eyelids. Very pretty. A slight, was it a cockney accent? Funny that.

'Let me help you with your pack.'

I'm dreaming, thought Jackson. There's one laid on in the billet for me. Couldn't be better. He struggled with his kit-bag and found himself behind her nice little rounded bum. That's funny. She was wearing very short, cut-down Army Tropical shorts. Funny. Then he took another look at her. Just a minute. She isn't a girl. I don't think. She's . . .

She interrupted his thoughts.

'They call me Rosie and I think you look a bit of all right.' She fluttered her eyelashes.

'Who do I report to?' Jackson felt weak.

Rosie nodded to a door at the end of the hall. 'Report to Sarge. Come on.'

He followed Rosie down the hall, leaving his kit in an untidy heap by the door. Rosie knocked on the door, opened it, winked. 'In you go, luv.'

A hairy-chested, heavily muscled man lay on a bed, dressed in none too clean underpants. A bottle of booze and a tin mug on the bedside table. He stared at Jackson and looked disgusted.

'Gawd. Here's another one.'

'Eh?'

'Another bleedin' fairy.'

'Where?' inquired Jackson, looking about him.

'You!' roared the Sergeant.

'Me?' Jackson laughed. 'Honest, Sarge, you're safe with me.'

The Sergeant studied Jackson, screwing up his face. 'Then why the bleedin' hell did they send you here?'

'Why did they send you?'

He sat up on the bed and poured a drink into the tin mug.

'The Sarn Major put me in charge of this lot. The lousy bastard. I got pissed out of me mind in the mess and told him his fortune.'

'Bit careless that. What's wrong with this place? Apart from Rosie. She had me fooled for a minute.'

'There's thirteen of them. Bleedin' thirteen. A new bleedin' intake of rejects, posted in from Gawd knows where.' A long, still highly suspicious look. 'That's why I thought you was another.'

Jackson started laughing again.

'It ain't funny. What's yer name?'

'Jackson.'

'Okay, Jackson. Me name's Brown. Like a drink? There's a glass over there.'

Jackson picked up a dirty glass, washed it and poured himself a generous helping of gin. He was about to sit on the edge of the bed, then changed his mind. He didn't want Brown to revert to his original impression of him.

'Thanks.' He took a drink, then moved back to the wash-stand basin and added water, then sat on a chair and waited.

Brown was looking moody as he stared into his tin mug. 'They've put me on the booze. I don't mind confessing I can't take this mob.'

'Must be a bit of a strain.' Jackson was still grinning.

'Now where shall I billet you?'

'You'd better give that some thought.'

'I'd never have believed it.' Brown stared earnestly at Jackson. 'I knew there was queers. Stands to reason. Reckoned some blokes I knew were. But when you get thirteen, bleedin' thirteen all together, prancing around, twittering away, wagging their arses, and listen to their chat.' He breathed heavily. 'It takes some bleedin' believing, it does.'

'I bet.' Give him sympathetic smile. 'Not bad this gin.'

'There's a big room on the top floor you can have.'

'Okay.'

'When you go to kip, shove the wardrobe against the door.'

'No need for that, Sarge. I can beat them off.'

'It ain't them,' roared Brown. 'It's the bleedin' guards!'

'Eh?'

'The guards. This mob goes out at nights and comes back with the bleedin' guards.'

Jackson was startled. 'Are you joking?'

'Wait till you see the bleedin' goings on. That you wouldn't believe, the screaming and the rest of it. I lock myself in and I ain't kidding.'

Jackson looked at the sweaty, hairy Sergeant, and thought, if he locks himself in, wow! Things must be dicey.

'What do the guards want with this lot? Isn't there any local talent in town?'

'Eh?'

'Girls.'

'They want free booze and a quid or two. Some of these

queers are loaded with money. That's all I can make of it.'

'What time does the party usually start?'

'When the pubs shut. Round eleven. By midnight the house is shaking.'

'I'll be back before then.'

'And lock yourself in.'

'I will,' agreed Jackson.

He returned to the billet at ten-thirty, made his way to his room. No key to the door so he manhandled the wardrobe and covered the door with it. He noted how heavy it was and thought, even the guards will have a job trying to break that down.

It was a comfortable room with a large bed, fitted carpet, a dressing table with a mirror and two side mirrors. He read for a short time, then placed the book on the bedside table, switched out the light and snuggled down in the clean sheets and easily and effortlessly fell asleep.

As he passed from sleep to awareness, the noises outside the door increased in volume. Heavy boots slamming on the stairs, hysterical laughter, a deep voice, a scream. A radio somewhere was turned on full blast, dance music. Then over it a loud voice shouting, 'I'll kick the shit out of you!' A door slammed. Then another. Jackson sat up in bed and nervously lit a cigarette. Drunken laughter, then heavy boots on the stairs and someone pounding on his door. 'Who's in there? Open up. Come on. Who's in there?'

Jackson thought, now I know how little Red Riding Hood felt.

Another voice. 'Door's locked, Bert. I'll break it down.'

Sound of wood splitting as a heavy body hurled itself at the door. The wardrobe shaking but holding up.

Jackson climbed out of bed, searching for something heavy. He found a poker. If anybody tries anything on me, I'll beat his bloody brains in.

A voice. 'Must be a wardrobe in the way, the crafty bastard.'

'I'm gonna bash another one, Bert.'

'Aw, leave it.' Then the voice raised. 'Be back for you sometime, don't fret.'

'I've gotta find another one to bash, Bert.'

Heavy boots on the stairs going away.

Jackson waiting, shivering. Wow! And they pay for it. They ought to be on danger money. He moved about the room. Then the house was silent again. He got back into bed. Good wardrobe. Thank God old Sarge tipped me off.

He awakened again from a crazy dream and then realized it hadn't been all a dream. Those boots pounding up the stairs. House quiet. Good. Now he remembered it was Sunday. Would there be a parade? Nobody had said anything about it. Forget it. He turned over. The sheets felt damp. Must have been sweating. Go back to sleep.

A light tapping on the door.

'Who's that?'

'Rosie?'

'What do you want?'

'I want to use the mirror.'

'Piss off.'

'But we always use the mirror.'

'I said, piss off.'

'Now, be nice.'

'I want to sleep.'

A giggle. 'I didn't much.'

'Come back later.'

Jackson dozed off and when he awakened it was almost midday. Missed breakfast. He climbed out of bed, had a strip-down wash, then moved the wardrobe back to its original position. Should be safe now. He got back into bed. Luxury. A bed, sheets. Luxury. Take the day off.

The door cautiously opened and Rosie entered. 'So you're awake.'

He . . . she looked fresh and wide awake and when she smiled she dimpled. She was wearing a hairnet and carried a make-up bag.

'They didn't beat you up then?'

A giggle. 'I never struggle, but some do get a bit stroppie.' She sat at the dressing table. 'Do you mind?'

'No.'

Rosie opened the bag and placed jars on the dressing table and began applying cream. Patting it on her fresh schoolgirl complexion. 'I hope you weren't bothered.'

Jackson was watching Rosie, fascinated. It was like being with a girl. No girl could be more feminine . . . well . . . appear to be more feminine. Every gesture. That flawless skin. There had been plenty of queers in NAAFI, but nothing quite like Rosie. She was way out on her own.

Rosie interrupted his thought. 'You don't talk much, do you, luv?'

'I'm listening.'

'You look a bit shook up. Didn't your Mum ever tell you the facts of life?'

'My old Mum would have to be put away if she ever learned there were people like you around,' grinned Jackson.

'Poor old thing. Well then, that's better.' Rosie finished rubbing the cream into her face and now patted cream under her chin. 'It's simple. Some are and some aren't. Haven't you ever tried it?'

'No thanks.'

Rosie giggled. 'I like you, I really do.'

'How do you get away with it?'

'What, luv?'

'Christ, you use make-up and everything.'

'Only recently and if something doesn't happen soon, I'm going into drag. They can't do it to me.'

'What are you talking about?'

'I've been in safe billets all through the war, waiting on the officers. Down base, of course, or working in the canteen or something. Then I'm posted to this lot. Should have gone for a conchie from the start but, you know, I couldn't. Couldn't stand up to them and say, look at me, luv, can't you see what I am, darling? I mean,' Rosie giggled again. 'How daft can you get calling me up for a soldier?'

'Makes sense.'

Rosie's voice indignant now. 'So they post me to this mob and any day now we're going up the front.'

'What?' Jackson sat up in bed.

'Didn't you know? So I'm camping it up all I can. What use would I be up there?'

Rosie's voice carried on and on protesting about how daft it was to send her up the front, but Jackson was hardly listening. So that's the game, he was thinking. So Cobbey's posted me to a company that's going to see action. And the bloody war is almost over.

Rosie was still talking. 'So we all decided to get together and really camp it and poor old Sarge is almost doing his nut. He's going to report us all. Just what we want him to do. He's going to have us all up in front of the Major and he's terrible. He wants everybody up in the front line. We call him Willie-Win-the-War, and I'm going to put on a real show for him, all of us are. We aren't going up the front.'

Jackson started thinking again. Willie-Win-the-War wow!

Jackson could feel his knees trembling as he faced Major Hanson, who wore a very tough expression. He was leaning back in his chair, looking impatient.

'Why do you want to see me?'

'Well . . .' Jackson hesitated.

'Spit it out.'

'I understand the company is going up the front line, sir.'

'What's so bloody strange about that?'

'I'm excused.'

'You're what?'

'Excused the front, sir.'

Hanson looked at the Sergeant Major. 'What's this bloody fool talking about?'

'Sounds to me like he's one of the dodgy boys.'

Hanson glared at Jackson. 'It won't wash. Soon there'll be one last drive. Final push, then it's Berlin. I want to be there and you'll be there.'

As Hanson was speaking, Jackson was fumbling with the breast pocket of his battle blouse. He produced his AB64, opened it on the magic page and placed it on the desk in front of Hanson, who picked it up, glanced at it indifferently, then threw it back across the desk to Jackson. 'I don't know anything about this.'

'But I do, sir.'

'We're hauling up tanks to the front and you'll be with us.' He grinned at the Sergeant Major.

'No, sir.'

Hanson stood up and roared. 'What! You arguing with me?'

That good old reckless feeling coming to the rescue again, and Jackson welcomed it. The war nearly over and he thinks he can bulldoze me into going into action, does he. His knees had stopped trembling.

'Not arguing, sir. Just stating a fact.'

'You do as I say.'

'A Medical Board . . .'

'I don't give a shit. You're going up front.'

'Forget it.' Jackson relaxed.

'What?' Hanson's eyes were mean, narrow slits.

'Request to be posted back to my old company.'

A grin. 'Forget it.'

'Then you'd better put me on a charge.'

Hanson glanced at the Sergeant Major, who was breathing heavily through his nose. 'That won't be difficult. Refusing to obey orders, for a start.'

'Refuse your punishment.'

Hanson sat down, then leaned forward over the desk, picked up Jackson's AB64, read it again, and threw it back on the desk. 'Want a court martial, do you?'

'Yes.'

'Yes, sir! Yes, sir!' shouted the Sergeant Major.

'Yes, sir.'

'You can have it and I'll be glad to see you go inside.'

'You won't be around, sir. You'll be up the front. Or, no, you won't. You'll have to hang on down here because you'll be the star witness.'

Jackson could see that Hanson hadn't thought of that and he was giving it some thought. Rub it in.

'And, sir, I'll win because all I'm doing is sticking up for my rights and I'm entitled to do that. It says in my AB-64 . . .'

'Base duty, you snivelling . . . I'm not wasting time on you.

Sergeant Major, return him to his company.'

'I'll do that, sir.'

'Anybody else?'

'Another thirteen outside, sir. Sergeant Brown's charging them with immoral practices in the billet, sir.'

'What were they up to?'

The Sergeant Major almost choked. 'Buggery, sir. They're all fairies and they've been having it off with the guards.'

'No,' said Hanson. 'Nobody in my company.'

'The new intake. Even got lipstick and stuff on their chops.'

Hanson was up on his feet shouting again. 'What a dirty bloody way to try and get out of action. Take 'em away. Scrub 'em and give them the shittiest jobs you can find. I'm not seeing them. I'm not pressing charges. You shut Brown up, understand? They're all going up the front! And you!' He glared at Jackson, who was now convinced he was quite insane. 'Get out. Pack your kit. I'm getting rid of you!'

The Area Commander was a full Colonel. Pink face, white moustache, and he struck Jackson as being incredibly stupid. Major Cobbey, trying to sound detached, as a good Commanding Officer should be, but not succeeding too well, had recited, at some length, the terrible things that Jackson had been up to. And judging by his expression, it really did not add up to very much. It did not sound half as awful when recited out loud as it must have sounded in his head when he had gone over Jackson's crimes, mainly against himself, before sending for the Area Commander and putting Jackson on the mat. The AWOL charge was about the only solid crime and Jackson had already been punished for that.

But the Colonel was giving Major Cobbey a sympathetic ear.

'Seems extraordinary. You post the chap to another company and in three days the chap's back here.'

'Yes, sir, and once before he was posted to another company. That was before my time, but it's in his record, and the same thing happened, sir. He was quickly posted back again. Obviously, sir, he must give the impression that he's absolutely useless, so they send him back.'

'Does seem extraordinary.' The Colonel glancing at Jackson. 'How does it happen, eh?'

'The first time, sir, they wanted me to drive an articulator-truck, and I couldn't handle it.'

'He didn't try,' growled Cobbey.

'Second time, sir, the company was being posted up front and I'm excused front line action, sir.'

'Extraordinary.' The Colonel turning to Cobbey. 'Y'know, I can't make head or tail of this chap. I'm rather convinced he's stark staring bonkers.'

A cunning look fleeting in and out of Jackson's eyes. 'If you don't mind, sir, I resent that remark. I know my father's in an asylum. Has been for fifteen years, but our doctor assured me it doesn't run in the family.'

'I think he's lying,' said Cobbey, in bitter anger.

'See what I mean,' said the Colonel, looking well pleased with himself. 'Think I've put my finger on it.' Tapping his head. 'Hasn't got all his chairs. Think I'll see if I can get through to him. Now look here, Jameson.'

'Jackson, sir.'

'As I said, now look here. You've obviously proved yourself to be rather a problem and we don't allow that in the army, y'know. Chaps do as they're told. Smartly and on the order. Absolutely no other way round it and you will do exactly that. We'll have no nonsense. Won't stand for any. Give you my word. Now you jolly well soldier on and don't give us any more trouble.'

'That's all I want to do, sir,' said Jackson, with his burning honesty look. 'Do my duty, sir. Soldier on, get on with the war, sir, and get it over with.'

'Oh, Christ,' Cobbey softly moaned.

'Then in future don't bugger up your good intentions. Well, that's about it, Jameson. Exactly what I was saying. Can't imagine why you interrupted me.'

'I didn't mean to, sir.'

'He's doing it again. All right, then. Jolly well soldier on, and let's have no more nonsense.' Turning to Cobbey. 'Think he'll be all right now. Can see you have a problem, though. Think I put my finger right on it. Chap hasn't got all his chairs.'

Chapter XVI

Dusty driving with blissful smile. Jackson tense in his seat next to him. Watching for snipers. They had just crossed the border and were in Germany, and Jackson was thinking they seem peaceful enough – old men, women and children clearing away the rubble. We made a bloody mess of this place. Then he remembered the letter. He had kept it all of four years.

It had been in a popular basement bar and restaurant in Piccadilly Circus with Edwardian decor, where everyone seemed to gather. British, Canadian, all ranks, no one barred, unless horribly drunk and wanting to smash up the place. It was there he had met Eli and her mother just before Christmas in 1939. He had started a party, gathering people from other tables, who joined him, and a small group of his friends, and soon more tables were lined up as more people joined them and he found himself seated next to Eli and her mother and Eli was pretty and charming and her mother sophisticated and charming. And, after the party, they had taken him to their flat overlooking Regents Park and he had been introduced to Eli's stepfather, very correct, very English and then he had discovered that Eli and her mother were German.

Eli's stepfather had been in business in Hamburg and soon Jackson was a friend of the family. They practically adopted him and he spent all his spare time with them until he was posted to France. He was in private billets in Croydon, so it was easy to get up to town.

On his return from France – he had continued to write to them – he spent his leave as their guest at Cookham on Thames, and another leave before he had been posted to the Middle East. On this occasion Eli's stepfather had given him a letter and asked him, if he ever got to Hamburg, to deliver the letter personally to Herr Strauss. Jackson had agreed to do it. The family had been very good to him. He had sometimes been curious and wondered what was inside the letter, but had not opened it. Eli's stepfather had assured him it was only a business letter but very important. So all the years, all the four years he had kept it. Maybe now he would get to Hamburg. He would do his best to get there anyway, and deliver it personally. He owed it to them.

Dusty was muttering to himself and grinning and Jackson looked out of the window again. Keeping a sharp eye out for snipers. The war was miles away, but if he knew anything about Germans, they were not going to allow the English, Yanks and Ruskies to sail through their Fatherland without some kind of protest.

Dusty laughed, 'Monty's done it again.'

'Done what?'

'Gone through them like a dose of salts like he did in Libya.'

'He didn't,' smiled Jackson.

' 'Course he did.'

'I should know,' lied Jackson. 'I was his batman.'

'You was?' Dusty's eyes opened wide. 'Monty's my hero.'

'Not mine.'

'He's my hero. Tell me about him, Johnnie.'

'You mean when I was his batman?'

'Yes. When you was his batman.'

'Well. He couldn't keep a batman. He was always finding fault and they kept coming and going, so finally they sent me to him and I must say he was trouble.'

'Where was this?'

'El-Alamein. Not long before the battle.'

'He did it there,' cackled Dusty. 'Went through them like a dose of salts.'

Jackson ignored the interruption. 'Just before the battle and there were Generals and staff officers all over his caravan and waiting outside it all spiffed up and looking smart and Monty was in his old baggy pants and his beret smothered in cap badges and I was kept busy making cups of tea. No booze and no smokes.'

'Very strict was Monty,' beamed Dusty. 'He's my hero.'

'And there was the map on the wall of the caravan with different coloured little flags stuck all over it.'

Dusty got so excited he nearly ran off the road.

'Careful, you silly bastard!' shouted Jackson.

'The battle plan for El-Alamein. Soon as you said that I knew what it was. It was the battle plan.'

'You're brilliant. It was, Dusty. It was the battle plan and Monty kept bashing away at it with his swagger cane – and here are the tanks, and here are the Australians and here are the New Zealanders and here are the Jocks. I'm sending them in bagpipes playing, and here are the rest of the British forces and here and here, of course, back here the artillery, a thousand guns, gentlemen, I say, Jackson, this tea is absolutely foul.'

'Did he say that, Johnnie?'

'He always said that except one day when I pissed in it and that was the only time he didn't complain.'

'You didn't?'

'Who's telling this story? So I brewed up some more tea and there he was still ranting and banging away on the map with his swagger cane and all the generals and that lot were being very respectful and saying, "I say really, that's a pretty sharp pincer movement . . . and that's rather a good stroke . . . catch them with their pants down there, I rather imagine." And then Monty said, in a sort of gloating way, "This time we're going to hit the Hun for six," and then when they began filing out, still listening to Monty, of course, he said, "The guns go off tonight with a big bang and I'm going to give it to them for twenty-four hours, then we go in and this time we win," and as he was leaving he turned to me and said, "Jackson, you really do make a foul cup of tea".'

'Johnnie, I never would have told you, but you do. You make bloody horrible tea. He's my hero, you know.'

'I know, but I was making good tea for him. It was the best. Twinings. The Prince of Wales blend, which I'd wan-

gled out of NAAFI and I was heating the pot first and all
that because I didn't want Monty to go into battle without a
good cup of tea under his belt, so I got mad with him. Really
mad, so I went to the map and I started moving the little
flags around.'

Dusty held his breath. 'What happened?'

'That was it.'

'That was what?'

'That was the battle of El-Alamein.'

'You mean . . . do you mean, Johnnie, that Monty didn't
come back and give you a rollocking and change the flags
back to where they were?'

'He came back.'

'Then what?'

'Looked at the map and kept saying, brilliant, never been
a battle like it before. Never be a battle like it again. Brilliant.
They won't know what's hit them.'

'Then you mean . . . you mean it was you, you, Johnnie,
you won the battle of El-Alamein?'

'That's right.'

'Then he didn't win it.'

'No.'

'You did.'

'Yes.'

'Then, Johnnie, that makes you my hero, don't it?'

'Yes,' said Jackson. 'Don't forget to keep your eyes open
for snipers.'

The convoy drove over the Bailey bridge and Jackson looked
down at the sunken ships in the harbour, then they were
over the bridge and in Hamburg and the convoy came to a
halt. Jackson got out of the cab of the truck and looked
about him. Then he moved to the back of the truck and got
his small pack and walked to the cab of the truck and
climbed in and opened his small pack and found the letter.
He had taken good care of it. It was wrinkled but comparatively clean. He found a pen, paper and uncensored envelope
and he wrote on the paper:

Dear George,
   I am in Hamburg and I cannot find it. I return your letter.
                    Regards,
                    Johnnie

   'Musso hanging upside down, fancy that,' said Dusty, keeping his eyes on the truck ahead of him.
   'Fancy that,' smiled Jackson. 'Was he one of your heroes?'
   Dusty simpered. 'He looked funny, didn't he? That hat. His girl was hanging upside down next to him. Fancy that.'
   'Yes. Just fancy that.'
   'In the picture she had black knickers.'
   'Well, it was a bloody newspaper picture.'
   'They could've been blue, Johnnie.'
   'Fancy that,' grinned Jackson.
   'Upside down showing her knickers.'
   'It wasn't her idea, Dusty.'
   'Might have been red.'
   'Or pink.'
   'He loved her, didn't he?'
   'Died bravely.'
   'Wonder if he did?'
   'The papers didn't say he didn't.'
   'Like you would've died, Johnnie. Bravely.'
   'Of course.'
   'I wouldn't.'
   'I've been trying to tell you you're brilliant.'
   'You're joking.'
   'No. You know how to die.'
   'I've thought about it, Johnnie. Specially after I've been to the flicks. You know, Clark Gable, Bogart, Cagney and them.'
   'Go out screaming.'
   'Screaming and shooting, eh?'
   'Shitting your pants, Dusty, and screaming for another chance.'
   'Musso didn't go that way.'
   'How did he go?'
   'Upside down.'

'You are a bloody genius, Dusty.'
'With his girl . . .'
'With black knickers.'
'Might have been green.'
'They were purple.'
'How do you know, Johnnie?'
'The Pope blessed them.'
'He wouldn't.'
'He did.'
A giggle. 'Can't be a bad old Pope. Bet they were black.'
Jackson yawned. 'Where are we?'
'Germany.' Then a side glance and a grin. 'And I ain't seen no snipers.'
'Know why?'
'Why?'
'Because there aren't any.'
'Didn't I tell you?'
'They've quit,' said Jackson, making himself comfortable. 'You know the war's over.'
'It ain't.'
'Yes, it is. I'm not scared any more. Wake me up when we get there.'
'Where?'
'How the hell do I know where? Somewhere. The next place. Wake me up.'
'When we get there you'll wake yourself up.'
'Why?'
'Because when we get there you'll know we're there.'
'Jesus. You are a bloody genius.'

It was another village, but this time it wasn't a school, it was a mill and a few girls were working the looms, and they showed a giggling interest when the soldiers moved into a spacious room and peered in at them and started whistling them up.

Jackson inspected the girls and decided two weren't bad. He had taken over a one-time office now unfurnished just off the main working area, and Paddy and Dusty had moved in with him, and they all agreed things didn't look too bad.

As the girls left the mill, Paddy was waiting outside. It had meant missing tea, but still. He grinned as Jackson joined him, winked and pointed.

'I know,' said Jackson. 'The skinny one for you. Come on.'

They caught up with the two girls, one on each side of them.

'Do yer speak English now?' inquired Paddy.

Giggles.

'You do or you don't.'

More giggles.

'Do you booze it up?'

Frantic giggles.

'Do you fuck?'

The girls stopped giggling.

'British Tommy's been here before us. They understood that,' smiled Jackson.

'Grub?' said Paddy, moving his hands to his mouth as though shovelling coal into a stove.

The girls looked serious.

'You eat. You drink. We fuck,' said Paddy.

'He's Don Juan,' said Jackson to the plump blonde.

'Do you or don't you, me dears?' demanded Paddy.

'I'll translate,' said Jackson. He spoke slowly, 'Do you eat and do you fuck?'

'Eat,' said the skinny girl.

'If they eat, they fuck,' said Paddy.

'But where's the grub?'

A knowing wink from Paddy. 'I can fix the cook.'

'Not Leadbetter.'

'You crazy now? It's the queer little fellow who's working for him now.'

'How can you fix him?'

'Never you mind,' grinned Paddy.

The girls seemingly couldn't stop eating the Spam and bully beef and tinned potatoes and peas, so Paddy loaded them up with a few more tins and the girls knew where they could get some whiskey from a farmer. He had his own still and it was instant brew and the roughest whiskey even Paddy had ever tasted and cost them forty cigarettes, and then they staggered back to the mill and made up beds, and Jackson helped the blonde to undress with drunken, shivering fingers and then, for how long he had no idea, he tried to get into her and couldn't. There was nothing wrong with him, yet he couldn't get into her and finally he fell into an exhausted, drunken sleep, still wondering why he couldn't get into her. When he woke she wasn't there, and yet she was. She was working one of the looms and all the girls working the looms were glancing his way and giggling.

Paddy awakened and discovered that he was alone, then he saw the skinny girl working another loom.

'How did you work out, Paddy?' inquired Jackson, hung-over and eye-weary in his bed.

Paddy gave him a cautious grin and the thumbs up sign.

'I didn't,' groaned Jackson. 'I couldn't get in.'

A moment of shock on Paddy's face. 'Jesus, and I couldn't . . .'

They discussed it at some length, both puzzled. Then, naked, got out of bed and faced the laughter and got dressed and began folding their blankets, then Jackson found a very small rubber ball in the blankets. He stared at it, puzzled, then he understood the secret of the plump blonde's chastity, and so did Paddy. They both grinned hungover grins, then Jackson bounced the small rubber ball to the plump blonde. 'Better hang on to this, darling, you may be needing it for some other innocents.'

The blonde caught the ball and laughed and looked as if she liked Jackson.

He had one leg and he used crutches. He was in his middle forties. A handsome man. He owned the mill and lived in a large modern house on the edge of the village. He spoke almost perfect English and had been wounded outside Leningrad, an ex-Major of an Infantry company. His name was Werner and he was strongly attracted to Jackson, who did not suspect that he was a latent homosexual. Werner had dread suspicions that possibly he was, but refused to face it.

Jackson was invited to the house. It was forbidden, of

course, to visit with or associate with Germans, not that anyone took it too seriously. It was a splendid house and Jackson noticed that Werner smoked cigarette butts that he picked up on the streets. On the first visit Jackson watched Werner roll the cigarette butts. He kept them in a silver box. He presented Werner with a packet of Players and it was interesting to watch his eyes light up as he accepted the gift.

Werner had two sisters. Lotte was aged thirty-five and plain. She also spoke almost perfect English. She was intelligent and helped to run the mill. Magda was blonde and beautiful, widowed and aged thirty. Before the war she had travelled extensively and was an ardent name dropper. She had met many famous people in the arts and politics during her travels. She was not only beautiful but also charming and witty. Jackson was in some awe of her and of course she knew it and it amused her. She accepted Jackson's cigarettes gracefully, but apart from the farmer's still – the crude instant whiskey – there was nothing to drink in the village except beer and it was so weak, about half per cent proof, that about the only effect it had was to flush the kidneys.

Jackson decided that he really needed something stronger to relax him and give him courage when he was in Magda's company, and Werner, by sheer chance, or so it seemed, made this possible. He casually mentioned that there was a distillery nearby that sold double corn whiskey, but it was for officers only. This set Jackson thinking. He badly wanted to impress Magda. More, he wanted to get into bed with her. How? The answer came to him. He gave it a great deal of thought before putting the plan into operation.

Getting into Major Cobbey's office was quite simple. A window was open. Typing the letter with one finger was more difficult, but he finally achieved it.

> The bearer of this note is
> entitled to fifty gallons of whiskey
> for the officers of 213 RASC Company,
> attached to GHQ Allied Command. This
> is not a request but an order.

Jackson then printed 'AMGOT' and just below that he

signed it 'Bernard Montgomery, General'. Then he found a stamp and blurred it over the signature.

He knew that Dare was going through a frightening dry spell. Should he let him in on it? He really had the shakes and was almost incapacitated. The poor old devil. Since the whiskey was for officers only, he really needed an officer to go along with him, and who was better than thirsty Dare.

'You're crazy,' snarled Dare. 'My God, if anyone twigged . . .' His hands were restless and he had a twitch in his left eye. 'War will be over almost any day now and then I get my damn bowler hat and all the damn whiskey I want.'

'Supposed to be rationed in England.'

'I'll damn well find it, Johnnie.'

'If you last that long.'

'Don't bloody well tell me something I'm only too bloody aware of,' yelled Dare. 'Christ, do you know the officer's ration?'

'One bottle whiskey or gin per fortnight,' intoned Jackson.

'Doesn't even touch the spot,' growled Dare. 'Just when the old body starts feeling normal, the bloody bottle's empty.'

'Well, if you want to chance it . . .'

'Isn't there some other damn way? God, I hate to turn down such a golden opportunity, but I simply can't afford to be involved.'

'Military Police on the gate guarding the damn place.'

'Of course, the stuff's more precious than gold dust, isn't it?'

'May need a travel/work ticket to get past them.'

'Ah, Johnnie, now there I may be useful. But my damn name won't be on it.'

Jackson stared at Dare's battle blouse hanging over the back of a chair.

'If I were an officer, less problems with the MPs at the gate.'

Dare looked at his battle blouse. 'Should be a reasonably good fit.'

'Brown shoes. What size do you take?'

'Nine.'

'I take eight and a half, so that's no problem.'

'God, Johnnie, if you're caught.'

'I pinched your kit, didn't I?'

'Of course I wouldn't be such a damn fool as to loan it to you, would I?'

'Of course not,' grinned Jackson.

Dare was worried. 'Johnnie, if you're rumbled, your feet won't touch, y'know that. You'll be in the can for an awfully long time. Do you honestly think it's worth it?'

Jackson grinned. 'If you could see her, you wouldn't ask that question.'

'She really must be something else and seven eights.'

'She is.'

'But fifty gallons. Isn't that pushing your luck?'

'I'll only be able to make the one trip.'

'Well, good luck, but don't whine to me if you come a cropper.'

Jackson nodded and picked up Dare's battle dress and tried it on. It was a good fit. The hat was a little large, so he stuffed strips of paper in the lining.

'And I'm in for a couple of gallons, right, Johnnie?'

'And you can refill at Werner's when you've got through that,' smiled Jackson.

'Good,' beamed Dare.

Jackson borrowed two milk churns from the farmer who owned the still, and stole a case of empty beer bottles from the canteen. And that night he and Paddy loaded the churns and bottles into a truck and the next morning Paddy picked him up just outside the village and Jackson, changed into Dare's battle dress, tied a tie about his neck and placed the slightly too large hat on his head and they drove to the distillery.

To Jackson's relief, there was no problem with the Military Police at the gate. A face peered into the cab of the truck, then moved back, a salute, which Jackson casually returned, the gate was opened and they drove into the distillery.

Jackson got out of the cab and waved his papers under

the nose of the owner or manager, who read the paper and then stared at Jackson, who decided on the spur of the moment that shouting was probably the best line to take.

'Hurry it up will you. I haven't got all day. We're giving a party tonight for the American GHQ lot and I've got to damn well get back and make all the arrangements.'

'AMGOT, sir?'

'Of course, AMGOT.'

Now the German started shouting and very quickly the milk churns were filled with whiskey and Jackson paid and found to his delight and surprise that the cost of the whiskey was about the equivalent of fifty cigarettes on the black market.

They drove away happily, and outside the village, Jackson demoted himself, and then they deposited the milk churns in Werner's living-room and Dare called with his own empty whiskey bottles and they all got very drunk, except Magda.

The booze should last a long while. He knew he could never go back for more. That piece of bumph with AMGOT and Montgomery's signature on it would have to land on a desk somewhere and cause raised eyebrows.

Magda was always charming and smiling and she would smoke his cigarettes and drink his whiskey and flirt a little, but she would only drink so much, then she would excuse herself and go to bed.

Jackson knew what the problem was. He should have been a colonel at least, then things would have been different.

Werner and he were always left at the end of the hard-drinking night. Werner would sit at the grand piano and sing. He had a fine tenor voice and he sang sentimental German songs. Jackson liked him, but a lot of the time when Werner was singing his mind was elsewhere. He wanted to make love to his sister. He thought that if he put the pressure on her he might come out a winner. He not only kept them supplied with cigarettes and whiskey, but with Paddy's help he was supplying them with food from the cookhouse. He would think about putting the pressure on her, but somehow he couldn't.

Werner told him about Leningrad, where he had been frost-bitten, starved, and finally wounded and luckily evacuated.

'Johnnie, before the siege, there were about three and a half million people in the city, at the end there were less than a million.'

The numbers didn't make any kind of sense to Jackson.

'More than the Americans have lost since they became a nation,' said Werner, who was an historian as well as a mill owner.

'You mean more than they have lost this war?'

'This war, and the First World War, all the wars they have fought. More Ruskies died in Leningrad than all of the Americans.'

It didn't make sense. 'And Germans?'

A shrug. 'We killed more Russians, but they killed plenty of us. We are thinned out.'

'Think you'll make a comeback, Werner?'

A smile. 'Watch us, Johnnie. We will not always be picking up cigarette ends from the gutters.'

'Fuck you,' grinned Jackson.

'You should love us, Johnnie. Us Germans. Who else understands you English?'

'Something wrong with your sense of humour.'

'Now you are going to point out what we did to the Jews.'

'Something like that.'

A shrug. 'There always have to be scapegoats. Hitler was determined to build a new Germany.'

'And now it's destroyed.'

'And it will awaken again.'

'Fuck all your Germans. You're trouble.'

'I like the English, Johnnie.'

'Not the Russians?'

Werner laughed. 'Fuck them.'

'What will happen?'

'No one can be sure, but I think the Russians will try and break us, the Americans will pay us, and help build up our nation again, and you English will make us feel guilty. Then you will be liberal and of course, in time, do business with us again.'

Jackson couldn't quite believe it. He knew he was pretty dim when it came to politics. He seldom read the papers or listened to the news. He hadn't even heard about Hamburg being destroyed.

'When it's over, what will happen to your leaders?'

A cynical smile. 'There will be a moral judgement and all the people in the western world will heap abuse on the terrible Germans. But we almost had the bomb.'

'What bomb?'

'The heavy water bomb.'

It rang a bell somewhere in Jackson's head. There was a raid on Norway someplace. He hadn't been too interested at the time and there were the rockets of course, landing on England.

'What about the bomb?'

A faraway look in Werner's eyes. 'It would have made all the difference.'

Jackson was getting bored with the conversation. 'Magda went to bed early again.'

Werner helped himself to one of Jackson's cigarettes, then poured himself a drink and smiled.

'People who are kind seldom win.'

Chapter XVII

Tompkins stopped him and smiled unpleasantly, yet Jackson suspected that he was attempting to be friendly.

'Well, well, if it ain't young Jackson.'

What's he want?

'What's your job then?'

How could he tell him he was in the ranks of the unemployed? Apart from keeping Werner and family in booze and cigarettes and the odd tins of grub that Paddy scrounged from the assistant cook.

'Well, sir, I'm sort of in transit.'

Tompkins tut-tutted. 'Can do better than that, can't we, Jackson.'

A gleam in the eyes. 'I hope so.'

'Now, let me see. Osnabruck.'

'Ah.' The gleam in the eyes brightening.

'Been there, Jackson?'

'No transport, sir.'

'Suppose you pay a visit with a reliable driver who I'll appoint. Yes, suppose you go.'

'Yes, sir. I'll need money.'

'Sergeants' mess funds in good order, Jackson.'

'Can't wait, sir.'

'Thought you'd catch on. No bleedin' fun and games now.'

Cameras, thought Jackson. Gold watches, diamond rings, beautiful girls. Wow! With a straight face, 'I can't afford another slip-up, sir.'

'Tomorrow morning. Report to the Sergeants' mess ten hundred hours.'

The reliable driver turned out to be the foxy-eyed Bell. Why was it everyone trusted him? You only had to look at his slack grin to know he wasn't reliable. But Jackson was in high spirits, so could afford to put up with Bell's company.

Werner had given him all the gen on the black market scene. Twenty cigarettes sold for the equivalent of five pounds sterling. It really made you whistle. Coffee – what a chance for the Yanks – was also incredibly expensive. Cameras, gold rings, diamonds. That was the stuff to collect.

They had to make a detour and then drive over a Bailey bridge. Jackson looked at the original bridge. A good fifty feet of the centre had been blown. He stared down at the roaring river below, then they were back on the main road.

An hour later they were in bomb-damaged Osnabruck. They parked outside the NAAFI Bulk Issue Store and with hope in his heart, Jackson entered the building. He scanned the faces behind the long counter with growing disappointment. Not a familiar face in sight. He moved along the counter. They were doing a brisk business. He looked longingly at the goods on display. The booze. The cigarettes. The tinned foods. Christ, there was a fortune here if he could only get his hands on it.

He tapped on a door and pushed it open. A Sergeant Major was seated behind a desk rustling papers, adding figures. Jackson instantly recognized him. He never had liked him much, but that didn't matter. Last time he had seen him he had been a Sergeant. Sergeant Pilgrim. Now he's a Sergeant Major.

Pilgrim looked blank for a moment, then recognition dawned.

'Remember me?' grinned Jackson.

Pilgrim had been in charge of the men's canteen in Benghazi. Oh, Christ, there had been a punch-up and the canteen had been closed on Captain Blacks' orders, and Pilgrim had got a bloody nose out of it. Never mind. I don't have to remind him of that night. Let's hope he's forgotten.

'Jackson. Yes, I remember you. What do you want?'

It was no great welcome. 'I'm stationed not far from here. It's good to see you.' Jackson now remembered that Pilgrim was queer. Well, who cares, I've never worried about anyone's politics.

'You were thrown out of NAAFI, weren't you?' The pursed lips. Femme hand gesture and so bloody ugly. Face like a death mask. Who could bed it down? Well, never mind.

'I didn't see eye to eye with the management,' smiled Jackson. 'It really is good to see you.'

'I'm very busy.'

'We've been on the move constantly for a month and haven't been able to draw our rations anywhere.'

'Put your order in in the usual way and you'll get what you're entitled to. If you can prove it. You know that as well as I do.'

'Can you let me have some extra stuff under the old pals' act?'

'We never were exactly the best of friends, were we, Jackson.'

'Now, come on,' smiled Jackson.

'I haven't forgotten Benghazi and that awful riot.'

'I didn't start it.'

'My impression was you did.'

'It was Meadows and Ted Abbot.'

'I think my memory is better than yours.'

'Honestly, I remember it well. But let's forget it. Can you help me out?'

'You're asking me to do something illegal, aren't you?'

'I'm asking you to help me.'

'So you can sell it on the black market.' A sniff. 'Think I don't know. Now. I'm very busy. Put your order through the normal channels.'

'So you won't help me?'

'No.'

Jackson knew he hadn't got a hope in hell with Pilgrim. The miserable bastard. He wouldn't give a man dying of thirst a glass of water. He also knew he was an ace fiddler. With a mean look in his eyes, Jackson said, 'So you won't let me have anything?'

'For the last time, no.'

Now a mean grin. 'I bet you're looking after the Hitler Youth mob, aren't you, darling? All those lovely blond boys.'

It was almost a female squeak. 'You get out of here, Jackson.' Pilgrim was shaking. 'I don't have to listen to your dirty talk and scandal.'

Jackson surveyed him for a long moment, enjoying his discomfort, then he left, slamming the door behind him.

One glance and Bell knew it was bad news. His friendly expression turned sour.

Jackson walked back to the truck.

'Now what?'

They were standing by the truck. 'Now what, what?' jeered Jackson, disliking Bell more than ever.

'Tompkins won't like it.' A snide grin on Bell's face now. 'He's not going to be any too bloody pleased with you, Jackson.'

A corporal and a private were loading cases on a truck parked next to them. The corporal was saying, 'What say we go to the Ratskellar and have a couple of pints, eh, Tom?'

'You took the words right out of me mouth, Charlie.'

They both laughed.

'Where's that?' inquired Jackson.

'The Ratskellar? It's the NAAFI joint. The only good beer in town.'

'Like to show us the way?'

'Yeah, you can follow.'

Jackson climbed into the cab and they followed close behind the other truck.

Bell said, 'Maybe you've got a reprieve.'

'Think I'm not praying.'

'If there's no one there you know, it's the rope for you, Jackson.'

The Ratskellar was jammed with happy beery soldiers. Pint bottles and mugs on all the tables.

Jackson pushed his way through the crowd at the bar, then he saw Weaver. A mutual look of delight and a hand came over the bar. 'Jackson.'

'Weaver.' Wow! God is good.

The last time Jackson had seen Weaver, well, almost the last time, was in Tobruk. Weaver lying on his bed repeating over and over, 'I'm on strike for better pay and better conditions' and finally Captain Morris had ordered Sergeant Dunne to throw a bucket of water over him and for a few moments Weaver hadn't moved. Just gasped and gone rigid. Then shook himself like a dog and said reproachfully, 'You didn't have to do that,' and then lay back and closed his eyes again and repeated, 'I'm on strike for better pay and better conditions.' Trying to work his ticket or out of his screaming mind, or both, and they had sent him to the crazy farm, and now here he was, a bright smiling Weaver. Just like his old self. The way he had been before nine months in Tobruk and Sergeant Weaver now. That was even better news.

'I've got someone with me, Bob.'

'Bring him along.'

Jackson beckoned to Bell and walked behind the counter

and followed Weaver into his office-cum-bedroom. Two beds, an office desk, a few sticks of furniture. Jackson introduced Bell, who was wearing his friendly expression again.

The door was closed and bottles of beer were opened. Weaver was taking the day off.

This is the way it should be, thought Jackson, when two old friends meet after a long absence. Good old Weaver. Always one of the best.

Jackson told him his adventures since he had been thrown out of NAAFI and they both laughed a lot. Then Weaver told his adventures. In the crazy house he had met a sympathetic Major who had put him through all the puzzle games and tests, rested him and finally returned him to NAAFI and duty.

'I had some trouble with some of the bloody idiots when I got back,' he confessed. 'The billet Sergeant Major, who'd taken over from old Dodds, for one. So I finally showed him my papers and said, look this is proof. I'm sane. It's signed by a Colonel of a hospital and six doctors. It says I'm sane. Where's your bloody document?'

They switched to whiskey and it was night before they knew it. They were all very drunk. Bell, worried drunk, kept saying, 'Better get back. Tompkins won't half give it to us.'

Weaver and Jackson, happy drunk, were getting sick of him and either ignored him or told him to shut up.

Around ten o'clock Bell lurched to his feet. 'Gotta get back. I'm going. You gonna load up the truck, I'm going.'

Another half-hour of argument, then cases of beer were loaded on the truck and Bell was groping his way to the driver's seat.

Weaver, a fond arm around Jackson's shoulder, 'You've gotta come back now, now don't forget, you've gotta. Long time no see. You come back now. Next trip see about the whiskey, gin and smokes. You come back now.'

The truck driving away and a voice fading, 'You come back now.'

Bell driving and Jackson thinking, come back. I'll be

back, try and keep me away, and next time he's laying on the girls. Good old Weaver. What a pal. His eyes closed. He began to doze. A bump, then another bump. It was hard to focus at first, then it slowly dawned on him Bell was driving on the pavement. Won't do, Jackson thought. Just won't do. 'You're driving on the pavement.'

Bell's voice, thick, 'Know what I'm doing.'

'No.' That's not logical, thought Jackson. No. He doesn't know what he's doing. 'Get off the pavement.'

'Know what I'm doing.' Bell swerved off the pavement.

'And keep on the right side of road.'

'Why don't you shut it.'

'Only telling you.'

'I'm driving.'

'Then drive on right side of road for Cris's sake.'

They were back on the pavement again.

'Bell, you're pissed.'

'Shut it.'

'I'll drive.'

'You? You?' Bell started laughing. 'You drive?'

'Me.'

'Don't make me laugh.'

'Still on the pavement, Bell. Get off the pavement.'

'I said, shut it!'

Jackson kicked Bell's boot off the gas pedal and pulled hard on the hand brake. The truck swerved and rocked a bit then finally stopped.

'Out!' shouted Jackson.

'You telling me ...'

'Out, prick.'

Jackson opened the door and pushed Bell out of the cab, then clumsily got into the driving seat. 'Get in.'

'I'll do you over!' In the dimmed headlights Bell's mouth an ugly gash, his eyes drunken and somewhat demented.

'You couldn't even swat a fly. Get in.' Maybe I should do him over, thought Jackson. Golden opportunity. I owe it to him. But he couldn't work up enough energy.

Bell stumbled to the cab door and climbed in.

Jackson drove the truck off the pavement, back on to the

road and away. A long silence, then Bell said, 'Maybe I am pissed.'

'Pissed out of your mind.'

'Had a skinful. Oh, had a skin.' Bell belched and fell asleep.

Jackson drove on, concentrating on the road, forcing himself to stay awake. Hardly any traffic, thank God. He came to with a start. Did I doze off? Blinking and rubbing his eyes. Must stay awake. The next thing he knew he was driving on the grass verge. He swung back on to the road again. Drove on for a while, wanted a cigarette. Tapped his pockets. Out of cigarettes. No good, can't stay awake. Pull in side of road and sleep it off.

When the truck stopped Bell woke up. 'What's up then?'

'Can't stay awake.'

'Gotta get back.'

'How?'

'Drive. I'll drive.' Bell didn't move.

'My foot you'll drive.'

'Can't make it, Johnnie, eh?'

'Can't make it is right.' Jackson was staring at the dim outline of a farmhouse. It was in darkness. 'Let's wake 'em up.'

'Who?'

'Them.'

'Who's them?'

'Bloody Germans.'

'Don't be daft.'

'Kip in a bed.'

'You're crazy.'

'Won't sleep in the cab.'

Jackson started the engine and slowly drove to the farmhouse and parked the truck.

'Now what, Johnnie?'

'Knock 'em up.'

'They won't like it.'

'We've got some beer.'

'Now steady now. You watch it. Tompkins . . .'

'Who's going to miss a case of beer? Come on.' He

approached the front door and banged on it. 'Open up! Amgot! Amgot!' I'll show them, he thought, as he waited. No noise from the house. Again he banged on the door. 'Open up! Amgot! Amgot! Police!'

A light appeared in one of the rooms and presently the door cautiously opened and an unshaved face peered at them.

'Sleep,' said Jackson as he pushed open the door. 'Sleep. Bell, bring in a case of beer.'

The German farmer was frightened and cringing.

'Beer!' shouted Jackson. 'Beer. Wow. Beer very good. Plenty beer, my old friend. Got to sleep. Understand?'

He was now in the main living-room and found the best armchair and made himself comfortable, and the farmer didn't know what was happening but wasn't saying anything, simply looking at Jackson and smiling and cringing a bit and probably wanting to kill him.

'Friend!' shouted Jackson. 'You my good friend!'

Bell staggered in with a case of beer, grinning foolishly. 'Beer. Like beer?'

'Beer very good!' Jackson shouted. 'We get pissed, friend. Open up some bottles!' He was still shouting but now at Bell, who couldn't wait to get the bottles open. He handed the first one to the farmer, who drank doubtfully, then greedily, then looked happy.

'Beer!' thundered Jackson.

'Beer!' yelled the farmer.

'English beer!' howled Jackson.

'English beer!' gloated the farmer and he finished it fast.

'German beer, piss!' thundered Jackson.

'Peace,' agreed the farmer.

'Another,' yelled Jackson, who was suddenly wide awake again. 'Give the Hun another beer.'

The Hun didn't have to be told. He had picked up the bottle opener and was tipping back another bottle.

'Drink to England!' yelled Jackson, who suddenly felt patriotic, for a change.

'England!' yelled the German farmer and tipped the bottle again.

'Germany!' thundered Jackson, toasting the farmer with his bottle.

'Where, sir?' Seemingly, the farmer hadn't followed Jackson's English.

'Right here. This is Germany.'

'Kaput,' shuddered the farmer and drank again.

'Get the family up,' demanded Jackson, but he was too late. Two young, pink-faced girls, looking frightened, were hovering about the open doorway. A tank of a woman wearing a cotton sleeping cap roughly pushed past them and started shouting at the farmer:

Jackson pressed a bottle of beer in her hand. She drank, stopped shouting at the farmer and smiled. Red apple cheeks and a gigantic belly.

'I love you, darling,' shouted Jackson, and put his arms around all of her and gave her a smacking kiss. 'Bring the tinned grub!' he yelled at Bell. 'Move!' He knew he should have been a general.

Bell moved and staggered back to the truck.

Jackson kissed the first girl, then the second girl and opened more bottles of beer. He felt like a millionaire.

'We will eat!' he thundered. 'Bully and Spam and spuds. Have you got spuds?'

No one understood.

Bell returned with some tins of Spam and bully beef and the tank lady got busy at the stove and the farmer was slapping Jackson on the back and Jackson was telling the girls that he was going to fuck them.

'Both together!' he said pleasantly. 'Never mind the weather.'

No one seemed to understand, or care.

More bottles were opened and the room seemed to be filling up with people, mostly middle-aged men, no girls. Two young men, one looked amused, the other angry, but he managed a smile every time Jackson handed him a beer.

The tank lady made dinner and there were spuds and delicious gravy.

'England,' the farmer kept toasting and winking at everybody and drinking like a fish.

'Germany,' Jackson always replied.

The girls giggled every time Jackson spoke to them.

Bell was kept busy hauling in the beer.

Jackson was concentrating on the farmer and reasoning, get old Dad to like me and he won't feel so bad when I fuck his daughters. I'll sort of be like one of the family. It made sense to him.

'You my friend,' he said with total drunken insincerity. 'You my good friend.'

'You my comrade,' said the farmer with a drunken smile.

'Bloody communist,' snarled Jackson.

'No!' roared the farmer. 'Fascist!'

'That's better,' said Jackson, calming down. 'At least you aren't giving me any shit.'

They embraced, then an accordion began to squeeze and fart and Jackson danced with the tank lady, thinking, get in with the old girl and she won't feel so badly when I fuck her daughters. It made sense. Then he danced with one daughter and then with the other and it was the other he found he was holding tighter and pushing up against more fiercely. So she was the one he was going to fuck. It all made sense.

Bell had fallen asleep in a chair so the guests were looking after the beer.

Decent lot, thought Jackson. He knew he was too drunk to carry the beer in.

Then everyone left except, of course, the tank lady and the old farmer and their daughters.

'Show me to my bed,' demanded Jackson of the girl he had been pushing up against the hardest. 'I'm going to give you some good old roast beef of old England.'

She led him to a bedroom and he pushed her on the bed and fell on it. Then she wasn't there. Funny girl, she was laughing and going under the bed, so he fell off the bed and crawled after her and then she was on top of the bed and when he fell on it, meaning to fall on her, she wasn't there, so he fell off the bed again and crawled after her under the bed and there she was again laughing on the bed. Funny girl, and when he fell on the bed again she wasn't there, so he fell off the bed and went under the bed and she was on the bed, under the bed, on the bed, under . . . and that was that.

When he woke up something inside his head was screaming at him and someone, he thought, was hitting him on the head with a hammer and he didn't feel very good. He turned, moaning, and was confronted with a hairy face and a lolling red tongue and it was a dog, paws over the sheets, grinning at him. Jackson wondered if he should check its sex but couldn't be bothered.

No sounds in the house. Nothing moving except Jackson's guts, so he found the place and took care of that. Then he found Bell and woke him up and then they left the house and found the truck parked further away than Jackson believed he had parked it. Then they discovered that there was no beer in the truck, not even a case, not even a bottle. Two mouths hanging open staring into the back of the truck. Then they stared at each other, and the first reaction was anger. Cheated, conned, robbed, taken. But Jackson could not retain his anger. He wasn't feeling like a general this morning. In fact, he wasn't feeling like anything. Muttering about what they would do to those bloody square heads, but the courage of last night had dissipated into a nervous hangover. They got into the truck and drove away.

They came to the detour, the forgotten detour, and they looked at each other and both realized at the same moment that if they hadn't got drunk and stayed overnight at the farmhouse they would, without a doubt, have missed the detour sign and driven over the original bridge and plunged down far below into the roaring river. They said it together, 'Christ!' Then grins swept over their white faces and somehow RSM Tompkins was less to be feared than he had been a moment ago.

But he had to be faced and he looked horrible. His face red as a beetroot, veins standing out on his forehead, eyes astonished, belligerent, and black with anger in turn. His voice as loud as the roaring river but somewhat incoherent. 'Not possible . . . no, no . . . pinched, no flogged, you mean . . . yes, that's it . . .' a howl. 'You bleedin' flogged it, don't tell me . . . yes, you two, and you Bell, you . . . bleedin' Bell . . . I trusted you . . . yes . . .' a scream. 'The mess funds! The mess . . . Bell . . . I hand picked you . . . this bleedin' abortion . . . this one . . . Jackson . . . He's only the bleedin' afterbirth . . . we all know that . . . but you Bell . . . trusted . . . yes . . . you two now . . . feet won't touch . . . no . . . I'll have you both . . . yes . . .'

He reeled off all the endless charges and although Jackson's stomach was practically turning over with fear, he had time to note that Bell's face had turned. It was, really was green, and he was on the point of blubbering.

Then Tompkins' voice came to a choking halt and Jackson noted that he seemed to have run out of steam and looked lost.

Jackson's hungover brain began to function. Not too well, but it was turning over. The missing mess funds. How would Tompkins explain that and to whom? To Major Cobbey? 'Sir, I sent Jackson to Osnabruck to – er – the NAAFI Bulk Issue Store, sir, to er, get some, er . . .'

'What! You did what?'

He could hardly do that, could he?

Jackson found the answer. 'Let me go back and load up again . . .'

Now Tompkins bellowed, 'What!'

'And I'll pay. It's all on me.'

Jackson, with some regret, saw that he had probably saved Tompkins' sanity.

'And this time,' yelled Tompkins, 'with a reliable driver!'

'Yes, yes,' agreed Jackson. 'Yes, of course.'

Christ, he had got Sergeant Leadbetter!

'I'll do the driving,' said Sergeant Leadbetter. 'You load, you pay, then we come right back. That's the drill.'

'Yes, Sarge,' said the limp Jackson.

They crossed the Bailey bridge and again Jackson looked at the destroyed bridge and this time he shuddered, but he didn't bother to mention it to Sergeant Leadbetter. Somehow he didn't think he would get much sympathy.

The Ratskellar wasn't quite so busy. Weaver's outstretched hand and delighted grin and not too much of a hangover by the look of him. What did they call him? Old iron guts. Behind the counter again and into the office-cum-bedroom and the first bottle of beer opened and another day off for Weaver.

'No, lad,' smiled Leadbetter. 'Jackson's not on the booze today. Just load up the truck and we're off.'

Jackson's eyes on the bottle of beer. A couple of those could only help. The opened bottle advanced towards him, it was second nature to Jackson to grab it.

'Good luck, Johnnie.'

'Gug, gug, gug.'

'No,' protested Leadbetter. 'No boozing. You heard what I said, Jackson. Put that bottle down.'

It hadn't left Jackson's lips. It was going down, bottle tilting, eyes on Weaver. He could see that Weaver didn't believe a word Leadbetter was saying.

A bottle was thrust into Leadbetter's hand. 'No boozing,' he said firmly, placing the bottle on the table.

'No boozing,' grinned Weaver. 'No booze.'

'Eh?'

'Jackson's my pal.'

'The RSM says to me, get the truck loaded and come straight back.'

'No,' said Weaver. 'Your RSM don't pay my wages. We have a few drinks, then we talk.'

'No,' protested Leadbetter.

'No beer, then.'

A silence as Leadbetter stared at Weaver. Then he said, 'Lad, do it my way, will you. There's all hell to pay right now. Load us up.'

'Gug, gug, gug.' Jackson stared at his almost empty bottle. He was wisely keeping out of the discussion.

'Okay,' smiled Weaver. 'I'll load the truck. How much do you want?'

'How much you got, Jackson?'

Before Jackson could reply, Weaver interrupted, 'What do you mean, how much has he got?'

'He's paying.'

'Johnnie paying?'

'I lost the last lot,' confessed Jackson.

Weaver laughed. 'You always were careless.' Then, turning to Leadbetter. 'He's not paying. Now, here's the game. I'll double the load. Free.'

'You'll what?' Leadbetter couldn't believe it.

'Double. No skin off my teeth. One condition.'

'What's that?'

'You leave Johnnie here for a week.'

'Now, lad, you know that's not possible. He ain't got a leave pass for a start. Say he got picked up.'

Weaver laughed. 'I can get away with anything in this town. No need to worry about Johnnie, he'll be with me.'

'Look, we'll load up and go back right now see, then I'll have a word with the RSM and I think maybe . . .'

'No dice.'

Leadbetter looked at the bottle of beer on the table. He was fighting duty and a greedy need to pick it up.

He picked it up and took a long satisfying swig. 'Ah.'

Weaver handed Jackson another bottle.

Leadbetter went 'Ah' again, then, 'You said a double load?'

'Yes.'

Thoughtfully to himself Leadbetter muttered, 'RSM can't complain about that, can he now?'

'Shouldn't think so.'

'Ah. It's good beer, and you want him to stay on a week?'

'Yes.'

Leadbetter whistled under his breath for a moment or two.

'The RSM likes his beer, who don't, but what he likes best is a tot of whiskey. Got any Scotch?'

'Sarge,' Jackson started laughing. 'You've turned into a bloody spiv.'

Leadbetter looked guilty, for a moment, then said gruffly, 'War's as good as over, son, so don't mind relaxing a bit.' Then he looked directly at Jackson and marvelled, 'If you fell in a sewer you'd come out smelling of roses.'

They had several beers and Leadbetter, as he was leaving,

in a high good humour, said, 'Don't worry, lad. I'll fix it with Tompkins. He tangled with me once and came off second best. So don't you worry, lad.'

They waved him off and Jackson shook his head. He's set in his tracks now, he thought. He's a bloody father figure.

'There's a dance hall,' said the drunken Weaver, weaving a bit. 'And this is it and I'm the king.'

They entered and he was. The girls were all around him, laughing, flirting, touching him. 'Told you,' grinned Weaver, not even attempting to beat them off. 'I'm lover boy, king of the rats. Pick any one you want. I'm also the local Frankie Sinatra.'

He went up on stage and the band gave him a big hand and he sang. He was really terrible, being so drunk, but he hit a few good notes and some of the girls even screamed. Then he was back with Jackson, arm about his shoulders. 'Pissed. Shouldn't try it pissed. Still, never mind, eh?'

Then he danced like crazy for an hour and must have sweated out the booze because he seemed to sober up again. Then he was back on the bandstand and this time he was hitting all the notes and he was good.

The king. Jackson could hardly believe it. Old Weaver lying on a bed in Tobruk, sand happy, and look at him now. Sinatra can't be having it any better.

Leaving the bandstand and walking into the smiling German girls, Weaver said, 'Made up your mind which one?'

Jackson had. She was for him. That smile. That body. That enchanting smile. Dirty. She was his. Eyes not begging. That enchanting, dirty grin. She was the one.

They made their way back to the darkened Ratskellar.

Weaver was a good chef and there was whiskey and gin and, God, champagne. How the hell had he ever learned to be such a good cook? And Weaver made it clear that he loved old Jackson as a real buddy. He laughed over all his jokes and almost drowned him in booze. They ate and drank and made love to the girls and didn't mind listening to the noises coming from the other bed. They were friends, couldn't be closer if they had been Siamese twins.

At dawn, Jackson awakened and looked at Inga asleep. A week of this . . . bliss. But he wasn't sure he could keep it up. Keep it up for a week. But then he didn't know Inga.

The week was incredible. Inga was insatiable and the wonder of it was she made him feel exactly the same way. She could awaken him any time. He could awaken her. There was no pretence about being in love. She was totally honest. She was surviving the only way she knew and the only way she could. But they had a genuine liking for each other. The week was eating and drinking and making love.

Chapter XVIII

For once Jackson listened to the radio. Incredible. He just couldn't believe the news. Hitler dead. It was hard to believe after all these years.

'There's still Japan, Johnnie,' said Weaver.

'Well, that's not for us, is it? The Yanks.'

'Don't know. They'll want us in on it.'

'Well, it's over. Let's celebrate. Let's have a drink.'

What was he talking about? He had a drink in his hand. That's all he'd been doing the past week and now he had to get back to his company, and about time, too. He couldn't take much more, but what a week it had been.

'Soon be in civvy street.' Was Weaver looking gloomy?

'What's wrong with that?'

'Nothing.'

'You're married, aren't you?' A grin. 'One of the few.'

'Yes, she wouldn't leave me.'

'Good for her.'

'Fuck.' Weaver lifted his glass. 'End of war, old buddy.'

'End of war.'

'She's a good wife.'

'Must be.'

'But I'm having a hell of a good time here. Never had it better.'

'You'll settle down.'

'Yeah. I've got a trade. Not badly paid, and a little box of a house in the suburbs.'

'Doesn't sound bad.'

'Work all the week, then I'm let out Saturday night for a few pints with the boys and Sunday lunchtime.'

'Wow!' Jackson grinned. 'You'll go mad with joy.'

'There'll be Mick there and Harry and Alf, Joe, Bernie, that is, if they survived. The pub serves cheese and pickled onions on the bar Sunday. Big deal, it's free.'

'If it's not bloody well rationed now.'

'Don't it sound bloody awful to you?'

'Here. Why not sign on with NAAFI again? They'll still be needing staff all over Germany and God knows where.'

'Can you imagine I'll go home and tell her that?'

'No. Suppose not. Oh, well, you'll settle down.'

'I was settled, Johnnie. Since then I've had a taste of life. I'm the bloody king here, aren't I?'

Jackson laughed. 'You bloody well are.'

'No. If I told May I was signing on again, I'd need a bucket and mop to swob up her tears. Don't think I haven't thought about it.'

How odd, Jackson thought. I've never seriously considered what I'll do when the war's over. Just prayed for it to end. But now what? No trade. No skill. Be free though. Free? Who's been freer than me recently? Who was freer than me when I was in NAAFI? And I didn't even know it. Just what the hell is freedom?

'Don't know what I'll do, Bob.'

'You'll find something.'

'Suppose so.'

'You'll get by.'

'Always managed to somehow.' Jackson thinking, if only I'd fiddled something, enough to open a business or buy a pub. But never did look to the future.

'She's a good wife but how the hell am I going to live with her?'

'Well, Bob. One for the road.'

'You're free, lucky bastard. Cheers, Johnnie.'

'Cheers.'

They drank and grinned at each other.

Jackson had said goodbye to Inga without sentiment. A long kiss, a laugh, and that was that. He was feeling more damn sentimental at parting with good old Weaver. What a friend he had been.

'You come back now.'

'I'll be back.'

'And stay.'

A grin. 'Doubt if I'll get away with that again.'

'Well, wangle something and don't forget you come and stay with me in England.'

'Of course.' And Jackson thought, wonder if she will stand for that? Something told him that maybe a boozy old wartime buddy might not be welcome.

'Come back.'

'I will. So long, Bob.'

'Don't forget now.'

They were all seated round the mess table.

'Hitler shot himself.' Dusty was smiling.

'No,' said Paddy. 'He was gassed.'

'Poisoned,' said Jackson. 'He took a bloody pill.'

'They burnt him,' grinned Dusty. 'How about that?'

'Who cares now?' Paddy glowered. 'The bloody war's over.'

A dreamy look in Simpson's eyes. 'I'll be back with my wife.'

'And some won't,' said Jackson. 'But they'll be back in one piece.'

'Bet he gave it to her first,' smirked Dusty. 'Bet Hitler gave it to her first.'

'The old Roger, Dusty?'

'The old Roger,' cackled Dusty.

'With the swastika stamped on it,' grinned Jackson.

'Goodbye cruel world. Remember this,' laughed Paddy.

'He's an old sex maniac,' smiled Jackson, nodding at Dusty.

'Dirty little bastard,' grunted Simpson.

'Never had it,' confessed Dusty. 'But when I go, that's the way I'll go.'

'Overrated,' said Leadbetter, leaning over the table. 'Now you lot get on your way, we've got to clean up.'

'I thought the bully beef was a little over-cooked, chef,' said Jackson.

'I'll over-cook you,' growled Leadbetter. 'Now the lot of you skat.'

'It's good news though, Sarge.'

'It's history, Jackson. Don't dirty it up.'

'Makes you think, though, Sarge. When you die, who the hell are you?'

'The great leader,' marvelled Paddy. 'What a way to go.'

'How would you go, Paddy?' inquired Dusty.

'Kicking the shit out of anybody who got in me way.'

Still the dreamy look in Simpson's eyes. 'Soon be back with my wife for keeps.'

It dawned on Jackson. World history toppled and all Simpson can think about is getting home to his wife. What a crazy world.

Jackson was still thinking about the war being over the next day. He just could not get it out of his mind. The war was over. It's over and I'm safe. I got through it lucky. I'm safe. No more problems. I'm alive. The last thing that Jackson would admit was his fearful dread of death. The end of cheerful smiling Johnnie Jackson. It was inconceivable. He loved life too much. It had made him a coward, but he loved just being alive and he had to see it through from the beginning to its ordered, very ordered end. A long life, of course, into the eighties, better still the nineties. How about a century? He could not bear the thought of being cheated a full life span. Now the war was over and he was safe and he had no hard feelings towards anybody. To his surprise, not even Major Cobbey. He decided that he had to see him and explain this. No good requesting an interview. He couldn't really talk to him standing at attention with RSM Tompkins breathing down his neck.

He stopped Major Cobbey as he was getting into his car.

'Sir.'

A bilious look. 'What is it?'

'The war's over, sir.'

'I'm quite aware of it. So what?'

'No hard feelings, sir.'

'What are you talking about?'

'Soon be home, sir.'

He almost stretched out his hand and said, put it there, then changed his mind when he caught Cobbey's expression, and then he realized, he's sorry. He's a regular. End of war, end of promotion. He had finally made Major. War is his career, and now what will happen to him? He's probably only Acting Major. So they'll demote him to Captain. Poor old bastard. Jackson began to feel sorry for him and it showed.

Cobbey gave Jackson a withering look and climbed into his car.

Jackson threw up a splendid salute and Cobbey automatically returned it. The car drove away.

Jackson watched it until it was out of sight, thinking, it must be rough on the old regulars. They wait year after year for promotion so that they can have some kind of pension at the end of their career. Old Cobbey hasn't had much of a life and he won't have much of a pension to look forward to. But for me life is just beginning. The war's over. Without knowing why he put his hand deep inside his trousers pocket and gripped hold of his cock and held it and thought, when this withers, then what? And wondered what he was thinking about. The deadly future was a long way away.

There was something wrong with Paddy. He sat around brooding a lot of the time. Not his usual happy-go-lucky self at all.

'What the hell is it, Paddy?'

'We had it made in Italy, Jackson, and then the bastards

transferred us to here. We were sitting on a bloody fortune.'

'And didn't know it,' agreed Jackson.

'And here we are now, the bloody Mecca, and all you can get your hands on is the bloody beer and the odd bottle of whiskey and its no price on the market at all.'

'Don't remind me.'

'And you the King Spiv.' Paddy sounded bitter. 'It's the smokes we need and the coffee and the grub and the war's over and I'll be going home broke and what the hell's the good of that.'

'And I'll be going home broke.'

'I thought you were a fella wid ambition.'

'You need the goodies.'

'Listen, Jackson, tyres fetch a good price, and I know some fellas in the market for them. Now, pinching them won't be so easy, but selling them will. How about you coming in wid me?'

Jackson thought about it, then shook his head. 'War's over, Paddy. I don't want to take the chance.'

'I always said you were a bloody coward. I'm not going home with empty pockets.' He lurched to his feet. He had been polishing off a bottle of Jackson's whiskey. There was still plenty left in Werner's house. 'I'll do it meself.'

'Think about it.'

'It don't need thinking on.'

'Tomorrow.'

'Tomorrow never comes, Jackson.'

Tomorrow came for Paddy. He was in jail. Everybody was buzzing over the news. False rumours at first, and then the truth.

Paddy stole six tyres and put them in a truck and drove to a garage in the village and dumped them off and was told to come back for the money, and when he came back there were six of them. Six rough-looking grinning Germans.

'Where's the money?'

All grinning. 'Goodbye, soldier.'

'No money?'

'Goodbye.'

'Only one thing to do so there is. Take it out of your hides. It's no problem.'

The first German got Paddy's head in his face and he floated away, blood streaming. The next got the head as well and a third got a left hook, then Paddy was down taking a kicking but he got up again. It was warming up and Paddy kept knocking them down but they were pretty rugged and came back for more and Paddy was happy. It was almost as good as money, and there was screaming going on all the time. Two of the men's women were there and they were out in the streets screaming and a Military Police Patrol drove by and had to investigate and they watched Paddy admiringly for a while before they interfered and they finally got hold of him and wanted to know what it was all about and with total honesty Paddy told them, so they had to arrest him. Paddy didn't seem to mind.

Why is everyone so interested in reading Company Orders, Jackson wondered as he pushed through the crowd. He read, Fitzroy, Patrick, 787, has escaped from the Field Punishment and Detention Holding Centre, where he has been detained awaiting a court martial. Anyone who sees him will apprehend him.

Jackson couldn't stop laughing.

The next night on his way to see Werner, Jackson was apprehended by Paddy, who came out of the darkness. 'Johnnie.'

'How did you get out?'

'Got over the wall. How else?'

He made it sound easy.

'Paddy, you were soon for home leave and demob.'

'Talking of leave, I'll need passes.'

'Passes? How am I going to . . .?'

'You can, and you will and I'll need shaving gear and me best battle dress and some travelling money as well.'

'And then what, Paddy?'

A chuckle. 'Then I'll go travelling.'

'You're crazy.'

'You'll do it for me.'

'I can't get the passes.'
'Dare.'
'He wouldn't do it, so don't be daft.'
'Then I'll look after that part of it meself. I'll need some-body else's AB64 and the leave pass will have to agree with it. That won't be so difficult.'
'Paddy, go back.'
'Be inside too long.'
'I'll get your things.'
'Then speed it up. I'll be waiting here.'
Paddy faded into the darkness.
Jackson returned in half an hour and handed a parcel to Paddy. 'Here it is, Paddy.'
'Thanks.'
'What're your plans?'
'I'll be travelling a while, then I'm going home.'
'Get out of Germany as fast as you can.'
'I've some business to do first.'
'You're a bloody fool.'
'I'll get home and I'll have enough to take care of me.'
'Tralee?'
'That should do as well as anyplace. Maybe you'll look me up after the war.'
'It's over.'
'When they demob you.'
'Look after yourself, Paddy.'
'Look me up now.'
They held hands a long while, then Paddy faded into the darkness again.
That was the last time Jackson saw Paddy.
Three weeks later he read on Company Orders that Paddy had been apprehended by the Military Police, but before they caught him he had shot and killed one Redcap and wounded two others.
He was court martialled and executed.

The train rattled on and on seemingly for ever, clattering through Germany, Holland, final destination Ostend, then a boat to England and ten days' leave. Wooden seats getting harder every minute. Jackson wanted to walk in the corridor, but it was impossible, bodies sprawled everywhere. Home for leave, but where to go? Look up Eli. Stay with her and her family for a time. Maybe her father would give him a job after the war. He had hinted that he might last time he saw him. When was that? Nineteen forty-one. So long ago. So much has happened. Well, go and see them anyway. Never know, George might give him a job. Must start thinking about the future now. All those years and he hadn't given it a thought. Well, there hadn't seemed to be a future.

'England,' said Simpson. He was bright-eyed and couldn't sleep.

'England,' said Jackson and groaned as he turned once again on the wooden seat. 'My bloody back.'

'I haven't told her I'm coming home,' Simpson confided. 'I want it to be a surprise. Can't wait to see the look in her eyes.'

England, thought Jackson. And I'm going there with Simpson. Funny old world.

Ostend was rain-drenched and the seas were stormy.

Jackson and Simpson booked into the transit camp. Wooden huts filled with bunk beds and the smell of long-travelled, unwashed bodies.

The notice read, 'No sailings today.'

Looking at the stormy sea with an anguished expression, Simpson said, 'Be calm tomorrow.'

'What about tonight?'

'What about it?'

'Let's have a look at the town.'

Simpson smiled. 'I've waited this long, I can wait another day.'

'Let's go to the NAAFI.'

Lukewarm tea, thin as cat's piss. Eggs and chips and warm beer.

'Can't take it,' said Jackson, heaving himself up from the table. 'I'm going into town.'

'Don't do anything crazy,' smiled Simpson with complete

disinterest, his eyes on the stormy sea, all his thoughts with his wife.

Jackson grunted and walked away.

Jackson found a bar run by a friendly Belgian and two girls, both pretty. He had a couple of drinks, then walked around the town, went to the cinema, and in the evening returned to the same bar. In a corner sat an RSM alone, drinking steadily. He didn't speak to anyone and Jackson took no notice of him. He was propped up on a bar stool, talking to the girls and the owner, buying them drinks and the owner bought drinks back. It was a pleasant cheerful evening and he left at midnight. The RSM was still seated in the corner drinking. Jackson returned to the transit camp and slept.

The next day was cold but the sea was calm. Jackson worked it out. His leave would not start until he reached England. He wasn't short of money, so why not have an extra day or two? What was the hurry? He liked Ostend and he was enjoying himself.

Simpson couldn't believe that Jackson was staying on an extra day or two.

'Your boarding card will be out of date, you bloody fool.'

Jackson decided to check out with the Sergeant who issued the boarding cards. Money changed hands and Jackson was issued a new boarding card.

He made his way to a café, had breakfast. Strolled round the town. Explored a few bars and in the evening returned to the friendly bar. The same RSM was seated in the same corner, steadily drinking alone. Jackson stayed on until two a.m., kissed the girls fondly goodbye, pumped the friendly owner's hand, and left.

The RSM was still seated in the corner, drinking alone.

The next day Jackson thought about it and then decided that one more day wouldn't hurt. He paid the Sergeant and got a red boarding card.

The next day blue.

The bar always welcomed him and he wasn't spending that much. The boss bought more drinks than he did.

This night was special. After the drinking and after the RSM left. It was upstairs and a game of strip poker and the boss didn't seem to be worried when Jackson won and went to bed with the laughing blonde.

The next day it was a pink card and Jackson wondered for a fleeting moment when he was finally going to get home to England. Tomorrow, he thought, without too much interest.

Drunk in the men's toilet watching the water gushing out of him, a voice behind him said, 'You seem to be here a long time.'

Jackson turned and grinned.

'It's a good bar.'

'What are you in?'

'RASC.'

No brass numbers on his battle dress.

'What company?'

'Five-o-one.'

'Canadian battle dress.'

'Better cut,' grinned Jackson, who had bought it for fifty cigarettes from a German.

'Let's see your leave pass.'

'Why?'

'I'm in the Military Police.'

Wow! Why didn't I trouble to look at his bloody cap badge, Jackson wondered.

'Here's the pass.'

The RSM examined it, couldn't fault it, handed it back. 'You're overstaying.'

'Bad weather.'

'We know better.'

Jackson's mind racing, wondering what the RSM had on him. 'What's the hurry?'

'No hurry. You're coming with me.'

'Why?'

'You'll find out.'

The RSM and two corporals, looking at Jackson, thin-lipped.

Jackson sobering up.

'501441. Funny number that.'

'NAAFI.'

'You in NAAFI?'

'No, kicked out.'

'Then why the number?'

'I was called up in the army in Egypt. National service call-up, then transferred to the army.'

'Canadian battle dress.'

'A buddy gave it to me.'

'Or you pinched it.'

'I don't give a fuck what you think. I'm going home to England.'

'I wonder.'

'What have I done wrong?'

'You stayed overnight in the café.'

'Well?'

'The boss is a well-known homosexual.'

'Fancy that,' grinned Jackson. 'The blonde certainly wasn't.'

'I'm wondering about you.'

'What about me?'

'Fucking queer.'

How many more times am I going to be accused of that, wondered Jackson. I'm getting bloody tired of it.

'Get a doctor.'

'What?' The RSM looked surprised.

'I want a physical examination. Right now, and if you're wrong, I'm pressing charges against you.'

'You watch what you say.'

'You'd better watch it. Now get the doctor.'

'You don't tell me . . .'

'You're a cunt,' said Jackson.

A corporal moved towards Jackson. The RSM waved him back.

'You're a deserter.'

'Cunt.'

'Put him in a cell.'

The corporal hovered in front of the open cell door. Jackson noticed his fists were bunched again.

'Help yourself,' said Jackson. 'And I'll have that doctor

checking me out for grievous bodily harm as well.'

The cell door slammed shut.

All Jackson's personal belongings were on the desk. The SIB Major was going through his wallet. He carefully opened a small thin paper package.

'What's this?'

'Corn.'

'Why are you carrying this about with you?'

The farmer who owned the still had wanted Jackson to get him some corn to make whiskey with. He had picked some ears, wrapped them in paper and shown them to another farmer to be sure that there was no mistake. It hadn't dawned on him that the name for corn, in Germany, was corn. Better not explain that though, Jackson thought.

'It reminds me of England,' smiled Jackson.

'What?'

'The cornfields of England.'

'Corn,' said the Major, as he spilled it over his desk. 'You've overstayed your leave.'

'Haven't even started my leave. It doesn't start until I get to England.'

'Then you're wangling a few extra days. Your boarding card for the boat expired yesterday.'

'Couldn't make it.'

'Why?'

'I was ill.'

'You were drunk in a bar last night.'

'Later on in the day I felt better.'

'You've been drunk in the bar for days.'

'That's the way it's been. Just before it's time to board the boat, I've been sick. Later in the day I seem to recover.'

'The Canadian battle dress.'

'A gift from a friend.'

'Why did he give it to you?'

'I saved his life. My leave pass is in order, isn't it?'

'I can hold it and check it with your company.'

'I wish you would do that.'

'All right, Jackson. We can keep track of you.'

'Why?'

Jackson knew that they had nothing on him.

The white cliffs of Dover and then a train to Victoria Station and no one to meet him, of course. A tour of some of his favourite pubs and then a phone call. The family were in Cookham. Another phone call and a happy voice told him the times of the trains and they would be there to meet him.

George was all friendly smiles and in the pub he insisted on buying all the drinks.

'Thanks for trying to deliver the letter, Johnnie. I knew, of course, before you got there.'

Jackson wasn't going to look stupid and say he didn't.

'It was just a bigger shambles than I imagined.'

'Terrible.' George sadly shook his head, but then hastily added, 'But that's war, I suppose.' He didn't want people to overhear him and think that he was unpatriotic.

Eli was charming, but she was treating him like a big brother and that was the last thing he needed.

She finally confessed that there was a prisoner of war in a nearby camp. She was very much in love with him and they had even, by letter, passed to and fro by one of the guards, arranged to get married as soon as possible.

'But how?'

'He'll be returned to Germany one day.'

'And then?'

'We plan to go back as soon as possible and George, of course, has many contacts in Germany.' A smile. 'Some are even known to be anti-Nazi, and anyway, Mummy has property over there.'

'It's a bit of a mess.'

'Not all of it. Anyway, we feel displaced here.' Huskily, 'Everyone's been marvellous, but, well, we're German.'

'How about George?'

'He'll come along, I suppose. Mummy and I will manage whether he does or not. His business over here isn't all that successful. He's convinced he can do better in Germany.'

Jackson was bewildered. The place a bloody shambles and George thinks he can do better over there, and Eli convinced and they're probably right.

'And er . . .'

'Hans?' Her face lighting up. 'Just fancy, he was in the same business as George before the war. George, of course, will employ him.'

End of prospects of a job. End of Eli.

Why not try Mildred? She won't be home. It's over four years, most probably married and she won't be living with her Mum, but still, she'll know where she is and give me all the news.

Mildred's Mum's voice on the phone. 'Yes, she's here, home on leave.'

'That must be nice for you, Mrs Henry,' enthused Jackson.

'Yes, it's lovely to have her home. Who shall I say . . .?'

'You remember me, don't you? Johnnie.'

'Oh, yes, yes of course, dear. How are you then?'

'I'm fine. I'm just back on leave.'

'It must be lovely for you to be home and the war over and everything.'

'Well, it's nice to be remembered.'

'Of course, so it is. What did you say your name was, dear?'

'Montague Burton.'

'Of course I remember you, Monty. How nice you're back. I'd better call her. Just a minute.'

A voice calling, 'Mildred . . . Mildred, it's a call for you. His name's . . . er . . . anyway, you'd better take it.'

'Hello.'

'Hello, Mildred.'

'Who is it calling?'

'Johnnie Jackson.'

A long pause. 'Where have you been?'

'Killing those bloody awful Germans.'

A giggle. 'Last time I saw you, you were scrounging for the NAAFI.'

'Just testing your memory.'

'Where are you?'

'In a phone box Piccadilly Underground.'

'You didn't write.'

'I lost your address.'

A pause. 'That's just like you. How long have you been home?'

'Just got in, so I thought I'd look you up in the phone book. How long will it take you to get here?'

'You could pick me up.'

'Haven't got any petrol coupons for the Rolls.'

'The trains are still running.'

'Okay. I'll be over.'

'No, there's no need to. Where shall we meet?'

'Same old place.'

'That dear old pub in Piccadilly.'

'I'll be there waiting for you, and then we'll do the town.'

'Just like old times.'

'The words out of my mouth, darling. Fantastic luck you should be on leave.'

'Isn't it? I'll be there in about an hour.'

'Marvellous.'

A pause. 'I'm glad you phoned, Johnnie.'

The line went dead.

Jackson hung up and smiled to himself. He had met her in 1939 and when he returned from France and was posted to the West Country, she had made three trips to see him. The last time they had stayed in a pub in Launceston. He had been working during the day in a canteen in a camp on the outskirts of the town, but he had the evenings off and he slept at the pub, of course, and they had a wonderful time. She was in the ATS and was a damn nice girl.

He watched her slim legs walking down the stairs, bright eyes searching. She was even prettier than he remembered. He stood up and grinned. Should he salute her, or what? She was a bloody officer now.

They shook hands but held hands quite a long while, smiling into each other's eyes.

Together, 'You haven't changed.' Then they laughed and he ordered the drinks.

It was a little difficult, though. Private soldier, lady officer. They laughed about old times and the tension of the reunion began to melt.

'Be problems, ma'am,' smiled Jackson.

'Not really.'

'Must be quite a few places Private Jackson can't take you.'

'Well . . . never mind.'

'I do.'

'What can you do?'

'Buy a suit.'

She brightened. 'Would help. But the coupons . . .'

'Buy the coupons.'

She laughed. 'You certainly haven't changed.' Then a pause. 'Before you phoned, I made a date. Well, he's an old friend.'

'Phone him and cancel.'

'He's just back, too. I'm supposed to be meeting him in the Savoy. You could come . . .'

He shook his head. 'Hardly.'

'Well . . .'

'Who is he?'

Vaguely, 'He's a Colonel. I know what. I'll go and meet him and think up something and get back as fast as I can.'

'When did you see him last?'

'Oh, about six months ago. He was in England most of the time. Went on, he said, a special mission to France six months ago. Now he's back.'

'What will you tell him?'

She smiled. 'Don't know, but I'll dream up something.'

'Hurry back.'

'Fast as I can.' A warm smile and she was gone.

She hadn't dreamed up anything, thought Jackson, as he watched her being escorted down the stairs by a spry, whippet-thin Colonel in his middle forties.

She was wearing a forced bright smile now and looking a little uncomfortable.

'Colonel Thompson . . . er . . . Johnnie Jackson.'

The Colonel nodded and ignored Jackson's outstretched hand. 'Better have a drink, don't you think?'

'Not a bad idea,' agreed Jackson. He looked at them both and wondered why people had bad memories.

'Back on leave?'

'Yes.'

Jackson got the impression that the Colonel expected him to call him sir.

The drinks arrived. The Colonel waved the waiter away.

'Let's have them again.' Then to Jackson, 'Have to knock 'em back fast before they run dry, and it takes all one's time rushing from place to place to find the next place that hasn't run dry.' A smile to Mildred. 'Unless times have changed, my dear.'

'Not much, Charles.'

'There are clubs, of course.' A knowing look. 'Ah, but . . . pity, can't take you along, can we?' Staring at Jackson's totally undecorated battle dress. 'You understand.'

'No,' smiled Jackson.

'Other ranks, I mean. Those places are out of bounds.'

Mildred looking more uncomfortable.

'Not this time,' smiled Jackson.

'I'm sorry?'

'Your memory.' Jackson shook his head, then turned to Mildred. 'And yours.'

They both looked puzzled.

'Tell you a little story,' said Jackson, finishing his drink as the next one was placed in front of him.

'There was a nice little pub in the country. Summer 1940. And a private and ATS bint were staying there and so was a Captain, and the Captain was awfully jolly and friendly with the private and used to have drinks and chat away . . .'

Mildred and the Colonel looking at each other, now showing slight embarrassment.

'Finally, ATS bint had to return to London. By some strange coincidence, gallant Captain had to go to London that very same day. Wouldn't it be rather jollier if he drove her in his little MG sports. Of course, why not? Private soldier waved them off. Place Launceston. Time, August. The pub, the Swan.'

Mildred pink-faced and eyes lowered.

The Colonel gave an embarrassed laugh. 'Moment I saw you, I thought, seen that chap before, but y' know, one meets so many people. You really have a jolly good memory.'

It had totally registered with Mildred, of course, and he could see by her expression exactly how she felt – why doesn't the ground just open and swallow me up.

First round to me, thought Jackson, as he looked at them both. They were finding it hard to look at him and even at each other. I've drawn first blood and soon I'll have the bloody Colonel on the run. Then the insult really registered. He had no claims on Mildred. He had not forgotten her address, just hadn't written. It hadn't been all that import-ant. But he had remembered the pub, the time, the place, the bed they had slept in, made love in, and the one-time Captain, now Colonel, who he had known all along had only been sucking up to him because he wanted to have it off with Mildred.

And he had thought he hadn't even a hope in hell.

And he had got into her knickers as easy as that.

And they've been seeing each other ever since.

And she had been really delighted to see him again. In her eyes, her expression, the way she touched his hand before she left to get rid of the Colonel, and couldn't, or didn't want to manage it.

But the real insult. She had forgotten. Forgotten where and when and the place of their love-making.

Hurt pride. Too damn right.

And he felt like a bloody fool.

He finished his drink, dropped a pound note on the table, stood up. 'Have fun.' And walked away.

Mildred caught up with him at the top of the stairs. 'Johnnie?'

'Yes?'

'Darling, I'm sorry. I feel such a bloody fool. I just forgot.'

'I know. Isn't that what I've been saying?'

'Look, I'm sure Charles will understand. He feels pretty uncomfortable as it is. He will understand. I don't even have to tell him . . .'

'Good old Charles,' mocked Jackson.

'Just wait here. I won't be long.'

'Change of plans,' said Jackson. 'I'm going to spend the rest of my leave in the West Country.' He walked away.

She called after him. 'Johnnie, Johnnie . . .'

He walked on.

Chapter XIX

Four years and eight months since he had first met Madge. Give a week or two, in this very pub. Nothing changed. Only time. Wonder how she looks. At least she'll bloody well remember me. Enough crazy letters passed between us until a year ago, no a year and a half ago. Christ, more than two years ago. What happened to time? He had stopped writing when he had fallen in love with Cristie. Surprised to find it still hurt. Hadn't thought of her in a long time, but it could still stab him. The ones that do the rejecting are the ones who stay in my mind.

Madge had finally rejected him.

'Being posted overseas?'

'Yes.'

'How long, do you think?'

'No idea.'

'Oh.'

And he had been thinking, I'm asking you to wait for me. I don't know how long it will be. I want you to wait. He wanted to know that there would be at least one person thinking about him, writing to him, loving him.

He picked up his pint of beer, drank, and smiled wryly. I was young, just a kid, and I thought I had it made. Charming Johnnie could get anything he wanted, yet screaming for security, for love. Afraid of dying and no one caring.

Getting maudlin, he confessed to himself.

And Madge had been thinking, I do love him but don't know that I trust him and then he'll be away years and what am I supposed to do, and his prospects, well, they're not too good. Dad took a liking to him, offered him the management of the other shop if he came back and we got married. Managing dad's shop, and he didn't turn it down. Where's his ambition? Another pint, thought Jackson, then I'd better go in search of her. Surprise, surprise. Then the wry grin again. Surprise for who?

A voice. 'Know you, don't I?'

Jackson turned. A big red-faced farmer. It took a moment or two to place him. A pal of Madge's dad. Had a few pints with him in the past.

'Johnnie Jackson.'

'Ah.' A sly smile. 'Chap from Lunnon. What yew doing these ways?'

'On leave.'

'It's been a long time now.'

'Four years.' Remembered his name. 'Harry, have a drink?'

They never refused. Open their purse and moths flew out.

'Why you's back then, boy?'

'Thought I'd take a look at the old place.'

'Ah.'

'How's Madge?'

Mouth shut like a trap. Then, 'We's ain't talkin', Madge and me.'

'Why's that?'

Jackson watched the pint he had just bought Harry disappear down his throat. The mug slammed on the counter. 'The Frog officer. A gennelman. The Pole, drunk us all unner the table. A nigger. No boy.'

Jackson watched his broad back as he walked out of the bar.

She was in the cocktail bar of the one good hotel in the village. She was alone, seated at a table. He stared at her. She hadn't noticed him as he walked in. She was reading a magazine, a drink in front of her. He got the impression that she was waiting for someone.

When he ordered his drink, she looked up. Complete total surprise. He smiled, waved, picked up his drink and sat down at her table, facing her as if it were yesterday.

It took her some time to recover.

'Well . . .'

'Hello.'

'Well, I never.' Then a quick flashing smile. 'Won any more medals?'

He roared with laughter and she joined in. 'I've kept it. It always gives me a laugh.'

He laughed again, but he wished she hadn't mentioned it. It was one of the most phoney, drunken stunts he had ever pulled and he wanted to be taken seriously.

'Why are you back?'

'I wanted to see you.'

'Now . . .' She was warning him.

'Why else would I come back?'

He knew she would have to give that some thought.

'This is my first leave home since I last saw you. I could have spent it in London.'

He still found her very attractive.

'I'm expected to take that as a compliment?'

Her voice was soft, the West Country burr still lingered, but less than before. He remembered that she was a snob. She would like to associate with the gentry, but her father was a small tradesman. Impossible. So she was displaced. He found himself feeling sorry for her.

'You still want to get away from here?'

'I will be.'

'Oh?'

'When he comes back.'

'Where is he now?'

'Germany.'

'Where will you go?'

'The States.'

My God, she's going to marry a nigger! His face registered shock.

'I thought I'd best tell you.'

'Where will you live, Harlem?' He hadn't meant to say that. 'That's where the . . .' a pause '. . . Negroes live?'

Her eyes angry. 'You've been talking.'

'Someone was talking to me. They couldn't wait to give me the good news.'

More angry now. 'There was some in a camp close by. No one hardly spoke to them. He was different and educated and wanted a girl to talk to, so I used to meet him. Nothing happened. A lot he said I didn't understand. It was politics. I never met anybody who talked like him and nothing happened. Nothing. Only who's going to believe it?'

Jackson felt that she was stating her defence. She had probably gone over and over it in her mind.

'They don't even listen.'

Exactly as he thought.

'And I can see you don't believe it. We never did.'

She protests too much.

'Even Dad doesn't believe me. Mum does.'

Mum would. The sun rose and set on Madge.

'If he had wanted to . . .' Now she looked puzzled. 'I don't know. I used to ask myself and never knew. He always behaved like a gentleman.'

He stared at her and believed her and then was surprised at his own thoughts. What difference would it make anyway? There had been him, and the Pole she had told him about, and the Free French officer, who had been shot down over France, where he spoke the language. Then a nigger. Now there was someone else.

'Madge, I don't care.'

She looked amazed. 'But I didn't.'

'I don't care.' Feeling rather noble, he noted, and didn't really like it.

Her expression softened and her hand touched his, just like in the old days, then was hastily drawn back. 'You were always . . .' She searched for a word. 'Unpredictable.' An embarrassed little smile. 'Is that the right word?'

'Yes.' He smiled.

'Thank you.' She sipped her drink.

He ordered two more. 'So you're getting married and going to the States?'

'Yes.'

'Where?'

'Texas.'

'Texas. How liberal is . . .'

'Hank.'

'Isn't that Henry in English?'

'Suppose so, but he likes Hank.'

'Does he know?'

She violently shook her head. 'I met him in Plymouth.
He's never been here.'

'You mean never? What about your family?'

'They met him in Plymouth.'

'Doesn't he wonder why you've never brought him home?'

'He can wonder all he likes. If he set his foot down here
the cat would be out of the bag and then . . .'

'That's not honest, Madge.'

Scornfully, then a smile. 'You can talk.'

Jackson grinned. 'But this is serious.'

The smile again. 'That's right. He's my ticket out of this
place.' The smile switched off. 'Where everybody talks scandal and treats me like . . .' Her voice fading. 'You don't know
how I hate them. People I've known all my days.'

'You don't love him.'

'He's kind.'

'Is that enough?'

'He's rich.'

'How do you know?'

'Seen photos of his house, his Mum and Dad, the cars. His
Mum writes to me. He's rich all right.'

She looked down at the hand he had not held. The diamond ring made Jackson gape. All he could think to say was,
'Good luck.'

She surprised him. 'You wouldn't marry me. Now you're
back, I mean.'

The answer was immediate. No. Not even if he could
afford to. He liked her. She wasn't terribly intelligent, but

she was so sexually attractive, and warm and, yes, she was honest.

'Knew you wouldn't.' Her smile again. 'I like you, could love you, but never would trust you.'

'Who are you waiting for?'

'Olive.'

The old bag who was with her the first time he had met her.

'She doesn't care what anybody thinks or says. She's my friend.'

Nice old bag.

'I'll be here a few days.'

Their eyes met and held.

'Or maybe you'd like to go somewhere else, Johnnie, where no one knows us?'

Their hands met. What a hell of a diamond ring, thought Jackson, and she's worth it.

'You know I'll always love you, Madge.'

'You know . . . somehow I think the same.'

'Well. Must go.'

'Suppose so.'

'Pretty stupid saying thank you.'

'I was so happy. Honest.'

Shouldn't end. 'Madge, you planted those things in the bedroom, didn't you? When you had to go away for the day.'

'What things?'

Laughing. 'Well, there was a pair of your panties hanging on my battle trousers when I woke up.'

'No!'

'And on that bloody crucifix. You remember that? There was hanging your medallion with the gold chain. Christ, I gave it to you.'

'I always seem to put things down places.'

'And your bedroom slippers. One was pointing to the bed and the other in the direction you were travelling.'

'Well, I'm always tidy.'

'Everywhere I looked was Madge.'

'Fancy that.'

'I love you, Madge.'

'Oh, Johnnie, I love you. When you coming back?'

'Near as I can work it out, end of December or early January. That's not far off. Six, seven months.'

'Oh, Johnnie . . . I . . .'

A long pause and Jackson, feeling most gentle, 'That's when Hank's expected?'

'Yes.'

'Then ?'

'Oh, I don't know.'

'Texas?'

'I don't know.'

'Big house, three cars, have to be four now.'

'It seems a long way away.'

'It is, from your village.'

'That place!'

'You'll never have to enter a pub again. Cocktail bars only from now on.'

A giggle. 'You're laughing at me.'

'No, darling.'

'Johnnie . . .'

'Know my prospects? Best offer to date. Your old man's promise of nearly five years ago – marry Madge and you can manage the other shop. Madge, wonder if he meant I could manage the shop but I'd never be able to manage you?'

A laugh, 'You've managed all right.'

'When's your sailing date?'

'Well, Hank said February or March. That's when we go to the States, but first we get married in Plymouth, then go to London for a bit. Then Portugal and Spain and, oh, I don't know.'

'How about throwing all that away and sharing a cold water flat in London with me, with a view of the gasworks. Rent? Pay you next week.'

A long wait, then her soft voice almost moaning, 'Johnnie . . .'

'Darling, tilt your head up. Look at me. It's Johnnie and he isn't going anywhere. He doesn't even know what he wants to do except enjoy life. And you're the cocktail bar girl and I can see you by that bloody swimming pool, and Hank's rich and he's kind and . . . want me to start blubbering?'

'Johnnie, I love you true.'

'Then you'd better keep in touch.'

'You'll be my cousin if he wants to know who's writing.'

'Keep in touch, because you never know . . .'

'Hank and I might break up.'

'What?'

'If I don't like it over there. If I was in love be different.'

'Stop reading my mind. I've had nearly a week of it.'

'We've talked it over. He said if we don't make out, meaning me, he wouldn't stop me if I wanted a divorce, he'd see I was well taken care of.'

'You've got to give it a try.'

'I will, but if it don't work out, I'll be coming back to you.'

'With your bloody alimony.' Jackson sounded bitter. Why, he wondered. Don't be a phoney. As she is now I would take her. With money wouldn't it be even better? But that poor kind-hearted, trusting bastard's money? Like robbing the poor box in a church. He didn't like it and she saw it.

'I'm not going over there to rob him. I'll do all I can to make it a success, but loving you isn't going to make it easier. How can we know that I won't fit in with all those rich people and he may go off me?'

'Madge.' He kissed her. 'He'd be crazy if he didn't stay in love with you.'

'Anyway, I want to know where you are and how you're getting on, so you write.'

'I will.'

'I love you because . . . you know I never swear.'

'And when I make love to you?'

'Those words!' She looked shocked and happy as she kissed him. 'I never swear, but I love you because really you're an honest bastard.'

'I said it first. I love you and I know I'll always love you.'

He yelled out of the carriage window a few moments later

as the train smoke began to envelope her. 'Don't forget, keep in touch.'

Osnabruck. The nearest point to his company and he would have to make his way back the best way he could.

All his kit piled around him on the station platform. Dump it in the RTO's office. I've got to get transport, can't carry this lot.

Might look up old Weaver. Might stay over a day or two. Inga? Right after Madge? No. Faithful Johnnie? He had to smile to himself. Nice girl, Inga, but Madge was something else. Be good to see old Weaver though.

The surly RTO Sergeant grunted and nodded to a corner in his office.

Walking through the bomb-shattered streets of Osnabruck, thinking, take a chance. I'm back late from leave as it is. So, you are, or you aren't, in trouble already. Bad weather, held up in Dover. Who's going to bother to check it out? And if they do, who the hell cares? The war's over, everybody's waiting for demob. That Japan business won't be for us. Not us old timers with nearly six years in. So relax.

Not many soldiers in the Ratskellar. Well, it's early. Jackson looked along the bar for Weaver's welcoming smile. Mustn't let him talk me into another week. Just a few drinks and so long.

Weaver's old faithful second in command, the corporal, was behind the bar.

'Hello, Phil. Where's Weaver?'

Phil scowled. 'On leave.'

'Oh. When did he go?'

'Yesterday.'

'I'll have a beer.'

'Not in the bloody office.'

'What's up with you?'

'Coming here, getting pissed up, bringing in whores.' Phil's face bitter and resentful. 'And we had to do all the bloody work.'

'Why didn't you tell Weaver that instead of kissing his arse?'

'I don't want any sarcastic remarks from you.'

'You ought to thank me.'

'What's that?'

'While me and old Weaver were pissed, you and your mob must have just about cleaned out the till.'

'You get out of here.'

'I want a beer.'

'I ain't serving you.'

'Weaver won't like to hear that.'

A sneer. 'Maybe when he gets back, what he likes and what he don't like won't count for much.'

'So you're going to pull the carpet from under him?'

'Is that your business?'

'I'd watch it. Weaver's a lot smarter than you.'

'We'll see.'

'You miserable bastard.'

'Get out. That's an order.'

As Jackson walked out of the bar, he remembered Weaver's home address. He would write to him and warn him that his old buddy, his second, was gunning for him, and be ready for trouble. He worried to himself, that's all I can do.

He made his way back to the station, collected his kit and waited outside. Trucks pulled up, deposited soldiers. Happy, home-leave-going soldiers, and drove away. Finally he found a truck that was going his way. Even going through the village. Luck.

Next morning Tompkins barked at him, 'Reported to the MO yet, Jackson?'

'No, sir. I was just going . . .'

'Yes. Just going. You get along there fast. You know the rules.'

On the way to the MO's office, Jackson thought, yes I know the rules. Report for medical inspection, which means, quite simply, a short-arm inspection. Charming. I don't mind all that much, but how about the married men? Spend a leave with their wives and then have to stand for a short-arm inspection. Bloody insulting.

Only Simpson there. Jackson greeted him with a broad

grin. 'Hello, Simpson. I bet you had a good leave.'

Simpson turned and glared at him and Jackson gaped back. Dark bruises showed around both eyes and when he spoke Jackson saw that some of his front teeth were missing, his expression savage. 'Mind your own bloody business.'

'Sorry.' Jackson sat down and picked up a magazine and thought, Simpson in a punch-up. What the hell could have happened?

The MO gave him a short-arm inspection, nodded curtly and Jackson pulled up his trousers.

'I'm fit, sir?'

'Yes.'

'Aren't I lucky, sir?'

'How do you mean?'

'I had a great leave, sir. I went with twelve Piccadilly whores.'

'Then I'll have to put you through further tests.'

Jackson laughed. 'I'm joking.'

'I'm not. Get on the slab.'

'Now look . . .'

'Do as I say.'

The MO picked up a steel rod and inserted it down Jackson's penis, and Jackson yelled in agony and regretted his misplaced sense of humour.

Simpson sat on his own at a table in the corner of the wet canteen and he was drunk.

Jackson picked up his bottle of beer and joined him.

'What do you want, Jackson?'

'A word with you.'

'Want to know all about it, you nosey bastard.'

'Yes.'

Simpson stared at his bottle of beer. 'Shouldn't be drinking. I ought to knock it off.'

'What happened?'

'Do you care?'

'Funny enough, yes.'

A pause. 'I gave you a hard time, didn't I?'

A grin. 'Yes.'

'For her. That's why I was doing it. For her.'

'I know.'

'Must knock off the booze. Okay. I got home. The kids were sort of scared of me at first but they eased up after a bit. She was a bit strange, too. Well, it had been a long time.' A gulp of beer. 'Four days later I woke up, went to the bathroom. I'd got a packet.'

Jackson thought, Oh, Christ.

'Told her, then she started to yell I'd brought it back from Germany, I'd been going with whores and I'd given it to her.' Another gulp of beer. 'Next thing she was down in the corner of the room. Only used the flat of me hand, but it sent her spinning. Couldn't punch her.' He made it sound like an apology. 'Nice to get a packet of gonorrhea from your wife after . . . well, you know.'

All Jackson could do was give a sympathetic nod.

'So I went out and checked in the local pub. Hadn't even been there. They were friends of mine and when I told them, they soon bloody well told me. I knew the bloke. Funny that. Used to drink with him. He'd been excused the bloody war. Reserved occupation. Been turned down by the medical board and he'd been studding for half of us who used the pub and he was handing out a packet to my wife. He must've known he had it. I found him in another pub and he put up a better bloody show than I expected. I mean, for someone who ain't even fit for the army. Finish. He went to the hospital, I saw to that. I went in the nick but they let me out next day. Johnnie, I've got to stop boozing or it won't never clear up, but I feel so bloody miserable.'

Jackson could see he was near to tears. A mixture of rage and self-pity. Poor old Simpson. Him of all people.

'Well, you've had a skinful, so another one won't make much difference, but you'd better quit drinking tomorrow. Why hasn't the doc put you in hospital?'

A cynical smile. 'Pox hospital's doing a roaring business. I'm waiting for a bed.'

They were crowding round the newspaper and grinning.

'Well, we won't be going to Japan, then, eh?'

'Wouldn't have gone anyways.'

'How'd you know?'

'Can't go now they've made a big hole in it.'

Jackson got hold of the newspaper and stared at the picture of a giant mushroom cloud and read the headlines, and then began to read the words and the words began to blur, so he stared horrified at the mushroom cloud again.

The sniggering voices faded out, yet stayed in his mind.

'Won't go to Japan.'

'There's a big hole in it.'

The clots. The stupid . . . can't they understand anything?

The children . . . we've won the war. The Yanks, Russians, us. We had it made, then the Yanks had to drop that.

The invasion of Japan would have cost countless lives . . .

The print blurred again.

But why drop that? Why bloody well make it in the first place?

Werner. The bomb. Germany nearly had it. He shivered. They would have dropped it. Goodbye London. Politicians. He couldn't laugh, but wanted to. They must all be crazy, and this one's only a baby. The first. What will big daddy be like?

He was sweating. What about the kids? The kids now? The kids waiting to be born? I've never been crazy about kids, never had any, and I'm not bringing any into this crazy world. What have they got to look forward to?

The war's over. Peace on earth, and then some crazy bastard comes up with the bomb.

He laughed as he threw the paper away and lit a cigarette. He knew life would never be the same again, God knows how it would be, and then a thought crossed his mind and for a moment he couldn't believe it, but it was true. Come what may, he was looking forward to the future anyway. A shout of laughter that startled the soldiers in the room. Then Jackson yelled, 'I must be crazy too!'

Mouths opened and laughed and heads nodded in agreement.